PRAISE FOR THE CHIMERA SEQUENCE

"Elliott Garber's debut thriller *The Chimera Sequence* has everything I love in a novel: great characters, a thrill ride of an adventure, and a looming global menace. But best of all, the story hooked me from the first intriguing page to the last illuminating line. Read Garber's first book, a thriller destined for bestsellerdom. I can't wait to see what this guy writes next!"

—James Rollins, *New York Times* bestseller of *The Sixth Extinction*

"Elliott Garber has delivered a high-stakes thriller that will earn your attention with clean, clear prose and a solid grasp of global geopolitics. *The Chimera Sequence* is terrifyingly realistic, chock-full of research that rings as true as today's headlines."

—Bob Mayer, Former Green Beret and *New York Times* bestselling author

"I couldn't put down Garber's engaging, rapid-paced, action-packed thriller. His riveting first novel benefits greatly from his experience as an Army veterinarian who has worked with a variety of unlikely animals around the world. The book even features important appearances from a military dog, a Secret Service dog, and a tracker bloodhound. What's not to love?"

Maria Goodavage, *New York Times* bestselling author of *Top Dog* and *Soldier Dogs*

"Animal lovers rejoice! Not since *Jurassic Park* has a science thriller of this magnitude been written just for us. While the story is filled with human characters you'll hate to love and love to hate, the real heroes (in my humble opinion) of *The Chimera Sequence* are an appealing supporting cast of mountain gorillas, working dogs, and other creatures great and small. One word of warning: don't pick up my fellow veterinarian Elliott Garber's book unless you're ready for an adventure. You won't be able to put it down until you reach the very last page!"

—Dr. Marty Becker, "America's Veterinarian" and *New York Times* bestselling author

THE
CHIMERA
SEQUENCE

A NOVEL

ELLIOTT GARBER

OSPREY
PRESS

OSPREY
PRESS

This is a work of fiction, except for the parts that aren't. Names, characters, places, and incidents either are the product of the author's imagination or are used fictitiously. Any resemblance to actual persons, living or dead, organizations, businesses, events, or locales is entirely coincidental.

The views expressed in this book are those of the author and do not reflect the official policy or position of the Department of Defense or the U.S. Government. Nothing in the contents should be construed as asserting or implying U.S. Government authentication of information or endorsement of the author's views. The manuscript has been reviewed by the Department of Defense to prevent disclosure of classified information.

BOOK DESIGN BY PHILLIP GESSERT

ISBN: 978-1-943968-01-5 (hardcover);
978-1-943968-00-8 (paperback); 978-1-943968-02-2 (electronic)

For Becca, who made this story possible.

TOP SECRET

THIS IS A COVER SHEET FOR CLASSIFIED INFORMATION

STATEMENT FOR THE RECORD BY
[E.G.]
AAAS SCIENCE & TECHNOLOGY POLICY FELLOW
BEFORE THE SENATE SELECT
COMMITTEE ON INTELLIGENCE
UNITED STATES SENATE

Madam Chairman, Mr. Vice Chairman, Members of the Committee, I am honored to come before you today to present the requested report detailing classified events surrounding this year's Independence Day.

As a military officer and veterinarian specializing in infectious disease, I am personally acquainted with several of the key players involved in this incident. The history of these relationships is such that I have complete confidence in the information shared with me, and the accuracy of the final text has been verified by multiple parties.

We cannot choose to ignore the difficult lessons here. Similar threats lurk even now, as a faceless enemy watches and waits, wondering if we have learned anything from our past. And this is why you, representatives of our most prominent body of elected officials, must absorb this report with an uncommon attention to detail and a unique willingness to act upon your convictions.

I was there on the Fourth. The President's team had been promoting his Celebration of America for months, and over 400,000 spectators packed themselves in between the Capitol and the Lincoln Memorial, ready to be dazzled. We might have chosen differently had we known what was really going on that day.

I present you now with the terrifying true account of the most dangerous threat our nation has ever faced.

This is how it happened.

SATURDAY, JANUARY 30

PORT SUDAN, SUDAN
6:48 P.M. EASTERN AFRICA TIME

Dominic Odhiambo was curiously content for a man who would be dead within the hour. He felt a weight lift from his shoulders as he turned off the highway and approached an imposing steel gate. They had finally arrived.

It was still dusk over the rugged Red Sea coastline, but the glaring fluorescent security lighting of Sudan's largest shipping port already illuminated the entire city with a sickly artificial glow.

Odhiambo punched the numbers he had carefully memorized into an old Nokia mobile phone.

A man's quiet voice answered, "Salaam."

"Yes, the product has arrived." Odhiambo repeated the words he was given with the telephone number earlier that day.

He watched as the gate slid open and returned a nod from the security officer sitting inside an air-conditioned booth. *If only things were always this easy.* The ancient Land Rover pulled forward with a groan. A quick glance in the rearview mirror confirmed that the truck was still right behind him.

It was a warm night, but not warm enough to explain the beads of sweat Odhiambo felt forming on his glistening forehead. Almost there. He carefully steered through the sprawling container terminus, all the way up to the main loading dock. The skeletal shapes of three cranes leaned out over the water like supersized praying mantises frozen mid-hunt.

"This is it, right?" he asked the man in the passenger seat beside him. Two others in the back leaned forward to hear.

"Looks like it, MV *Panagia*." Vincent Lukwiya was like a brother to Odhiambo. They had worked side by side for almost twenty years and together were given this most important task by their leader. Now, six weeks and over three thousand miles later, the end was in sight.

Odhiambo eased off the gas and let the Land Rover drift to a stop, idling the engine as he peered into the maze of massive shipping containers to his left. They were stacked five—even six—high, like toy blocks for the children of giants. He imagined the lengthy journeys that each of these faded orange, red, and blue boxes would make in the months and years ahead. First by ship, like the monstrosity looming in the water to his right, then onto trains and finally trucks, ending up in every far-flung corner of the world that he would never get to see. Odhiambo had dreams that were so much bigger than his little corner of war-torn central Africa, but a nagging feeling told him it was too late to escape.

He unconsciously felt for a crumpled piece of paper in his pocket. It had been his constant companion ever since it fell from the sky—along with thousands more just like it—several months earlier. Odhiambo wasn't stupid. He knew who it was from: another bunch of white men thinking they knew what was best for Africa. But it promised a way out of this prison that was his life and a path forward.

It was all he had.

The creak and then bang of a large metal door broke the silence. Odhiambo wiped a sweaty hand on his jeans and felt for the distinct solid form at his left hip. They said no weapons, but who did they think they were dealing with?

"Look," Lukwiya whispered, nodding at several dark human shapes emerging from the shadowy stacks ahead of them. "Must be them."

"What are we waiting for?" Odhiambo reached for the door handle. "Let's go."

All four men eased out of the vehicle. Odhiambo looked back to see another two jump down from the passenger side of the dust-covered Volvo truck.

"Do you have what we were promised?" A tall man strode purposefully toward Odhiambo and his men. No greeting or thanks for making the long trek. Only business. The man's charcoal suit looked expensive. Too nice for the occasion. But then, Odhiambo's boss had never thought it necessary to tell him who they were doing business with.

"Of course," Odhiambo said. "My men will unload it now."

"Get on with it then." The tall man turned and said something soft and guttural to one of the others. Odhiambo was expecting to hear the Arabic they had been listening to on the radio while driving across Sudan over the last few days. But there was something unfamiliar about these sounds. The other two men, similarly olive-skinned and dark-haired, led the way to the back of the truck. Odhiambo looked carefully for any signs that they were breaking their own prohibition. Maybe that left side of the stocky one's jacket hung just a little too low? But it was tough to tell in this light.

He watched his men—really only teenagers—struggle to unload the painted blue iron drums from the truck. Each one weighed over a hundred pounds, and their shape made it hard to handle them delicately. But delicacy was exactly what was needed, in more ways than one. They arranged the eight drums in two rows and then waited.

"You realize of course that any trickery is easily detected in this business," the buyer said. "We will screen each drum here, but the conclusive tests will be done at our final destination."

The stocky man pulled a black device with a small LCD screen out of the inside of his jacket. Odhiambo turned his head slightly toward Lukwiya and whispered in their native Acholi, "Now you will regret it."

The man stooped to scan the first drum from top to bottom, nodding slightly as he scrolled through numbers on the screen. Odhiambo watched every movement with growing dread. He knew they shouldn't have tried their old game of skimming off the top with this deal, but Lukwiya had convinced him otherwise. How could he really have believed his friend's vain promises about coming out on top, profit in hand and finally able to leave this life behind?

The others stood silently as they observed the man move from one drum to the next. Five done, and apparently passed the test. Now he paused and swept the device again along the side of the sixth drum. He turned to look at the leader and shook his head as he stepped toward him.

"So, you thought it might be so easy to fool us?" The tall man took the device and motioned with his other hand for Odhiambo to come to him. "Let me show you the problem."

Odhiambo stepped forward and peered into the glowing screen. He didn't know what he was supposed to be looking for, but he wasn't about to admit that now.

IT HAPPENED IN an instant. Vincent Lukwiya saw the leader turn slightly, his head moving in an almost imperceptible nod. Behind him, the stockier man pulled a SIG P226 from his belt and fired straight into the back of Odhiambo's head from five feet away. A soft whoosh from the silenced pistol was accompanied by the simultaneous impact of the bullet with his friend's skull. It burst open, sending fragments of bone and brain in every direction, while his body stumbled forward and fell hard against one of the iron drums.

Lukwiya jumped forward, reaching for his own hidden weapon, when a blinding spotlight caught him in its beam.

"Don't move!" shouted the tall man.

Shading his eyes from the bright light, the veteran fighter looked around and saw ten more men stepping out from the shipping containers, their assault rifles trained on him. Two of his own had managed to pull their pistols but dropped them just as quickly. They all knew resistance would be worthless.

"Now, shall we continue?" The leader picked up the measuring device and handed it to his partner. "You should know that we do not tolerate cheating in our business arrangements. I thought I had made that clear to your boss."

The stocky man finished scanning and said something incomprehensible to the others.

"At least only one of them needs to die today." The leader motioned to Lukwiya with his weapon. "You should go now. Payment will be arranged if we find the product satisfactory for our needs."

"That is not what we agreed to." Lukwiya spoke through gritted teeth, fighting back the blend of shock and hatred that surged inside him. Any last chance of self-preservation depended on his ability to keep himself under control. "Half the money here and half later."

"Yes, but that was before you broke the terms of this agreement. I'm not sure your jungle prophet really understood who he was doing business with, but I think he will soon realize just where he stands. Now leave before we must provide any further encouragement."

Vincent Lukwiya had never been forced to acknowledge defeat so clearly. He was not stupid, though.

"Get the body," he muttered, jogging back to the old Land Rover.

A minute later, the two vehicles had left the port and were speeding south down the dark coastal highway, back into the heart of Africa.

MONDAY, JUNE 28

VIRUNGA NATIONAL PARK
DEMOCRATIC REPUBLIC OF THE CONGO
7:03 A.M. CENTRAL AFRICA TIME

You gents ready for this?" Marna Van Wyk could barely hear her own voice over the Eurocopter AS350's thumping rotors. "We're heading in!" The anticipation was killing her. After weeks of delays due to the increased rebel fighting on the ground, they had finally crossed the border and were flying over Virunga National Park. It wasn't just the oldest park in Africa, but one of the best. What would her parents think of that? Quite a claim, coming from the girl who had grown up right in Kruger's backyard.

Marna watched the landscape unfold beneath her in total awe. The immense cones of eight ancient volcanoes broke through a rumpled blanket of thick green forest, and her eyes were instantly drawn to a white river of smoke streaming from Nyiragongo's active volcanic crater. *Better hope the wind doesn't shift in our direction.* She could just make out Goma's sprawling slums clinging miserably to the edges of Lake Kivu far to her left. What a godforsaken little city that was, ruined over the years by a constant cycle of disasters in every flavor. Stretching out in the foreground, the change in vegetation marking the border of the park was coming into view, revealing the patchwork of tiny fields and tin-roofed huts that made up the villages on the other side.

"Okay, I see it!" she shouted, looking toward a small clearing in the forest below them. Marna brought the helicopter down quickly, but she knew her practiced touch on the controls meant her passengers would barely feel the rapid twisting descent. She loved everything about her job, and it didn't hurt that she was so damned good at it. Perched just above the jungle canopy, she made a split-second assessment that the clearing would accommodate them, if only by a hair, and continued down.

The noise increased to a deafening roar as displaced air tore through thick foliage, sending a vibrant green storm of leaves, vines, and branches out in all directions. Finally, her giant dragonfly of a machine hovered for a moment before settling down to rest in the brushy undergrowth.

As the rotor blades slowed, Marna checked her mirror just in time to see Bonny's lanky red and brown body leaping out of the helicopter's open hatch. She couldn't help but smile as the bloodhound's ridiculously long ears opened in mid-air like Dumbo reincarnate. Thick loose folds of skin slid forward with the impact of those massive front paws on the ground, then rebounded, quivering, back into position. Two thin men in olive fatigues and black rubber boots followed immediately behind the dog. Innocence and Proper Kambale, brothers and career Virunga rangers, swung their AK-47s into the ready position and pushed into waist-high vegetation.

The Kambale brothers had pointed to the clearing as they circled over the forested flanks of the extinct Mount Mikeno, recognizing a favorite old spot for a cool drink and debrief with tourists high off their first gorilla sightings. The clearing was born years earlier, with the cutting of an ancient hardwood for charcoal production, but it was overgrown now and quickly on its way to being completely reclaimed by the encroaching jungle. This park had been a home to the brothers for thirty tumultuous years, and Marna watched them drink in its verdant air anticipating a familiar recognition.

The disturbed glance said it all. Something was off. Marna smelled it too, a faint tanginess mixing weakly with the dissipating fumes of the engine.

"What's that stench?" The distinct male voice came from right behind her, still inside the helicopter. His accent was an almost neutral American, just slightly affected by a hint of rural drawl.

Cole McBride.

Only three months since she'd first met this crazy wildlife veterinarian, and he had already won every competition for sending the most confusing romantic signals ever. But that was not her concern today.

"Could an elephant have wandered up this far to die?" he continued.

"You smell it too?" Marna asked.

"Yes, something has died here." Innocence Kambale turned back at the edge of the clearing, struggling to pull a determined Bonny out of the brush. She was onto something. The Virunga bloodhounds were trained to track both individual human scents and generic dead animal odor—useful for finding both the poachers and the poached. "Very close."

Marna swung her door open and leaned out of the pilot's seat. Behind her, Cole appeared in the open hatch before jumping smoothly into the knee-high vegetation. He was just over six feet tall and well proportioned for his height, not too gangly but not a bulked up bodybuilder either. She'd had her fill of that type down in Joburg—rich Afrikaner guys who had nothing better to do than spend all day in the gym. But Cole was different. Decked out in rugged hiking boots, dark khaki pants, and a faded plaid button-down, he looked as if he could have stepped right off the pages of *Outside* magazine. The overgrown hair and closely cropped beard served to complete the picture. Not that she'd ever tell him so—his head was big enough already.

Yes, he wasn't only smart, but quite nice to look at, too.

And he knew it.

THE EUROCOPTER'S MECHANICAL roar had now been replaced by the screeching and scolding of an assortment of birds and small primates still upset by this monster's invasion. Cole looked up into the trees and caught a flash of orangey-brown fur high in the canopy.

"At least the golden monkeys are alive and well," he said, bringing a pair of binoculars up to his eyes. After a few seconds' observation, though, he wasn't so sure. These dachshund-sized little balls of energy normally spent the majority of their time further down the slopes where their favorite meal of bamboo grew more abundantly. *Why are they way up here?* It looked like there were only about ten of them bouncing around in the branches, when normally this group had over sixty individuals. Some of the gorilla trackers had been working on habituating the family before last year's flare up of violence, so it had been quite a while since the monkeys had seen any friendly human faces.

A quick burst of popping machine gun fire rang out from slopes below, silencing them momentarily. After a second's pause, the animals' screaming started up at an even higher volume than before. *That probably has something to do with it.* Cole hoisted a large backpack out of the helicopter's open bay and settled it onto his shoulders.

"Doesn't sound like we have much time for exploring." Marna hopped out of the cockpit, then turned to rub a hand affectionately against the helicopter's shiny green finish. "You guys know I can't risk damaging this little beauty!"

"What," Cole said, "you're worried she can't handle an adventure?"

He knew the Eurocopter's thin fiberglass fuselage wouldn't stand much of a chance under fire, unlike the armored skins of the Blackhawks and Chinooks he was used to flying around in. But no reason to get Marna more worried than she already was. This early morning excursion across the border was not exactly internationally sanctioned, and he was fully aware of the potential repercussions of being apprehended by one of the rebel groups camping out in the park. Cole swore under his breath as he imagined what might be in store for Marna as the only woman on this somewhat reckless outing. The odds of coming away from a confrontation unharmed were not in her favor. Maybe the politically savvy warlords would understand her value as a bargaining chip, but those teenage foot soldiers high on superglue would have only one thing on their minds.

"Oh she'd do just fine, thank you very much," Marna said. "It's just that this two million dollar flying machine is technically still on loan from South African National Parks, and she's definitely not supposed to be in the Congo this morning. Don't want to take any chances."

"I gotcha, don't you worry." Cole looked back into the helicopter for the final member of their group. "What do you think, doc?"

"Just loading the last dart."

Dr. Antoine Musamba's stocky frame was hunched over a large backpack full of the expedition's medical supplies, the Pneu-Dart 389 tranquilizing rifle already slung over one shoulder. He pushed a fogged up pair of wire-rimmed glasses onto the top of his smooth bald head, adding to the aura of intense concentration. Cole watched as he injected a potent combination of two anesthetic drugs, tiletamine and zolazepam, into a long silver dart. He knew the cocktail would quickly and safely immobilize a five-hundred pound full-grown silverback, and that Musamba would already have other darts in the backpack pre-loaded with the right volumes for average adult females and juvenile gorillas. The Congo-based veterinarian for the Gorilla Doctors—the organization hosting Cole in central Africa—was an expert in the field anesthesia of large primates, his skills developed over many years working among these volcanoes.

Musamba started putting the filled dart into its carrying case, but then paused, letting the rifle swing down off his shoulder.

"Always ready, right?" Cole said.

"Exactly." Musamba loaded the powerful dart into the rifle and climbed out of the helicopter. "Let's get going."

Cole knew how much this long-awaited return to Virunga meant to Musamba and the Kambale brothers. The rebel fighters controlling the park had been messing with their country's future for too long. There was a hardened resolve in his colleague's dark eyes that Cole hadn't seen before. Sure, they were there first for the gorillas, but the expression made him realize Musamba probably wouldn't be completely opposed to using the Pneu-Dart in his own defense. Only difference between shooting a gorilla and shooting a human was that the much smaller rebel might never wake up.

"I will stay here with Marna to watch the helicopter." Proper Kambale's French-accented English was surprisingly good, given its status as the fourth language in his repertoire. "You three must go now to discover what has died and find our gorillas. We will stay on the radios, yes?"

"Yep, sounds good," Cole said. "We need to get our eyes on some gorillas and then hurry on back out of here. You good, Marna?"

"We'll be fine." There it was again, the playful smile that made it hard to focus on anything else. "Just don't make us wait too long!"

"No danger of that," Cole said. "Much as I love Virunga, definitely don't feel like messing around with its current human residents."

He followed Innocence and Musamba into the forest. *At least not with only this crew to back me up.*

IT HAD BEEN seven months since anyone from the park staff or the Gorilla Doctors had laid eyes on Virunga's mountain gorillas, and they had no idea how the critically endangered animals were being affected by this constant violence. There were supposed to be over two-hundred of them in the park, almost a quarter of the world's total population, but Cole didn't know how well they could survive without the intensive protection and monitoring that was responsible for bringing the species back from the brink of extinction over the last forty years. Ever since the naturalist Dian Fossey—and her film version Sigourney Weaver—made them famous with *Gorillas in the Mist*, the mountain gorillas were enduring favorites of conservation organizations and animal lovers all over the world. Unfortunately, even their fame couldn't protect them from the violent human conflicts that were an almost constant presence.

The last visit to the park came at the official invitation of General Ntaganda himself, head of the M23 militia, a group of disaffected Tutsi soldiers who at the time were reigning supreme over the various other rebel organizations in the region. Cole remembered the general as a media-whore with a misguided public relations sensibility. He repeatedly emphasized that his soldiers were specifically instructed not to harm the gorillas, all while openly profiting from an illegal charcoal industry that was quickly destroying their last remaining home range. The invited team, including Cole, the Kambales, and several Fossey Fund trackers, was able to account for all three habituated mountain gorilla families during that visit, but since then the fighting had gotten completely out of control.

There were rumors that a new group had entered the fray, eager to take over not only the charcoal production but also the much more valuable mineral mines in and around the park. Unlike most of the factions vying for control of the area, the new fighters had shunned any media attention and were shrouded in a seemingly self-imposed mantle of mystery.

"You really think it could be Kony and his gang of misfits?" Cole had asked Marna the week before over a couple big bottles of Primus. The glass and labels on Rwanda's most popular beer were clearly recycled one too many times, but that didn't take away from the refreshment it provided after a long day sweating in the forest. "All the guys from Virunga seem to think he's finally found his way out of the Central African Republic—even managed to do some recruiting along the way."

"I seriously doubt it." Marna took a long slow drink. "Ever since your president sent those military advisors to hunt the lunatic down, he's apparently done a pretty tidy job of staying under the radar. Why choose now of all moments to risk entering the mess across the border?"

Military advisors, right. Wonder where Jake and his guys are now, anyway? Cole had thought, before answering her with a sarcastic smile, "Well, a few million bucks in black market minerals has been incentive enough for plenty of other guys through history, right? Why should poor old Joe miss out on all that?"

INNOCENCE HAD GIVEN Bonny a long leash, and she trotted along an over-grown trail leading through the thick forest, her nose alternating every few seconds between the soft earth below and the pungent air above. Another quick burst of automatic weapons fire cut through the silence, clearly startling Musamba from his steady pace just a few steps ahead of Cole. This time the faint popping was answered by several louder explosions. Some of these militias were made up of Congolese army defectors, and they had brought halfway decent artillery into the mix.

"You okay there, doc?" Cole said. "Sounds like we've got some serious firepower in the park this morning."

"Yes, and that was quite a bit closer than the first bunch."

Dr. Musamba had grown up and attended university in the capital city of Kinshasa. He spent most of his career working as a consultant on animal health and agriculture to various international development organizations intent on spending their millions in his country, and his English was flaw-less. Cole knew the sharp and proper enunciation of each word had evolved out of years of friendship with a never-ending stream of idealistic young foreigners like himself—men and women from all corners of the wealthy world, coming with dreams of saving the Congo from itself.

But they always left disappointed. Not Cole, though. He was working hard to be different. After a year playing witness to and occasional par-ticipant in an unending series of impossible battles in Afghanistan, how could he not?

"Everything alright, boys?" Marna's voice crackled over the radio at Cole's belt. "You're out of sight now and those guns are making us jumpy back here."

Cole dropped the large net he had been dragging through the under-growth and smiled to himself as he tried to think of a witty response. *Why does that South African accent have to be so damn sexy?* And the girl behind the voice didn't make it any easier. Her classic Dutch features, easygoing humor, and confident competence were difficult to resist.

But Cole had not come to Africa for romance. Just the opposite—he'd been hoping it would be an escape, a time to focus on his research, forget about military life for a while, and recover from the disastrous relationship he'd left behind. Marna was making this resolution way too difficult.

He opted for brevity over wit. "Roger that," he answered. "We're doing just fine so far."

COLE PICKED UP the heavy-duty butterfly net and continued dragging it through the brush along his right side. It was already filling up with a va-riety of flies, mosquitos and other more alien insect species disturbed by its movement. In his left hand, he held a large white flannel flag tied onto a broom handle. The flannel was perfect for gathering ticks, easily fooling them into thinking it was some tasty mammal walking by.

"Not the most glamorous part of my job," he had admitted to Marna a few weeks earlier. "But someone's got to do it. Do you realize how many diseases are carried by these creepy crawlies?"

"Right, and this is how you're gonna find the next Ebola?" Marna said, a little too cynically for his liking.

"Exactly." He left it at that. Let her be skeptical—she'd come around eventually.

Cole was pretty faithful in taking these decidedly low-tech tools of the trade with him every time he went out trekking. He first learned the method during a summer project combing the manicured forest paths of Martha's Vineyard. A vet school professor had recruited him as an enthusiastic young student to do the legwork in figuring out why this glamorous holiday island off the coast of Massachusetts was seeing far more than its fair share of tick-borne diseases. Rich people didn't like worrying about scary diseases like tularemia, Rocky Mountain spotted fever, and Lyme. It was too great a price to pay for the simple task of taking their fat Labradors out for a summer stroll in the woods.

Even though he hadn't come up with an answer worthy of publication in *Science* or *Nature,* Cole caught the research bug and had been looking forward to getting back in the field for a long time. And now, Africa.

After an hour of insect hunting in these tropical forests, he usually had enough bugs to keep his team busy in the lab for a couple of days. First they had to identify each and every little creature, pulling out a variety of South African field guides and local university publications to make up for the fact that no one cared enough about Congolese insects to merit the production of a full textbook.

The more interesting part came next. Each little test subject was dropped in a pricey machine—kind of like a miniature food processor—and combined with just the right cocktail of chemical solutions. Turn the blender on for a few seconds, push the eject button, and out popped a one milliliter vial of genetic stew that could then be searched for any number of known and more mysterious disease agents.

Although Cole didn't mind the insect work, it didn't excite him in same way as trapping and tranquilizing animals from the seemingly boundless menagerie of mammalian species endemic to the region. After nine months on site, he had obtained blood and tissue samples on everything from the tiny chisel-toothed shrew to the majestic African elephant, with a whole bunch of bizarre-looking bats and vicious little monkeys in between.

These samples went into the same mini-food processor to produce their own molecular smoothies, and Cole had already identified some intriguing new viruses. Would one of them be responsible for humanity's next big pandemic, just like so many others jumpstarted by the zoonotic transmission of an unknown pathogen from animals to humans? Another HIV, Ebola, or SARS? Much as he hoped not, this was exactly how it happened, time and time again. The whole point of the project was to learn about these viruses before they made the lethal jump out of their natural habitat. His role with the mountain gorillas was just icing on the cake of this whole year. An almost inaccessible dream of an experience that every animal lover, biology major, and veterinarian would have killed for, and he was right there living it.

"WE'RE GETTING CLOSE," Dr. Musamba said quietly.

"I think Bonny agrees." Cole noticed that Innocence was having a hard time keeping the strong young dog at a controlled walk as she pushed her way through a lush patch of nettles. The overwhelming scent of death was now at a gag-worthy level, but Cole was no virgin when it came to the wonders of decomposing flesh.

He remembered two dead rhinoceroses in Kruger National Park, poached overnight for their precious horns and left to rot in the searing South African sun that faithfully rose the next morning. It was the first day of a three-week internship during his last year of vet school, and he already had a nasty case of travelers' diarrhea. Thank you, Johannesburg street vendor, but that *braai*—grilled lamb chops—was definitely worth it.

Forensic investigations can't wait for a vet student with a weak constitution, though. So he'd jumped in a Land Cruiser with the rest of the team and bumped along twenty miles of backcountry safari track just hoping he wasn't going to be sick and ruin an otherwise decent first impression with his veterinary idols. At about fifty yards out, a giant cloud of scavenging vultures lifted off the rhino carcasses and sent a wafting aroma that hit Cole just at the point where he couldn't hold it in any more. Fortunately, everyone else was so intent on scoping out the surroundings that they didn't seem to notice as he crept off into the bush to find some relief.

That scent of the two aging rhino corpses was about equal to what Cole smelled now.

INNOCENCE KAMBALE STOPPED suddenly.

"*Oh, mon Dieu.*"

The trail opened ahead of them into another small clearing, but Cole couldn't initially see what caused the park ranger's uncharacteristic exclamation. He stretched to his full height, peering over the two shorter men. "Damn."

A coarsely-haired black shape lay motionless in a packed-down circle of green vegetation. *There's no way that gorilla is still alive.* It would have heard them approaching and sounded the alarm long before they were close enough to get a visual. Not only that, Innocence and Bonny were familiar enough with the gorillas' stealthy movements that they would have already identified the presence of a family group foraging in the area.

The ranger let loose some low grunting sounds, gorilla-speak meaning something like, *Just so you know, there are some friendly humans approaching.* No reason to surprise the animal in case it was really only sleeping. The three families of mountain gorillas in the Mikeno sector of Virunga National Park had all been habituated to human observation over almost ten years, and the relational understanding that the Kambales had with them was uncanny to an outside observer. It was as if the gorillas knew they had to subject themselves to the *oohs* and *awws* of the camera-toting tourists in order to secure their continued existence as a species.

Cole and the other veterinarians, on the other hand, were always a bit jealous of this unspoken camaraderie. The gorillas were smart enough to recognize every well-meaning vet who had ever been involved in an unwanted medical procedure, and they were especially wary when they spotted the dart gun. Smart as they were, these still very *non*-human primates could not seem to understand that the veterinary interventions were only being done to save their lives.

The lack of any response to Innocence's grunts confirmed Cole's fears. Not only confirmed them, but widened them into something he hadn't even considered. One dead mountain gorilla could not be responsible for the stench of death permeating this whole section of forest. He had thought for sure it must be an elephant, or maybe a couple of them, slaughtered and half-butchered by rebels a few days ago for the tusks and whatever meat they could carry back to camp. But a gorilla, one of their gorillas—that idea had not even crossed his mind. *What if there are more?*

"Adult female," Dr. Musamba said. His voice had a matter-of-fact tone that could only come from someone who had seen more than his fair share of tragedy. "Can't tell which one yet."

"Poor girl." Cole crouched down with the other two men. "What the hell happened?"

The body was already covered with flies and beetles, nature's scavengers quickly finishing off the nutritional recycling job of an efficient jungle ecosystem. What was left of the gorilla was curled up on its stomach in the leafy depression on the soft ground—her final resting spot. One arm was wrapped over the closer side of her head, as if to block out the filtered morning light she would never see again. The female must have made the nest before she died, maybe hoping that a good long sleep would do the trick of letting her live another day.

"Only one way to find out." Musamba tightened his lips and looked across at Innocence, eyebrows raised. *You know what to do*, the expression clearly said. The Virunga ranger stood up and used the butt of his AK-47 to flip the stiffened corpse over.

An angry mass of flies lifted off and immediately began settling on the three men's glistening faces and exposed forearms. It wasn't even worth trying to swat them away. The abdominal cavity had been opened up and most of its contents already eaten by another scavenger, probably some type of forest rat based on the lack of any more obvious trauma. The eyeballs were also gone, and the exposed black skin of her face and chest was chewed up and beginning to rot.

Not a pretty sight.

"So where's the entrance wound?" he asked, wondering aloud what he knew the others were also thinking. There was no doubt in his mind she'd been wounded and left to die by a gun-toting rebel out for live-action target practice.

"It can be hard to find under the thick coat," Musamba said. "When Senkwekwe and the others were killed, we had to comb through carefully in order to find each one."

"The kill shots were obvious enough, though, right?" Cole said. "I mean, weren't they all hit at pretty close range—almost execution-style?"

"Yes, they all took direct shots to the head and chest, but there were other wounds also. We did not find them all until the necropsies were done."

Musamba had been one of the first to the scene on that horrific morning. Seven well-known mountain gorillas slaughtered, simply because their presence in the park made it harder for corrupt officials to profit from illegal charcoal and mining operations. The story was big enough to merit an iconic photo on the cover of *National Geographic*—the dead silverback being carried through a cornfield on the edge of the park, his five-hundred and thirty pound body tied to a makeshift bamboo stretcher on the shoulders of no less than fifteen grieving villagers—which was how Cole first heard of it. That photo was the reason Cole even started thinking about mountain gorillas and dreaming of how he might be able to get involved. Fast forward a few years, through two deployments and his PhD coursework, and here he was.

Musamba continued, "Let's say this girl got hit by a single bullet, lived long enough to clean herself up and allow the wound to contract a little. It's going to take a careful exam to find what we're looking for."

Cole was impressed with his colleague's assessment. Wildlife medicine involved a lot of forensic pathology, and Antoine Musamba had become the Gorilla Doctors' resident expert over the last few years. It helped that almost all the gorilla killings had happened in the Congo, so the veterinarians based at the other parks in Rwanda and Uganda had a distinct disadvantage on that front. Not that they minded, of course. Even the most natural pathologists among them never looked forward to an autopsy of a gorilla they knew personally, though it often meant unlocking the mysteries of how they could better protect these vulnerable animals in the future.

They all paused to listen to an extended exchange of gunfire. When the last echo faded, Innocence looked up at the two veterinarians with an impatient look on his face. "Time for a careful exam is something you do not have, my friends. Those guns are getting closer, and we must not be caught here so far from the helicopter."

"He's right," Cole said, opening the backpack. "Let's glove and mask up for a quick once-over and then—"

"Wait," Musamba interrupted. "There's something else over here."

Cole jumped to his feet. They'd been so focused on the discovery, no one had done even a superficial assessment of their surroundings. Now he could see that the Congolese veterinarian was walking towards what looked like another dead gorilla. Its massive black form was about ten yards away, partially shielded from where the others were standing by a thick cluster of prehistoric-looking ferns.

"Oh, no," Musamba said, pointing at the body. "Can you see the left front limb there?"

Innocence and Bonny were right behind him.

"It's Rugendo."

"You know I'm still the new guy around here," Cole said, jogging over to the second gorilla's final nest. "How in the world do you recognize him already?"

"Rugendo is the only silverback we've known to lose an entire hand to a hunter's snare and recover to do just fine," Musamba explained. "We intervened about two years ago, removing the necrotic tissue and shooting him up with long-acting ceftiofur. He was head of a family of twelve. That must be one of his females back there."

The silverback was resting on his right side, and Cole did his best to ignore the deathly stench as he crouched down to look at the stump of a limb. The hand and wrist were missing, but the gorilla's long dark hair had grown over the area, covering up any sign of the old wounds.

"Looks like this guy Rugendo knew he was going to die, just like the female. You two agree?"

"Yes," Innocence answered. "I can see he made a proper nest here. He must have been sick for some time, you know. Gorillas are not messy creatures, and he did not take care of his toilet properly."

That's a generous way of putting it. Rugendo probably weighed in at somewhere near four-hundred pounds, and the amount of jungle vegetation required to provide the calories for his active lifestyle contained an awful lot of fiber. Trackers often used the nest droppings to determine how recently a gorilla was in the area, and they were also studied by scientists doing population and disease surveys.

Cole stood up and pulled the radio off his belt. "McBride to Big Bird, do you copy?"

"Is that what you're calling my pretty lady now?" Marna's voice came through clearly this time. "Yes, I can hear you fine. Where are you guys?"

"Just about half a kilometer from you," Cole answered. He heard an edge in Marna's voice that wasn't normally there. "We've found two dead gorillas. Not sure what did it yet, but we're about to get our hands on them and find out."

"Seriously? Shit." She paused. "Hey, our man Proper here is pretty sure we've got some fighters headed this way. Can you hear them much where you are?"

So that explains it. Cole knew Marna wasn't one to get worried unless the threat was real, and if Proper Kambale thought the threat was real, then it most definitely was. "Alright, well sit tight and we'll get back there as soon as we can. Keep us posted if anything changes. Out here."

"So much for a thorough necropsy."

Cole was disappointed. Even though he hated that these two beautiful creatures were dead, he still wanted to take advantage of the situation by doing some comprehensive sampling for the emerging infectious disease study. Time was running short for his data collection, and he wasn't about to miss out on a rare opportunity like this one.

"What do you guys think we have time for?"

Musamba had already slid an N95 respirator mask over his face and was pulling on a latex glove.

"No sense taking unnecessary risks just because we're in a hurry." He snapped the second one tight and knelt down over the silverback's putrid body.

"Two gorillas," Cole said, "and both had time to find a place to die."

"Probably not trauma, then." Musamba was moving his gloved hands through the silverback's long coarse hair. "Though that would have been the easier explanation. Why must these tragedies always happen on my watch?"

Cole followed his example with the mask and gloves, and they examined the carcass together while Innocence and Bonny stood guard a few yards away. "Looks like he's a couple of days fresher than the female."

"Yes, most of his soft tissues are still intact. No evidence of obvious bleeding here, either."

"That's good," Cole said. "I've got to admit, I was getting a little worried that we had walked right into an Ebola outbreak." Ebola virus was one of the top infectious killers of wild gorillas in central Africa, but it often caused vomiting, diarrhea, and sometimes even visible hemorrhage from bodily openings. "That would have been more obvious by now, though, I assume?"

"Probably, yes," Musamba said. "If Rugendo had died from Ebola he would not have this normal pile of stool produced in the days before death."

Cole watched him running gloved fingers over the gorilla's left foot, then caught his breath as he saw what had grabbed the other vet's attention. "That's not something you see every day."

The thick black skin was covered in raised bumps, mostly round and somewhat flattened on top, which had not been obvious from a distance but were easy to see now. Several of them had burst open in what looked like scabby ulcers, but others still had a head of yellow-white pus visible just under the dimpled surface.

"Look at this, his hand and face have the same lesions," Musamba said, moving his own hands up the silverback's immense body. "No, it wasn't Ebola or even our rebel friends that killed Rugendo. Probably some kind of virus—maybe monkeypox. Don't you think?"

"Can't say I've ever seen a case myself, but that's definitely how I would expect it to look." Cole traced his fingers through the hair of the gorilla's broad back. "The skin feels pretty normal through here, though. Would that be a typical distribution?"

"Yes, monkeypox lesions are usually focused around the face and extremities, just like smallpox used to be."

"That's right, and chicken pox stays around the torso more. I can still remember those itchy sores all over my chest, but the worst were the ones my little eight-year old arms couldn't reach in the middle of my back."

Cole thought of his littlest brother and sister, not yet born when the rest of his family suffered through those couple of weeks of *Varicella* infection. They were the only ones of his siblings who got immunity the easy way, after the chicken pox vaccine was finally approved.

"Okay, give me two minutes to take a couple samples of these lesions." Cole slid a new scalpel blade onto the slightly rusted handle in his other hand. "Then we'll get out of here."

"Here, this should be a good spot," Musamba said, pointing at a pus-filled lump on the bare underside of Rugendo's swollen forearm. It was still intact—hadn't had time to open up while the gorilla was still alive.

Cole lowered the scalpel blade towards the skin for the initial incision.

"Alrighty, cover your eyes just in case we've got any pressure in there."

His warning was a split second too late. A tiny geyser of pus just missed Cole's face and hit Innocence Kambale right at the corner of the mouth.

"Zoba!" The ranger jumped back, and Bonny whined, looking at Cole suspiciously. *Good thing I don't understand Lingala.* He hadn't even realized Innocence was there, leaning in behind them, when he started cutting.

"Oh, man, did I get you?" He hoped his genuine concern was clear.

"I am fine." Innocence was not wearing a mask. "Did not expect it to jump out at me like that. Next time, some more warning maybe?"

Cole knew he wouldn't have been able to regain his own composure so quickly had their roles been reversed. But like most African guides and park rangers who spent their lives working with foreigners, Innocence had developed an incredible level of patience with his *wazungu*. Some criticized it as leftover colonial subservience, but it also meant job security.

Musamba tore open an alcohol wipe and reached it toward the younger man's scarred face. "Just a small spot, I think. You didn't feel anything inside your mouth?"

"No, I will be fine," Innocence said. He let out Bonny's lead and she immediately plunged ahead into the brush. "I will make a quick circle to see if there are any others."

"Let's hope he *will* be fine," Cole said under his breath, watching Innocence lift his weapon and disappear behind the bloodhound. "I'll feel horrible if he comes down with something from that."

"Don't worry too much. Doesn't look like it got on his mucous membranes, and these guys who grew up in the forest have incredible immune systems anyway." Musamba circled another lesion on the gorilla's arm with one finger. "Here's a good one. Just leave a wider margin so you don't burst the lesion this time."

Cole carved a perfect elliptical pattern around the lump—just like removing a little skin tumor from an old golden retriever. He realized he was unconsciously allowing himself room for a tension-free closure, momentarily forgetting that this patient was way too far gone to be worrying about proper wound healing.

"Could you hand me a rat tooth forceps?" he asked. "Need to elevate this bit of skin so I can see what I'm doing when I cut it away from the underlying tissue."

Musamba tore open one end of a small paper sterile pack from his bag and folded back the ends, allowing Cole to reach in for the forceps. Using the forceps in his left hand and the scalpel in his right, the veterinarian lifted the free piece of skin and smoothly cut through its subcutaneous roots.

"Well, let's see what that can tell us," he said, dropping the dime-sized sample into the sterile cup Musamba had opened for him.

"Why don't you get a couple more while we have everything opened up. Maybe this one next to his eye, and another on his foot?"

"Sure, just give me a second." Cole felt his hands remembering their old familiarity with these surgical tools and quickly added two more skin biopsies to the sample cup. As he twisted the lid securely in place, he couldn't help but imagine the headline on tomorrow's *ProMED* e-mail alert, "Possible Monkeypox Outbreak Among Congo's Mountain Gorillas." Maybe it would even make CNN?

A LOW GROAN interrupted Cole's thoughts. He looked up and caught Musamba's questioning glance.

"Innocence, everything okay over there?" He couldn't see the park ranger anymore and realized that the sound of his steady movements through the undergrowth had stopped a few moments earlier.

"Oh, no." Innocence's voice was thick with tortured agony. "Come and you will see."

Both veterinarians jumped up and pushed through the thick vegetation, following the voice as it changed from human moans to low gorilla grunting. After about thirty yards, Cole saw the park ranger's thin frame hunched down over another black form. Bonny lay on the ground beside him, chin resting across one paw. Her job was done.

The stench here was overpowering, and a quick scan of the area revealed at least eight other dead gorillas huddled in makeshift death nests.

"Shit," Musamba muttered.

Cole felt like an awkward outsider who, while walking with a new friend, has just come upon the scene of a car accident in which this friend's entire family has been killed. Although he had loved working with the mountain gorillas over the last few months, he knew that he didn't yet share in the unique bond the other two men had with these majestic creatures. They *knew* these animals like family. They had dedicated their entire lives to protecting them.

He and Musamba cleared the remaining distance and crouched down beside the park ranger. *What's with the grunting?* Then he saw it, the slightest stirring of hair on the body just in front of them.

Another movement revealed a tiny black hand reaching out from under the dead female gorilla's prone form. Five perfect fingers slowly extended and then folded back into a clenched fist, holding tightly to their mother's coarse black hair.

VIRUNGA NATIONAL PARK
8:14 A.M.

The lone survivor," Cole murmured.

"And it's only an infant," Musamba added. "Not who we might expect as the last one standing here."

Innocence reached toward the baby gorilla's tiny arm, but the Congolese veterinarian caught his wrist just in time.

"At least get some gloves on, my friend. You've already had one close call today."

The park ranger withdrew his hand, nodding slowly.

"You are right." His voice quavered with conviction. "But I am not leaving this one behind."

Cole watched the two men closely. The park rangers and gorilla trackers spent hours every day following and observing their subjects. They naturally grew close to these adopted families and developed a sense of relationship and responsibility that far exceeded even the strongest connections he had observed between pet owners and their dogs and cats. Did this personal attachment go beyond the boundaries of what would normally be considered appropriate for true scientific endeavors? Maybe. But it was hard to imagine how the emotional involvement could be avoided, given the time invested by these men and the uncanny humanity of their subjects.

"Probably we will take it, yes. But be careful with yourself." Dr. Musamba's voice had a hint of emotion in it as well. "You do not want to be the next victim of whatever has killed all these old friends."

Cole moved around to the other side of the dead female and lifted her stiffened torso up just enough for the two men to gently pull the infant out from underneath her. Innocence held the five-pound gorilla cupped in his huge hands, while Musamba worked to free its tiny fingers from the dead mother's hair. The baby's body was limp and unmoving in their hands, and it had not uttered even the smallest sound of protest. Yet somehow its little hands maintained an incredible grip, only releasing their hold when the veterinarian pried each black finger open individually and replaced them onto Innocence's waiting hand.

Cole was struck by the eerie resemblance of these two sets of hands, the fragile wildness of the newborn mountain gorilla gripping for protection on the man who had spent his life providing just that.

"He's not in very good shape, that's for certain," Musamba said.

"Looks like his mom must have died overnight." Cole gently lowered the body back down to the ground. "The rigor mortis has already kicked in, but she's not beginning to putrefy yet. Just a little bloated in the abdomen, I think."

Innocence cradled the infant up against his chest with one hand and pulled the edges of his rain jacket over the frail body with the other. It was a cool sixty degrees high on the slopes of Mount Mikeno, and Cole knew the baby's temperature had probably already dropped dangerously low without its mother's body heat and constant nourishment to sustain it.

"Doesn't look like he's completely missed the bullet on this disease, though." Cole looked closely at the baby gorilla's wrinkled face. "Do you see this little rash around his lips?"

ALL THREE RADIOS crackled with static at the same time, and Proper's deliberate voice came through. "You must come back here *now*. The rebels are moving in our direction."

"Good copy," Cole replied. Why was Proper doing the talking now, though? He was normally the strong silent type. "Everyone okay?"

"Marna is preparing the helicopter—be ready to jump in and fly."

"Gotcha." It was like Proper had read his mind. "We're headed your way with all the speed we've got."

It was true—the three men were already jogging back to where they had left their bags near Rugendo's massive body.

"Say goodbye to your papa, little one," Innocence whispered. He had slung the M16 across his back before freeing the infant minutes earlier, but now Cole lifted it over his head.

"There's no way you can run very well with this banging against you," he said, already turning away down the path. The heavy steel felt like it belonged there in his hands, an extension of his own body that had been absent for far too long. Strange thing was, he'd never thought to miss it until that very moment. He was loving every day of this break from the military, and he definitely hadn't planned on getting back into the saddle so quickly.

"Yes, but are you comfortable with that thing?" Musamba looked skeptical.

"I think I'll manage. Now let's move!"

Had it really been two years since he turned in his own weapons and hopped on that C-17 out of Bagram? Two years, and yet the memories—and the nightmares—were as fresh as the day he left. Cole wondered again if he should have been more open about his career path with these guys. Might have come in handy for a time like this. But no, he was usually quite content to be the young American researcher simply tagging along for the ride.

They crashed through the understory now, spurred on by spitting bursts of automatic weapon fire coming from the direction of the helicopter. The quiet purposefulness of their outbound journey was long gone, replaced by an uneasy realization that this little foray might not turn out well at all. There was no predicting the behavior of these desperate men who were temporarily making the park their home.

Bonny led the way now, apparently needing no guidance from Innocence to track their own scent trail back to the helicopter. Cole followed right behind her, moving at a quick jog while grasping the rifle in one hand and holding onto his bouncing backpack with the other. It was coming back to him fast, this feeling of being totally present in the moment, every bit of mental agility and physical strength focused on the task at hand. Each low-hanging branch and fallen log was an obstacle to be subconsciously analyzed and instinctively overcome before moving on to the next one.

He glanced over his shoulder to make sure the others were still right behind him. Musamba wasn't quite as graceful on his feet, but he still ran surprisingly well for a man of his age.

"Go, go faster, Doctor," shouted Innocence, right at Musamba's heels. He was still holding the infant gorilla up against his chest, protecting him with his body from the twisting vines that seemed to reach out against their progress every few feet.

Cole heard a sharp yell behind him and turned to see the Congolese veterinarian fly through the air and then hit the soft forest floor with a thud. Innocence managed to leap to the side of the path just in time, narrowly avoiding a nasty fall that could have been fatal for his tiny charge. The tranquilizer gun and supply bag had gone airborne as well, but Musamba was already on his feet and gathering them up before Cole arrived to help.

"You okay?" he asked, doing a quick sweep for any obvious injuries.

"Yes, let's go."

He took off again in the direction of the helicopter. The forest was quiet except for the sound of their own pounding feet and the sporadic gunfire. *Guess the birds are smarter than us.* They gave their warning calls and made an escape, rather than continuing straight into the danger zone. Unfortunately for a bunch of earthbound humans, the mechanical bird waiting ahead was the only way out. Two quick bursts of fire were accompanied by the ripping sound of speeding metal passing through dense foliage, then heavy thuds as the stray rounds slammed into a waiting tree trunk.

They were getting close.

An image flashed through Cole's head. Dark skin and trembling pink muscle, bright arterial blood coating his face in a pulsing spray of death. It was two years since that freak wandering bullet found its home in the soft flesh of his veterinary technician Ben's thick neck. Replace the cool wetness of this mountain rainforest with the withering summer heat of the Korengal Valley, and that urgent evac was really not so different from this one. Speed and chaos and a hidden enemy—the memory raged on, in all its gruesome glory. The sound of an engine sputtering to life jarred him out of the flashback and was followed by the intense thwacking of rotors, moving faster and faster with each powerful slice through the air.

"There it is," he shouted over his shoulder. Bright sunlight from the clearing ahead beamed into the trees to meet them. The blast of air from the rotor wash caught his hair as he dropped to one knee beside the panting bloodhound and shouldered his rifle. Seconds later, the other two men were behind him.

"Are we clear to move to you?" Cole asked over the radio.

He could see Marna sitting in the cockpit looking out toward them. She held her Beretta M9 in one hand and motioned them forward with the other. He knew she had cross-trained as an armed park ranger back in South Africa, but this was the first time he had actually seen her pull a weapon out.

She carried it well.

"Yeah, we've got you covered best we can." The slightly higher pitch of Marna's voice was the only indication that she was sitting exposed right in the middle of a firefight. Brave girl. "Proper's returning fire on the other side of the bird."

Cole looked back over his shoulder.

"You gentlemen first, with Bonny too. Fastest you've ever run in your life."

They jumped into the clearing and took off sprinting across the remaining thirty yards. A burst of automatic fire erupted from the trees on the other side of the clearing, but it was too late. Within seconds, both men were scrambling safely behind the dog into the open hatch of the helicopter.

Cole raised his eyes to the vivid blue sky for a moment. First, do no harm. That phrase from his veterinary oath had taken on a new meaning the first time he found another human being in his sights and squeezed the trigger. But sometimes, he now knew well, the innocent needed an avenger. He moved the selector switch on the rifle from safe all the way over to burst and fired off an extended spray of 45-millimeter rounds.

"Cover me!" he shouted.

MARNA WATCHED AS Cole rose up from the kneeling position and took off running toward her in one fluid motion. She was firing blindly out the other side of the cockpit—probably not the wisest decision—but couldn't take her eyes off him. He played American football in college, she knew that, but she'd never really seen him in action before. There was something else about the way he moved, though—more than just the athleticism—that she couldn't put a finger on.

The sound of the weapons now reached a fevered pitch, coming from the surrounding forest in an unceasing wave. *There's no way he's going to make it.*

And then Cole went flying through the air, hitting the ground facedown with a crash.

"No!" she screamed, rising up from her seat in panic.

But he was moving again, rolling to the side and then back on his elbows in a prone position, rifle at his shoulder, firing across the clearing. Another smooth jump to his feet, and he covered the remaining ten yards with a burst of speed, launching himself in a soaring leap through the open hatch.

At that moment, Marna pulled back on the collective lever. The helicopter leapt off the ground, shooting up above the forest—as if it had been waiting for just that moment all morning long—and rapidly ascending into the open sky above.

They were safe.

WASHINGTON, D.C.
7:12 A.M. EASTERN STANDARD TIME

Anna flashed her ID badge along with an especially winning smile as she ran up to the employee access gate.

"Rough morning?" the Secret Service agent asked, grinning quizzically as he gave her handbag a quick look and waved her in.

"No—well, yes—but it wasn't my fault! I swear I was waiting on the Red Line at Union Station for twenty minutes." Anna tucked a strand of wavy hair behind an ear and took off at a quick walk up the curved drive. "I should have just biked!"

"Well hey, take care of yourself today," the agent called after her.

"Thanks," she answered, before spinning around to face him again. "I almost forgot! Can you give this to Tyson for me?" She dug into her briefcase, pulled out a small waxed paper bag stamped Metro Mutts in large block letters, and tossed it into the surprised agent's hands.

"Not while he's working, but he'll thank you later." He laughed. "Now get out of here before you get me in trouble!"

Anna turned and continued up to the entrance, a faint smile on her lips. This agent was younger than most of them, and cuter, too. They all looked so tough and official with their black uniforms and big guns, but his face revealed a touch of humanity she hadn't found in the severe looks of the other agents. Best of all, though, was that he worked side by side with an even more handsome Belgian Malinois. Tyson wasn't supposed to interact with people on the job, at least not in a friendly way, but his handler had let Anna sneak a couple of head scratches the previous week, and she was in love.

Not just with the dog, or his handler, but with her whole life right now. Only a few weeks into her summer internship in the White House Press Office, and she was thriving in the new role. The press secretary himself, Andrew Mills, had asked her to be his personal assistant for the summer. Even though that meant more responsibility and longer hours than some of her fellow interns, she jumped at the opportunity. She'd also fallen in love with D.C. and all that urban living had to offer. Who said a country girl from Wyoming couldn't make it in the big city?

"I'M SO SORRY I'm late, Mr. Mills," Anna said, pushing on the door to his West Wing office.

Her boss was there, standing behind his desk. But he was clearly talking to someone else, now blocked from view by the open door. His eyes opened wide as he said, "Good morning, Anna."

She stepped into the room and tried to muffle a gasp. President David Rogers turned to face her with an impatient look. His expression instantly softened, however, and he extended a large wrinkled hand.

"I don't think we've met. You probably know me, but you are—?"

"Anna. Anna McBride, sir. Mr. President, sir." She felt the hot flush of blood spread across her face. "I'm so sorry for interrupting. I'll just wait outside now. Thank you, sir."

"This is my summer intern," Mills said. "Apparently she hasn't yet learned the importance of knocking on doors before entering." He looked pointedly at Anna as he said these last words, but the grave expression quickly broke into a grin. "Just get yourself some coffee—I'll be out in a minute."

"No, I insist that she stay with us. Coffee can wait, but urgent discussions of international significance cannot. This is what she is here to learn, is it not?"

"Well, sir, I guess you're right. This will be good for her."

Anna couldn't resist one more face-saving plea. "Really, I'll be very happy to wait outside."

"Too late, Anna," Mills said. "Just listen and learn and remember your non-disclosure agreements." He turned back to the president. "I just don't see how you can go forward with this speech on conflict minerals in light of the disaster of a storm brewing in the Caribbean this morning."

Anna's ears perked up at the mention of conflict minerals. Her boss had given her the draft press releases to review last week, and she was immediately captivated by the story. Ever a faithful fan of Leonardo DiCaprio, she had seen and loved *Blood Diamond* years ago. Since then, she'd maintained a vague impression that the issue was pretty much taken care of. Something about the Kimberley Process, right? Now Anna knew that she had been wrong. Yes, the diamond industry was a little cleaner, but in its place were the gold, tin, and tantalum that now lined the pockets of governments and criminals alike throughout central Africa. This was something she could get excited about. But now a darn hurricane had to come and spoil the party!

"We've kept these people waiting for three years now," President Rogers responded. "It's not just a pet concern of mine. I thought you agreed that there are genuine national security implications here?"

Mills took a sip of coffee before replying. "You know I do. We've committed to addressing the issue, and today's conference would've been the perfect venue."

"Would have been?" The president's forehead was deeply furrowed.

"I just don't think you can afford another criticism over misguided priorities. Not with the election only four months away. Your challenger will love portraying you as too focused on a mysterious African mining problem when you should be worrying about this monster of a hurricane here at home. Remember Bush's mess with Katrina?"

"You're right, of course. But this is important."

Anna was surprised at the president's apparently genuine interest in the issue.

"It is," the press secretary agreed. "There are lots of important things happening in the world, every day. And they're all vying for your attention. But with all due respect, sir, we've reached our current quota of hot-button is-sues. First the Israeli retaliation in southern Lebanon, now the storm, and I know you haven't forgotten all the planning we've done for this Celebration of America on the Fourth."

"Anna, what do you think?"

The president's question caught her off-guard. She looked up into his intense green eyes, her mind racing to formulate a response worthy of this first presidential interaction. Thank God for all those years of speech and debate. Thinking on her feet and speaking with poise were talents Anna had worked hard to develop.

"I really admire you for getting behind the conflict mineral issue, Mr. President, and I agree that it needs your support in order to facilitate real change in the region. There are a lot of young voters who would love to see you taking more of a leadership role in promoting peace and economic growth in Africa."

President Rogers' eyebrows went up. "Well thank you, young lady."

"But I also have to agree with Mr. Mills," Anna continued. "We can't risk the comparisons to Katrina. Today this office needs to be all hurricane, all the time."

"Much as I hate to say it, you're exactly right." The president smiled. A smile that made Anna cringe inside. "At this point in the election cycle we can't afford any mistakes."

"And there you have it," Mills said. "We'll put these press releases on the back burner for today, at least. Now let's see where we're at with this storm."

4:47 P.M.

Anna hopped off her old purple Schwinn and squeezed it into a crowded bike rack. She had lost the original seat to an enterprising thief on her sec-ond day in D.C., and the new one was now securely bolted in place. They'd have to work a little harder for this one. She spun the combination lock and gave it a good tug. Life in the city did come with its own annoyances, but she could adjust, no problem.

Turning the corner onto 7th Street Southeast, she glanced at her reflection in the big windows of a French café. Although the temperature itself wasn't unbearable yet, this East Coast humidity was going to take some getting used to. Her normally tame hair had frizzed up like crazy, and she'd also learned just how quickly she could break a sweat. The day's walk from Union Station back to her apartment on East Capitol was so bad she hopped in a thirty second cold shower before running right out the door again. Back in her native garb of jean shorts, comfy t-shirt, and Chacos, she could manage much more easily. The dark business suits she had taken such care to pick out for the internship were quite obviously not made for summer in D.C.

Anna caught sight of her twin brother as she approached a wall of glass fronting the coffee shop. *Now that is a good-looking guy.* She took great pride in Chase's appearance and even felt an odd sense of ownership—those first nine months of extremely close quarters had served to create a unique bond.

His tall frame was hunched over a little table just inside the glass, clearly absorbed in the stack of papers covering the keyboard of his open Macbook. Chase had the same dark chocolate hair as the rest of the family, and she was still surprised to see it so uncharacteristically under control. Three weeks earlier, he had been sporting Wranglers and boots as the new state rodeo champion, so the transformation to classic khaki-wearing Capitol Hill intern was remarkable. The dark stitched leather of his favorite Tony Lamas crossed under the table was the only remaining hint of regular life back in Wyoming.

Chase glanced up at the door as it swung open with a rush of hot air.

"Hey, you finally made it!"

"Yeah, sorry. Had to jump in the shower after that walk from the Metro. Can you believe this humidity?"

"Makes you miss the mountain air back home, that's for sure." Chase pulled his navy blazer off the neighboring chair and laid it across his lap. "How was your day?"

"Oh, you know, just hanging out with the POTUS and shaping world history, as usual. Let me get a drink, though. What do you have?"

"Just the house blend. I would have gone for something cold, but Mr. Hipster behind the counter let me know that Peregrine doesn't ruin coffee like that. Hmpf."

Anna looked around the room as she waited for her turn to order. People watching was one of her favorite parts of any coffee shop experience, and Peregrine Espresso never disappointed. Behind the counter, three of the rotating crew of pierced and skinny-jeaned barristas fussed over hand-poured coffee. The hipster look hadn't been taken up with quite as much vigor yet back home, and Anna was intrigued. In fact, just yesterday she e-mailed her mom to ask about sending some of her old t-shirts. The agricultural and Wild West themes she grew up with would be perfect. Of course, no one needed to know that they had originally been designed and proudly worn without a hint of irony.

A couple of staffer-types like Chase stood in line ahead of her, engaged in a hushed but easily eavesdropped discussion about their well-meaning older congressman's latest social media blunder. At the bar, a bearded thirty-something juggled his espresso with a couple of yogurts, somehow managing to get the snacks into twin toddlers' hands without spilling a drop. The golden retriever and monstrous stroller parked outside must have been theirs. Stay-at-home dad, or just back from work early? She had noticed a few like him chatting away together as she jogged through Lincoln Park last week. Quickly caught up in a highly realistic daydream featuring Anna McBride as the powerful career woman supported by a similarly domestic hunk, she tripped over a beagle and landed in a heap on the concrete. Whoops.

"So what's the inside scoop on this storm?" Chase asked, closing the computer. "I'm sure you guys must have access to all sorts of top-secret meteorological data, right?"

"Don't know about that, but I guess NOAA does keep us in the loop pretty well. Everyone thinks it'll be a bad one, even though it's still early for hurricane season."

"Right, thanks for that detailed analysis." Chase gave her an exasperated look. "I was just looking at the satellite images online, and it's still building strength and picking up speed over the water."

He'd always been a bit of a weather geek, and Anna couldn't hide the amused smirk as she watched his enthusiasm build.

"It's already done some serious damage in the Bahamas, but this landfall on the Florida coast is taking longer than everyone expected."

"Mmhmm, I have no doubt you will keep me fully updated." Anna's eyes lit up with indignation as she remembered her big disappointment. "The worst part about it is that we had to cancel the president's speech on conflict minerals! Of course, we could have done it after all, seeing as the storm hasn't even hit the U.S. yet."

"Oh sorry, sis. I know you were excited about that. You had me kind of interested, too, especially with Cole right in the middle of things over there."

"Not exactly in the center of it, as long as he stays put in Rwanda. But yes, still right in his neighborhood."

Chase gave her a questioning look.

"Haven't you checked your e-mail? He was in the DRC today, trying to find the Virunga gorillas."

"No, I came straight over here, and you know I can't check Gmail at work." Anna was worried now. Her research over the weekend for the day's canceled event had made her realize just how unstable the area around Virunga National Park really was. "What else did he say? Dang it, yet another reason I need a data plan on this stupid old phone!"

"That was pretty much it, unfortunately. Just a typical two-liner."

Anna pulled the laptop over and opened it up, scanning through her brother's inbox until she found what she was looking for.

"They're back in Rwanda now," he said. "So it's too late to do much worrying."

He was right. There wasn't much more to the brief note from Cole. But Anna also knew he had a tendency to hide things that might worry their parents.

"Why does he keep mentioning this South African pilot girl?" Her tone betrayed a playful disapproval. "You don't think he likes her, do you?"

Chase raised a hand to his chin as his face took on an exaggerated expression of contemplation.

"Let me think about that for a minute." A sly smile broke through the mask. "Umm, yes. What's not to like about a helicopter-flying tall blond with an exotic accent?"

"Ugh, you guys are all the same!" Anna reached across the table to lightly slap her brother's arm. "What's wrong with us plain ol' American brunettes?"

"You know I love you, Anna." His smile had broken into a full grin. "But I'm going to ask Cole if that Marna chick has a younger sister."

TUESDAY, JUNE 29

Marna Van Wyk was as African as any white woman could claim to be. Her mother traced a direct descent from Jan van Riebeeck, founder of Cape Town and considered by most Afrikaners to be the father of their country. Way back in 1652, Van Riebeeck commanded the Dutch East India Company's expedition to establish the first European settlement on the rugged coastline of the Cape of Good Hope. Her dad's history was a little more ambiguous, but she did know that one great-grandfather was alone among his parents' eight children to survive confinement in a British concentration camp during the Second Boer War.

Now Marna had grown up in the new South Africa, and she embraced a slightly different take on things than most of her Afrikaner forebears. Her parents' education and vast farms around Nelspruit still set her apart from the majority of her fellow citizens, but she couldn't be held responsible for that, could she?

So Marna was an African. More African than Cole was American, she'd dryly pointed out when he tried to protest her claim to that title. His family had only been in the States since the late nineteenth century, when a young Aonghus McBride arrived from Scotland. Aonghus promptly enlisted in the Army and was shipped out west to join the 7th Cavalry's questionable campaign in defense of the new American frontier.

"The only difference between my white ancestors and yours," Marna remembered adding, "is that mine were not quite so successful in their efforts to wipe out the natives. A fact I'm quite proud of."

He took this quite well, she thought. Even though Cole occasionally liked to brag on his cowboy heritage, Marna knew he was a little more nuanced in his understanding of the world than he usually let on. Which was one of things she especially liked about this mysterious American veterinarian who had unexpectedly crashed into her life a few months earlier.

But where was he, anyway? Marna glanced up from her book and out a screened window into the cool darkness. Across the yard, a lone shadow moved across the brightly lit window of the lab. He was still at it.

She sat back in the old recliner and adjusted her mask for what must have been the tenth time in as many minutes. How did people ever get used to wearing these things? Yet another reason she couldn't have become a vet herself. Of course, that failing grade in organic chemistry didn't exactly help her chances, so Marna had gone another route and trained as a helicopter pilot in the South African Air Force. Every game farm and wildlife preserve in the country needed its own pilot, and she knew that these sky cowboys worked right alongside their veterinary colleagues. After her commitment to the SAAF was up, Marna landed a dream job just up the road from her parents' farm in Kruger National Park.

And now here she was in Rwanda, doing just what she always imagined but never really thought would happen. South African National Parks had loaned her along with the helicopter to Rwanda's fledgling park system back in March. The new president's recent commitment of tourism training and resources for other countries on their shared continent had raised some eyebrows among those more aware of just how competitive Africa's safari dollars really were. But when Marna proposed the loan and got initial approval, she flew north before hardly anyone in her organization even knew what was happening.

The helicopter. Those ugly gashes in the fiberglass skin would be tough to explain, if the previously immaculate machine ever made it back down to Kruger. But that was only one of several major concerns competing for attention over the last eighteen hours.

She looked around the makeshift isolation nursery she and the others had set up in one room of the veterinary hospital's temporary holding facility. The Gorilla Doctors' headquarters campus wasn't built to house gorillas for more than a few days, but it seemed to be holding up reasonably well. The three older orphans were moved from Virunga National Park's more permanent facility during a break in the fighting earlier in the year. They didn't have the same outdoor spaces to explore here in Musanze, of course, but Marna thought they still seemed pretty pleased with themselves most of the time.

That changed with the sick infant's arrival earlier in the day. The older orphans could tell that something was up, and they made it clear to everyone that they were not happy about being kept out of the loop. Marna looked down at the tiny creature clinging to a blanket in the crook of her left arm. Her gloved fingers crept up his wooly black back and traced around a perfect little ear, so very human in every way. He was sleeping peacefully now, but she knew he wasn't out of the woods yet. Even though the baby gorilla had quickly revived with some IV fluids and several good feedings, the discolored rash spreading across his skin told a different story.

"HEY, YOU STILL awake in there?"

Cole peered through the screen and watched as Marna shifted slightly and then slowly opened her eyes. The beam from her headlamp shone brightly down at an open book in her lap. An amused smile crept over his lips as the beam began moving across the floor and up the wall to the window, following the sound of his voice.

"Careful, that thing is bright!" he said, bringing a hand to his eyes.

"Oof, sorry about that," Marna answered groggily, reaching behind her head. The room went dark. "I guess I fell asleep after all."

"That's okay," Cole said. "It's past midnight, so Innocence should be coming by any minute to take over. How's our little man?"

"Pretty good, I think. He's been asleep since the last bottle at ten."

"Nice. Just sit tight for a minute while I get geared up. I want to take another look at him before I head back to the lab."

Cole stepped back from the window, brushing against the glossy leaves of the mango tree that provided such welcome shade during the day. He took a deep breath of the cool mountain air. At over six thousand feet in elevation, Musanze enjoyed some of the nicest weather in Rwanda.

And wow, had it been a long day. Even though a part of him felt exhausted, his mind wouldn't stop racing. There was no way he could get to sleep anytime soon, not with the biggest discovery of his brief scientific career still cooking in the darkened lab across the yard and working its evil magic in that tiny gorilla sleeping in Marna's arms. *Still, he's a lucky little guy.* Not just for the choice real estate the infant was currently enjoying, although that was hard to beat. How had Innocence even spotted him, a barely perceptible movement beneath his dead mother? Cole was sure he wouldn't have been so observant, only moments before their frenzied run back to the helicopter. He pictured that final sprint across the clearing. Who in the world would be so stupid as to actually fire on them? Was it really just some desperate rebels looking for ransom money?

The insistent tug of competing priorities was hard to ignore. Focus on the science first, knowing what it might mean for his own professional advancement? Or direct more attention and resources to the actual gorilla deaths and the violence his team had narrowly escaped on the ground?

He pulled thin white Tyvek coveralls over his clothes and topped the outfit off with a mask and gloves. Now that he'd gotten the preliminary lab results, they really couldn't mess around with any more human exposures, cute as this little orphan was.

"You look exhausted," Marna said. The genuine concern in her voice filled Cole with a quiet warmth. "Are you really going to keep working in that lab all night?"

"Probably. I've gone through one whole set of real-time cycles but I want to repeat everything before I sound any false alarms."

"So does that mean you found something?" Marna carefully handed him the still sleeping gorilla and switched her headlamp back on.

"Yeah, it looks like a definite match for monkeypox. I've gotten clear positive reactions for the two most commonly used genes on my PCR assays."

"Slow down, you lost me there."

"Sorry, polymerase chain reaction. It's kind of the bread and butter of molecular diagnostics right now—basically lets me look through those tissue samples from the dead gorillas for a specific sequence of a virus or bacteria's DNA—and allows for much quicker answers than we could otherwise get in a place like this."

"So how do you know you can really trust the answers this fancy machine is spitting out?"

"Good question, and sometimes we don't," he said. "But in this case I'm pretty confident. The genetic sequences of both the viral proteins I targeted are supposed to be one hundred percent specific to monkeypox, which helps rule out the possibility of any of the virus's nasty cousins."

"Like smallpox, you mean? I can't help but think about those awful pictures in my parents' old *National Geographic* magazines. The lumps and bumps completely covering those poor little kids' bodies look a lot like these ones."

"Yes, that would be a surprise. But fortunately not one our generation has to worry about. Even though it could infect other animals in lab experiments, smallpox only lived naturally in the human population. That's what made its eradication possible to begin with."

Marna slowly moved her headlamp's beam across the little gorilla's skeletal arms. "I could only hear bits and pieces of your conversation with Dr. Musamba on our trip back this morning. You said monkeypox is actually a rodent virus?"

"Yep. It was first discovered in lab monkeys back in the '50s, so that's where it got the name."

Cole parted the baby gorilla's thick hair and gently ran a finger over the diffuse spotted rash. It was already worse than when they found him earlier in the day. The gorilla was awake now and moved around in his hands with surprising strength.

"Since then," he continued, "people like me tromping around in central Africa found out that in reality the virus spends most of its time hanging out in a few species of squirrels. Every few years it makes these crazy jumps into humans and other primates, but we haven't really figured out why that happens or how we can predict and prevent it."

Although Cole's hands were still moving across his patient's little body, his eyes had unconsciously moved several inches higher to rest momentarily on the appealing curves of Marna's scrub top.

She lifted her head with a smile. "Ah, I get it. Predict like PREDICT, the program you're funded by, right?"

Didn't look like she had noticed his straying eyes, Cole saw with embarrassed relief. Why did he always find himself in these awkward situations? Late nights with attractive colleagues were recipes for disaster. Fun disaster, sure, but not what he was really looking for right now.

"Exactly. My doctoral research here is part of USAID's Emerging Pandemic Threats program, and PREDICT is a branch of that whole initiative. Basically, the U.S. government has given a nice pot of money to a bunch of groups like the Gorilla Doctors so they can study the emergence of new infectious diseases in geographic hot spots around the world. It just happens that many of these diseases jump out of high-risk wildlife like some of the ones we've been working with here."

Was she really so interested in research funding mechanisms? Her eyes hadn't left his own through that whole long-winded explanation. Or was she actually onto him and just wanted to see how long he would hold her gaze? Well, he wasn't going to be the one to look away.

A NOISE AT the door interrupted his plotting.

"Oh, you're both here now?" Innocence's resonant voice broke the hushed silence of the moment. "How is this little baby of ours?" He finished adjusting his mask as he crossed the room.

"Seems to be pretty stable. Still eating well and just the slightest fever," Cole said. "But unfortunately my tests confirmed our suspicions of monkeypox, so you're going to need to put on some coveralls before you take over."

"Cole, my friend." The exasperation was clear in this native Congolese's accented voice. "You know I have lived in these forests and worked with these animals my whole life without any Tyvek to protect me."

Cole smiled. The park ranger had a point. But he was the doctor and protector of the public health here, much as he hated bossing people around.

"Innocence, you *are* my friend and that is why I don't want any more responsibility for getting you sick."

Marna turned to look at him quizzically. "Any *more* responsibility?"

Cole contorted his face in exaggerated embarrassment. "I may have burst one of these lesions right in Innocence's face back on Mount Mikeno this morning. He was very generous to forgive me, but I just hope he's not incubating the virus even now because of my clumsiness."

"I am fine," Innocence said.

He took one final look at his adopted charge now struggling to gain a higher perch on Cole's shoulder and turned back toward the door.

"And you are right, I accepted your apology. So please, say nothing more about it."

TINY WHITE FLOWERS liberally adorned the unassuming green vines climbing along the plastered walls outside the building. Marna had always loved the strong dark scent of jasmine. She took a deep breath, filling her mouth and lungs with the cool night air.

"Can't you just taste it?" she asked Cole in a hushed whisper. They stood at the window looking in on Innocence's preparations for a night with the orphaned gorilla.

"What, the flowers?"

"Yeah, take a mouthful of air and hold it a few seconds. Think of it like wine-tasting. Swirl it around. Now, do you taste it?"

She watched Cole deliberately follow her instructions. He was doing it again, holding her eyes in that grip of focused attention. From any other guy, she would have known, no question, the desire of possession behind that intense look. With Cole, though, she was confused. He'd let three months go by without moving on from these occasional intimate stares. They'd even gotten tipsy together a few times, but nothing. Just a casual goodnight, and then back the next morning to the friendly banter of daily life and work.

Cole released the air and smiled. "That's nice, you're right. I've never thought about tasting scents like that."

He turned back to the window and Marna stepped in beside him. Not quite on purpose, she let her bare elbow brush and then rest again Cole's forearm. He didn't move. It was silly, especially with everything else going on, but there was something intensely comforting about this simple human contact.

They stood there, watching as the Virguna park ranger finished piling old blankets in a far corner of the room. The constant refrain of low hums and grunts came drifting through the screen to them—yet another way he put his tiny charge at ease. She might need to get some lessons on this mysterious mountain gorilla language if she was going to stay on as a foster parent. Innocence knelt down and then stretched out in the nest of blankets, cuddling the infant in one arm while resting his scarred cheek on the other. She kept meaning to ask Cole about the scar. All she knew was that it happened at the same time he and Proper's parents were killed. How could a child who had witnessed such horror mature into the kind and gentle man she now watched soothing this sick baby gorilla to sleep?

"You should get to bed."

Cole gave her shoulder a squeeze. There it was again. How could he not realize what his touch did to her?

"I know, I'm exhausted," she whispered. "You too?"

"Yeah, long day. I'm feeling okay, though, and need to go finish this second round of tests. I'll walk you back first."

Marna started down the hard dirt path toward the apartments on the other side of the complex. They walked in silence. She listened to the repetitive call of a lonely tree frog. *You're not the only one, little guy.* A dog barked in the distance.

She finally spoke again when they reached her door. "So remind me why these tests can't wait until morning?"

Yikes, she didn't intend for it to come out quite so boldly. But he was either denser or more skilled at hiding his true understanding than she expected.

"I need to at least confirm the results of the assays I've already done before getting the word out more widely tomorrow. If it's really monkeypox that's killing those gorillas, then this is a much more virulent strain than anyone's ever seen before."

"And if it's not?"

"Then we're in even more trouble," Cole answered. "And I'm on my way to infectious disease fame, or at least my first paper in one of the major journals."

Marna usually loved that playful grin, but his eyes betrayed the hungry ambition behind his humor.

"So that's what this is all about, then? Getting your name in the papers and moving on up in the world?"

He looked hurt. "Marna, I'm just kidding around. Sure, I want to be successful in my work, but I hope you know how much I care, too. If I only wanted to be rich and famous I definitely shouldn't have spent most of my life in school becoming a research veterinarian."

"I know, sorry." And she was. His unconscious rejection stung a little, but that was no reason to respond in kind. "I guess I'm just tired, that's all."

She unlocked the door. Better not to go down that road tonight, anyway.

"Hey." Cole reached out and grasped her hand, gently pulling her whole body into his. "You're beautiful when you're tired, then, you know that?"

Marna let herself fold into his steady arms as she felt three months' worth of unfulfilled tension lift off into the dark Rwandan night.

A BLISSFUL MINUTE passed before they were discovered. The pesky whine at Marna's ear stopped abruptly to reveal itself as a hungry mosquito on the side of Cole's neck. She jumped out of his embrace and smacked him with a practiced hand.

"You still haven't gotten your malaria meds refilled, have you?" she asked, laughing and opening her fingers to show an incredulous Cole the culprit smeared across her palm.

"Well, no, but I would have happily accepted the risk for another few minutes like that!" He pulled her back in.

But now the tides were turned, and Marna knew she had broken his resolve. She looked up at him happily and then moved her hands up along his body and against his chest to push him away.

"I hate to do this to you now, but you really do need to get back to that lab."

"Woah, woah, just when you finally convinced me it could wait?"

"I know, but I guess that mosquito brought me back to reality. I will remain ready to hear about how beautiful I am any time you please."

The look of resigned angst on Cole's face was irresistible, and she couldn't stop herself from reaching up to plant a light kiss on his scruffy cheek.

"Now take that with you back to the lab and be ready to tell me everything over breakfast."

"Ugh. You're a cruel woman, you know that?"

He took her head in both hands, leaned in, and gently rubbed his nose against her own. She felt his lips brush hers for the briefest second, and then he was gone.

GOMA, DEMOCRATIC REPUBLIC OF THE CONGO
9:24 A.M.

L ars Olsson nodded to the two guards as he stepped between them and pushed through the heavy white canvas flap into the tiny space that served as office, bank, and bedroom. Lowering himself onto the cot, he took a deep breath of the cool clean air. It was a welcome respite from the oppressive heat outside, even worse than usual due to the stench of burning tires wafting over the entire city.

The portable air conditioning unit and accompanying HEPA filter were unnecessary luxuries in a place like this. He knew that, of course. But after thirty years of moving from one hot and smelly location to the next, he was ready for a taste of luxury.

Had it really been thirty years since he hopped on that flight to Addis, a starry-eyed volunteer full of plans to save the starving children of Ethiopia? It was the day after his graduation from the University of Copenhagen as a newly minted physician. Thirty years. His tall wiry frame and full head of sandy blond hair might keep people guessing about his age, but he knew the deepening creases in his tanned face would give him away soon enough.

Olsson leaned into the tent's solid corner post and opened up his laptop. It always took several minutes for the mobile data link to find a connection, but he had to resist the urge to tap aggressively on the touchpad while he waited. Even the satellites did their best to avoid this god-forsaken rubbish heap.

Thirty years was a long time. A long time to devote to a cause that never seemed to get any better. The faces changed, the skin color changed, and the diseases changed. But everything else was constant, disaster after disaster, year after year. He loved it, this never-ending challenge of broken people needing his healing touch and organizational expertise. But he was tired.

A chime let him know the connection was live, and he watched his inbox fill with news from the outside world. His boss in Nairobi wanted an update. A nurse needed confirmation that they could still use her before starting the long journey from the States. Some freelance journalist requesting an interview. You'd think they would realize their readers didn't want to hear about it every time Africans start killing each other again.

And then the ProMED e-mails, this steady stream of reports detailing all the different ways people and animals got sick and died. Lars skimmed the subject lines with a passing interest. Another outbreak of cholera in Haiti, that came as no surprise. He spent two years running a post-earthquake field hospital in Port-au-Prince and saw enough watery diarrhea to last a lifetime. Wild ducks dying in Mongolia from the latest strain of influenza. Worrisome, but probably just another false alarm. He was tired of the media's feeding frenzy every time *the next big flu pandemic* loomed on the horizon.

"Dr. Lars, you have a visitor outside." The booming voice of one of the guards interrupted his reading.

"Right, who is it?"

"She says she is from the magazine, that she sent you a message this morning."

Well that was a bit presumptuous. The lines around his mouth deepened in an angry grimace, but the bolded subject line of one more e-mail caught his eye as he reached to close the laptop:

PROMED > MONKEYPOX, GORILLA - VIRUNGA, DRC;
UNCONFIRMED REPORT

The grimace changed to an open-mouthed gape as he opened the message. "How the hell did someone manage to get into Virunga?" he said out loud.

"That's what I'm here to find out, too."

Olsson looked up toward the crisp British voice and saw a slender white hand pushing through the tent flaps.

"Excuse me, Miss—" The guard's voice was firm.

"Get your filthy hands off me!" The woman's hand drew back through the flaps. "Do you have any idea who I am?"

Olsson stood up.

"No, he doesn't. And neither do I, for that matter." He glanced one more time at the open message on his computer screen before walking to the front of the tent. "It's okay, Pierre, you can let her in."

JUST WHAT HE needed, some distant cousin of the royal family who fancied herself a writer. Couldn't she have gone chasing rhinos in South Africa instead? God knows they needed all the help they could get. But no, this second-tier future duchess would take nothing less than the deepest heart of darkness for her big breakthrough story as a serious journalist.

Claire Clifford, only child and heir apparent of the Earl of St. Andrews. Did she really think he would be impressed? Ha. But if she wanted a story, it was hard to go wrong with the mountain gorillas. They had been tugging at the heartstrings and pocketbooks of the adoring Western world for a hundred years.

She wasn't bad to look at, though. Olsson fixed his eyes on the back end of the woman's skinny jeans as she turned to leave his tent. Yes, he would be quite happy to spend a few days showing her around. In three months he'd already slept his way through what was left of Goma's female expats, but he wasn't quite ready to start breaking the official prohibition on romantic interludes with his colleagues at the field hospital. This feisty royal visitor could not have come at a better time.

"So you really thought you would be able to get up into the park to see the gorillas?"

She might be pretty, but she clearly didn't understand the realities of war in central Africa. Olsson nodded to the guards as he left the tent.

"I may be new to this journalism game, Dr. Olsson, but I'm not ignorant of the advantages that come along with my family's connections."

"Call me Lars, please." He could play nice, when he wanted to. The doctor slowed his pace slightly so her Ladyship would not have to jog quite so obviously beside him. "And yet, you do seem to be ignorant of the fact that we are in the Belgian Congo. This is not Kenya, or Uganda, or another one of your cousin's former colonies."

He glanced at his guest to appreciate the effect of his words, then continued on. "I can guarantee you that your family's name and history are meaningless to the average rebel commander staking his claim here in North Kivu province."

They stopped outside the main entrance to the large hospital tent.

"Lars, darling, if that's what you prefer." Her facial muscles relaxed into a practiced smile as she stepped forward to place a hand on his arm. "Thank you for the history lesson. I'm sure I don't need to remind you that there are in fact no former Danish colonies here in Africa, or anywhere else in the world, for that matter."

"If you say so," he replied with a smile. He couldn't care less about the relative lack of empire-building ambition among his forebears, and he would wait for another day to remind her of Greenland and the Faroes.

"I'm also aware of certain other advantages I have that often help to open closed doors in a world so unapologetically run by men."

Olsson felt her hand tighten in a gentle squeeze. She released slightly and let her fingers slip down over his tanned arm.

"And a week of closed doors here in Goma has left you ready to start playing with these advantages?"

She brushed a strand of strawberry blond hair behind an ear and crossed her arms over her chest. "You only wish it were so easy, don't you, doctor?"

"Oh, I'm not worried about myself, Claire." This was a lie, of course, but he wasn't going to crawl into her lap so easily. "You should be careful with those tender touches, though. Some of the locals might not like it when they realize you're not really inviting them in for more."

"And what makes you think I won't be?"

Olsson looked into her eyes, waiting for the smile to break. But it never did.

"Just be careful. We're a long way from Scotland Yard, you know." He ducked in through the tent's entrance. "Enough of that. Didn't you want to see some of our patients?"

CLAIRE FOLLOWED THE doctor through the canvas flaps and welcomed the wave of cool air that rushed over her glistening face. The window unit in her room at the lakeside Ihusi Hotel had coughed up a blast of musty warm air when she first checked in a week ago, and—despite several visits from an overly confident in-house electrician—it was still losing the battle against the pervasive tropical heat.

"Welcome to Goma General Hospital, your highness," Olsson swung out an arm in an exaggerated flourish. "Proudly representing the finest medical care in the eastern Congo."

Claire raised her eyebrows. Was he being serious? She knew Doctors Without Borders was the real deal, but this seemed like a very basic operation.

"Yes ma'am, ever since the last of Goma's local doctors fled to Kinshasa last month, we're the only shop in town."

"Well, can't say I'd like to find myself in need of your services."

Claire felt her eyes adjusting to the dim filtered light glowing through the white canvas tent. Everything was white, she noticed. White folding cots arranged in long rows, made up with white cotton sheets. White doctors and nurses dressed in white scrubs and lab coats. A glaring white surgical light at the far corner of the tent. Everything except the patients, that is, who were *black black black*. Claire wasn't a racist, she was sure of that. But it was harder than she expected to be in the minority all the time.

"If anything happens to you, we might be willing to do some initial stabilization before putting you on a chartered flight back to London." He lingered on the *might* a little longer than Claire would have liked. "If you play nice, that is."

"I don't plan on getting myself shot or blown up, but thank you for that assurance. I'll be sure to behave myself."

She followed as he stepped towards the nearest cot and knelt down beside a sleeping child. "Most of our patients don't have that option, to simply fly on out of here. We're their only hope, and unfortunately we can't save everyone."

He pulled the sheet back to reveal a bandaged stump just below the girl's left knee. Claire exhaled slowly.

"What happened?"

"Wrong place at the wrong time, just like most of the civilians we're taking care of." He adjusted the flow of intravenous fluids running into the girl's arm. "The hardest thing is that we often don't know who's innocent and who's not. A little girl like this, that's easy. But almost anyone else could have blood on their hands."

"And so you would turn them away, let them die on the street, if you just knew their crimes?"

"There are only a hundred beds in this little inflatable hospital of ours, Claire. We try to focus resources on those who are not instigators in the conflict, but in reality it's almost impossible to discriminate." He stood up again and started walking down the central aisle. "As long as they don't come in with a rifle strapped to their backs, we'll do what we can to provide a healing touch."

Claire's eyes lingered on each cot as she passed. She had never seen such a concentrated display of human suffering. Every combination of missing limbs was joined by burned faces and bandaged heads. Those were the obvious injuries, though. She couldn't tell what was wrong with most of these anonymous Africans, and she honestly didn't want to know. Claire felt the heaviness lift off as she refocused on the real reason she was here. There would always be more humans living and dying and destroying the rest of the earth while they were at it. The mountain gorillas, though, that was a species she could really care about. And they needed her help.

She quickened her pace to catch up with Olsson, who was bent over a bed at the other end of the tent.

"Thank you for the tour, Lars," she called out, realizing too late that her volume was several levels too high for the hospital setting. Claire reached his side and continued in an exaggerated whisper that seemed more appropriate. "I appreciate this little peek into your operation here, but you promised that we could discuss that report about the gorillas."

He put one finger to his lips and adjusted the position of a stethoscope with the other hand. Claire clenched her teeth but remained silent. She was not used to being shushed or ignored, especially when she had so clearly made her needs known. The man lying in front of her seemed to be in worse shape than most. He was in a real adjustable bed and hooked up to equipment that looked like it could have come straight out of a posh private hospital in London.

"I guess this is your little ICU ward, then?"

Another finger to the lips as Lars continued moving the silver bell over different areas of the man's bandaged chest. *He's doing that just to spite me.* Claire knew it wasn't true as soon as the thought crossed her mind, but did this guy really need such an extended listening session? Finally the doctor removed the buds from his ears and replaced the stethoscope around the back of his neck.

"Sorry about that, but this gentleman is in a pretty bad way."

Claire nodded her head and tried to force an understanding smile.

"You want to talk about the gorillas, then? Interestingly enough, our friend here might have been a good source of information. He was found a couple of nights ago near the old park headquarters at Rumangabo. Dropped off outside the hospital here nearly unconscious."

"And that's just outside the gorilla sector, right?" Now Claire was more interested.

"You've done your homework, yes. I can guarantee you that he wasn't out there gorilla trekking, though, so I highly doubt he would have anything of interest to tell you."

"Can I ask him some questions when he wakes up?" She looked into the man's face, wondering if he might have seen anything that could jumpstart her unsuccessful investigation. *Endangered Mountain Gorillas Threatened by Warring Rebels in the Congo.* She already had the basic story written out, but it still needed at least a couple of decent quotations and all the photographs before it was ready for the public eye.

"If he wakes up, you mean? He's only just hanging on." Olsson shook his head and glanced at a clipboard that was hanging off the side of the bed. "Three gunshots to the chest and abdomen have left him septic and with only one healthy lung. Who knows how he crawled out of those mountains."

Claire looked down at the man's hand, resting along his side just inches from her own leg. An IV catheter was taped in place on top of it, feeding a steady stream of fluid and drugs in this last-ditch effort to keep him alive. Who was this dying rebel? Did he ever catch a glimpse of the majestic creatures who shared the forest with him? She gave in to a sudden impulse to run her fingers along the top of his arm, realizing with mild surprise that it was the first time she had ever touched a black man. Or maybe he wasn't a rebel at all, but actually a gorilla tracker out to check on his endangered charges, ignoring the risk to himself?

"So quick to ignore my advice about those gentle caresses?"

The doctor's words pulled her back to the present, and she jerked her hand away. Not because of what he said, though.

"Why does he have these little bumps on his skin?" Claire rubbed her fingertips instinctively against her jeans, then looked up. "I'm not going to come down with one of those flesh-eating worms or something awful like that, am I?"

"What do you mean, bumps?"

Olsson reached across her and began moving his own fingers across the man's arm. She saw him pause in several places, pushing into the skin and tracing invisible circles with a long index finger. It looked like he was holding his breath. Suddenly he grasped the man's hand in his own and lifted it into the air, turning it over to bring the palm up toward his face. It was covered in dark rounded bumps, even more obvious against the lighter pigmentation of the man's palm.

Claire watched as he shook his head slowly and dropped the hand. It caught on the side of the bed before rolling off the edge in a heavy collapse.

"Oh, shit," he whispered.

Cole stepped into a pair of giant rubber boots as he pulled the latex glove tight over his left hand. Protection complete. He smiled as he realized what a far cry this was from the Biosafety Level 4 labs he trained in at USAMRIID the year before. The U.S. Army Medical Research Institute for Infectious Disease. He had spent three months at the sprawling research complex in Frederick, Maryland, mastering some of the molecular techniques he was now using in Rwanda.

The Tyvek suit and N95 respirator mask were not really an adequate substitute for the positive pressure space suits he'd used at USAMRIID, and after the all-nighter in the lab he wished he had more. It didn't make a lot of sense—the clinical signs and genetic testing both indicated monkeypox all the way, but monkeypox didn't usually kill so efficiently. The speed with which the virus must have gone through those mountain gorillas was incredible.

At least the world of science had never formally documented an outbreak like this. It was rare to find a virus that spread so quickly and easily while also causing severe disease and death. Highly transmissible and highly pathogenic at the very same time. Bugs like that tended to burn themselves out, plowing through a susceptible population until there was nobody left to infect. It wasn't a great strategy for long-term survival, and that's why most diseases stayed away from the deadly combination.

There was a lot of life and death happening in central Africa that was invisible to the rest of the world, though. Someone had to be there to find the dead, identify what killed them, and tell the story. Cole knew he was lucky to be in the right place at the right time.

This was his chance to be that someone.

"Hey, you planning to stand out there all day?" Marna's voice brought him back to the little entry area outside the infant gorilla's nursery room. "Poor little Endo has been waiting all morning to say hi!"

"Yeah, sorry, just gearing up out here." He opened the door and stepped into the improvised isolation ward. "Someone's got to stay alive to tell the rest of the world what happened here, you know."

"Very funny." Marna's inviting smile was a welcome sight. Or at least the peripheral evidence of it was—the bright eyes and tone of voice. The smile itself was hidden behind her round white mask. "Don't worry, though, as much as I hate this protective equipment stuff, I've been doing everything just like you said."

Cole walked across the room to the recliner. She was curled up looking relatively comfortable, feet tucked under her and a book resting on one arm of the chair. If it weren't for the biohazard gear and infant gorilla sleeping on her chest, she would have made for a perfect picture of home.

"Endo, you said?"

"Yep, the Virunga rangers decided to name him after his dad, Rugendo."

"Gotcha." Was it really only yesterday that they discovered the massive silverback's stiffened form? "At least we assume he's Rugendo's baby. You know those blackbacks occasionally get a little action on the side, too." Each mountain gorilla family was usually made up of one mature silverback male, several younger blackback males who weren't really supposed to be breeding, and a larger number of females with their young.

Cole caught the sly humor creeping around Marna's eyes.

"Yes, I've heard," she said. "No reason the big old daddies should be the only ones having fun, right?"

"Exactly."

He knelt down beside the chair and pulled a small digital thermometer from the pocket of his coveralls. There was a quick vibration against his leg. An incoming text message. It would have to wait.

"So how do you think he's doing this morning?"

"Not great, honestly. He's hardly woken up for me since I took over from Innocence a couple of hours ago, and he would only drink about half an ounce of the formula."

She was right. The fluffy black form nestled against her had barely stirred when he entered the room and started talking. He watched the long dark hair rise and fall rapidly. The respiratory rate was obviously higher, and there seemed to be an increased effort behind each breath.

"I'm going to get a temperature on him, see if that fever has changed at all."

He placed one hand over the gorilla's tiny rump, rotating it away off Marna's chest. It reminded him of similar slightly awkward interactions with female pet owners over the years. Why did they always insist on holding those puppies and kittens so close to themselves?

He glanced up at Marna's face. "Sorry, not trying to come on to you here!"

She laughed, an open and honest laugh he had come to love over the past few months.

"Really? I think you've just been looking for an excuse."

He felt the blood rush to his cheeks and thought of that hint of a kiss they shared the night before.

"Guess I can't deny that." All those hours in the lab had given Cole time to think, and he was finally ready to see where this thing might go. "But I've gotta be honest, any daydreaming I may or may not have done on this subject definitely didn't involve so many layers of synthetic petroleum byproducts."

She raised her eyebrows.

"You know, all this latex, Tyvek, nylon, that's what it's made of."

"Well, if you can one day learn to tone down your science-speak for us regular ol' countryfolk, you might just have a chance to fulfill some of those daydreams of yours."

Cole's quick smile froze when the thermometer beeped three times, and he pulled it out of the infant gorilla's tiny rear end. The fact that Endo had barely stirred when subjected to such an indignity was not a good sign. Neither were the numbers that flashed on the instrument's stamp-sized screen.

"Well, what is it?" Marna asked.

"101.8. A little higher than what Dr. Musamba got overnight. He's still fighting the infection, but we don't want to see it get any higher than that."

"And if it does?"

"Then we might start thinking about some meds. Anti-inflammatories, maybe even one of the anti-virals we've got back in the pharmacy."

Cole wiped the thermometer with an alcohol swab and put it back in the coverall pocket. He looked at the gorilla's fragile black hands, clasped tightly on another old blanket. It was a poor substitute for his mother's long dark hair. Why did those little hands keep drawing his attention? Each petite fingernail seemed a stark reminder of the creature's strange humanity.

Cole felt the vibration against his leg again, but this time it continued. That was a major problem with the full biohazard get-up—it was impossible to access anything left inside the suit.

He ran an index finger along one of the little gorilla's hairless forearms. The rash had turned into barely perceptible bumps in the paper-thin skin. Classic monkeypox, sure, but why was each stage moving so quickly? It didn't match any of the case reports he read through in the lab overnight.

"Let's see if he'll eat anything for you," Marna said, reaching for a formula bottle on the table beside her. She moved the nipple gently across Endo's pouting lips. After a few seconds, they responded, answering the instinctive call known by every newborn, and opened just enough for her to push it all the way in. A few tiny bubbles rose inside the bottle.

"Hey hey, success!"

But he'd spoken too soon. The baby gorilla erupted in a series of fragile coughs, spraying formula in a fine mist through the air. The coughing sputtered out, and with a delicate moan Endo turned his face away from the still-hovering bottle and into the blanket.

"And that's why we wear these masks," Cole said, unconsciously checking the seal of his own where it crossed the bridge of his nose.

"I'm beginning to understand how all those new mothers feel when they complain about their kiddos not wanting to eat." Marna shook her head. "I mean, how long can he survive if he doesn't start taking more of this stuff?"

"Not more than—"

A quick pounding on the door startled them both.

"Dr. Cole, Dr. Cole, are you there?" Proper Kambale's voice.

"Yeah, everything okay?" He stood up and strode over to the door, which had now been opened a crack from the other side.

"We have been trying to reach you from the office. Someone is waiting on the phone for you, calling from Goma."

So that explained the repeated calls to his cell. "Thanks, Proper. Let me just get out of this stuff and I'll be right behind you."

The tall man nodded his head. He looked very similar to his brother, Innocence, but without the disfiguring scar across his cheek. Cole turned back into the room with a quick shrug and a wave for Marna, and then stepped out into the entry area.

"Any idea who he is?" Cole called after the departing park ranger.

Proper turned around.

"A doctor, from Médecins Sans Frontières." The French rolled off his tongue easily. "He says it is about your ProMED message."

"Hello, this Dr. McBride." Cole spoke into the phone, trying to mask the breathlessness resulting from his run across the grounds. He was on a landline in the Gorilla Doctors administrative office.

"Dr. McBride, nice of you to take my call." There was a characteristic northern European flourish to the man's sarcastic introduction. "I'm Lars Olsson, medical director of the MSF hospital across the border from you here in Goma."

"And I'm Cole McBride, veterinarian and PhD student here with Gorilla Doctors."

"Ah, a veterinary doctor. I wondered."

Cole frowned. Always playing second fiddle to the *real* doctors, there was no way around it.

"I heard you were calling in reference to my message through ProMED this morning?"

"Yes, I've got something interesting for you here at the hospital."

"What, did someone bring in one of the dead gorillas or something?" The situation had just gone from bad to worse. "I hope you've got it appropriately quarantined."

"No, no, much more serious than that. It's a human."

Cole held his breath.

"A live human. I believe we have the first human case."

GOMA
3:08 P.M.

Lars Olsson pulled out of the gated Doctors Without Borders compound with two honks on the horn and a harsh spinning of tires on gravel. He peeked at his only passenger and smirked with satisfaction at her white-knuckled grip on the armrest. This was going to be fun.

"How far did you say it was to the border?"

Claire had to shout over the fast Congolese rumba beat blasting from the truck's rugged speakers. She had already undergone a regrettable transformation in his mind from intriguing to annoying. It was to be expected, of course, but most women lasted longer than a few hours. Half a day suffering through the self-important Brit's questioning had been enough.

"The border?" He shook his head, dismayed. "It's just across town, twenty minutes at most."

Had she really spent a week in Goma without grasping this most basic fact of the city's geography? Its proximity to the Rwandan border was the root cause of so much grief over the past twenty years. After a triumphant Tutsi victory ending the infamous genocide, millions of Hutu refugees had poured into Goma and brought their violence with them.

"And from there to this gorilla vet headquarters?" she asked.

"Musanze. Shouldn't be more than an hour or so, depending on the roads." The doctor slammed a hand down onto the steering wheel, but the blasting horn had no effect on three old women crossing the dirt road in front of the vehicle. The wrinkled skin drooping off their bare arms provided a sharp contrast to the bright patterns bursting from their flowing dresses. After what seemed like an eternity, they reached the other side, and Lars stepped on the gas briefly before bringing the truck to a screeching stop again. This time it was a group of goats, grazing contentedly on a pile of trash in the middle of the road.

"And traffic," he added. Car traffic was rare in all but the biggest African cities, but the never-ending stream of people and animals apparently intent on obstructing his forward movement more than made up for its absence.

"You mean this gigantic Land Cruiser doesn't have the desired imposing effect?" Claire laughed.

"Sadly, it's just the opposite," he admitted. The trademark vehicle of the humanitarian community attracted the needy masses like moths to a light bulb.

"Well you can't blame them. Every time your type pulls up in a big white SUV it means free goodies, right?"

"Something like that," he said dryly. He was past the point of trying to keep up their flirting banter. She did have a point, but his days of handouts and photo opportunities were long gone. Leave that to the celebrities out on their annual poverty safaris.

He turned the volume up several notches.

"I guess they don't want what we're carrying this time, though." The wannabe journalist was leaning across the center console now, her shouting mouth almost touching his ear. She just wouldn't give up.

He glanced in the rearview mirror at the cooler tied down between benches in the back of the Land Cruiser. She was right. No one in their right mind would want anything to do with the special cargo they carried. Ten kilos of ice surrounded three layers of sealed sample bags, delicately packed just twenty minutes earlier. It was a lot of effort for one little biopsy cup and a tube of freshly-drawn blood. But it was worth it, if that American veterinarian turned out to be right.

Olsson shifted his line of sight just over to the right. He couldn't help but admire the woman's high-cheekbones and full lips, all framed by rosy blond waves cascading down past her shoulders. Something about her appearance seemed to exude the noble genes of which she was so consciously proud. It would be a conquest to remember, and even better, to regale his old med school friends with back in Denmark. *Might as well give her another chance.* He relented, and turned the volume back down.

CLAIRE TAPPED A hand against the side of her seat and crossed her legs again. The urge to pee had been growing ever since they left the compound. Why didn't she go before they left? Somehow she'd never grown out of this childish lack of foresight, and she often suffered through embarrassing situations as a consequence.

Like now.

At least Olsson had started being friendly again and wasn't giving her too difficult a time about it. He promised that there was a somewhat private hole-in-the-ground she could use at the border station up ahead. But the long line of cars they had been sitting in for the last twenty minutes wasn't moving at all. The heavy black smoke billowing up from over the last hill before the Rwandan border only added to her anxiety. Of course, in most situations she would have swallowed her pride and done the deed right on the side of the road, royal honor be damned. But the line of vehicles they sat in was surrounded by a swelling crowd of angry-looking Africans, and there was no way in hell she was going to pop a squat right in the middle of this chaos.

"You holding up okay there?" Lars asked. She still couldn't tell when he was being genuine.

"Not really, actually." She wanted to scream, but they weren't quite close enough for that yet. "How long do you honestly think we could be stuck here?"

"No way to know." He laid on the horn again.

"I wish you would stop doing that. It just makes them look at us with even more evil in those dark eyes."

She hated that the men passing the Land Cruiser could peer right in through the window, their bitter faces just inches from her own. The women and children walking with them seemed more content keeping their eyes to themselves.

"So you're done pretending you actually care for the people here?"

"It's not that," she said. "Just that I didn't come here for the people. You know my story focuses on the plight of the gorillas." Couldn't he appreciate that?

"Ah yes, your precious gorillas. And yet you've never even seen one, have you, in its natural habitat?"

"Don't start that again, please. You're much more fun to be around when you're playing nice."

"We Westerners will shell out our gold and even lay down our lives for the endangered mountain gorilla," he continued. "But does anyone raise a finger when five million human souls are sent to hell?"

"Five million?" Was he being serious? She knew a lot of people had died, but that seemed like an exaggeration.

"Even more than that. All killed here in the Congo over the last two decades of conflict." The doctor shook his head, and his face showed a confusing mix of disgust and pity. "But no, please go ahead and write your story about the mountain gorillas. At least it puts this place on the map."

"And you think that could help somehow? With the greater conflict?" Claire felt an amplified sense of purpose surging inside her. It was a rare sensation.

"As long as the mountain gorillas are alive and well, the rest of the world has a reason to care about Virunga and the Congo. Kill them off, and it's all over."

"What is? I mean, are you saying the gorillas have something to do with everything else that's going on here?"

Claire wanted to make sure she understood the connection clearly. It might be just the unique angle she needed to get her story published with one of the big-name magazines. She glanced out the window and noticed that the crowd was moving more quickly.

"Well good, I guess you've got a head on your shoulders after all." The doctor smiled wryly. It was an attractive smile, in that alluring middle-aged guy kind of way.

"Go on."

"What I'm saying is that people care a lot more about the plight of eight-hundred endangered mountain gorillas than they do five million anonymous Africans."

He stared at her, his ice blue eyes drilling a hole into her soul. "The world doesn't care about one more African boy being forced to kill his parents as initiation into a tragic life as a child soldier. It doesn't care about one more little African girl being kidnapped and forced into bondage as a sexual plaything for warlords four times her age. What the world cares about are cute baby mountain gorillas losing their jungle homes."

A single bead of sweat broke free from his forehead and traced a path down the doctor's dusty cheek.

"Take the gorillas out of the equation, and this place descends into an even greater hellhole of violence and economic exploitation than ever before. Journalists like you stop coming, donor money stops coming, international organizations pull out, and the heart of darkness reigns supreme."

"Wow."

Claire wouldn't have guessed such an emotional diatribe could come from the rather cynical aid worker's mouth, but there it was. The sense of greater conviction that had been hiding under too many layers of her own psyche crested a wave of new inspiration.

A fist slammed against the driver's side window, just as the hideous rattle of a machine gun sounded in the distance.

Claire jumped halfway out of her seat and felt her head smack against one of the hardened steel roll bars along the Land Cruiser's roof. A wet warmth spread between her thighs.

"What the—" Lars yelled. She saw him tug on the wheel as the SUV lurched away from the offending contact.

But the fist followed, and now it was pounding again and again. A large black face pressed against the window.

"Doctor Lars, doctor Lars!"

"Oh shit," Lars said. "Guess I know this guy."

The cars in front of them started moving, and the mass of people outside was now running, frantic faces and crying children. She crossed her legs and pulled a bag up onto her lap. Not perfect, but it did the job.

Lars rolled down the window a few inches.

"Doctor Lars, you treat my son at hospital, two weeks past." The man was breathless, an expression of uncontrolled fear glowing in his brown eyes.

"*Eh bien. Je vois.*"

Claire swore under her breath as Lars and the man carried out a hurried exchange in French. The only words she could pick out were what sounded like three letters repeated over and over. *L-R-A.*

"LRA *viennent,*" the man was whispering. "*Vous devez échapper. Evadez-vous maintenant!*"

"*Merci, mon ami,*" Lars replied. "*Allez avec Dieu.*"

The man disappeared into the crowd as Lars stepped on the gas and swerved onto a small rutted track cutting off the main road.

"What did he say? What are you doing?" Claire realized she was shouting. She tried to continue more calmly. "My French is horrible already, but I can't understand anything with that awful African accent."

Lars kept his eyes ahead as he responded quietly. "He seems to think that the LRA is here."

"LRA?" She recognized the letters from somewhere, but there were too many acronyms in this swarm of rebel groups and government forces to keep track of them all.

"Lord's Resistance Army. Joseph Kony and his crazies. That LRA."

Now she remembered. Kony 2012 and all that YouTube hype. Hadn't they caught him already? Claire knew the psychotic Ugandan warlord was famous for his brutality, but she was still shocked to see the change that had come over Olsson's face. It looked as though all the healthy tanned color had drained away, leaving a much frailer old man in its place.

"Where are we going?"

Claire laid a hand on his wiry arm, feeling her own fear dissipate slightly as an honest tenderness welled up within her. Did he have some kind of history with them?

"There's another route that can get us to the border," he said. "Runs parallel to the Goma-Gisenyi road."

The color was already returning to his face, accompanied by a fierce look of hardened resolve. But that didn't change what Claire had seen moments before. He was vulnerable after all, this jaded humanitarian who seemed to take such pleasure in making her feel small.

"Won't they close the border station?"

"They might try," he said. "As long as we can get there we should be okay. I've been known to play the doctor card to great effect."

"Doctor card?"

"Here in Africa they love us white doctors." He shrugged.

Claire looked out the window as they bumped along the muddy track. Dilapidated tents were crammed one after another on either side, and there was no sign of a cross path that might let them continue eastward toward the Rwandan border. She hadn't spent much time in the informal refugee camps surrounding the city, but something seemed to be wrong here. Where were all the people?

There. A break in the tents opened up ahead. The SUV skidded to a stop, and Olsson began turning the wheel to maneuver it onto an impossibly narrow path. Now they were going in the right direction, at least.

Claire gasped.

A monstrous black pick-up truck turned into their path, not more than fifty yards ahead. She could see four men above the darkly tinted windshield, their arms cradling scary-looking guns as they leaned casually over the top of the cab. As if on cue, the men raised their weapons.

"Well that throws a wrench in our plans." Lars slammed on the brakes and then shifted into reverse, sending Claire flying forward against the windshield. "Sorry about that, better buckle up and hold on tight, sweetie."

She lifted one hand to her throbbing forehead as she fastened the seat belt with the other. A knot was already forming, and her fingers came away slick with blood. What the hell did he think he was doing, trying to outrun these guys? She could just make out the look of astonishment on their faces, and one of the men pointed his rifle to the sky and fired off a quick burst.

"Stop!" she shouted. "You want to get us both killed?"

No response. He spun the wheel as they flew back into the intersection, the truck knocking a corner out from the closest tent as it pulled sharply back onto the original rutted track. Claire was shocked to see the fearful dark eyes of a child staring out at her as the tent collapsed, and then they were moving forward again, engine roaring. She caught a glimpse of the black truck speeding toward them, and heard another burst of gunfire at the same moment that one of the rear windows shattered in an explosion of broken glass.

"Keep your head down."

The doctor's voice had not changed, which only made her angrier. As if he went running for his life from armed militias on a regular basis. They were picking up speed now, bouncing dangerously between the unbroken rows of tents on either side.

"We don't lose anything by trying to evade them now," he said. "If they had wanted to kill us, they could have done that right from the start."

"Fine," she yelled from the floor. "But you really don't think we should just see what they're after?"

"Want an honest opinion?" He didn't wait for an answer. "I've seen enough LRA victims to know we'd be better off dead."

Claire wanted to cry. Why had she come along on this little adventure, anyway? To get the inside scoop on the gorillas. Ah, yes. Those men in the truck looked a little bit like gorillas—did that count? She regretted the decision to come to Africa in the first place. Why couldn't she have been content with her sheltered London existence, without a care or responsibility in the world? What was she trying to prove?

She felt the deep thumping bass from the truck behind them before she could hear it. Steadily growing louder, vying for dominance over the growling of the Land Cruiser's overworked engine. The rebels were getting closer.

"They found the chase scene soundtrack, at least." With her face to her knees and hands locked over her head, Claire could barely hear Lars' voice over the uproar. "A nice touch, really."

A sharp pop interrupted the rhythm, and the back right corner of the vehicle dropped. One tire down.

"That might be it for us," Lars said quietly, as the SUV continued tearing down the track.

Another burst of gunfire, a loud hiss, and the rear end evened out.

"Yep, that's the game."

Claire heard the doctor inhale deeply and felt the damaged vehicle drag on its back rims to a rapid stop. She turned her head just in time to see him turn the key in the ignition, and the engine went silent. Now the full blast of the pursuing truck's music hit them, a profanity-laced ode to the American gangster life. It continued for what seemed like several minutes before cutting out mid-sentence.

Silence.

Lars leaned forward and reached a hand under his seat. A single shot rang out as the glass of his side-view mirror shattered. He slowly raised both hands back up to his head, a stethoscope clenched in one fist.

"Time to try out that doctor card?" Claire whispered.

"Exactly. Be smart here, and follow my example."

Claire released what was left in her bladder. Might as well make herself as unappealing as possible. She sat up slowly and watched in her own mirror as four black men jumped out of the bed of the truck. They wore smart-looking jeans with fitted t-shirts, not the ragged old military uniforms she had seen on other rebel fighters around Goma.

One of them jogged up to the Land Cruiser and rapped against the hood with the butt of his rifle. The whites of his eyes seemed far too big as he stood there grinning at her.

"Out!" He shouted suddenly. "You must get out now."

ATLANTA, GEORGIA
6:17 A.M.

Bill Shackleton poured a generous helping of milk over his cereal and sat down in front of the laptop. The morning routine. He'd been eating Wheaties for thirty years, ever since General Mills first signed on as his only sponsor for that ill-fated rookie season. The company hadn't stayed loyal to him, after the torn ACL and botched repair, but he was a man of simple needs and saw no reason to mix things up. He unconsciously glanced up at the framed box cover hanging above him. A much younger and leaner looking version of Willy Shackleton, first-round NBA draft pick, smiled down at him. It had been a fleeting taste of the high life, and he didn't miss it.

The injury forced him to move on, and he finally found what he was looking for. Work that actually meant something in the grand scheme of life.

Chief, Viral Special Pathogens Branch.

The title had a certain ring to it, something that made people react with a slight shiver when he told them what he did. It also meant he was responsible for tracking and stopping the scariest diseases the world had ever known. Ebola, hantavirus, Kyasanur forest disease, Crimean-Congo hemorrhagic fever. And of course, smallpox. Bill Shackleton held the key to one of the world's two known remaining stockpiles of the otherwise extinct virus. It was a weighty calling, and he was proud to bear it.

Shackleton knew he didn't have to check his work e-mail at home, but he felt a sense of duty that had grown over his years at the Centers for Disease Control and Prevention. If he wasn't available around the clock, who would be? He had worked hard to get where he was, and he wasn't going to drop the ball on the American people.

The dining room windows lit up with a bright white flash, and he paused with the spoon halfway to his mouth. *One, one-thousand, two, one-thousand.*

Crack! His hand shook, spilling milk on his khakis. *Damn, and I was expecting that one.* So the storm had arrived. Good thing, since that's all anyone could talk about on the news last night. Keep those guys in business one more day. Lightning in a hurricane, though? That was a little out of the ordinary.

He scanned through the inbox, almost hoping for something that actually needed his attention. There were always reports from the regional offices and teams working out in the field. But it had been a quiet couple of months. Yes, that was good for the public health. Good for all the people who weren't dying scary deaths from mysterious diseases. But it wasn't ideal for ensuring that his office got appropriate federal funding for the next fiscal year. He needed to prove that his unit was doing something worthwhile in order to maintain the allocation of money they would need in the case of a real emergency. Just another inefficiency that came along with working for the government.

And quite simply, he was bored. Bored with a slight trace of nervousness. As an infectious disease epidemiologist and veterinarian used to chasing the worst of the worst from one global hotspot to the next, Shackleton didn't like to sit around twiddling his thumbs.

He clicked on the filtered folder titled, "ProMED," and smiled as the messages loaded up. Five years as moderator of the zoonotic and vector-borne disease list had given the online disease reporting system a special place in Shackleton's heart. It wasn't just an e-mail list—the community it represented was a treasure-trove. Where else could you find such a diverse collection of educated and well-intentioned professionals, all likeminded in their desire to protect the public health?

He scanned the subject lines for any mention of his own special pathogens. One line almost jumped off the screen:

PROMED > MONKEYPOX, GORILLA - VIRUNGA, DRC;
UNCONFIRMED REPORT

That was one of his, alright. Not the most thrilling, but it always had potential. Monkeypox had stayed on the CDC's radar ever since the big U.S. outbreak in 2003. Stupid pet stores importing exotic African rodents ended up causing a bunch of unsuspecting prairie dog owners to get pretty sick for a few days. Anyone in the market for a friendly Gambian giant forest rat? You couldn't make this stuff up.

But unconfirmed report? He always liked that. It proved that ProMED still had a unique role to play in the public health arena—the means by which the very first reports got sent around. Too bad if an unconfirmed report turned out to be unfounded. It was better to be safe and prepared than to regret missing a few hours or even days because someone wanted to wait for the gold standard testing to come back.

It was a simple e-mail message, apparently submitted to ProMED sometime overnight and forwarded immediately by the moderator.

Dear Colleagues,

I am writing to report on an emerging outbreak of suspected monkeypox disease in the mountain gorilla population of Virunga National Park, Democratic Republic of the Congo. During a brief foray into the park on June 28 to check on the health status of these endangered great apes, I observed at least ten recently dead animals from one family group. Rebel violence on the ground prevented further investigation.

All carcasses showed signs of fulminant pox-like disease, and biopsies were taken from one specimen. I conducted two real-time PCR assays targeting monkeypox genes in the laboratory here at the Gorilla Doctors Regional Headquarters. Each assay was repeated twice, and all have shown strong positive reactions.

A live infant gorilla was also removed from his mother's carcass and taken back to our isolation facility for monitoring. The patient has a fever and is beginning to develop cutaneous lesions similar to the ones observed on the other dead gorillas.

Please contact me with any collaborating information or for further details.

Respectfully,
Cole McBride, DVM, MPH
USAID PREDICT Research Fellow
Musanze, Rwanda

Cole McBride. Why did he know that name? The veterinary world was a small one, but Shackleton couldn't immediately place it. A quick Google image search brought up a man's smiling face from the website of a recent infectious disease conference. And then it came to him. He had mentored this guy years ago as a veterinary student summer intern. Didn't he join the Army, though? Shackleton tried to keep track of promising young veterinarians like him, maybe convince them to apply for the Epidemic Intelligence Service one day. It was a route that had worked for him, and he did his best to make sure there would always be a few vets to balance out all the other health professionals at the CDC.

ANOTHER FLASH OF lightning was followed immediately by a deafening thunderclap. There was a scraping sound against the roof, and then a large branch fell past the windows. He'd been meaning to get that old oak trimmed for years. As he stood up to assess the damage, the kitchen light went out and his laptop screen dimmed. The power was out. Perfect timing.

Shackleton looked at the wireless signal on his screen just as it turned from black to gray. So the internet was out, too. He closed up the machine and stuffed it in an old leather briefcase.

Upstairs in the spacious master bedroom, he leaned over his wife's sleeping form.

"Sweetie, you awake?"

She opened one eye. "You think I could sleep through that?"

He smiled and let his fingers run across her forehead and down one cheek. "The power and internet are out. I'm heading into work now—just got word that something big might be starting up in the Congo."

"Let me guess, Ebola again?" Michelle Shackleton was a family practice physician and her husband's biggest fan.

"Nope, they think it's monkeypox, but just in gorillas so far. Sounds like an especially bad strain, though."

He felt her hand reach up to squeeze his own.

"We'll be fine," she said. "Now get out of here before this storm picks up even more."

Shackleton turned back at the door.

"Love you. I'll let you know when I get in."

He wanted to look in at the kids but decided against it. No reason to wake them up now, with school already called off for the day.

THE RAIN WAS coming down in sheets as Shackleton turned slowly out onto the deserted cul-de-sac. He was confident in the Suburban's capabilities, but no reason to take any chances. He reached for the radio and hit preset number one for the local public radio station. A woman's excited voice cut through the chaos of wind and water.

"—special update on hurricane Diana, who has officially made landfall here on our Georgia coast."

He shook his head in disgust. The faux gravity in her voice wasn't fooling anyone. This was clearly the most exciting moment yet in the local weather forecaster's brief career.

"Winds at the center of the storm are currently topping 130 miles per hour and don't show any signs of calming down. Fortunately for us, Diana appears to be heading back out to sea, so the severe loss of life and property damage we've already witnessed in Florida are unlikely to be as much of a worry here."

The disappointment in her voice was obvious. But what happened in Florida?

A monstrous tree limb appeared in the road ahead of him, and Shackleton slammed a foot on the brakes just in time.

"That doesn't mean we're totally out of danger yet, though."

Phew.

"Torrential showers and high winds are raging across the state now, and hundreds of thousands have just lost power here in the Atlanta metro area."

The veterinarian felt his phone start to buzz in his chest pocket. He turned off the radio and pulled over to the side of the highway. Who would be trying him this early?

The caller ID simply said "CDC." Every call made from a landline at work showed up with the same generic four-digit extension, so it was impossible to tell who was on the other end without actually taking the call.

"Yeah, this is Bill." He half-expected to hear the grating voice of the automatic messaging system, telling him to stay home for a weather delay.

"Bill, it's Jen. Are you at home?"

His eyebrows lifted. Dr. Jen Vincent was his direct supervisor and head of the Division of High-Consequence Pathogens and Pathology.

"Good morning to you, too. Nope, on my way in already, but it's taking forever in this storm."

"Great, so you must have seen ProMED, then?" Her voice exuded the smooth confidence that had paved her rapid ascent through the CDC's management hierarchy.

"Yeah, thought I'd try to get a call over to Rwanda from the office. I didn't think a few dead gorillas would merit an early morning call from the big boss, though."

She paused. "Unfortunately it's not just the gorillas anymore."

Shackleton caught his breath.

"Another message just came through, this time from a Danish physician with MSF."

"And?"

"He thinks he's got a human patient. Our index case."

Bill Shackleton felt his heart rate speed up. He watched the rain batter relentlessly against the windshield, his mind racing. Funny how the excitement of an outbreak never got old.

"Bill?"

"Yeah, still here. You know me, already thinking through a plan of attack."

"Just get in here safely and we'll go from there. You got anyone who might be interested in a free vacation to the Congo?"

"Ha." And yet, he knew she was deadly serious. "See you soon."

GOMA
3:42 P.M.

Vincent Lukwiya sat in the driver's seat watching the scene unfold in front of him. His scouts were right—this was definitely the doctor from the big aid hospital in Goma. The white Land Cruiser had a fancy logo plastered across each side, and the old man was waving a stethoscope in one hand. Maybe the obvious display of affiliation usually provided some protection to the vehicle's occupants? No such luck this time.

"Out!" One of his soldiers shouted aggressively at the two *wazungu* still sitting frozen in their seats. "Get out with your hands above your heads!"

Lukwiya smiled. He relished the sight of such terror in the white woman's eyes. Everything changed with Odhiambo's death in Port Sudan. The tension that had been building up in him for years—the desire to escape his life of violence—all came crashing down when their exit plan was so decisively defeated. In the months leading up to that fateful night, he might have felt some pangs of regret, even pity for these innocent foreigners.

But no more.

Those misguided dreams were long gone. He had decided to embrace the life he'd been given.

It had paid off, too. Over the last five months, he moved into the inner circle of top LRA lieutenants and was now one of Kony's most trusted assistants. The little mining enterprise that was launched with the exchange in Sudan had significantly improved the group's financial standing, and the paltry sums promised to defectors by the aid organizations were no longer quite so appealing. Lukwiya ran one hand down the smooth leather sleeve of his tailored Italian jacket. The future looked bright.

Or it had, until two days ago.

"Please do not hurt us." Lukwiya opened his window a crack so he could hear the white man speaking. "I am a doctor, and my friend here is a journalist. We have nothing of value for you."

The doctor began to lower his hands.

"Stop, don't move!" the soldier shouted, stepping forward until the muzzle of his AK-47 was almost touching the doctor's forehead.

"I only want to show you our identification papers," the doctor said. "You can verify that we represent no threat and then release us."

The soldier raised his chin and startled laughing hysterically. "We have no use for your papers."

With a twist of his wrist he flipped the rifle and brought the solid stock up with a crack against the doctor's chin. The man stumbled and fell, a trickle of blood spilling from one corner of his mouth.

His soldiers were still high on the meth he'd given them in preparation for the afternoon's raid. It did wonders, this crystal candy generously donated by his new trading partners. The Prophet didn't approve of drug use in his ranks—he preferred a more pure psychological form of exploitation. But Lukwiya was impressed with the uninhibited fearlessness it seemed to instill in his men. Their new capacity for violence was unmatched by anything he had ever seen in the past.

They needed this man alive though. It was time for him to step in as the good guy.

"Enough." He spoke sharply as he jumped out of the truck. His soldiers fell back, almost cowering at the sound of his voice.

"Let me apologize for this boy's action, doctor."

Lukwiya knelt down in the muddy road, pulled a silk handkerchief from his breast pocket, and wiped the blood away from the man's mouth. It was true—the soldier was no more than a boy, maybe fifteen at most. He was captured during a routine raid in the Central African Republic and forced to kill his own parents with the family machete as a first step in his indoctrination. After two years of emotional oppression and ever-escalating violence, the boy was turning into one of their most promising fighters.

"You have come to Africa to help the people, yes?" Lukwiya asked, making no effort to hide the sneer on his face. "We have an opportunity for you to carry out this wish."

"Yes, my friend," the doctor answered through clenched jaws. "But you must know that I focus my efforts on those who are not contributing so directly to their own people's destruction."

Lukwiya jumped up and swung a booted foot directly into the doctor's unprotected stomach. He watched the man fall to his side, an agonized groan escaping from his stoic features. Beside him, the woman screamed in shock.

"Stop!"

"Your friend here will be better off if he learns to control his tongue," Lukwiya said quietly, letting his eyes wander across the woman's body. She was beautiful, even with the dark stain spreading from her crotch. It was not the first time he had caused a woman to piss herself in fear, and it would not be the last. He reached a hand to her face and let his fingers move slowly down her tear-stained ivory cheek and across one corner of the small mouth, resting them too long against lips painted a deep red. Her look of stunned horror grew as the seconds passed. This pitiful creature had lived her life too far from the violence that was his everyday reality. He lowered his hand slowly and dropped down to a knee again. He would have to work on this good guy routine.

"You must be more careful, doctor." He placed his hand on the man's shoulder and held it firmly, trying to cultivate an expression of genuine concern on his face. "We have been looking for you, yes, but my leader does not tolerate insolence and will readily seek another's skill if you prove unsuitable to the task."

OLSSON OPENED HIS eyes at the rebel leader's words. They needed a doctor? He clutched at his abdomen and groaned again. Yes, the kick had hurt, but nothing worthy of this exaggerated show of agony. It was always better to be underestimated.

He brought a hand to his face and opened his mouth, moving the hand across his lower jaw. Give them a moment to feel some remorse.

Finally, he spoke.

"So the LRA needs a doctor?"

Olsson stood up, steadying himself against the muscled shoulder of this ridiculously dressed warlord. Italian calfskin and a fancy Swiss watch in the Congo? He shook his head. Claire stepped closer and clung with both hands onto his right arm. Her manicured nails dug into his bare skin, but he welcomed the contact. "You probably know I can't do much by myself, without any equipment or supplies."

"We can get whatever you need," the man said. "Money is not an issue."

Olsson did his best to stifle a smile. *You've made quite an effort to make that obvious.* Last he heard, the LRA was short on both funding and soldiers as the group struggled to push into its third decade of meaningless terror campaigns. What was with this newfound display of wealth? And why had they chosen this moment to insert themselves into the fighting around Goma?

"This girl, she will only get in the way." The leader turned to the young fighters behind him and continued in English. "You think we should kill her now?"

The pressure of Claire's fingers on his arm released and he felt her whole body tense. A quick glance revealed a look of complete desperation painted across her distorted facial features. Didn't she realize the man was bluffing?

"Stay calm," he whispered.

It was too late. She broke into a run.

"Stop, Claire!" Lars stood deathly still, watching as she cleared the truck and continued at a full sprint back in the direction they had come from.

The rebel leader looked over his shoulder.

"Get her." He spoke softly—through gritted teeth—before turning back to watch the chase.

Olsson looked on helplessly as three of the teenaged soldiers leapt into action, but the fourth simply readjusted the old AK-47 against his shoulder.

He must have misunderstood the command.

He was going to shoot.

Olsson crouched and dove.

A deafening burst of gunfire exploded in his ears just as one shoulder slammed into the boy's chest, sending the rifle flying as they both collapsed in a tangle on the muddy track beneath them. Olsson struggled to get up, straining to see around the rest of the rebels, now frozen in place.

He heard a weak cough. She was alive.

Now he was up, yelling, trying to run to the crumpled mass lying in the mud thirty yards away. But strong hands held his arms, and he felt the hard steel point of a gun pressed into his spine. He fell silent, watching the dark crimson stain spread across Claire's sky blue blouse. It had been a rare sensation in his life to feel so totally powerless, especially when confronted with a situation that matched his own professional training. He bit down hard on the corner of a cheek until the taste of warm blood washed over his tongue. If she was going to bleed, so would he.

"You've killed her, you stupid, stupid, boy."

Olsson spit a mouthful of bloody saliva at the boy's shiny patent leather shoes. The gesture was reciprocated with a sharp kick to the back of his locked knees, and he collapsed to the ground for the second time.

"Yes, he is a stupid boy, this one."

The tall rebel leader turned and strode across to the killer, a small black handgun stretched in front of him.

The gloating amusement that was painted across the boy's face changed instantly to abject terror.

"No, sir, I'm sorry, sir, you said—"

The leader stopped, his face just inches from the boy's own. Slowly shaking his head back and forth, he shoved the pistol between them, fired a single shot, and stepped away. The terror now changed to shock as Claire's killer brought his hands to his crotch before dropping heavily onto both knees.

Olsson almost felt sorry for him. Almost.

"I did not say to kill her." The leader was still shaking his head, pacing back and forth. "I said get her. Get her. You should have known this white bitch was worth far more to us alive than dead. And now, you will pay."

He turned to the other three young fighters. The easy confidence that had characterized them just minutes earlier was gone.

"Kill him. Make it hurt. No guns."

Olsson turned his head away, but that didn't keep him from hearing the brutal assault being carried out just a few yards away. Heavy thuds of feet connecting with soft flesh. Ripping and popping of joints irreparably torn and twisted out of place. And laughter, only laughter. At least the dying boy had the dignity to keep his own mouth shut. Or maybe he was already too far gone.

Another minute, and it was finished. The laughter died down, replaced by an uneasy silence.

"Come, we must get rid of these bodies." The older man's voice had no shame or sorrow in it, only business.

Olsson sat alone in the mud, staring vacantly up into a cloudless sky, barely aware of the two limp bodies being carried separately into the sea of tents. He might have spent the last thirty years working at the most dangerous margins of life, but he would never get used to such senseless violence.

A heavy thud brought him back to the present, and he let his eyes focus on the two young fighters now standing in front of him. The large sample cooler from the back seat of the Land Cruiser lay open at their feet.

"Ah, I see you discovered our hidden cargo," he said.

The leather-jacketed leader frowned.

"What if I told you these are dangerous medical samples?"

The two teenagers shifted nervously, eyebrows raised.

"And that this lady and I were already exposed to the same disease?"

The rebel leader cocked his head to the side. "What are you trying to say? We have no time for games here."

Olsson looked him directly in the eyes, channeling all the grimness he could muster.

"You've heard of Ebola, yes?" He watched the leader's face, trying gauge the reaction to this slight spin on the truth. "We suspect that this new disease is even worse."

"Yes, we know Ebola well. But we have heard of no such sickness in Goma."

"Many have died already." Olsson didn't like the clear skepticism in the man's squinting eyes. "Simply being near me will put you in severe danger of catching this disease and dying yourselves."

The rebel leader laughed. It was a chilling laugh, and Olsson realized his ploy had failed. The young soldiers looked at each other, confused.

"Dying ourselves, doctor?" The man's face turned stony cold. "Do you think we in the Lord's Resistance Army have any fear of death? Have you not seen what just happened here? We lose that fear in the very first hours of our service. Those who cannot face it as men are sent on their way to the evil one."

Olsson noticed that the younger men did not look quite so convinced.

"And what will Mr. Kony think if you bring home this plague to decimate his army?"

"Doctor." The tall man stepped up to him and placed a rough ashen hand against Olsson's cheek. "You have missed the point. The plague is already upon us."

Anna McBride heard her stomach growl angrily as she dug into the generous serving of hummus with a triangular section of steaming pita bread. The appetizer was a house specialty at The Lonely Cedar, and it was delicious. She just hoped her boss wasn't listening too carefully.

He looked up from his phone and continued where he had left off a minute earlier.

"I don't see how we can get it right," he said. Dark circles framed his drooping eyes. "I'd take a terrorist attack any day over another one of these natural disasters."

Anna didn't respond. She furrowed her brow and let her head tilt slightly to the side. Couldn't he see that they weren't alone? A young olive-skinned man stood at the end of their table with a pitcher of iced tea in his hand.

"Sorry to interrupt," he said. Anna couldn't detect any hint of an accent. "Would either of you like a refill?"

Andrew Mills pointed quickly to his glass and continued on, apparently unperturbed.

"I mean, you know the statistics as well as I do."

No. No, she probably didn't.

"A terrorist attack—coupled with our decisive response—gives us an easy ten percent bump in the polls. Easy." He paused to stuff a piece of pita into his mouth. "Okay, maybe five percent if it's a small one. Either way, it gives him a chance to show some strength, and that's what we desperately need right now."

Anna watched in horror as a half-chewed glob of bread and hummus spilled out of the man's mouth. He didn't seem to notice.

"And yet look at us now, with this damned hurricane. Six point drop overnight, and all because the president hasn't personally gone wading around in the floods yet? It's pathetic, really."

The man could keep talking for hours. And he would, if Anna didn't jump in somewhere to stop him. Maybe that's why he liked her so much already? Because she was willing to set him straight, lowly intern that she was? The rest of the staff in the press office seemed to have given up on the task—they rarely interrupted his verbal crisis-of-the-day diarrhea. *Here goes nothing.*

"I'm sorry, Mr. Mills," she started. "But I think that if your well-rested, pre-political self could only hear the way you're droning on right now, he would probably throw up even more of that pita than you already have."

Mills stopped mid-chew, picked up a napkin, and wiped his mouth. It worked. He scrunched up his large nose and tilted his head.

"I mean, just listen to yourself!" Or maybe the reason he liked her was because she shared this tendency to let loose with impassioned rants on a fairly regular basis. "Here you are, comparing a terrorist incident—no, almost asking for one—to a hurricane, judging them only on the way they impact our president's poll numbers? Is that really the only thing that matters to you? I'm sorry, but that's what's pathetic. Not the allegedly fickle emotions of the American people."

The press secretary finished chewing and swallowed his bite. He looked at her with what seemed like a bewildered awe in his eyes.

"Anna McBride."

"That's my name."

"Who knew that the token cowgirl intern from Wyoming could turn out to be such a little firecracker?"

Anna felt the blood rush to her cheeks. She hated the way she blushed so easily.

"You know," Mills continued, "the president was really impressed with you yesterday. That little encounter in my office might turn out to be your lucky break."

She brushed a loose strand of hair behind her ear. Another nervous habit she would be happy to do without.

"You think so?"

"I know so," he said. "He specifically asked me to include you at the highest level as we continue to mold his image for the upcoming election. Finger on the pulse of America's youth—I think those were the exact words he used, if you must know."

Not that she was surprised. Anna was quite familiar with the incredulous look the president had given her the day before. Apparently there was something about her first impression that gave older WASP-y men low expectations for her in the wit and intellect departments. Even though she didn't like being so thoroughly misjudged based on these superficial assessments, she was quickly learning that the stereotypes could also be used to her own advantage.

"I'm not sure how similar I am to the rest of America's youth," she said. "But I'm honored he mentioned me, and you know I want to contribute however I can." Did she really, though? After just two weeks at the White House, Anna wasn't quite so sure a second term was really in the country's best interests.

"Long as you keep working your ass off and making friends like you're already doing, you're on track for a pretty eye-opening summer. Access most interns could only dream about." Mills scooped up another bite. "You like the hummus? This is the only place in D.C. to get the real thing, you know. I fell in love with the stuff in Beirut."

"I love it!" She really did. "When were you in Beirut?" It sounded like such a romantic city, in the fullest sense of the word.

"Way back when you were still running around barefoot on that ranch of yours, probably." He rested his chin in one hand, his face relaxing for a rare second. "I ran public affairs at the embassy for a couple of years."

"But you've barely said a thing about what's going on in Lebanon right now!"

She hardly knew the story herself.

Anna watched as his cheeks tightened up and the lines around his eyes reappeared.

"You're right," he said. "It's a tough one for me, personally."

"How so?"

"The president and I don't exactly see eye to eye on Israel's place in the world, that's all. So on that issue, I hold the party line but otherwise keep my mouth shut."

This was unexpected. Somehow it made her boss seem much more real.

"But anyway," he continued. "I'm going to keep you busy this summer."

Back to business.

"We'll let you run with the conflict minerals project, see if you can find another good venue for that speech we missed yesterday."

"Sounds perfect," she said. "I've already been in touch with—"

"Then there's the big party at the Capitol coming up at the end of the week," he interrupted. "We've got to do everything we can to keep the press selling it for us big time. Of course, that's not going to be easy with this damn storm grabbing for everyone's attention. We need to dream up some creative ways to tell the public about the president's involvement."

Anna frowned.

"Even though you've already told me he has no intention of getting more involved?"

"It's all about perceptions, my dear." Mills grinned across the table. "That's a lesson you need to learn early in this business."

Her frown changed into a scowl. Was there really no other way to run a country?

The savory smell of grilled meat interrupted her thoughts.

"*Marhaba*, Mr. Andrew, my friend." A man arrived at the end of their table carrying a huge platter filled with bite-sized pieces of lamb and vegetables. His kind face was darkened with what looked to be a permanent five o'clock shadow extending most of the way up his round cheeks.

"Fadi, I didn't know you were here."

Anna was again surprised at the clear change in her boss's demeanor. He looked so much better without that stressed out grimace she was used to.

"I want you to meet my new intern, Ms. Anna McBride."

"It is my pleasure." The man set the platter down on their table and bowed his head, one hand over his heart. "Any friend of Andrew's is most welcome at my restaurant."

SHE WAS BEAUTIFUL, this new intern. Andrew did know how to pick them. But it wasn't the regal beauty of his own wife and daughter. The blended Mediterranean features of Lebanese women had been making the world's men swoon for thousands of years, and Fadi Haddad took great pride in that fact.

"So how long have you been coming here, anyway, Mr. Mills?"

The girl spoke with a comfortable confidence that Haddad had grudgingly come to admire in American women. How could he not, with his own daughter Myriam embracing the trait so fully?

"Too long," Andrew replied with a grin. "I first stepped into The Lonely Cedar as a lowly college intern with the State Department, what, almost twenty years ago now?"

"Yes, that must be right," Haddad said. "You didn't look so different then. Only a skinnier and happier version of yourself."

It was true. His friend's slow deterioration over the past three years had been obvious, one lunchtime conversation at a time. The big job at the White House had not been good for him, even if it represented the realization of so many dreams.

Friend. It was a funny word to use, given their diverse stations in life—a devout Muslim immigrant and the blue-blooded voice of the American president—but there it was. And it was the same with many of his customers at the restaurant. Unlikely friendships forged over hummus and baklava. The conversations ran deep and the mutual affection was genuine. These pillars of Western power had been coming to his little restaurant for almost thirty years to share their hopes and fears. And for what? Simply because they enjoyed his generous welcomes and savory snacks?

But what if these men and women knew the truth? He could barely restrain a shudder from rippling through his heavy frame.

"I must get back to the kitchen," Haddad said, bowing again. "If you will excuse me, my friends."

"Thanks, Fadi." Andrew waved a hand over the table. "I don't know what I would do without your feasts to look forward to every week."

The girl nodded and looked up at him with an honest smile. "Yes, thank you. I already know I'll be back!"

Haddad turned away from the table. Why didn't he ask about the attacks in Lebanon? He had promised himself that he would, if the press secretary showed up for his regular Tuesday lunch. Maybe there was something that could be done? Maybe the United States didn't really understand the suffering that was being inflicted on his people by those Zionist invaders? He wanted to believe it, with all his heart.

But he didn't ask.

He couldn't.

Not now.

A message had appeared in the Drafts folder of his shared Gmail account the day before.

A message that would change everything.

Still no answer?" Marna Van Wyk watched Cole slide the phone back into his pocket. She could tell he was nervous. He had already reached the limits of what his own basic lab could do, and Dr. Musamba just stopped by with a report that the little orphaned gorilla was taking a turn for the worse. Not like they needed another complication added into the mix.

"Nope," Cole said. "This time it went straight to the doctor's voicemail, like the phone is turned off."

"Well shit."

"My feelings exactly." He sat down again at the desk. "Let me try the hospital one more time. If they're still not picking up we'll see if we can reach the main Doctors Without Borders office in Nairobi."

Marna felt another wave of dizziness come over her. She leaned against the doorframe and closed her eyes. This was the third time in as many hours, and she was getting worried. The South African helicopter pilot had always prided herself on a robust immune system—she was always the one person among her friends who somehow avoided coming down with the flu every year. But now she felt downright nasty. The dizziness she could handle. It was the throbbing headache that made it hard for her to concentrate on anything else.

"Are you sure you're alright?" Marna opened her eyes and saw Cole staring at her.

"Yeah, fine," she lied. "Think I'm just tired. I'll head back to my room as soon as we figure out what's up with these visitors."

Cole pulled out his phone and started dialing.

"Yes, hello, is this the field hospital in Goma?"

He raised his eyebrows and gave Marna a thumbs up.

"Perfect, great. This is Dr. Cole McBride, calling from Rwanda. We were expecting your director, Dr. Lars Olsson, and another visitor here in Musanze some time ago."

Cole paused as he listened, then his whole body slumped into the chair.

"Wow, I'm sorry to hear that. And you have no other way to get in touch or track them down?"

He pushed one hand into his thick dark hair.

"I understand. Yes, that sounds like the best course." He paused to listen. "And the patient, the one Dr. Olsson suspected of monkeypox, how is he?"

Another pause, longer this time. Marna wanted to care, but the pain in her temples made it almost impossible.

"Well that's bit of good news, I guess. Although it might be easier on you if he just died already. I imagine you're not fully equipped for true isolation procedures?"

Cole stood up and walked around the desk. He held the phone to his ear with one hand, nodding his head. Marna gave him a questioning look as he raised the other hand to her forehead and rested it there for a few seconds.

"I understand," he said, his lips forming a thin line. "Please keep us updated on Dr. Olsson and the journalist. And let me know if you identify any other possible cases."

He wrote down two phone numbers and gave his own.

"Thanks again, we'll be in touch." Cole placed his phone on the desk and put an arm behind Marna's back. A comforting strength radiated from his touch. She realized she was shivering.

"Marna, you're sick," he said.

And that was the last thing she heard.

ATLANTA
7:45 P.M.

"Ladies and gentlemen, we've just received some good news from the flight deck." The flight attendant's amplified sweet southern drawl broke through even the highest setting on Dr. Bill Shackleton's noise-canceling headphones. "We're anticipating a brief respite from the high winds over the next twenty minutes or so, and we are now number five for takeoff. Please turn your cell phones to airplane mode and discontinue use of any larger electronic devices."

He would believe it once they were in the air. But Shackleton still lifted the headphones off his shiny brown scalp. No reason to make things difficult for the flight crew. They looked stressed enough as it was.

The flight had already been delayed for three hours, and his initial optimism about their chances of beating the brunt of the storm was long gone. As if sixteen hours squeezed into a coach class seat meant for someone half his height wasn't enough. But that came with the territory as a government employee in an age of fiscal restraint.

"Hey Bill," a man's voice called across the aisle. Travis Grinley was a promising young virologist—recently graduated with a PhD in molecular virology from Columbia—who Shackleton had handpicked for the mission. He was responsible for most of the high-tech toys packed safely below them in the plane's hold. "Think we might really get off the ground this time?"

"Sadly, no," he replied. "But you know I want this trip as much as the rest of you guys."

"Ha, I believe it. Can't say I'm jealous of desk jockeys like you."

It was true. The worst part about taking over as head of Viral Special Pathogens was that he rarely got out of the office anymore. All the things he loved about outbreak investigations were still happening, but now he was reading the reports about his subordinates' international adventures rather than leading them himself.

Not this time, though. Somehow he had managed to convince his boss that he was needed on the ground. Pox viruses were his specialty, after all, and this was an opportunity to pass on some of the practical skills he had picked up over the years. Tricks of the trade. He smiled. How else were all these junior scientists going to learn the best way to bleed an angry baboon? Or what to do when accidentally poked with a used needle in some mud hut a hundred miles from the nearest hospital? You just couldn't learn this stuff from a book.

"So are you gentlemen heading to South Africa?" The woman in the middle seat beside him turned her bulky shoulders in his direction. *Oh God, no.* Shackleton hated airplane talkers and thought he might have gotten lucky this time.

"No, actually, just passing through." Rule number one: never volunteer additional information. She didn't take the hint.

"Oh, that's too bad," the woman said. She wore a bright turquoise t-shirt emblazoned with the words *New Hope Community Church Summer Mission Trip* across the chest. It was oversized even for her generous proportions. "I've been twice before and it's just an amazing place. So many needy people and they just love it when we can provide a helping hand here and there."

I'm sure they do. But Shackleton was a kind man, even if he didn't always feel that way. "Well that sounds very nice, I wish you a successful trip this time around."

Again, end of conversation.

But alas, she chose to elevate her airplane talker status and proceeded from basic pleasantries to persistent interrogation.

"So if you're not staying in South Africa, where y'all going instead?"

She gazed at him, apparently oblivious to his growing impatience.

"Heading on to Rwanda, but I'm afraid this delay means we'll probably miss our connecting flight in Johannesburg."

"Rwanda, wow." Her jaw dropped. "That's a little scary for my taste, but I guess it's good some people are willing to go places like that. They must need your help real bad since the genocide, huh?"

Shackleton was consistently surprised by the ignorance of his fellow Americans. At least she knew the term genocide and could connect it with Rwanda—that was better than most. But hello, those horrific events were over twenty years ago, and Rwanda was now the poster child for successful economic development in Africa.

It was time to implement the next level of preemptive antisocial tactics. He pulled a book out of the seat pocket.

"If you'll excuse me, ma'am."

"Oh, so you're a reader too?" She reached into the Hudson Booksellers bag on her lap and took out a new copy of *The Hot Zone*. "Have you read this one? I was trying to find something about Africa and Sandra here convinced me to pick this up."

She nodded to a tiny woman in the seat beside her sporting the same turquoise t-shirt.

Shackleton forced a smile. The situation had just gone from bad to catastrophic. He didn't like to lie, but sometimes it was for the best.

"No, doesn't really look like something I'd be interested in."

He opened his book randomly and brought it up to his face. Maybe he was farsighted?

The intercom crackled to life. Salvation could sometimes be found in the strangest ways.

"Well folks, we're so sorry to get your hopes up."

Shackleton crouched down to look out the small oval window. The horizontal downpour made it impossible to see anything past the Boeing 777's gigantic wing.

"They were able to get four flights off, but we aren't going to be so lucky." A chorus of groans rolled through the plane. "Hartsfield-Jackson Atlanta International Airport is officially closed to any further air traffic, so we will be returning to the terminal."

Crap. This was going to put a serious wrinkle in their plans.

HE CAUGHT UP with the rest of the team back at the gate.

"Well this is a literal shit-storm, right?" Travis Grinley was grinning. Go figure.

A small Asian woman laughed, but sobered up on seeing Shackleton's approach. She was a new Epidemic Intelligence Service officer recently assigned to Viral Special Pathogens and still seemed somewhat intimidated by him.

"Don't worry," he said. He wasn't going to let this chance for some field-work slip through his fingers. "I'm disappointed, of course, but we'll make something else work. Anyone have updates on other airports in the area?"

"Yeah, doesn't look good." Travis nodded at his phone. "Pretty much everything in the southeastern U.S. is closed for the night."

"Seriously?" Shackleton found that hard to believe. "Anyway, as long as we can get to New York tonight, we should still be able to reroute through Europe and be on the ground in Kigali by tomorrow afternoon."

"Love the optimism, boss, but that's going to be impossible." Travis looked up from his phone again. "The skies are shut down between here and D.C. We're looking at a twenty-four hour delay, minimum."

Shackleton closed his eyes and tried to release the tension in his broad shoulders. He should have known it was too good to be true. But that left them with a real problem.

"Who else do we have in Africa right now?" He looked from face to face. "This investigation can't wait twenty-four hours, you guys know that."

The new EIS officer spoke up. "Leila's at that conference in Gabon— that's not too far, right?"

She was right. Leila Torabi was a second year EIS officer presenting her research on filoviruses at the International Medical Research Centre's annual meeting in Libreville. It would still take her a few hours by air to reach Kigali, but that was better than delaying the official CDC response by a whole day. At the very least she could pick up samples to hand carry back to Atlanta.

"Perfect," Shackleton said. "Don't know why I didn't think of her before. Any of you have a good mobile number for our favorite Iranian princess?"

He looked at Travis, eyebrows raised. It was tough to keep a workplace romance secret anywhere, but the CDC rumor mill was especially active.

"Yeah, let me find it." Travis tapped the screen a couple of times. "It's a bit late to call her now, though, don't you think?"

Shackleton smiled. This could just work.

"Give me that phone."

WEDNESDAY, JUNE 30

The land of a thousand hills, wasn't that what they called it? Leila Torabi pressed her forehead against the small oval window and watched as a patchwork quilt of green and brown appeared below the plane.

Rwanda. The country and its people had fascinated Leila for years, but this would be her first visit. Too bad it was going to be so short, really just a twenty-four hour layover on her way back to Atlanta. But such was life for a globetrotting officer in the CDC's Epidemic Intelligence Service. In all honesty, the thrill of being involved in an exciting outbreak like this was well worth the jet lag and missed tourism possibilities.

She gripped the armrests and tucked her head slightly as the tarmac rushed up to meet them. Over thirty years of international flights, and yet she still freaked out over the landings.

A couple of bounces, and they were safe. Leila stretched her arms.

Thirty-four years, to be exact. She didn't remember that first flight as a four-month-old infant, of course, but her brother loved to tell the story of the family's infamous exit from the United States. He always made it sound like they were fleeing for their lives, and the two of them spent many happy hours reenacting the adventure as children. She knew better now.

"Ladies and gentlemen, it is my pleasure to welcome you to Rwanda."

The female voice bounced with a joyful African lilt. Leila nodded along as the flight attendant repeated herself. The French was easy—she had studied it all the way through high school. But Kinyarwanda? Not so much. That would take at least one more visit.

"So, have you come for business or for pleasure?"

The short round man beside her had mercifully stayed busy on a laptop for most of the flight. Now he turned to her, white teeth gleaming in a friendly smile.

"Ah, business only this time, I'm afraid."

Leila was not quite so generous with her teeth.

"That is good," the man said. "You must know, Rwanda loves business."

"Yes, I know it's seen some impressive economic growth over the last few years."

Leila looked at him more closely. All those years as a diplomat's daughter had given her an especially sensitive radar to the strange race of men who spent their lives pretending to solve the world's problems.

"But please, it will be your pleasure to visit the mountain gorillas." He stood and pulled a sleek leather carry-on from the overhead bin. "They are my country's most treasured resource."

Leila smiled as she followed him into the aisle. He wasn't kidding. She had just read in the airline's seat-back magazine that mountain gorilla tourism brought in several million dollars of valuable foreign exchange every year. But this guy must not read ProMED.

"You know," she said. "I've always dreamed of doing that, but unfortunately I just won't have the time."

Leila was actually terrified of the creatures—thank you, *Goodnight Gorilla*—but there was no reason to go down that road now. She didn't think she would be seeing any gorillas in Musanze, anyway. Her job was simply to act as an overnight courier, bringing protected samples back to the CDC for further analysis. Bill Shackleton's middle-of-the-night call had made that clear. Not the most glamorous of assignments, but at least it got her out of that dreaded presentation in Libreville.

A blast of humid warm air met her at the plane's open door.

The man looked back at her before stepping out onto the stairs.

"Welcome to Rwanda!"

Leila nodded, a faint smile on her lips. It was hard to get annoyed with someone so genuine.

She pulled out her phone as she walked across the asphalt towards the terminal. There it was, the phone number for Dr. Cole McBride. What kind of a name was that, anyway? Almost too American for its own good.

Leila typed a simple message.

Just arrived. Will meet you as planned.

And pressed send.

SHE WAS A looker, no question about that. But was she really the best the CDC had to offer? It was clear they weren't taking his outbreak very seriously yet. Cole gave a wave and lowered his simple printed sign as the woman strode purposefully in his direction. Leila Torabi. Her caramel skin, green eyes and closely cropped dark hair matched the exotic sound of her name perfectly.

He stepped forward with a smile, shouldering his way past a tour operator trying to steal his prime location.

"You must be Leila?" he said, extending a hand.

"Dr. McBride, it's a pleasure." The accent was unexpected, mostly British but with something else there too.

"Call me Cole, please," he said, reaching for her roller bag. "Let me get that for you."

She held up a hand. "Oh, it's no problem. I take this thing everywhere with me these days."

Right.

"Let's just head out to the truck, then." Beautiful, and Miss Independent, too. "Plenty of time to get caught up on things once we're on the road."

He wove his way through the crowd, checking over his shoulder every few seconds to make sure Leila stayed right behind him. She navigated the chaos surprisingly well. Not quite like Marna, though, whose tall strong body demanded attention and deference wherever she went.

Marna. Cole thought of her body, now racked with fever and shivering painfully in bed back in Musanze. He had left her there hours earlier, with Musamba promising to stay by her side and call him if anything changed. At least this lonely emissary from the CDC was a physician, and apparently a pretty smart one at that. He looked her up that morning after receiving Dr. Shackleton's call: undergrad at Oxford, medical school and residency at Harvard, and then an infectious disease fellowship at Hopkins. You couldn't ask for a better pedigree, but did she have any real world experience to back it up? Still, it would be good to have her on Marna's case for a few hours.

COLE SWERVED TO avoid a dog that jumped in front of his speeding pick-up.

"Crap, that was close. It's like they have a death wish or something!"

"I'm impressed," Leila said, laughing. "Even though I grew up overseas, I never had to do any of the driving."

"So that explains the accent? I've been trying to place it, but the closest I got was some kind of generic international school hybrid."

"Well that *is* about as close as it gets," she said. "My dad was a diplomat, so—"

"Wait, but I thought EIS officers had to be American citizens." He'd been waiting for a chance to ask. "Or is there some kind of exchange program you're part of?"

"Seriously?" He caught her raised eyebrows out of the corner of his eye. "I *am* an American citizen, same as you. And we have a bunch of foreign national trainees in the program too."

"But you just said—"

"—that my dad was a diplomat, yes." Her tone made it clear this was a conversation she had far more often than she liked. "And I know, my accent is confusing. I was born while he was studying in the U.S., and some loophole made it possible for me to claim citizenship when I came back for med school."

"Gotcha," Cole said. "Sorry, don't mean to pry too much."

"No, that's okay, I know it's a little out of the ordinary."

"Just one more question, I promise." Cole glanced at her with a wry grin.

"Fine, fine."

"Where's your family actually from, then?"

She paused, and then said more quietly. "I'm Persian."

It took him a minute. That wasn't something you heard every day.

"Ah, Iran, that's—"

"—all we need to say about that." She started digging through her purse. "Sorry, it's just a part of my past I'm not very proud of, that's all."

"Hey, no worries."

Cole stared at the road ahead of him. Why such a touchy subject? Yes, Iran had been in the news a lot recently, but it's not as if she needed to be ashamed about that. He tried to remember the article he read the day before, some fanatic government official spouting off about nuclear sovereignty and the Great Satan, as usual.

Torabi. The name had rung a bell when Shackleton first mentioned it on the phone. Torabi. Yeah, that was definitely it. Farrukh Torabi.

He stole a glance at Leila, who was reading something on her phone. It must be a fairly common name, right?

She looked up.

"So tell me a little more about these gorillas."

The devastation was worse than he had ever seen.

And that meant a lot, for someone who was among the first on the ground during two Ebola outbreaks and managed more cholera epidemics than he cared to remember. Dr. Lars Olsson pulled on another pair of gloves and turned to the thin woman beside him.

"Could you hold off the vein for me?"

She knelt on the dirt floor of the dark tent and pressed a bare thumb into the angle of the moaning teenager's arm. Although she was reluctant to say much, Olsson had managed to piece together the basics of the woman's story. Newly minted in Kampala as a graduate nurse's assistant, Grace returned to her family's village in northeastern Uganda for her own wedding to a local shopkeeper. The raid was sudden and unexpected, crazed men appearing out of the forest with guns and machetes. After seeing her husband of only an hour hacked to pieces, she was handpicked for captivity by Kony himself. Now two decades later, the woman was long retired from the royal harem and had only been kept around for her medical expertise.

The large firm nodules ravaging the boy's skin made it difficult to find a decent spot for the stick. Olsson ran an index finger slowly across the forearm and finally inserted the needle with a confident jab. He released a breath as the welcome flash of blood flowed back into the hub, then used one finger to push the rest of the catheter into the vein while removing the needle in a single fluid motion.

"You have a steady hand, doctor." Grace withdrew her thumb and handed him the tape.

"Only because I haven't always had competent assistants like you," he said, a brief smile flashing on his tired face. He watched as the woman slowly injected a simple combination of saline solution and anti-inflammatory drugs. It wouldn't do much in the face of such a nasty infection, but at least the medication might keep this suffering terrorist slightly more comfortable as he fought for his life.

A suffering terrorist. Olsson shook his head. Why did he even care about this teenaged killer's fate? It wasn't the first time, either, that he had been faced with the contradictory proposition of fighting for the life of one who had caused so much suffering. But such was the profession he had chosen, and now was not the time or place to begin making moral judgments about his patients' life choices. Or lack thereof, as was the case for most of these LRA soldiers. He tried to remember that, as he moved on to the next patient. They were both victims and perpetrators of some of the most atrocious crimes ever recorded.

Olsson grimaced as he watched Grace pull an old glass thermometer from the man's mouth and place it behind her ear. Oh well, there really wasn't much of a point in the standard safety precautions at this point. If they were susceptible to the virus, so be it. They would be spiking fevers within days, or even hours, if the story Lukwiya had told him was true.

"What's this one at?" Olsson asked, crouching down beside the tall form. He recognized the face and involuntarily reached up to feel his own bruised and swollen jaw. The man was almost completely unresponsive—quite the contrast from his flaunting show of violence outside Goma the day before.

"103.7. He's in the worst of it now."

"But no sign of the rash yet?" Olsson answered his own question by pulling back the man's lower lip with a gloved finger. The gums were bright red with inflammation, coalescing ulcers oozing a sticky yellow fluid into the otherwise bone-dry mouth. It was not a pretty sight. And yet it fit the course of disease so perfectly. First, the general achiness and exhaustion, followed by a rapidly rising temperature. Then the rash and ulcers in the mouth, which quickly spread to the face and neck before making a leap down through the rest of the body. The centrifugal distribution of the rash, and growing pus-filled nodules which followed, was classic. Face, arms, legs, hands, and feet, with just a thin scattering across the back and torso.

Classic, yes. But classic for what? In all his forays into Africa, Olsson had never seen a case of monkeypox. Chickenpox, sure, that was everywhere. Even a few cases of camel pox during those first years in Ethiopia. But the monkeypox virus only rarely made the jump into humans, and when it did, it was usually suffered silently among jungle tribes far outside the reach of even his brand of Western medicine.

"Grace, you said you have seen this disease before, yes?"

"Yes, doctor." She was wiping the man's sweating face with a wet rag. "But it was not like this."

He looked at her expectantly.

"The speed, doctor."

"Yes?" She was clearly not one to volunteer any extra information.

"That other time, there were many days of fever, many days of rash, and many days of the lumps. Now it is all in just one day, maybe two."

"Anything else?"

"So many are sick, and dying." She turned away. Olsson knew that one of her sons had been among the first to succumb to the disease. "That other time, there were only three who showed these signs, and one who died. Now, you can see what has happened."

And so he could.

Five large olive-green canvas tents were packed with over one-hundred young men, women, and children at every stage of the disease. The segregation had only started the night before, when he arrived and found the sick scattered throughout the camp. One pit grave on the edge of the forest clearing was already filled with the first twenty to die, and a second waited for its final occupants before being closed up as well. The only age group that seemed to have been spared so far was the older generation of top LRA commanders and a few mature women like Grace.

A quick assessment had confirmed Olsson's suspicions. All those over about forty years old bore the telltale dark scarring on the left shoulder of a childhood smallpox vaccination. Unfortunately, these universal vaccination campaigns tapered off and then stopped completely a few years after the final push for eradication of the disease back in the 1970s. What was the point of spending so much money and effort vaccinating against a disease that no longer existed?

That was the theory, at least. But it left billions of the world's youth unprotected from the most destructive virus ever known. The virus responsible for hundreds of millions of human deaths in the twentieth century alone—a much more prolific killer than the combined efforts of all that century's violent wars. A virus that in reality had only been contained, not annihilated. Olsson had followed the debate with interest over the years—should the remaining stock of smallpox virus be destroyed, once and for all? Or was there some valid scientific reason to keep holding on to it, year after year, deep in the most secure inner sanctums of the CDC and VECTOR labs? The Americans he could trust, but Olsson had met one too many unsavory Russians trying to profit off the world's disasters to be completely confident in the Biopreparat.

Olsson rubbed the raised scar on his own shoulder. He hardly remembered getting the vaccine as a young child. Was it really going to have some sort of protective effect now?

He hoped so.

And it did make a lot of sense. In the eighteenth century, the English physician Edward Jenner pioneered the development of the smallpox vaccine using cowpox lesions from a milkmaid's hands. The same vaccine had been used with positive effect in that unexpected monkeypox outbreak in the States a few years ago. So the potential for cross-immunity with different types of pox viruses was clear.

There was another possibility, though, one that Olsson couldn't get out of his head. What if his vaccination was only slowing down the course of this disease? Maybe his body, recognizing something similar to those viral particles it was exposed to so many years ago, could hold off the virus for a few extra days. But would it be enough to spare him completely?

Only time would tell.

"DOCTOR LARS!" A harsh voice interrupted his reflections, and Lars turned to see Vincent Lukwiya entering the tent. Grace froze, a mask of fear settling on her face.

"Mr. Lukwiya," he replied, setting down a clear bag of saline solution on the edge of a blanket. "I hope you come with good news?"

"You will continue the treatments with the medicines we have provided." Lukwiya spat at one of the sick men's feet.

"That's a given, yes," Olsson said. It wasn't easy to keep the bitter sarcasm out of his voice. "But what of the antivirals? You said they could be flown in today."

"You will continue with what you have."

Olsson jumped up and lunged at the rebel leader, catching his leather jacket at the collar.

"And do you realize that your soldiers will continue to die, then?"

A bemused look grew on the man's face, and Lars could hardly believe his own recklessness.

"There won't be much of an army left to resist anything, regardless of what your prophet wants to believe."

Lukwiya grabbed him by both shoulders and tossed him effortlessly against the side of the tent. Olsson bounced off the canvas and tripped over a leg, landing in a heap with one cheek resting awkwardly against the pocked face of a comatose patient. He rolled to his stomach and pulled his feet under him, tempted to try again.

But then he bowed his head and let out a strangled laugh. What was the point? Let them all die, if that's what they wanted. Lars felt his fleeting rage dissipate into the stifling heat of the tent as he stood up and brushed himself off.

"That will be all, doctor." Lukwiya turned to leave the tent but stopped just outside the entrance. "If you have any desire to leave these mountains alive, you would do better in the future to keep your emotions in check."

LUKWIYA COLLAPSED INTO a rusty folding chair at the makeshift desk in his own tent. He felt for the scar on his shoulder again and ran his tongue across his gums. The doctor said he would be immune. Then why did he feel so tired, more tired than he should have been after a slow morning milling around the camp?

Doctor Lars. He was proving to be more trouble than he was worth. As long as there was some chance of getting resupplied, though, he could still serve a purpose.

Lukwiya looked at the shiny iPhone sitting on his desk. It was a Chinese fake, like everything else in the Congo. He knew that, but at least it impressed the young recruits.

And now it sat there, taunting him with its silence.

He had to try again.

The SIM cards were taped one to a page in a small green notebook, each one marked with the dates and locations at which it had previously been used. Those Special Forces swine had made the business of communication much more difficult ever since they joined the hunt, but Lukwiya's quick implementation of strict controls had done the trick so far. At least the vast web of roaming mobile networks made this itinerate lifestyle somewhat more viable than it would have been otherwise.

He chose a Ugandan SIM that was last used in South Sudan five months earlier and touched a long number that appeared first in the list of recent calls.

Nothing.

He slammed a fist down on the plywood.

No ring. Not even a busy signal. Just a long beep, and then silence.

There would be no antivirals, no face masks, and no new needles. But those were the least of his concerns now. What of the money, and the blue iron drums guarded so carefully in the tent next to his own? It had been over a week since the last communication.

They were cutting ties.

MUSANZE
1:24 P.M.

"You really mean to tell me that you just left her here?" Leila shook her head slowly as she looked up at him. "And with a Congolese veterinarian, no less?"

Veterinarian. Somehow she made it sound like a dirty word.

Cole glanced at his friend and mentor, Antoine Musamba, who was standing silently in the corner of the room.

"I trust Dr. Musamba's judgment more than any of the physicians here in Musanze," he said. "We knew your arrival was the best thing that could happen for Marna right now."

"I'm sorry." Leila turned to Musamba, eyebrows raised. The biohazard mask made it tough to interpret her actual feelings. "I'm just very concerned about Marna right now—I hope you can understand that."

"Don't even think of it," the veterinarian replied. "We're glad you are here to help."

Cole let his eyes rest on Marna, even though it pained him to do so. Sweet Marna. Was it really only two nights ago that those flawless lips had brushed far too briefly against his own?

Her body contracted in an alarming dry heave, then went back to its persistent shivering. The effort added nothing to a half-filled bucket of vomit that sat at the edge of her bed. Glazed eyes stared into the distance, as they had ever since he and Leila arrived minutes earlier.

"So tell me again the course of her illness," Leila said. She moved her gloved hands gently down Marna's swollen neck. "You said she only spiked a fever last night?"

"Yeah," Cole said. "I wondered if something was up earlier in the day, but she swore up and down that she was feeling fine."

"And didn't the thought at least cross your mind that she could have been infected with the same thing that's also killing the baby gorilla she's been fondling for the last couple days?" She paused. "You know, the virus that's apparently spreading like wildfire through an aid hospital in Goma right now? The reason I just flew halfway across Africa this morning on official—"

"Of course I thought of it." Cole couldn't listen to this any longer. "We all did."

Why not give him the benefit of the doubt here? He kneeled down at the foot of the bed and laid a firm hand on the mountain of blankets over Marna's trembling legs.

"I realize it may be hard for you to believe this, but I'm actually not completely off my rocker."

«Convince me.»

"Are you serious?" It had been a long time since someone had questioned his judgment so blatantly. "You do realize that the normal incubation period for monkeypox is between ten and fourteen days, right? We haven't even hit forty-eight hours yet. And around here, a fever with headache and abdominal cramping usually just means you ate something you shouldn't have at the local market."

"I know, you're right." Leila stood up and took a step back from the bed. "Look, again, I'm sorry. I realize I'm doing an awesome job of making friends here."

Her eyes softened.

"You're fine, no worries."

Cole felt his heart slow down.

"You guys can see she's in a seriously bad way just as well as I can, M.D. or not," she said. "The real question is where do we go from here?"

"The only hospital that's worth much is back in Kigali—"

"Hang on, meant to check one more thing," Leila interrupted, pulling another latex glove over the one already on her right hand. She bent over the bed and lifted Marna's upper lip. "Nothing there, at least."

Cole stepped to the other side of the bed for a closer look.

"Mmm, do you have a flashlight in here?" Leila had inserted a thumb wrapped in gauze between Marna's molars on one side.

He looked to the small table in front of him. There it was, behind a journal and a couple worn paperbacks.

"Here you go."

"No, just shine it right in here for me."

He clicked the headlamp onto its brightest setting and set it at a good angle.

"That's what I was afraid of." Leila tilted Marna's head back with her other hand. "See those little raised lesions on her mucosal palate?"

He did.

"That's often one of the first signs. At least according to the case reports I was reading on the plane." She pulled her thumb out and straightened back up. "I haven't seen it myself before—that pet store outbreak happened while I was still an undergrad—but the overall picture here seems to fit the diagnostic criteria pretty well."

"Back to your question then," Cole said. "What's next?"

"Well how can we get her out of here? She needed to be in an ICU isolation ward yesterday. Is that even available here?"

"Like I said, the King Faisal Hospital in Kigali is the best we've got. They do have an ICU which is pretty well-equipped, but most expats prefer to get evacced straight out to Nairobi or Pretoria."

"How about health insurance, emergency medical evacuation, that kind of thing? Didn't you say she was actually employed by South African National Parks?"

"True," Cole said. "Best case scenario would probably be to get her on a chartered flight straight back home to South Africa."

"And start spreading this thing even further?"

"That's what isolation procedures are for, right? I know some of those medevac companies are set up for it." He looked to Musamba. "Can you see what kind of wheels we can get rolling down at SANParks? They'd have to be the ones to initiate anything like this."

"Of course," Musamba said. "I'll let you know."

LEILA WATCHED THE older veterinarian leave the room. How could she have been so cruel earlier? He seemed like a nice enough guy. They couldn't blame her, though. This was not how she had expected the visit to start out. Yes, she was an infectious disease doc, and she loved the patient care side of things just as much as the bigger picture epidemiology. But not out here in the bush. Not where she didn't have the people and the resources she needed to save this poor woman's life.

She turned back to the bed and saw Cole use a gloved hand to brush a strand of blond hair out of Marna's face. There must have been something going on between these two. Leila had broken enough hearts to know the look in Cole's eyes anywhere. That could complicate things just slightly.

"Cole, let me ask you something, one professional to another."

"Go for it."

"Do you have any reason to think that you might have suffered a more serious exposure of some kind? He cocked his head to the side. "Through your interactions with Marna, I mean."

"Oh, ha." He pulled his hand back. "No, I could only wish. She's way out of my league."

"Okay." She was skeptical. "Let me know if you change your mind on that."

"Besides," Cole continued. "I had the smallpox vaccine just a few years ago, so my titers should still be pretty protective."

Leila nodded. "You know that hasn't actually been proven, for monkeypox. But yeah, you're probably right."

Why hadn't she thought of that? She took off her gloves and felt her shoulder reflexively, imagining the oozing wound that had resulted from her own vaccination. It lasted for weeks before finally drying up into a nasty-looking scab. Everyone in Viral Special Pathogens had to get it, along with the more experimental vaccines for a whole slew of other scary diseases. Not that they got to play with the real thing down in that most-guarded of all the frozen vaults—only her boss had that access—but the vaccine's effectiveness in inducing immunity against most of the other orthopox viruses meant it was included with all the others. That, and because the powers-that-be thought it might be a good idea for a few health professionals to be ready just in case the virus ever reared its ugly head again. God forbid.

"Why'd you get the vaccine, though?" she asked. It wasn't a bad idea, given the nature of his work here in Rwanda, but wasn't it pretty difficult to get for someone without an official requirement?

"Good question. I guess I may as well tell you."

He sounded uncomfortable.

"Oh, this sounds exciting."

Or not.

"I'm actually active duty military, if you can believe it."

She rotated her head slightly. That was not what she expected. There was the heavy scruff poking out from his mask, the overgrown mop hanging way past his ears. But then, she had noticed a certain efficiency in his movements—a distinctive intensity—in that first moment together in the airport earlier.

"Maybe," she said slowly. "Tell me more."

"Well, it's pretty simple, really." Even with the mask on it was clear he was smiling. "I deployed to Afghanistan a couple years back and got the vaccination along with every other soldier heading that way. You know, just in case the Taliban is hoarding old smallpox scabs in some remote mountain cave."

"You know that's not what I meant," Leila said. "What are you doing hunting gorilla viruses in Africa while looking like some kind of outdoorsy frat boy?"

"Ouch." Cole lifted a hand to his cheek. "You mean this stuff? I admit, I kind of like being so far from the proverbial flagpole."

"Flagpole?"

"Sorry, in Army-speak, that just means it's nice not to have my bosses right here looking over my shoulder all the time."

"I see."

Was he deliberately trying to avoid answering her question?

"Here's the deal," he said. "I'm on an academic assignment right now. Basically getting paid my regular officer salary to turn myself into some kind of expert on emerging infectious diseases."

"Okay, now you're making a little more sense. Kind of like how we sometimes get Army docs in the Epidemic Intelligence Service?"

"Exactly."

"And why does the military think it's worth taxpayer dollars to send a someone like you back to school?"

She knew the answer as soon as the question left her mouth, but she wanted to hear his version.

"Honestly, for situations just like this one. Can you imagine what this virus could do if it got into the wrong hands?"

"Yeah, I guess I can."

It wouldn't be pretty, no question there.

"People like you at the CDC will help figure out what's going on behind the scenes, sure. But at the end of the day, you probably won't be the ones on the receiving end of an actual biological warfare attack."

"I guess I can't argue with that."

As much as she usually loved to hate all things military-related, Leila knew he was right. She was glad to be on her own side of the fence in this division of labor.

"That's enough about me, though," he said. "You know how I got my smallpox vaccination, and I assume you're protected too?"

"Yeah, all of us—"

"Perfect, then back to Marna. Anything else you want to do while we work on getting her out of here?"

Leila looked back at the bed, almost wishing her patient had miraculously disappeared and become someone else's responsibility. She felt so useless here on her own.

"Do you have anything in the pharmacy that might help? Even Tamiflu would be worth a shot."

At least it was an antiviral, if that's really what they were dealing with.

"I think so, but I'll have to run over there to check."

"Let's go ahead and get some samples, though, before we start her on anything else. I'll take hers back to Atlanta along with the ones you already got from those gorillas."

"What're you going to need?"

She thought for a minute.

"Just the basics for blood and some mucosal swabs. You don't have any viral culture media, do you?"

"Ha, that's one thing we've got plenty of around here. How do you think I'm sending all these new viruses back to my advisor's lab?"

A quick knock at the window startled her. Musamba was standing outside.

"Just got off the phone with Marna's parents. They'll have a plane on the ground in Kigali six hours from now."

"A plane? That's all they said?"

"International SOS," Musamba said. "Straight from Joburg. They'll have a medical crew ready for isolation procedures and full life support."

Cole turned back to Leila.

"You hear that? She just might beat this thing."

T hank you for stopping by, Sohrab."
"Of course."

Sohrab closed the door behind him and stood silently before the desk that filled his boss's tiny office.

"Take a seat, please." The man motioned to the only other chair in the room. "And don't look so forlorn—you are not in trouble."

Sohrab sat down and relaxed his shoulders slightly. That was good news. He had been a government employee long enough to know that it was never a good thing to be called into a private meeting with one's supervisor. But maybe this was different? Dr. Rahmani actually looked somewhat pleased with the whole situation.

"I saw your father at a meeting today," the older man continued. "He gives you his greetings."

"Thank you, doctor. I'm glad he is still in good health."

The tension returned. This was strange.

"He told me about your mother. I'm very sorry to hear of her illness."

Sohrab bowed his head. "May Allah be merciful to her."

"If you need any time away from the lab, just say the word. It is not good to be far from her during these last days."

"Again, I thank you."

This was the first time Dr. Rahmani had ever shown any interest in his personal life. What was he trying to get at?

"She has my wife with her now."

"But that is not why I called you here this afternoon."

Not a big shock there. Sohrab racked his brain. Had something gone wrong with one of the experimental trials?

"I was surprised to learn that your father is not aware of what you actually do for us here. I know your family has been living with them at the official residence, so I assumed you might have shared about your work."

"I take my security clearance very seriously, doctor." Sohrab tried to keep his hands still, resting on the edges of the chair. Did this really have something to do with his father's job after all? "It would not be my place to discuss our work with anyone else, regardless of family relations."

"That is good, Sohrab, very good. I respect that about you."

The older man placed his elbows on the desk and rested his chin on clasped hands. A thin band of pure white hair was plastered against his otherwise bare head. Sohrab had seen photos of him when he was younger, back when he sported an unwieldy thick dark mane. At that time, he was being welcomed as a somewhat famous scientist who had made a name for himself abroad, triumphantly returning home to Iran and bringing modern molecular biology with him.

"Is there something else you wanted to speak with me about, Doctor?"

Sohrab was confused. Normally his boss did not have any trouble getting right to the point. Now he watched as a sly smile crept onto the man's aging features.

"Yes, I respect that you know how to keep your mouth shut. That is a great gift in the world today." He paused, his eyes widening as he shifted slightly in his chair. "Congratulations, Sohrab. Our project has proved to be successful."

«Our project?»

"The work that I started, yes, so long ago. You have brought it further than I ever imagined possible." The old man sat up straight, a triumphant look growing on his face. "And now I have learned today, from your father, no less, that this shared life's work has reached its fulfillment. I was somewhat amused when I realized he did not even know of your involvement, but this is what proved to me that you could be trusted with the news."

Sohrab stared at him, not moving a muscle. This couldn't be right. Theirs was a defensive project only, a doomsday threat to be pulled out only when under the most extreme duress—just like the nuclear devices his father was working so hard to develop. His father. What could he possibly have to do with this?

Sohrab shook his head slowly.

"I know this comes as a surprise to you," his boss continued. "But we must be proud. Our creation is now free to serve its purpose in the world."

"Purpose? What purpose?" He couldn't restrain himself any longer. "It was never meant to be free, you know that as well as I do."

"What purpose, Sohrab?" The old scientist's tone now carried the hint of a threat. "The same purpose behind all our work, of course."

Sohrab stood.

"Today," Dr. Rahmani said, "we bring great honor and power to the Persian people."

Three short beeps meant the real-time thermal cycler had finished its analysis. Cole stepped across the tiny room that served as his lab and selected *Print Results* on the touch-screen monitor in front of him.

He and Leila had been reviewing all the monkeypox papers they could find online while they waited. Cole wasn't convinced that a simple swab of those lesions on the roof of Marna's mouth was going to yield enough DNA to give any definitive answers, but he agreed that it was still worth trying. They had to wait for her flight anyway—might as well see if they could actually confirm this crazy diagnosis.

And it *was* crazy, even if Leila didn't seem to think so. No one had ever reported on a pox-like disease with this short of an incubation period. These viruses usually needed weeks to get established in their hosts' bodies before they started causing any real signs of illness. But here they were, only two days since the big adventure in Virunga, and Marna was sick.

The phone call from Goma gave them even more reason to be suspicious, there was no question about that. Still no word from their director and his journalist friend, and the crisis at the hospital itself wasn't leaving the rest of the staff much time to get serious about tracking them down. Three nurses and one physician so far, along with about a quarter of the other inpatients at the facility, all experiencing early stages of what seemed to be a scarily familiar disease process. Fever, malaise, and body aches, followed quickly by this steady progression of the rash and nodules across their bodies.

Cole pulled a single piece of paper off the printer.

Crap.

"So what do you think?"

Leila stood up and reached for the page.

"Not good, for Marna, at least."

Not good at all. What was this going to mean for her, for them? He let Leila take the paper from his hands. Did she even know what she was looking at?

"I guess this will make your outbreak investigation a little more exciting, though."

Cole didn't make much of an effort to keep the cynicism out of his voice. Ever since Marna's collapse in the office the day before, he'd been doing a lot of thinking about things. He would quite willingly give up every shot at infectious disease fame, his PhD, and a whole lot more, if he could somehow get a guarantee that she was going to make it through alive.

He watched Leila skim over the summarized results from the two re-al-time PCR assays.

"Can you tell me what I'm looking at?" Leila asked. "I'm not going to pretend to be much of a molecular biologist here—I've focused more on the field work part of the job."

No surprise there. For some reason, a lot of the physicians Cole had worked with over the years seemed to look down on those who spent any time toiling over the bench. It didn't make sense, since it was here in the lab that diagnoses were confirmed, vaccines designed, and medications discovered. Although he could appreciate the sentiment, and he personally liked the hands-on animal work more than pipetting solutions from one vial to another, he was still glad he could play both sides.

"So basically, we ran two unrelated assays, each of them targeting a total-ly different gene that is part of the monkeypox virus's DNA." He took the paper back and pulled a pen from behind his ear. "I'm about to get kind of technical on you here, so feel free to stop me at any point."

"Go for it."

"Here's the first one." He circled a spot on the page. "The E9L-NVAR probe is looking for a particular DNA polymerase gene found in all the Eurasian orthopoxviruses except our favorite extinct cousin, Mr. Smallpox himself."

"And I assume that graph is showing a positive?"

"Yep, that tall peak means that the probe successfully found its target gene and caused it to multiply out a bunch of times over the course of each heat cycle. So we can check that box: yes it's in the orthopox family, but no it's not smallpox."

"Go on."

"The second set here is a hybridization assay," he said. "It uses a different type of probe that targets the B6R envelope protein gene."

"In English, please?"

"Well, the important thing is that this gene is totally specific to the monkeypox virus. The fact that our probe found its target yet again means we can be almost one hundred percent confident in our identification."

"Two different assays, two different genes, both pointing to—"

"Monkeypox, yep." At least she didn't need it explained more than once. "That's what's currently growing on the roof of Marna's mouth. And most likely circulating through the rest of her, too."

"It does make sense," Leila said. "But have these assays been verified and published anywhere? Or is it a method you've just developed on your own here in Rwanda?"

"Please, I'm not that much of a prodigy." He could understand her skepticism, but that didn't mean he liked it. "The whole system was actually developed by some of your CDC colleagues to help track the 2003 outbreak. I think I've got the paper saved on my hard drive here if you really want to see it."

"Don't worry about it, no." She kept looking back to the print-out, now resting on the lab bench in front of them. "I might give my friend in the virology lab a call, just to see what he thinks."

"Because you still don't believe that I know what I'm doing."

"Cole, get over yourself." She rolled her eyes. "This is science. Regardless of what you find here, we'll still need to grow this thing out in culture and run a full genomic sequencing back in Atlanta. There's got to be something different that can account for these superpox symptoms, right?"

There was a knock at the door.

"Dr. Cole, are you in there?"

It was Innocence Kambale's vibrant voice. Cole opened the door a crack.

"Yeah, what's going on?"

"We just now heard from Akagera Aviation, and they will not be coming."

"What do you mean, not coming?" Cole looked over his shoulder at Leila. "They're the only air ambulance service in the country."

"The owner himself expresses his sincerest apologies, but the helicopter is grounded for maintenance, waiting on a part to arrive from Nairobi."

Sincerest apologies, right. Always with the superlatives here, but sometimes that just wasn't enough. This would make things a lot more difficult. Cole had been counting on the company's new Augusta A109 helicopter, brightly painted in Rwandan blue, yellow, and green, to get Marna to the airport. The fledgling service recently evacuated a tourist off a gorilla trek, bravely landing right in the little clearing at the Karisoke research station. The overweight American had apparently suffered a mild heart attack when a playful young blackback mock charged him. Should have settled for *National Geographic* if he wasn't prepared for the real thing, but there wasn't a good system in place for properly screening tourists before sending them up on the mountain.

Now they would have to get a ground ambulance for Marna, and he knew that could be totally hit or miss. Why was it that the only pilot among them was the first person to get sick?

"One more thing," the tall park ranger said. "Not such bad news, this part. Little Endo's fever has broken."

LEILA STILL COULDN'T believe she agreed to take a closer look at this sick gorilla. They had passed by an outdoor enclosure on the way across the Gorilla Doctors compound, interrupting the three healthy orphans in the middle of a rambunctious play wrestling session. When she and Cole stopped to watch their antics through the fence, all three jumped up on their hind legs and stood there staring right at her, as if they knew she didn't belong. They looked more like children in gorilla costumes than the actual animals themselves, and the irrational fear that had been nagging at her ever since she stepped off the plane reached its climax. These creatures were just too much like humans for their own good.

"Try to imagine that he's one of your sick infants on the NICU." Cole looked up at her from across the small entryway that had been turned into their biohazard prep area. "At this age there's really not much of a difference at all, right? I mean, some babies are even born with that weird dark hair all over their bodies."

"Lanugo, you mean?" Leila pulled the Tyvek coveralls over her clothes. No stripping down and showering in here, fortunately, even though she knew it would probably be a safer bet. But she sure as hell wasn't going to be the one to suggest it.

"Guess so," Cole said. "Can't say I have a whole lot of experience with human infants yet."

"You mean you didn't leave some poor woman back home taking care of your mini-McBrides when you ran off to Africa?"

"Come on, what kind of a guy do you think I am?" He stood up and stepped into tall rubber boots. "Last time I spent much time with baby humans was after my little brother and sister were born."

"Twins?"

"Yep, they're the last of us five, and I was the first, so there's ten years between us."

For some reason he struck her as just the type that would come from a big family. Too much American wholesomeness there for her taste, thank you very much. And of course, he had to be polite and ask her right back.

"How about you? What's your family like?"

She bit the inside of her cheek. Why were they talking about this again?

"I'm not really in touch with them anymore."

That usually did the trick, but Cole seemed like the annoyingly persistent type.

"Oh wow, I'm sorry. That must be tough." He stood up and placed a hand on the doorknob.

A pleasant surprise—he was going to let it rest. She got up to follow him and suddenly found herself sharing something she hadn't even told Travis yet.

"I do hear from my brother over e-mail every now and then, though, so that's nice."

She regretted saying it even as the words left her mouth. But her brother's name and the subject line of the message she had just seen on her phone burned brightly at the front of her mind. When was she going to be able to read it, in the middle of all this chaos?

"Cool, that's a start at least," Cole said. He looked into her eyes for just a second beyond what was comfortable, and then opened the door. "Welcome to Endo's world!"

Leila expected the wafting nastiness of a zoo's great ape house to envelope her the moment she stepped inside the room, but she was happy to be wrong in this case. It really looked more like a baby's nursery than an animal cage. An old plush recliner sat in one corner next to a dim incandescent floor lamp. Along the other wall was a changing table, and in the far corner a big pile of blankets.

Sitting in the blankets was a tall black man she hadn't met yet. This must be the other brother from Virunga. He looked up at her and nodded, a kind smile on his face.

"Proper Kambale, meet Dr. Leila Torabi." Cole stepped forward and immediately knelt down on the blankets. "She's from the Centers for Disease Control, back in the U.S., and she's going to help us figure out what killed those gorillas."

The man made a move to stand but Leila held up a hand.

"Please, don't get up. It's very nice to meet you."

"And you, Madame."

It took a moment for her eyes to adjust to the dim green light filtered through a single window on the opposite wall.

Then she saw it.

The tiny creature was huddled against the man's chest, two beady eyes staring out at her from a ball of fluffy black hair. Leila felt her throat tighten, and her heart started pounding more quickly. This was the moment she had been dreaming about and dreading ever since she was a child.

Deep breath.

She was a doctor, a scientist. There was no reason this irrational physiological response should be so crippling.

"Well, aren't you going to come and say hello?" The dizziness subsided, and she saw Cole looking up at her, a quizzical expression in his goggled eyes. The baby gorilla squirmed in his hands, looking for all the world as if it was trying to get back to the warmth and safety of Proper's comforting hold.

"I hate to admit this now," she said, still frozen to the ground just inside the closed door. "But I'm actually not much of an animal person. I can say hello from here."

She waved uncertainly.

Cole let out a muffled snort from behind the mask. "Oh come on, poor Endo here is about the least scary animal you could imagine. Unless you just can't stand a good pus-filled nodule, but I can't believe that's the case."

Leila did want to see the lesions, and she could already imagine the hard time Dr. Shackleton would give her if she told him she didn't even take a look at the sick gorilla.

She took a hesitant step forward, then another. The infant must have seen her moving—he froze in Cole's hands and turned his head in her direction. What was she afraid of, anyway? Not that it was going to bite her. There couldn't be any teeth in that tiny mouth yet. The disease didn't bother her either. The same virus was coursing through Marna's body, and she hadn't had any problem with that. Maybe she could do this.

The gorilla pulled one frail arm out of Cole's hand and lifted it toward her.

"Look at that," Proper said quietly.

"See, he's trying to tell you there's nothing to be afraid of." Cole shifted in the blankets and motioned with his free hand. "Keep on coming, looks like he's asking for some female attention."

Leila took another step and then crouched down beside the nest of blankets. She felt her fear dissipating into the peaceful stillness of the quiet room. The gorilla still held his arm out, tiny fingers waving slowly in the air in her direction. Now she could really see his face, the tiny wrinkles around his pouty mouth and shining eyes full of life. Something in her cracked as she gazed at this innocent creature, and somehow the likeness to humans that had always been so scary and off-putting now seemed a comfort. She knew what to do. This sick little boy was just like all the others she had toiled over through her residency.

She slowly reached out a gloved hand and watched as the gorilla's tiny black fingers closed onto one of her own.

"He's beautiful," she whispered.

"Does that mean you've changed your mind?" Cole said.

Leila placed her other hand under the animal's tiny rump and lifted him out of Cole's hands. The infant relaxed against her chest, his trusting gaze locked on her face. A novel sensation rushed through her veins, some strange combination of instinct and hormones that no human baby had ever triggered.

"You could say that, yes," she answered, now running her free hand down the gorilla's furry back. "I never thought I could feel this way about an animal."

"You're not the first to have that reaction, if it makes you feel any better." Cole pulled a long cigar-shaped plastic container out of his coverall pocket. "Ever since Dian Fossey and *Gorillas in the Mist* hit the big time, these mountain gorillas have been doing their best to convince us humans that they're worth keeping around."

Leila looked up at Proper Kambale, sitting silently in the blankets. A bright blue surgical mask hid most of his long face, but the expression around his dark eyes added to the overwhelming sense of acceptance and purpose that was welling up inside her. She could understand a little better now why someone like this would risk life and limb to protect a forgotten corner of the world like Virunga National Park. What was that statistic Cole had shared on their drive up from the airport? Over one hundred and fifty Virunga park rangers killed on the job in the last twenty years alone. Men like the Kambale brothers, leaving their legacy of blood and toil on the slopes of the Virunga volcanoes.

The tiny creature began to move against her, rubbing his little forehead and one open hand up along her chest. She flushed with embarrassment as the gorilla began to smack his lips on finding the target.

"Hang on, I think we have some formula made up already," Cole said.

"Uh-uh, no way." Leila shook her head as Cole pressed a bottle into her free hand.

"Yes, Madame," Proper said. "I am trying to feed him all afternoon with no success, but now I see what I was missing."

Leila reluctantly took the bottle and inserted it gently into Endo's waiting mouth. Now with his face still and only inches from her own, she remembered the reason for their visit. The bare black skin around the gorilla's lips and nose was covered in raised pustular lesions, all equal in size and developmental stage. They were just beginning to form the characteristic umbilication, caving in at the center like a volcanic crater, and several oozed a viscous milky yellow fluid. Perfect for a viral culture. She glanced at the hairless underside of the forearm stretched out along the baby's emaciated torso. More of the same lesions, and there they were on the palms of his otherwise beautiful little hands, too.

"What did you say these lesions looked like when you first picked him up?"

Cole answered, "The rash was just barely visible."

"So you're saying a disease process that normally takes a couple weeks to play itself out has sped by in just forty-eight hours?"

Leila genuinely had a hard time believing it. But the evidence was right here in front of her, sucking away hungrily at the almost-empty bottle in her hand.

"Exactly," Cole said. He pulled a long cotton-tipped probe out of its plastic packaging. "You still counting yourself among the doubters?"

"No, I guess I really can't anymore." She pointed to an open pustule on the gorilla's forearm. "That looks like a good spot."

"Alright, do you have a good hold on him?"

She nodded. "Go for it."

Cole held the probe like a pencil, guiding it steadily into position and rolling it along the oozing skin several times. He raised his other hand, which held the clear plastic tube filled with viral culture media, and inserted the probe deep down into the gel. Then he broke off the protruding end and pushed the rubber stopper back into the top of the tube. There was something in the confident manner with which he went about the procedure that appealed to Leila's geeky scientific core, but a rapid knock on the door and resulting movement of her startled patient prevented her from pursuing that line of thought any further.

Innocence Kambale poked his face into the room.

"Cole, Dr. Torabi, you must come!" he said breathlessly. "Marna cannot breathe—Musamba says run quickly."

F adi Haddad looked up from his computer screen to peer through the cheap white aluminum blinds. The window gave him a clear view out over the long curved drive leading up from Fairfax County Parkway.

Still nothing.

A glistening mirage shimmered on a patch of asphalt, but the rest of the drive was mercifully protected by a towering forest of oaks and tulip poplars. The trees were everywhere, healthy and vibrant in their summer foliage, and they were a comforting presence in this little suburban oasis. It was really only a half-hour drive but always seemed a world away from the buildings and bustle of his downtown restaurant. Growing up on the rocky hillsides of the Bekaa Valley, where Solomon's famous grove of ancient cedars were the only trees left, Haddad had never seen such abundance. The trees were only one of so many things he had come to love about this adopted home.

He tried to imagine those rocky slopes, which would now be fading from their spring lushness to summer's dry golden brown. There would be mixed flocks of sheep and goats picking their way around the boulders, and bored teenagers, like he used to be, half-heartedly following behind, dreaming of greater things. Would he do it again, answer that call that had taken him out of one world and into another? In a heartbeat, yes. But not, perhaps, for the same foolish reasons that once so captivated him.

Lebanon, land of his fathers. His *real* home. Why was it so hard to convince himself now that he was still doing the right thing?

Haddad looked back to his screen and reread the message in his Drafts folder for the hundredth time. Nothing on the "To" or "Subject" lines, just a simple block of Arabic text in the main content box. It was meant to look like a letter from one relative to another about an upcoming family wedding. Fresh eggs for cooking up copious quantities of a favorite Lebanese omelet, insulin syringes for the visiting diabetic grandmother, and space heaters to ensure the newborn nieces and nephews were warm enough. The quantities were a bit off, but it would take an especially attentive analyst to catch that fact.

It was a curious combination, but Haddad followed the instructions to the smallest detail. Eggs from his restaurant's food service contractor. Bulk syringes from a medical supply company out in Leesburg. And the space heaters from Walmart.

Not because he wanted anything to do with whatever horror was now taking shape. No, Haddad complied because he was terrified of what would happen if he did not.

Where were they, anyway?

He looked around the simple office, grasping for something to organize, some way to take his mind off the one thing he couldn't stop thinking about. But there was nothing left to do. He had sent the self-storage facility's only employee home the day before, promising to pay twice his hourly wage if the simple man would stay home for the week. An allusion to needing a location for an adulterous sexual liaison was all Haddad needed to let slip, and the employee was all grins and encouragement as he willingly agreed to the underhanded arrangement. The thought made him sick. Regardless of his current reluctance to embrace the cause like he once had, Haddad was a faithful man. A good Muslim.

A movement in the corner of his eye caught his attention.

Two vehicles were making their way slowly up the drive. One of them, an older F-150 pickup with Maryland plates, belonged to his cousin. The other was a new Toyota compact, a rental that had been picked up near Dulles airport earlier that morning.

The moment had arrived.

Plane hasn't even left South Africa yet." Cole stepped back into the room and closed the door gently. "Apparently one of the doctors on call backed out when he got briefed on the details of Marna's disease. They're still waiting at Tambo International for his backup."

"Hope that costs him his job, cowardly asshole," Leila whispered.

"My thoughts exactly."

He sat down beside the bed and shook his head in anger. Didn't they realize a delay could cost Marna her life? She looked awful, stretched out there with her head cocked back at an unnatural angle, the plastic endotracheal tube sticking out of her gaping mouth. It wasn't hooked up to anything—they never used gas on the gorillas and weren't equipped with even the most basic anesthesia unit—but at least the tube let her rapid, shallow breaths flow freely. Leila sat on the other side of the bed, injecting small amounts of milky white propofol into an intravenous catheter whenever her patient showed signs of discomfort. The drug kept Marna just unconscious enough so that she wouldn't fight the tube uncomfortably filling her trachea. Not ideal, but at least it was keeping her alive while they waited for the ambulance to arrive from Kigali.

Musamba was in the middle of intubating Marna himself when they arrived at the room an hour earlier, and Cole could tell that Leila was about to go off on him again for acting way outside his scope of practice. Marna's gasping breath, and the rapid return of color to her lips when the tube slid into position, must have changed Leila's mind, though, and Cole was glad she held her tongue. He would have done the same thing if he'd been in Musamba's place, and he didn't have anywhere near the same experience intubating large primates. Who was going to argue that the veterinarian should have just watched her suffocate right in front of him?

"Shit, her blood pressure just won't stay where I want it." Leila took the stethoscope from her ears and removed the manual cuff from the pilot's toned bicep. "What I would do for a little dobutamine right now."

"You really think she's in danger of some kind of catastrophic heart failure?"

As much as he hated to acknowledge it, Cole knew there was a chance she could simply die on them right there.

"Yeah, she's dancing along the sharp edge of septic shock right now, and I'm afraid all the indicators are going in the wrong directions." Leila had two fingers on Marna's wrist. "Pulse and respiratory rates are through the roof, and I'm beginning to think more fluids might push her straight into ARDS."

Acute respiratory distress syndrome. It was often a point of no return for septic patients, especially when mechanical ventilation wasn't available. Where in the world was that ambulance? It was supposed to have left Kigali two hours ago.

"Isn't there something more we can do for her, with what we've got here?"

Cole didn't like the first hint of a defeated look in Leila's eyes. He knew she was in over her head, that she had never been forced to take care of a crashing patient in this type of setting, with two veterinarians to assist her and almost none of the drugs or equipment she needed. But still, she was the physician, a trained infectious disease doctor at that, and Marna was dying from an infectious disease. Couldn't she come up with something?

"I'm doing the best I can," Leila said softly. "Dr. Shackleton promised me that this was going to be a simple courier mission, in and out with the samples, that's it."

Cole felt the blood rush to his face.

"Feel free to call yourself a taxi back to Kigali, if that's how you feel." Now he was pissed. He wasn't going to just sit here and watch another friend die right in front of his eyes.

Leila glared right back at him, her lips pressed thin and tight.

He knew he was being harsh, but was this really the best the U.S. government could send in the face of a potential pandemic? "When you get back to Atlanta, though, could you ask your boss to send over the big guns next time?"

"Sure," she spat back, shaking her head. "I'll put in a special request so that our team is able to fly through the middle of a hurricane. Definitely don't want you or your investigation to be inconvenienced in any way, asshole."

"Look, I'm sorry." He took a deep breath. As much as he wanted to keep pushing, there was no use in escalating the already charged emotional atmosphere. "I know you're doing all you can."

Their painful vigil was interrupted by Katy Perry's powerful voice coming from somewhere deep within Leila's Tyvek suit.

"Shit, thought I changed that." She stood up. "I need to get this—probably my boss."

"Go for it, maybe he's got some good news for us."

Unlikely, but it was hard to imagine things getting worse than they already were. Cole watched her step out into the fading light, then turned back to the bed. How many cool evenings just like this one had he and Marna spent over good books and a bottle of wine? He would never have pushed so hard for that quick excursion across the border if he'd had any idea that their peaceful shared existence was going to come crashing down so dramatically. If they had not been there to find the dead gorillas and sound the early alarm, though, would it really have made any difference? The hospital outbreak in Goma would have gotten noticed eventually, but the international response could have been delayed by several days. Enough to make a difference, in the grand scheme of things? That remained to be seen.

"Come on, Marna," he whispered over her. "You've got to pull through here."

LEILA TORE OFF her gloves, mask and goggles and was working on the coveralls when her phone stopped ringing. She froze, then finally released the full-body sob that had been working its way out ever since Cole started attacking her with his nasty comments. Was she really this desperate for contact with the outside world? Apparently so.

A chorus of invisible insects droned on from the vegetation around Marna's cabin, but they weren't quite loud enough to drown out one more sob. *Stop it.* She could handle this.

At least the cool evening air was an unexpected mercy. It settled onto her exposed face and arms, almost seeming to lift away some of the tension from this day filled with unpleasant surprises. She dug into the pocket of her jeans and pulled out the phone. Just like she thought—one missed call from the CDC. Couldn't she get a break?

She was about to put it back in her pocket and start in with the personal protective equipment again when the phone started buzzing in her hand.

"This is Leila."

"Leila, it's Bill Shackleton, and I've got Travis on the line, too." Her boss's deep round voice was comforting and intimidating at the same time. What was he going to think of her progress so far? "Is everything okay over there? We haven't heard from you all day."

"Yes, sorry, everything's fine." She paused. Might need to clarify that. "We've been crazy busy ever since I landed in Kigali this morning, but I have the samples and should be on my way back to you first thing tomorrow."

"Leila, it's me, Travis." They had only been dating for a few weeks, but his voice had an immediate soothing effect on her. "You don't sound like everything's fine. What's going on over there?"

She took a deep breath.

"There's a girl here, a South African helicopter pilot working with the park system, who's sick. Really sick. She might die on me right here."

"Is it the same virus, Leila?" It was Shackleton again. "Do you have a human case there in Rwanda?"

"According to the tests Dr. McBride is using, yes." She looked in through the window to see Cole leaning over the bed. It didn't look like he could hear her, but she lowered her voice anyway. "I can't say I'm totally convinced he knows what he's doing, but he promises these assays were developed at the CDC a few years ago."

"He's right," Travis said. "I've been looking over the results he e-mailed from the dead Virunga gorillas, and it's definitely a dead-on match for monkeypox."

"Well that's what I'm skeptical about. Sure, the disease looks like monkeypox and tests like monkeypox, but it's not acting like any monkeypox virus we've ever seen before. If this girl really caught the virus from the dead gorillas, or more likely from the orphan that she's been helping to care for, then we're looking at an incubation period of less than forty-eight hours."

"Right," Shackleton said. "And that wouldn't just be unique for monkeypox, but for any of the poxviruses known to science."

"It's not just the incubation period, though," Leila continued. "The lesions on this sick orphan gorilla have progressed through all the classic pox stages since they picked him up off his dead mother a couple of days ago. He was right on the edge yesterday, high fever, labored breathing, no appetite, but as of an hour ago he seems to be doing a lot better."

"Did you get some kind of samples from him?"

"Yeah, fortunately Dr. McBride has a bunch of viral culture transport kits laying around." She felt for the hard plastic tube in her other pocket. "How am I going to get all this stuff through customs?"

"Don't worry about it," Travis said. "We'll send the export paperwork over to you there."

"And what about—"

Her boss interrupted. "Our bigger concern, Leila, is whether or not we can even let you travel, now that you've theoretically been exposed to the virus."

She caught her breath. That thought had not even crossed her mind.

"Seriously, Bill? You personally inspected my smallpox vaccination to make sure it took, remember?" She wasn't going to get stuck there in Rwanda. Not as the only real doctor and representative of the CDC just as a full-blown epidemic reared its ugly head. "And we've been following strict BSL-3 precautions. There's absolutely no chance I've been exposed."

She knew she was stretching the truth just slightly.

No response.

"Look, lock me down in the slammer when I get back there, for all I care. Just don't make me stay here."

Still silence. The slammer was a Biosafety Level 4 isolation suite at the CDC, the nickname adopted from an equivalent setup at USAMRIID. Scientists who had been exposed to dangerous pathogens were quarantined there until it was clear they were not actually infected.

Maybe she could try a more noble argument.

"The samples need to get back to you now, if we're going to figure out what's really going on with this virus."

"Much as I hate to say it," Shackleton finally said, "That might just be your ticket home. We already checked with DHL and FedEx, and neither of them is willing to touch the samples. We need to start the full genomic sequencing as soon as possible, and there's nowhere in Rwanda that's set up for that level of molecular analysis. If this virus isn't monkeypox, or it's some new mutant strain, we need to know and adapt our response accordingly."

"Your response," Leila said. "Does that mean there's more of a response in the works than sending your newest EIS officer straight into the hornet's nest?"

The words came out with more stinging accusation than she intended.

"It's tricky," Shackleton answered. "All air travel is shut down here on the East Coast due to this hurricane. And now we've gotten confirmation that both the airport in Goma and the Congo-Rwanda border crossing are effectively shut down due to the increased rebel activity in the area. The World Health Organization and MSF chartered a flight trying to send a team from Nairobi, but they got turned around mid-way to Goma."

"Wow." Leila suddenly felt even more alone.

"If you think you're in a bad way, just be glad you're not at that aid hospital in Goma right now. Half their staff and patients are sick, and they've just started getting reports of the disease in other parts of the city."

"I heard," Leila said. "Apparently their director was supposed to be arriving here last night with samples from the index case, but he never showed up."

"Not a lot of good news right now." Shackleton's voice was steady. "But you're right. We need those samples, and you're our safest bet on bringing them back here. Just promise me you'll be on that plane tomorrow."

"Yeah, take care of yourself, Leila."

She could see Travis saying the words in her mind and wished she were already back there, curled up in his arms.

"Bye for now. I'll let you know if anything changes."

LEILA LOWERED THE phone from her ear. She unconsciously reached for a new set of protective gear from a box beside the door, her professional call of duty overruling the aching hunger that had hit minutes earlier. But then she paused, remembering the e-mail from her brother that still sat unread in her inbox. Maybe there was time now? A quick peek through the window showed nothing had changed. Cole sat at the bedside, the fingers of one hand wresting against the inside of Marna's wrist while the other held the propofol syringe.

Maman.

That was all she had seen as she watched the messages slowly load on the lab's borrowed wireless. The craziness of the last few hours had made it easy to push to the back of her mind.

Such a blunt and unnerving subject line. *Maman.* Momma. And so typical of her brother. She was always glad to hear from him, relieved when he had first reached across the void three years ago to begin mending their fractured relationship. But his messages never brought the healing and reconciliation she was really hoping for. He seemed to believe she was still going to come back one day—to Iran, her parents, and even Islam.

My dear sister.

Sohrab always wrote in their native Farsi, even though his English was still just as good as her own.

Maman is dying of lung cancer. She begs you to come home, to kiss her on the cheek. It is her only wish, and Baba has given his consent. There is not much time.

She read the message again and shuddered.

That was it.

Why this? Wasn't one woman's imminent death enough for the day? Leila felt the anger welling up in her chest. Fifteen years of rejection and silence, and now Maman was asking this of her? The last time Leila had seen her parents, she was a fresh-faced, rebellious eighteen-year-old, stepping on a plane to London to begin her biology studies at Oxford. They had drawn the line at an American university—there was just no way to make that work given Baba's position in the government. But once she tasted that freedom, even the stodgy British version of it, there was no turning back. And when Harvard accepted her for medical school, she'd been issued an ultimatum. *Come home now, or you will have no home with us.* It was an easy decision.

The cigarettes, those hated cigarettes. All the arguments with her mother as a newly health-conscious teenager and aspiring doctor—all for nothing. Leila could almost hear her own pestering voice, watching her mom dig a crumpled pack of Winstons from the trash one more time. *Don't you want to live to see your grandchildren, Maman?* And yet, somehow Leila never believed she was really going to die from it. Or from anything.

And now this.

Leila closed her eyes. The anger had spread out from her chest to the very tips of her fingers and toes. She wanted to run, and keep running, until she was in a place where no one knew her, no one expected anything of her, no one loved her with such a broken, hurtful love.

The rain started slowly, one drop hitting her bare cheek, then another. Within seconds, it was a downpour, silencing the insects and filling the air with the heavy scent of the eucalyptus above her. Leila relaxed her shoulders slowly, and her eyes spilled over, tears mixing with the rain now soaking her face.

Of course she would go.

She had to.

NORTH KIVU PROVINCE
DEMOCRATIC REPUBLIC OF THE CONGO
6:44 P.M.

It was getting loud out there. Too loud. Captain Jake Russell stepped out of his tent and walked over toward the enormous bonfire in the center of the camp. The laughter was universal, but he still had a hard time making much sense of the rapid French that had by necessity become the language du jour with their newest hosts. Apparently a year of Swahili at the Defense Language Institute in Monterey was not enough when you were chasing terrorists across international borders. Jake's team had started off in South Sudan, spent a few months in the Central African Republic, and just a week ago made the hop down into the Congo. He had yet to figure out how this crazy self-proclaimed prophet and his ragtag army simply melted into the landscape.

The overpowering scent of roasting meat was hard to resist, and as he got closer he could see that his guys were looking longingly at the evening fare of their Congolese counterparts. The carcasses of three young goats, purchased with U.S. taxpayer dollars and slaughtered on site that afternoon, were now stretched out over the open flames.

"Hey Mikey," he called.

Master Sergeant Mike Denison was his chief enlisted soldier and non-commissioned officer in charge of their twelve-man team. He was also the team's dog handler. Even though Jake had a good six inches on him, he knew he wouldn't stand a chance against the career Special Forces operator. Mikey was built like a bull.

The sergeant stepped away from the group around the fire. He held a short black leather leash in one hand but didn't seem to need it. His multipurpose canine, a tall fawn Belgian Malinois named Rico, stayed right by his side. This was Jake's first time working closely with a special ops dog team, and he was hooked.

"Yeah, what's up?"

Jake waited until the two were right beside him, looking back towards the fire.

"That goat smells pretty good, huh." He stroked his chin thoughtfully.

"Me and Rico here won't argue with that. Hell of a lot better than whatever MRE I'll have to suffer through later on tonight."

The Meal, Ready-to-Eat was the military's answer to unsanitary and unpredictable local food on missions like this one. Jake's team had been relatively content to follow the rules so far, but there was no fire-roasted goat menu option in the MREs to go along with the chili and macaroni, pork rib, and hated veggie omelet. And that goat was calling his name, just like he knew it was for the rest of his soldiers. Canine included.

"You know, Mikey, as a commissioned officer in the United States Army, I'm occasionally called upon to use appropriate discretion when faced with what might seem to be contradictory directions."

Jake spoke slowly and deliberately, letting loose with the south Texas twang that he usually tried harder to mask.

"This is true."

"On one hand, we've been instructed to fraternize with our host nation's military, learn about their culture and strengths as we work alongside them to achieve our goals. But on the other, we're told to stick with our provided rations, not endanger the health of the troops by experimenting with local cuisine."

"It ain't easy, sir."

"Well I'll tell you what." He threw his head to the side, catching a quizzical expression on Mikey's face. "I'm going to make an executive decision here." "I think I like where this is going."

A high-pitched beeping interrupted them.

"That's the sat phone, shit. They might have something for us."

Jake took off jogging back to his tent.

"Oh come on, man," the sergeant yelled after him, and Rico let out a single bark. "You're really gonna leave us hanging like that?"

Jake stopped at the entrance.

"The goats are fair game—just save some for me!"

"JAKE, IT'S ME, Ed." Colonel Ed Alsina was his boss's boss, commanding officer of the whole Kony-hunting task force based out of Camp Lemonnier, Djibouti. Jake loved the way everyone in the special ops community was on a first name basis. Even though this relatively small point was often the main thing outsiders noticed, it was really just one of a hundred ways their world was different from the larger military culture. "You guys holding up okay over there?"

"Oh you know us, sir, just sitting around the campfire, holding hands and singing Kumbaya."

He had filed a SITREP just twenty minutes earlier, so the colonel already knew what they had seen and learned that day.

"Of course, I wouldn't expect any less of you." A deep laugh. "Going to patch you through to someone from the NSA. They got in touch with us just now, wanted to share some intel with guys like you who might actually be able to act on it."

Jake's eyebrows went up. The National Security Agency did not make a habit of getting in touch, at least not with his little team of operators on their wild goose chase across central Africa. This could be interesting.

There was a series of clicks, then Ed's voice again. "Okay, we should all be on the line now. Could the NSA go ahead and repeat your summary for our team leader? Captain Jake Russell is currently on the ground in the DRC, just west of Virunga National Park."

A confident and alluring female voice started right in. "Thank you, sir, and hello. This is Morgan Andrews with the Central Africa desk."

If this were the NSA, he wouldn't mind if they wanted to get in touch on a more regular basis. His team's four-month deployment was now nine-going-on-ten, and Jake was starved for female attention.

"As discussed earlier, our systems have picked up an increased frequency of outgoing calls to Iran made from an area along the eastern border of the Congo."

"Ma'am," Jake interrupted. "I'm going to have to ask you to repeat that for me. I thought you just said Iran, but that couldn't be right."

"Yes, the Islamic Republic of Iran. I was surprised too when I first received the automatically flagged report, so I followed up and did a little more digging into the data. Turns out none of these calls have been answered, ten to fifteen of them every day for the last week, and they're all going to one number on the Iranian government's secure network."

Jake let out a low whistle.

"Exactly." He thought he heard a smile in her voice. "Fortunately for us, the mobile networks that are carrying these outgoing calls are anything but secure. We believe it's most likely there is only one target behind these calls, and that this person is rotating SIMs."

"Wow." Jake was stunned. "I've gotta be honest, that's not the type of intelligence I was expecting tonight. I assume you know why me and my guys are out here, trying to track down old Mr. Kony and his army?"

"Yes, we're quite aware of your mission."

"So am I supposed to conclude that you think these calls may have something to do with all that?"

"That's a question mark, Jake." It was the colonel now. "But this intel has gone up the chain, and we're being directed to devote some resources here, dig around a little bit. Even if it doesn't end up having anything to do with our main man Kony, there's really no good reason anyone in the Congo needs to be trying so hard to get in touch with Iran. Weapons, minerals, ivory—there are no good options here."

"Well alrighty then," Jake said. He was pacing back and forth in the tiny open area inside the tent that served as his operations center. "Ma'am, can you tell me where those two mobile towers are located? Might help us to know where to begin looking."

"They're the only ones in the area. One in the little town of Rumangabo, and the other on the northwestern outskirts of Goma. We'll send those coordinates to you now. The Virunga mountains along the border with Rwanda and Uganda make a hard stop to any mobile communications."

"So basically anywhere between those two towers and the snow-covered peaks of a bunch of active volcanoes?" He exhaled sharply through his nose. "Sounds like a piece of cake."

"It's a large area to cover, yes." She was all business. "We're going to work on getting a better pinpoint location for you, but this is all we have right now. Good luck."

A click, and then his commander's voice again. "I know this sounds like needles in a haystack, Jake, but sometimes that needle is so important it's worth the effort. Shouldn't have to argue that point with you, I don't think."

"No sir."

"I want you to send up a Puma for a few hours tonight. Make yourself a nice little grid pattern to start sweeping this area. Looks like most of it falls within the national park, right?"

"Yep, that's what I'm seeing too."

Jake held the phone's receiver against his shoulder as he typed in the grid coordinates for the two mobile phone towers.

"Focus on the thermal imaging, and don't spend too long looking at any one thing this first time around. Remember, you've got elephants, go-rillas, probably some illegal charcoal operations in there. That stuff's going to throw you off if you're not careful."

"Watch out for the elephants and gorillas, check." He hoped his sarcasm was transmitting loud and clear over the satellite phone.

"Whoever's trying to get in touch with our friend the Grand Ayatollah is almost definitely not working alone. We're looking for large groups of people, evidence of electricity, illegal mining, stuff that'll pop so hot on your screen you won't have any doubt."

"We're on it."

He was ready to go make this happen.

"Out for now. Stay in touch."

"Will do, sir."

It was going to be a long night.

"You think this'll work?"

Jake peered through the darkness ahead of him. The sounds of the rest of the men around the fire had faded to an indistinct murmur. They were somewhat exposed out here on their own, but Rico's invisible presence made Jake a whole lot more comfortable than he would have been otherwise. He could barely make out Mikey's silhouette, already on the ground unpacking the Puma UAV from its long backpack. The Puma was a mini-drone, a next-generation unmanned aerial vehicle that took both color and infrared video and weighed in at only thirteen pounds.

"Yeah," Mikey said. "She doesn't need much."

He snapped the six-foot wings onto the drone's tiny body and lifted it high into the air over his head.

"Okay, ready when you are."

Jake held the tablet-sized ground control station in both hands, ready to guide the Puma into action. He watched Mikey cock his arm and take a step back, looking for all the world like he was getting ready to launch a giant paper airplane.

And then she was free, sailing across the open field of cassava and above the tree tops before disappearing into the inky blackness.

"Let's go hunt us some bad guys, right?"

"Hooah, sir. Hooah."

KIGALI
10:01 P.M.

The pulse oximeter's high-pitched beeping stopped for a second, hiccuped, and then continued on at a rapidly increasing rate.

"Come on, Marna," Cole muttered. "You can't give up on us now."

He looked up at Leila across the stretcher. She was rhythmically squeezing a large rubber Ambu bag, eyes on her patient's chest, watching for even the slightest rise and fall that should have come with each mechanical breath. Of course there was no ventilator on this emergency vehicle. Not even an EKG.

"You really think we can't risk pushing any more fluids?"

She shook her head. "Not until these diuretics kick in and start pulling some of the fluid from her lungs."

What should have been an uneventful hour's ride down to the international airport had turned into a two-hour nightmare with a crashing patient in stop-and-go traffic. But Leila's instincts were proving to be right on the money every time. And they were so close, with an airplane and experienced medical crew on the ground waiting for their arrival.

Cole turned to the two Rwandan paramedics squeezed onto a narrow folding bench along one side of the ambulance, silent for the last half-hour. "How far out are we?"

One of them stood and peered through a small window in the back door. "Very close now, doctor. Ten minutes, no more."

Exactly what he said ten minutes ago. But it wasn't worth fighting over. The back of the ambulance was a mess. Equipment in disarray, empty drawers hanging open, and discarded supplies sliding across the floor every time the driver stepped on the brakes.

"Heart rate's still increasing," Leila said. "Not what we need right now."

A wet crackling sound came from the tube in Marna's mouth. Cole looked across her body to Leila, who shook her head slowly, lips pressed tightly together. The cautious optimism that had characterized the doctor's expression was fading, replaced by a distant look in her unfocused eyes.

"We're too late—her lungs are totally flooded." A pause. "This might be it."

"Don't say that!" Cole's knuckles were white as he gripped the edge of the stretcher.

"Oxygen saturation's dropping fast." Leila spoke softly now.

Cole picked up the handheld pulse oximeter, the same one they used to monitor vitals on anesthetized gorillas up in the mountains. Eighty-nine percent. Marna's lungs were not doing their job, not getting that life-giving oxygen from the air into the blood. Any lower and her systems would start shutting down. He pounded hard on the partition separating the patient area from the driver's cab.

"*Dépêchez-vous! Plus vite!*" Hurry up! Faster!

And then it happened. The heart monitor stopped beeping.

One, one-thousand, two, one-thousand, three, one-thousand. Cole grabbed for the syringe of epinephrine and pushed it through the open port on the intravenous catheter in Marna's wrist.

Five seconds passed, then three more staggered beeps, and silence.

Another syringe. It was all they had.

No response this time.

Cole threw both hands on Marna's sternum. Up and down and up and down. Ribs creaked, then snapped, under the force of his weight on her chest. Leila stood stoic, silent, still squeezing the bag, ignoring the sickening mix of blood and mucus bubbling up through the endotracheal tube.

CPR was never quite as pretty as it looked on TV.

And rarely successful in real life.

Minutes passed, sweat pouring from his face, soaking his clothes underneath the Tyvek. But the monitor stayed silent, and Cole fought off the growing consciousness of a dreaded conclusion. Their life-saving quest transformed into a morbid vigil. And yet he continued to fight, putting every ounce of anger and frustration and grief into these futile efforts to bring a silenced heart back to life.

He barely noticed when the ambulance screeched to a halt behind the terminal, the doors flying open, red lights flashing over his hunched shoulders and pumping arms.

And then gloved hands, pulling him away, unloading Marna's limp body. Ghostly figures in white positive pressure suits, huddled in a group around the stretcher, shaking their heads. Snippets of conversation drifting across the tarmac, the South African voices distorted and muffled by each suit's hissing self-contained air supply.

"—has died."

"Too late for—"

"—instructed to take the body."

He sat down on the asphalt, head in his hands, and cried.

11:52 P.M.

"It's just not safe, Cole." A light turned on at the top of the stairs. "Even if I thought it was a good idea, you know I can't authorize something like that at my level."

"Dave, are you talking to someone down there?" A woman's voice called down to them.

«Yeah, honey.» Lieutenant colonel Dave Wong, defense attaché at the embassy, turned away from Cole and put one foot on the bottom step. "It's Cole McBride, down from Musanze, along with a doctor from the CDC. You'll want to hear this."

"She doesn't need to come down for us," Cole whispered.

"But she will. She likes you, Cole. Always talking about taking the kids up to see those orphaned gorillas of yours one of these days." He brought a hand to his forehead and pushed the fingers through thinning black hair, longer than any Marine Corps officer would dare to grow back in the States. "Liked Marna, too. Been rooting for you two to get together ever since you brought her to the Memorial Day party last month."

Cole could read the unspoken question in the man's concerned eyes.

"No, we weren't dating. But it was close, and I really cared about her." He bit the inside of his cheek. "Shit. It happened so fast."

The older man reached out and touched his arm.

A door opened, and Leila stepped out of the bathroom. The fresh coat of makeup didn't hide that she was still a complete wreck.

"Refreshed?" Dave smiled at her kindly. "Let's go sit down."

Cole followed him down the hall into an enormous living room, its floor covered with toys and books. "Way more house than we need, of course," the attaché had said, giving him a full tour six months earlier. "But it was the only place that met DoD's security requirements, so we weren't going to complain." Cole had shown up at the embassy for what he thought was an unnecessary introduction, letting Big Brother officially know that there was one more rogue military officer wandering around the country. But he and the attaché ended up hitting it off, and the Wong's house quickly became Cole's default whenever he needed a place to stay in Kigali. It was one of hundreds of palatial villas that made up the wealthy Nyarutarama neighborhood, and it felt as close to the States as he could get anywhere in Rwanda.

Dave motioned to a couple of recliners.

"You two make yourselves at home—I'll be right back."

Cole didn't need to be told twice. He collapsed into the welcome comfort and closed his eyes.

A moment later, a hand touched his shoulder, jolting him out of a light sleep.

"I'm so sorry, Cole."

He opened his eyes and jumped to his feet. Katie was there now, making no attempt to hide her recent tears. She reached up and kissed his cheek, then turned to Leila and squeezed her hand.

"Welcome to our little castle. I'm Katie."

"Thanks for giving us a place to stay tonight," Leila said. "If it's too much trouble—"

"It's not, and I always keep a bed made up just in case." Katie walked into the open kitchen. "You two want a drink? Coffee, beer, something stronger?"

She was a petite brunette, pretty and perpetually put together. A good match for Dave, an Academy grad who had taken the fast track into the world of diplomacy and was already on his third posting as an embassy attaché.

"Water's fine, thank you, ma'am," Cole said. He wasn't planning on sticking around long.

"I would love a shot of something—take the edge off—if that's alright." Leila looked questioningly across the large kitchen island.

"I've got just the thing." Katie reached high into a butler's pantry and pulled down a tall pale green bottle. "Have you tried this stuff? Think I'll join you."

Cole saw the curly cursive logo identifying it as Double Chocolate Vodka and felt his stomach churn. Those liquor companies were getting too creative for their own good.

"Sure you don't want something, Cole?" The senior officer was moving bottles around on the same shelf. "I've been looking for an excuse to open up this Johnnie Walker Blue. Ambassador back in Prague gave it to me at the going-away party."

Now that was an offer he couldn't refuse.

"Just one drink, then," Cole said. "No way you're getting me to stay the night. Hope you know that."

LEILA SWISHED THE sugary liqueur around her mouth. She would have preferred the real thing and almost said so, but didn't want to make this sweet lady feel silly. Sweet, yes, that was really the best word for her. Not like Leila's usual drinking crew back in Atlanta.

Yes, a doctor in the Epidemic Intelligence Service. No, never seen Ebola in real life. Yes, first time to Rwanda. Couldn't they appreciate that she wasn't exactly in the mood for small talk? A patient in her care had just died a horrible death, her estranged mother was dying too, thousands of miles away, and it was already past midnight. Enough already.

Cole saved her, setting his tumbler down firmly on the coffee table.

"This has been fun, thanks, Katie." He stood up, and the rest of them followed. "We should let you get to bed, though. I know those kids will have you up before sunrise."

"Well they're not quite that bad, but you're right."

Leila caught the questioning look Katie aimed at her husband, and his subtle nod in response.

"Just let me know if you need anything at all tonight. Hope to see you *both* in the morning."

"The three of us are going to make some calls from the basement," Dave said, kissing his wife's forehead. "I'll be up in a little while."

Leila followed the men down a narrow set of stairs into a large, unfinished basement. It was wide open except for a square section in one corner.

"Guess that's where we're headed?" Cole said. "You've never shown me this little spot."

"You've never needed to know." Dave raised an index finger and placed it against a smooth white panel set in the wall beside the door. "Now you do."

There was a short tone, and a tiny green light flashed above the panel. Leila heard the smooth turning of what sounded like way too much steel inside the door, and then a click.

"Welcome to my secure communications center." He pushed the heavy door open and walked inside. "Also serves as a temporary shelter that could hold our family for a week, God forbid the nineties' genocide ever repeats itself."

He flipped a switch and bright fluorescent lights flickered to life overhead.

Leila looked around the room in awe. One wall was dominated by a large desk holding two computers, a phone, and other equipment she couldn't identify. Maybe some kind of radio? Under the desk were several large backup power sources and a mess of wires. Shelving filled with bottled water and MREs covered the back wall, and stacked opposite the desk were a few folding cots. She couldn't imagine spending an hour, let alone a week, in this place. Especially with kids. But she also couldn't imagine the horrible circumstances that might drive them in there in the first place. More power to him.

"So who first?"

Dave sat down at the desk and picked up the phone, motioning for them to join him.

"We need to update Bill Shackleton at the CDC," Cole said. "Leila's working under him in Viral Special Pathogens, and he's also an old mentor of mine."

Leila nodded her head. She hadn't had the nerve to let Bill know about Marna's death yet.

"If his word on the importance of this outbreak isn't enough for you," Cole continued, "we can try to get Colonel Sam Simmons at USAMRIID on the line too. He's commander there, and I managed to rope him in as one of my thesis advisors for this PhD project."

Of course you did. Leila was finally beginning to realize what an annoyingly determined wunderkind this vet was, and it made her dislike him even more. Was it because she was so similar in all the worst ways? Maybe so, but that didn't change anything. She was done with Rwanda, monkeypox, and Cole McBride. Maman wanted to see her. Baba had given his blessing. That's where she needed to be.

"BUT HANG ON, who did you say you just got an e-mail from?" Cole couldn't believe the news of his virus had already reached the White House. What must Anna be thinking, knowing he was right there in the center of it?

"Andrew Mills, White House press secretary." Bill Shackleton's voice came through strong and clear over the speakerphone. "Like I said, this story has gone all the way to the top. The media loves a good feeding frenzy whenever there's even a hint of the next big global pandemic, and those videos from the hospital in Goma are starting to go viral online."

"Okay, but why the White House?" Cole was honestly confused. "Don't they have bigger fish to fry, with Lebanon and now that hurricane?"

"The election is four months away, Cole. You know how much the president likes to reassure his citizens that he's got everything under control."

Dave Wong jumped in.

"Think I've heard enough here, and I'm convinced." He looked up at Cole as he continued. "It's good to know my junior Veterinary Corps officer here isn't completely crazy for wanting to get back across the border."

"Well I didn't say that, but I do agree that it'll be vital in helping us understand what's actually going on with this virus. He'll be a couple days ahead of any other international response that's currently in the works, and that could translate into who knows how many thousands of lives saved."

"Understood. But I also need you to realize that even though we both think it would be useful for him to continue the investigation in Virunga, that doesn't mean I can authorize the mission. I also need to chat with USAMRIID and then get final clearance from AFRICOM for that."

"Don't let me hold you up, then. Thanks for the update, everyone. Leila, I'll see you tomorrow evening with those samples?"

She spoke up for the first time since saying hello. "Maybe not. I should have told you, but I'm putting in for emergency leave. My mother is close to dying, back in Iran."

"Okay, that complicates things, doesn't it?" Shackleton said. "I'm very sorry to hear that, though. I didn't know."

Cole looked at her quizzically. Why hadn't she said anything?

"More details to follow in an e-mail as soon as we get off the phone. But don't worry about the samples—I'll hand them off to Travis at the airport in Atlanta tomorrow, then continue on from there."

"Right," Shackleton didn't sound completely convinced. "We'll be in touch."

Dave leaned in to the microphone. "Thanks, Bill, for taking the time to chat. We'll let you go now."

"Pleasure's all mine. Now that you've got a confirmed human death there in Rwanda, I can almost guarantee we'll be spending a lot of time on conference calls together over the next few days."

COLE LET OUT a sigh of relief. Another thirty minutes on the phone, and Colonel Simmons from USAMRIID had also signed off on the plan. He emphasized that Cole's early return to the Congo could be their best and only chance of identifying the outbreak as an intentional release rather than a natural phenomenon. Unlikely, he admitted, but his job was to be suspicious. Now after being passed from someone at AFRICOM to the duty officer with Special Operations Command Africa, both in Stuttgart, Germany, they were finally waiting to be patched through to the Kony task force commander in Djibouti.

"Colonel Ed Alsina here, you're on a secure line."

Cole's eyes got big.

"Sir, this is Lieutenant Colonel Dave Wong, defense attaché at the embassy here in Kigali. Also listening in are Captain Cole McBride and a CDC physician named Leila Torabi."

"Cole McBride—you shitting me?" The senior officer's gravelly voice was unmistakable.

Dave looked across at Cole, eyebrows raised.

"Yes, sir," Cole started, a smile growing on his face, "You may have thought you'd never hear from that damn vet of yours after he left 10th Group, but here I am in the flesh, ready to haunt your nightmares once again."

Dave shook his head, giving Cole a look that could only mean *you lucky bastard*. "You two know each other, I take it?"

"Indeed we do. Cole served as a royal pain in my ass for almost three years, right up until he decided he'd rather play around with gorillas than keep taking care of my working dogs. Is he giving you any trouble over there?"

"I guess you could say that, sir."

Cole tried to catch his friend's eye, shaking his head from side to side. He knew Dave was genuinely concerned for his safety, but he wasn't going to let him jeopardize this mission.

Dave continued, "You're probably aware of the disease outbreak in Goma?"

"As of about an hour ago, yes."

"Well Captain McBride here is convinced that he personally needs to illegally cross the border into the Congo, by himself, in an attempt to trace the origin of this virus."

"What in—"

"Not by myself, Colonel. I would have two of the most experienced rangers from Virunga National Park with me, along with one of their tracking bloodhounds."

"I could give a rat's ass who's with you, son. First I need to know why you think this is even necessary."

Cole loved that about the colonel—he would always hear his men out.

"I can answer that, sir, because I needed some convincing as well," Dave said. "We've just gotten off the line with both the director of Viral Special Pathogens at the CDC and the Army commander at USAMRIID. Much as I hate to tell you this, they're in agreement that the mission is critical in stopping this outbreak before it gets out of hand. With the rebels closing both the airport and the only legal border crossing, there's no good way to get anyone else in there for a more comprehensive response and investigation."

"Well they're the subject matter experts, so it's not my place to question that assessment. I'm more concerned about Cole's safety and the implications of an unsanctioned international excursion by the U.S. military."

"Exactly," Dave said. "And that's why I don't think we can let him do it."

There was a pause, and Cole's wavering optimism began to fade. He couldn't just sit there and do nothing, though, not after what happened to Marna. Not with the devastation he knew was burning through the population, both human and gorilla, right across the border. He'd been battling this feeling of responsibility all night. Why did he have to be the one to go back out there? Hadn't he seen enough suffering and paid his dues already? The self-centered loner in him was tempted to simply hop on the first flight out of there, data in hand, and leave this mess for someone else to sort out. But he knew that wasn't the man he wanted to be—not the man his parents had raised him to be. He'd been given this extensive education, the military training, even his combat experience, for a reason, and he knew that reason did not involve his own safety or selfish academic ambitions. No, he couldn't turn his back now.

"You're in a secure area, correct?"

Cole's head shot up at the change in tone of the colonel's voice.

"Roger that."

"And everyone's got their clearances, I assume?"

"Affirmative." Dave's immediate answer caught Cole by surprise. He looked across at Leila, but she only nodded.

"I might have a way to make this work. We've got a small team just west of Virunga National Park right now, part of my task force hunting Joseph Kony."

"I didn't realize they were in the Congo," Dave Wong said.

"Arrived there last week, acting on reports from Invisible Children's Early Warning Radio Network, along with our own intercepts through the NSA. Looks like the main body of fighters is camping out right there in the park."

Cole remembered the purposeful attack on their helicopter only two days earlier. Had he really returned fire from the LRA?

"We got some new intelligence today, top secret only, that an individual in the same area has been making repeated calls in a failed attempt to reach an unknown contact within the Iranian government."

Cole couldn't help glancing at Leila and thought he saw the slightest flash of fear dance across her dark eyes.

"I'm wondering if we can kill two birds with one stone here," the Special Forces colonel continued. "It does seem like quite the coincidence, but you remember what I always say about that, right Cole?"

"That true coincidences are a heck of a lot less common than most people think? Don't worry, sir, I don't plan on forgetting it." It was one of Ed Alsina's favorite phrases, and it had served them well, tracking down Taliban fighters across Afghanistan.

"Well that's the censored version, but yes. I tend to believe these things happen for a reason. My guys would have been going into the park blind— the Congolese unit they're with is from Kinshasa and scared stiff of the jungle—so these two park rangers would definitely come in handy."

"And I know I don't have to convince you, sir, after everything we saw in Afghanistan, of how useful a dog with a good nose could be. I hate to admit it, but these bloodhounds might even be a step above our malligators in that department."

"I hear you," the colonel said. "And I think it's clear that my team would benefit from joining up with these guys. They do have a dog already, but he's obviously not as familiar with the local terrain or scents as this hound would be. But what about the virus—the outbreak?"

"I'll be collecting samples from everything I can get my hands on along the way, and I might be even more successful interviewing some of the locals if I've got a bunch of big guys with guns at my back. I think we can make this work for both sides. I really do."

Cole felt his heart pounding. He was so close.

"So what would this actually look like, your little expedition across the volcanoes to meet my team?"

"If we left at first light tomorrow and spent the night at an abandoned research camp just across the border, we could be with your guys near Rumangabo by the afternoon of the second day."

"Cole, I need you to be honest with me here. How sure are you that you can make this happen—make it through in one piece?"

"I'm safer in that park with the Kambale brothers than I would be with all of 10th Group backing me up. That's the honest truth, sir. They'll keep us far from any human activity until we've connected with your team."

There was another pause, and Cole realized he had broken a sweat again.

"What are you going to do if I say no?"

Straight to the point, as always.

"You really want to ask me that question, sir?"

"Cole, you know I have no command authority over you right now. It doesn't really matter what I say, does it?"

"Sir."

"But if you're confident, and you think these Virunga rangers of yours will give our guys a better chance of success, then go for it. I trust your judgment."

Cole exhaled.

"Thank you, sir. Which team is over there, anyway? Anyone I know?"

"Didn't want to tell you this earlier, but yes, the team leader is someone you'll get along with. I think you and Jake Russell got to be pretty buddy buddy up in Afghanistan, isn't that right?"

"Yes, sir, he's a good friend."

Cole could barely get the words around the massive grin plastered across his face. Jake wasn't just a good friend, he was one of his best friends in the world. Ten months of combat had a way of doing that. He knew Jake had followed the colonel over to this Kony task force, but last he heard his friend had been playing desk jockey in Kampala.

"One more thing," Alsina said. "You know this conversation never happened, right?"

"Roger that, sir."

"BIKE'S IN THE garage." The defense attaché had a look of resignation on his face as Cole took the single key from his outstretched hand. Their eyes met, and held. "Be careful, Cole."

"Will do, and thanks. It'll be waiting for you up in Musanze, just as pretty as ever."

"I wasn't talking about the bike, but yes, it better be." Dave Wong smiled, and looked to the door.

Cole started slow on the winding road leading out of the neighborhood, getting a feel for the black Ducati Monster beneath him. He still couldn't believe the senior officer had brought this beautiful machine to Rwanda, of all places, but he wasn't complaining now. Except for a dog barking in the distance, the street was silent. What a difference from the nocturnal symphony he knew to expect high in the Kabara meadow the next night. He passed one compound after another, each guarded by an imposing iron gate topped with concertina wire and multiple remote cameras watching, waiting. The sleeping ruling class of Rwanda. No combination of concrete and metal would protect them if this virus got out of hand. Cole was glad to be leaving the illusion of safety behind. Glad to have a purpose, to be on a mission that would require him to push past the comforts and limitations of the day-to-day routine.

He turned out onto the main commercial stretch, passing coffee shops and restaurants that most of the country's population would never be able to afford. He'd taken Marna for sushi a month earlier. Sakae—the best raw fish in Rwanda. She was skeptical, but it wasn't half bad, and killer views over the city made up for any deficiencies in the cuisine. He remembered the lingering conversation now, discovering their shared vision for future life and work in Africa, and the way she'd looked at him when they finally said goodnight. Why hadn't he taken the hint and made his move right there? It all came back to his own selfishness, and not wanting to risk the time, effort, and emotion that a relationship would require. He hated to admit it, even to himself, but it was an unavoidable truth.

That month together would have been heaven.

Cole revved the engine and felt the bike leap with expectation as he left the city behind. For the first time in nine months, the Kigali-Musanze road was completely deserted. It'd been too long since he'd looked out on a lonely road like this with a powerful bike underneath him, ready to do his bidding. Ever since his first night back home at Fort Carson, only hours after climbing out of the huge C-17 that had flown them all the way from Afghanistan, and he couldn't sleep. He'd only been responsible for one person on the deployment, just one soldier. Not a whole team, or even a company, like most non-veterinary captains. And yet he'd failed to bring his tech, Ben, back home. *Screw it*, he remembered thinking. *I need to ride.* Minutes later, he was flying up I-25 North, the cool Colorado night air rushing past him. It was good to be back on the 1958 Harley Panhead again. Best present he'd ever gotten, especially because his dad had been the bike's only owner since it first came off the lot. Denver, Fort Collins, and Cheyenne all passed by in a blur before he chased Ben's demon across the wide open spaces of Wyoming in record time. He finally crossed the cattle guard onto his parents' ranch just north of Jackson, right as the sun's first rays lit up the snowy heights of Grand Teton.

Home. It was a world away right now.

He picked up speed, tearing across the dark hills of Rwanda, and embraced the memories of the lost again. Ben, and now Marna. Both gone.

So what was the answer? Stop letting people get so close, and do an even better job of focusing solely on Cole McBride, selfish bastard number one? Not this time. Not any time. He needed to get back in the action. Back to where he could measure the results of a day's work in lives saved and justice dealt.

Time to tear a little corner off of the darkness.

He was headed into the park.

Wait for it…wait for it…" Anna held the Frisbee next to her waist. "Good boy, Tyson. Okay, go!"

The disk shot from her hand like a bullet, and the dog was right behind it, tearing across the lush grass of the Capitol's West Lawn in a brindle blur of strength and speed. She lifted one hand to her forehead, shielding her eyes from the setting sun at the other end of the National Mall.

There, almost fifty yards away. The Frisbee had reached its highest point now. It stopped and floated for the briefest second, then took off at another angle, almost as it was purposefully trying to fool its pursuer. But it didn't have a chance. As soon as Tyson got a reading on the new trajectory, he took off again at a sprint and was waiting in the perfect position to make a beautiful but completely unnecessary leaping catch.

Success.

"You've got quite an arm there," Danny said. "I mean, it's not often…"

"…you meet a girl who can actually throw a Frisbee?"

"I was thinking a little more generally, but you said it, not me."

The Secret Service agent looked at her with a wry smile, as if he were daring her to take their flirtatious banter to the next level. Anna had never really been attracted to a black man before, but that probably had more to do with their relative scarcity back home than any underlying prejudice on her part. At least that's what she wanted to believe. When Special Agent Danny Walker stopped her as she left the White House the day before, asking if she'd like to play with Tyson off the clock sometime, she jumped at the chance. This was a summer for new experiences, right?

"Well I can't take all the credit for it," Anna said. "I wouldn't have survived in my family if I didn't keep up with my brothers' athletic prowess."

"Oh yeah? So what sports did they get into way out there in Wyoming?"

"You make it sound like outer space or something!" Anna laughed and gave the impatient Tyson a scratch between the ears. "They've all played at least one type of college ball, but my oldest brother Cole was the only real standout. Two-time All-American defensive back, and the Cowboys even made it to a decent bowl game to finish out his senior year."

"Very cool," Danny said. "I played football in college too—sounds like I was lucky never to meet this brother of yours coming across the middle of the field."

She knew it. There was something about the way he moved that reminded Anna of all her athlete crushes over the years. And the thick arms emerging from his form-fitting white polo looked like they were more than just a recent acquisition at the gym.

"But no luck in the draft for you, either, I guess?"

"No, there was never really a chance. Not quite fast enough to be a running back in the big leagues." He bent over to lift the Frisbee from where it rested on Tyson's front paws. "That's okay, though, I never would've gotten to work with this guy if there had been a place for me in the NFL."

Tyson jumped to his feet, dark eyes completely focused on the disk in his handler's hands. His rippling muscles trembled under a short hair coat streaked with every shade of brown. The brindle pattern, combined with tall ears always on the alert and a long dark muzzle, gave the dog an almost unearthly appearance—a wild creature of the night, straight out of one of those silly paranormal romances Anna had been reading too much of. Danny gave the Frisbee a quick backhanded flick, sending it sailing out across an open stretch of grass. Tyson didn't move though, his eyes now locked on Danny's, waiting for the cue. And then the spell was broken, and he went flying off in another sprinting burst.

"I missed it!" Anna said, her mouth gaping and eyebrows furrowed in unbelief. "What did you do?"

"Ha, we have our own little system. Gotta keep those bad guys on their toes, right?"

"Well that was pretty impressive, I have to admit."

Not just the uncanny communication between man and dog, but also that this football-playing black guy even knew how to hold a Frisbee, let alone toss it with such finesse. She had a feeling the surprises would only keep coming.

"That's nothing," Danny said. "You should see him doing bite work. Might make you rethink all those little pats on the head you keep indulging him with."

"Oh, that reminds me! I keep meaning to tell you why I was so excited to meet Tyson a few weeks ago."

"Other than the fact that his handler seemed like a pretty nice guy, and wasn't bad to look at either?"

"Right." Anna tilted her head to the side and gave him her best accusatory look. "No, it's because my brother Cole is actually a vet in the military. He convinced my parents to adopt one of the working dogs he treated over in Afghanistan a couple of years ago, and it was basically love at first sight for me and Solo."

"That's cool. What'd Solo get retired for?"

"Not a fun story, since his handler didn't make it out. But Solo got hit pretty bad by some kind of explosion and lost one of his back legs and most of his tail. He gets around just fine now, though. Might even give Tyson here some decent competition in the Frisbee-catching department!"

"I highly doubt that, but maybe we'll get 'em together one day and see." Danny paused for a second, eyebrows raised, like he wanted her to read every possible implication into that loaded statement. "We use the Army clinic down at Fort Belvoir for all our routine vet care, you know. Tyson's probably given a few of your brother's friends a good scare."

"Meaning what?"

"He's just not a big fan of going to the vet, that's all. Tends to save his scariest growls for when they're going in for the old prostate exam."

"I don't blame him!" She knelt down beside the handsome dog, already back and waiting for the next game. "Such indignity, huh, Tyson?"

He looked up at her, tongue hanging out one side of his mouth. Not even the slightest sign of being tired after all that running on this warm summer evening.

"He's a Belgian Malinois, right?"

"Yes ma'am," Danny answered. "That's pretty good—most people have never even heard of them."

"Oh, I only know because my brother told me that's what you guys have. The special ops unit Cole was with switched over to the malligators too, even though the rest of the military seems to be mostly sticking with German shepherds for now."

"Yeah, some of the older guys weren't so sure about the breed, but now they'll never go back. These dogs are just the perfect combination of size, speed, and drive." The special agent gazed at Tyson with open admiration. "They've got a nasty bite, too."

"Pretty cool that he gets to go home with you at night. I don't see why the military hasn't caught on to that concept yet, still keeping them kenneled up on base all the time."

"Exactly," Danny said. "You can see how happy he is to be out here right now, not cooped up in some noisy kennel. And he knows when he's off duty, too—I can trust him completely even in a public place like this."

Anna looked up just in time to see a smoldering orange sun dip behind the towering Washington Monument in the distance. It was a quiet evening on the Capitol grounds, with only a few tourists wandering around taking pictures. She had noticed a young couple when they first arrived, seated on a blanket and enjoying what appeared to be a blissfully romantic picnic. They were finished now, stretched out on their backs, laughing and talking easily. Maybe that would be her in a few weeks?

She realized where the daydream was going and blushed. *Don't get ahead of yourself, silly.* Even if the internship did leave enough time for a real relationship to get started—which seemed unlikely—she had absolutely no reason to believe Danny was interested in anything more than friendship at this point.

A MECHANICAL BUZZING sound interrupted her thoughts, and Tyson cocked his head slightly, watching as one front paw lifted slowly off the ground. Then he jumped up, on the alert and staring at the small black sprinkler head that was now poking out of the grass.

"Run!"

Danny grabbed her hand and took off at a jog just as the sprinkler system turned on. Within seconds, the air was filled with a fine mist that felt incredibly refreshing as it settled on Anna's exposed skin. Her eyes met Danny's, and then they both burst out laughing. Unable to run and laugh at the same time, she pulled him to a stop and then let go of his hand, waving both her arms high in the air. Tyson was bounding across the grass from one sprinkler to the next, pouncing at each one and sticking his face right in the center of the spray before looking back to his handler and moving on to the next spot. The mist coated Danny's face and arms, leaving a glistening sheen of tiny droplets that only served to make him even more attractive in the glowing evening light.

"I guess we can blame the federal government, then, for all this humidity?" Anna said. "And here I thought it was a natural phenomenon all along!"

Danny still hadn't stopped laughing. It was a full, natural laugh, the kind that made you want to join in just for the fun of it. He finally paused and raised a hand to motion around them.

"Can't imagine this irrigation system is doing much for the grass, so I guess you must be right!" He wiped his eyes with the edge of a sleeve. "Me and Tyson have been here a few times before when this happens, but it's always been a regular sprinkler spray. The kind that actually gets the ground wet, you know?"

"Well I'm not complaining. It's kind of like those new misters that are getting so popular at all the amusement parks now. A perfect way to end what has turned out to be a very enjoyable evening with you two."

She gave what she hoped was a cute little curtsy.

"Who said anything about ending our evening? It's early!" He looked sincerely surprised. "Why don't we drop Tyson off at my place up in Chinatown and then get something to eat?"

Tyson was apparently bored with the sprinklers and sat patiently by Danny's side. Anna had not had any intention of turning this first hang out session into a real date, but why not? She knelt down next to the dog and brushed some of the excess water off his coat.

"What do you think, Tyson? Should I let your dad take me out tonight?"

He barked. A short, friendly bark, and Anna's jaw dropped.

"That's a yes." Danny smiled down at her, one thin black eyebrow raised. "Come on, we can swing by your place first if you need to change into something dry."

She nodded her head slowly.

"Fine, but only because Tyson is a very effective wingman." At that moment, her phone started vibrating in the pocket of her jean shorts. She pulled it out and looked at the tiny screen. "It's Chase, give me a second."

"Hey," she said, walking away from Danny and Tyson. "Whatcha up to?"

"Hey yourself, where are you?" Her brother sounded excited.

"Just hanging out with my own little Secret Service escort here at the Capitol. Everything okay?"

"Yeah, I'm fine," he said. "Have you seen the news, though?"

"No, why?"

"You know the gorilla deaths Cole is trying to figure out? It just hit CNN, big time."

"Wait, what?"

Since when was a disease outbreak in African gorillas worthy of CNN? She looked over her shoulder to see Danny attaching a dark leather leash to Tyson's collar.

"Just get over here. You need to see this."

THURSDAY, JULY 1

VOLCANOES NATIONAL PARK, RWANDA
5:14 A.M.

Cole clenched his jaw at the first burning brush of stinging nettle on the back of a hand. There would be plenty more where that came from. A heavy fog had descended on the mountains overnight, and at this darkest hour before dawn it was impossible to see more than a few feet in any direction. Bonny led the way, stopping for an extended sniff at the edge of the maize field before pushing straight into the dense brush that marked the border of the park.

"Come. This is the place." Innocence Kambale looked over a shoulder, his normally booming voice now a hushed whisper. Then he followed the bloodhound, giving her a long lead as she moved steadily into the thick bamboo. How they chose that particular spot to begin the trek was beyond Cole, but he trusted the pair completely.

He had pulled in on the Ducati a couple of hours earlier, exhausted but relieved to have found some initial closure in the speed and freedom of the open road. He knew it would take a few million miles like that before he would stop blaming himself for Marna's death, even though he knew deep down it wasn't his fault. But now he needed to regain focus for the tasks ahead.

First on the list was to wake and brief the Kambale brothers. There was no doubt in his mind that they would join him, if only out of professional loyalty to the park they were sworn to protect. And he was right. But the silent looks they exchanged when he mentioned Kony and the LRA made him wonder if there might also be something else in the men's complex personal history that made the decision to accompany him so easy. They would enter the park before first light, taking a little-used path at the base of Mount Karisimbi, far from the watchful eyes of both local farmers and Rwanda's park guards who stayed closer to the main entrance. No reason for anyone to raise eyebrows and start talking about this quick-moving group of three armed men and a strange-looking dog.

An unearthly scream shattered the air, and Cole froze.

Again, but this time it was answered, high on the invisible slopes above them. He brought his cradled Kalashnikov up into a ready position. Not quite an M4, but it would get the job done. The screams sounded like an evil combination of a hyena's laughter with the wails of a woman being choked to death, and within seconds they echoed from every direction.

Then a hand on the shoulder, and Proper Kambale's whispered voice in his ear.

"The tree hyrax is the least of our concerns on this day."

Cole nodded in embarrassment and continued on up the trail. How could he have forgotten? Every classic book on the region made at least one reference to the harmless creature's horrifying mating calls, and he had promised himself he wouldn't freak out like every other visitor to the Virunga volcanoes lucky enough for a serenade. Yes, it would be a good day if the rabbit-sized hyrax was the only enemy they encountered.

THE FOG LIFTED over the next hour, burning off slowly in the warming rays of the morning sun as they filtered through the towering bamboo in a glow of verdant green. The tall reedy plants were too thick to allow for much undergrowth, so the silent group's progress was mercifully free from the nettles and grasping vines Cole knew would soon plague them when they moved into the higher elevation Hagenia forest. A chorus of invisible birds joined the ever-present drone of insects. Would he even be able to hear another person approaching them, tracking them? Maybe not, but that's why he was glad to be in such good company. Nothing could sneak past Bonny's notice, even if her almost cartoonish features—the quivering nose, drooping eyes, and floppy ears—were sometimes hard to take seriously.

As if in answer to Cole's thoughts, the dog froze. She put her nose to the ground, then threw her head up into the air and turned from side to side. Within seconds, Cole thought he heard something in the distance. A rustling of leaves somewhere up ahead, then silence. Whoever or whatever was up there was now aware of their presence. An angry buffalo or bull elephant could mean serious trouble, but he was far more worried about other humans.

"Gorilla."

Proper's soft voice behind him brought a quick smile to Cole's face. Gorillas they could deal with. Maybe he'd even have a chance to make a quick health assessment. The biggest question right now was whether or not the virus had moved beyond the Rugendo family into the rest of the mountain gorilla population.

The hollow thumping of a gorilla's rapid chest beat broke through the forest's morning symphony, followed quickly by a burst of breaking branches and low grunts. And then he was there with them, a massive silverback in the path just ten feet ahead of a now extremely tense Bonny. The gorilla crouched on all fours, staring at them for thirty seconds... a minute. He rested lightly on giant knuckled fingers, the muscles of his broad back and shoulders rippling with every movement. Cole could clearly see the unblemished inky black skin of hands and face. No sign of infection meant no reason to knock him down for samples, not when they had so much ground to cover.

"I don't know him." Innocence spoke slowly and gently.

"Wild?" Cole tried to respond in the same unthreatening tone. Only a fraction of the gorillas were members of tourist-friendly habituated groups. Those that were not were much less predictable.

Innocence nodded in reply, then started in with the low grunting. *Just let us pass, old man. We are not here for you.* Even Cole could see the surprise on the silverback's face. The animal tilted his head to the side, as if deciding how to respond to this strange creature speaking his own language. In an instant, he was standing upright, an ear-splitting roar coming from deep within gaping jaws. King Kong in the flesh. Cupped hands rose to his chest again in a blur of action, the rapid slapping accompanied by a crescendo of angry bellows.

Then he was gone, disappeared into the bamboo as quickly as he had come. Cole knew that violent confrontations with wild silverbacks were possible, but this show of strength and hasty retreat were far more common.

Bonny took one tentative step forward, then another.

Time to go.

COLE LIFTED THE satellite phone from the top of his pack. Another loan from Dave Wong. This one wasn't quite as valuable as the Ducati, but much more useful for the journey ahead. At over eight thousand feet in elevation along the northern slopes of Mount Karisimbi, they were outside the range of the local mobile networks. Not that it would have mattered for this particular call. He dialed the number Colonel Alsina had given him.

"I seriously couldn't believe it when the colonel got in touch last night." Jake Russell sounded the same as ever. "How the hell did you convince him this was a good idea?"

"I have my ways," Cole said. "Great to hear that ol' Texas twang again."

"Right. Not that I'm complaining. I mean, we'll take all the help we can get. But still, it's been a while since you've even touched a weapon, right?"

"Yes and no," Cole said, glancing at the rifle resting easily against his leg. "I've been surprised how much the old skill set has come in handy working out here."

After ten months supporting Operation Enduring Freedom as Green Berets with the 10th Special Forces Group, the two young officers had convinced Colonel Alsina to send them to Fort Benning for Ranger school. Bonus for a job well done on the deployment, they said, and he took the bait. It was sixty-one days of hell in the mountains of Georgia, but Cole knew the training had prepared him well.

"Lots to catch up on both sides, sounds like," Jake said. "But we should have plenty of time for that, if we can actually find each other. Any chance you can make it all the way across today?"

"No way. I know the distances don't look like much, but the terrain is a game changer. Ravines and creeks make it impossible to go in a straight line, and we're staying far from all the more trafficked routes for now."

"That's alright, it'll give us more time to get up into the park ourselves."

"So where are you thinking for a rendezvous?" Cole didn't really care, as long as he got to make some basic assessments of the other gorilla families in the area. Their exposure and disease status would help pinpoint where the initial outbreak had occurred. He looked out over the velvety green forest carpeting the wide saddle below. The rocky outcropping they had chosen for their break provided the first full view of Mount Mikeno, only a couple miles across the invisible international border to the northeast. Its ancient volcanic cone jutted sharply out of the forest and into a now cloudless sky. The mountain was over a thousand feet taller than Grand Teton in Wyoming, but its solitary stretch for the heavens made it impossible to compare the two. Literally a world apart.

"After five hours on the Puma last night," Jake continued, "I'm pretty sure our targets are camped out right about halfway between Mikeno and Sabyinyo. Kind of a no man's land, from what I can tell."

"Nice, didn't realize you had a drone over there."

In Afghanistan they'd almost always had full coverage from the big boys—Predators and Global Hawks. The added layers of information and security couldn't be beat, but those full-size drones also required a secured runway and support team on the ground. The next-generation mini-flyers like the Puma were proving themselves a whole lot more useful for situations like this.

"Yeah, she picked up a pretty clear mother lode of human thermal patterns, along with what looked like a couple generators. We're gonna send her back out as soon as she's charged up again—try to get some regular video for confirmation."

"And where exactly are you now?"

"Just about ten klicks south of Rumangabo, hanging out next to an old military post of some sort."

"Okay, why don't you move out now for the Bukima tented camp on the northern slopes of Mount Mikeno. It's one of the old Virunga tourist accommodations and should be a good base for tracking your guys. I wanted to check out the area anyway—it's pretty close to where we found the first dead gorillas a few days ago."

"Sounds like a plan. Just check in with me this evening sometime. You know, to let me know you haven't been eaten by a leopard?"

COLE WAS PUTTING the phone away when Innocence and Bonny appeared from behind a large fallen Hagenia trunk. The park ranger had a finger to his lips.

Never a good sign.

"Eight men, coming this way. They speak Acholi, language of the LRA."

Even worse.

D istant voices of shouting men floated in on a warm breeze through the open flaps of the tent. Lars Olsson stopped writing and listened. He would welcome almost any interruption of this extended vigil. They had exhausted what was left of the medical supplies the night before, so there was no question anymore of even the most basic support for the dying patients in his care. And dying they were. There were now over fifty bodies dumped unceremoniously in the mass graves at the edge of the camp, and about that many still suffering. He couldn't make them better, or even more comfortable, but at least he could record his observations. Hope that someone might find the notes and understand what tragedy had come to this lonely spot. So that is what the physician turned to—documenting in careful detail the hour by hour progression of signs and symptoms as the virus ravaged the bodies of its forgotten victims.

The noise outside increased. Olsson looked across the tent and met Grace's eyes. Even after two long days working side by side, he still couldn't read anything in his assistant's detached expression. The walls of grief and resignation were too thick, layered as they were with two decades of death and disappointment. She rose and walked slowly to the entrance. The deep lines in her face and weariness of her stride made the woman look far older than her forty years.

"What is it?"

Lars stood up and joined her just outside the tent. A small group of armed men were entering the camp from one of the roughly cut forest trails. Two of them dragged another man between them.

"They are saying FDLR," Grace said. "This man is FDLR."

The Democratic Forces for the Liberation of Rwanda. Olsson knew some of his patients back in Goma had come from the same rebel group. Formed twenty years earlier by genocidal Hutus who had fled justice in their own country, they were now firmly embedded as an ongoing source of instability and destruction in the Virunga region.

The group stopped outside Lukwiya's tent, and he appeared now, looking angry. "Where did you find him?"

The oldest among them responded. "At the mine, last night, with three others."

The mine? Olsson knew the FDLR and other rebel groups made a killing with their low-tech and completely illegal open pit mines, digging for gold, coltan, and more all over North Kivu. There would always be buyers, as long as the price was right. But this was the first he heard of his own captor's involvement.

"And what of them?"

"Dead. This one, he try to hide in the forest, but we find him."

Lukwiya stepped forward and grabbed the captive by the chin. "What has he told you?"

"Nothing, sir. He will not speak."

The man's hands were tied behind his back with a piece of twine, and a dirty rag covered his eyes. Better for him to have died with his friends.

"We will see about that."

Lukwiya brought a knee up hard between the man's legs, and Olsson felt his own stomach turn. The captive let out a grunt as his knees buckled, and the two men on either side let him collapse into the dirt.

"Tell me, Hutu pig, what were you doing at our mine?"

Nothing. Lukwiya bent over and pulled the blindfold from his head.

"Look at me." The man only cowered further into the ground.

But Olsson looked. Not at the victim, but at Lukwiya himself. Yes, it was still there—the fear that had been growing in the senior LRA commander's eyes over the past couple of days. Olsson was trying harder to stay on Lukwiya's good side, now that his own role as doctor was somewhat superfluous. How to manipulate this fear, though, encourage it, play off of it, those were the questions of the hour.

Without another word, Lukwiya turned back into his tent, only to reappear seconds later holding a long *panga* machete in one hand. He motioned to his two men to lift the captive up.

The whites of the man's eyes, flashing in stark contrast against the midnight black of his sweating face, called out to Olsson across the clearing. But it was too late. Lukwiya grabbed one of his ears, lifted the machete above his head, and came down fast.

"No." Grace's voice beside him was barely audible.

There was a struggle, and then the captured man was on the ground again, deep red blood streaming from a gash on the side of his head. He was crying now—hoarse, angry screams—as he thrashed helplessly in the dirt, flailing his arms behind him.

Olsson's medical sense kicked into high gear. He couldn't just watch this and do nothing. It was as if Lukwiya read his mind, though. The commander turned to look directly at him, still holding the severed ear in one hand, blood dripping down his fingers, and shook his head. It was a warning. *This is not your conflict.* Olsson stayed where he was and hated himself for it.

Lukwiya said something to the gathered crowd, and in seconds a young boy came running up holding a long smoking branch in one hand. A hiss of steam puffed from the man's head as Lukwiya plunged the glowing embers into the wound and held it there for seconds that seemed like minutes. The man's screams jumped an octave. Olsson didn't want to watch but couldn't pull his eyes away from the gruesome spectacle. So this is what torture looked like. He'd seen the aftermath, too many times, but never the act itself. Lukwiya's face showed complete detachment, but the younger fighters were excited, ready for more.

Slowly, the screams faded to sobs, and then stopped completely. The man was pulled to his feet, and Olsson could see that the bleeding had stopped, the wounded side of his head now a clotted mess of mud and ash. The primitive cauterizing heat had done its job. Lukwiya brought his own face just inches from that of the much shorter captive's.

"Now, will you speak," the leader said. "Or do we take the other ear?"

The FDLR rebel stood motionless, his face a mask.

Lukwiya turned toward Olsson and shouted something in Acholi. Grace moved back into the tent and returned pulling one of their patients by the arm. The boy was one of Olsson's favorites, a tiny child who couldn't have been more than ten. He was among the first to make it over the hump of this pox disease, his fever breaking and appetite returning the night before. His body was covered with hard raised lumps, but the respiratory signs seemed to be resolving. None of this was what made the boy really unique, though. Fresh pink scars burst like cartoon explosions across his head and face—they were all that remained in the place of ears, nose and lips. And yet somehow there was still a will to live, hiding deep inside all that brokenness. Olsson wanted to bring him to Paris, set him up with one of MSF's partner organizations that offered plastic surgery. The boy's face would never be perfect, but he shouldn't have to live the rest of his life as a misunderstood monster.

Now the boy was being paraded in front of a new victim. *This is what we can do to you.* And it worked. The man started sobbing again, but this time quick words spilled between each breath.

"They said…"

Lars couldn't hear. He took a few steps across the clearing.

"… new mine, something valuable."

Lukwiya looked up and met his eyes. "Get back in the tent, or you will be next."

Shit. Olsson stopped and slowly turned back. So much for understanding what was really going on here—why the LRA had decided to set up in Virunga in the first place. But he liked his ears. He glanced over his shoulder one more time and stepped back into the darkness of the tent.

LUKWIYA TURNED BACK to the pitiful creature in front of him. So the FDLR knew they were making money—something about a new mineral from a hidden mine—and they wanted a piece of the pie. No way the Prophet would agree to that. Now with the market for illegal coltan drying up, this mine was the LRA's lifeblood. Of course, Kony was still hidden away up north. No reason to bother him with the small problem of the disappearing buyer. Yet.

If this Hutu scum was telling the truth, though, there was quick work to be done. "What do they say we have discovered, then, these bosses of yours?"

The man spoke through gritted teeth, his head tilted to one side. "Diamonds, going to Zim."

"Yes," Lukwiya said, a hint of a smile on his lips. "Maybe it is diamonds."

"Or something new, for China?" The shorter man spoke earnestly, as if he really thought Lukwiya would tell him a secret the miners themselves did not know. "Only guesses. This is why they send us, to scout and report back. We do not want a fight, only our fair share."

Lukwiya didn't doubt that. From what he had heard, the FDLR was far more concerned with growing their business empire than in toppling the Tutsi government next door. Cash could corrupt even the most passionate convictions. But no, there would be no sharing of this mine. Not as long as he was still alive to enjoy the very welcome rewards that resulted from controlling such a rare commodity. Lukwiya eyed the Breguet Marine watch resting comfortably on his wrist. A special gift from the buyer, personally delivered after their first completed transaction. He'd been on the run too long, slept under the stars too many times, to let it all go so easily.

"Take him." Lukwiya dismissed the man with a flick of his hand and turned back to the tent. He pulled out his phone. Still nothing. He would try one more time, then move on. The Persians were not the only ones interested in what he was selling.

FAIRFAX
4:03 A.M.

The insistent buzzing finally shifted from its role in his confused night-mare into a barely conscious reality. Fadi Haddad swung a heavy hand across the edge of the bed and felt for the phone in the darkness. He brought the glowing screen just inches from his sleep-blurred eyes. Give them a minute to adjust, and then: *Incoming call: Myriam's Mobile.*

That woke him up.

"Myriam, where are you?" Out of bed now, pulling back the blinds to look for her car, always the third one at the very end of the driveway. It wasn't there.

Sniffling on the other end. She was crying.

"Myriam, where are you?" He tried not to sound mad. This was the third time in as many months that she had gotten herself into some kind of late-night trouble. A light turned on behind him. Nour was up.

He tried again: "Answer me. Are you okay?"

A deep breath, then a pause. Another car accident? Arrested at a club? She had always been a strong girl, able to control her emotions, even use them to her advantage. And she knew how to play him, his little girl, too grown up at nineteen for her own good.

When the words finally came, they were worse than he ever expected.

"Aba, why?" Her voice was hard with anger, even betrayal. "How could you do this to us."

It was a statement, not a question. And then she was sobbing again, and another voice said something in the background. There was only one thing she could be referring to—the same thing that had been giving him nightmares all night, and the night before. But how? Haddad felt his wife's warm hand on his bare arm and pulled away. She couldn't know about this too. Not yet.

"She's fine," he said, walking toward the door. "I'll take care of it. Just get some sleep." She wouldn't—sleep, that is—he knew that much. Even though Nour trusted him completely, she loved their only child too much to turn off the worry switch that easily. And the last few months had been hell in that regard.

He was already on the stairs when a man's voice came on the line.

"*Kaif halak, ya akhi.*" How are you, my brother. Lebanese Arabic. The nightmare became reality. How did they find her? "We have your daughter, at the shop. She would be pleased to see you here very soon."

THE SHOP WAS the term they had agreed to for his self storage facility. A simple measure, but these days Haddad never knew who might be listening. The roads were completely empty as he flew past block after block of cookie-cutter McMansions and onto the parkway that would take him straight there. He was going to make it in record time.

Or at least he would have. Blue lights in the rearview mirror. He automatically looked at the speedometer and slammed on the brakes. Was he really going that fast? *Allah, not tonight.* The siren came on as a Fairfax County Police cruiser pulled up behind him. Allah wasn't going to help this time.

"License and registration." The cop's massive body almost filled the driver's side window when he leaned down to look inside. Haddad felt his heart pounding recklessly. Thirty years in the States, and tonight, of all nights, was the first time he'd ever been pulled over. At least this guy looked more bored than angry. Haddad handed him the documents and leaned back into his seat, trying to look calm. The cop straightened up and stepped back from the car, looked through the papers, then leaned back in. His eyes drilled into Haddad's, an expression that could only be suspicion growing on his face. Haddad nodded and tried to smile, but the cop just turned and walked back to his cruiser.

Did he know something? Broken bits and pieces of a hundred disastrous scenarios raced through Haddad's mind. Or was it just guilt by association, the almost daily judgment Haddad felt from other Americans simply for having a name that looked Muslim? But why tonight?

"Mr. Haddad." He was back. "Looks like you've done a pretty good job of staying safe on our roads for quite a while now."

"Thank you, sir."

"So what made you think it'd be a good idea to drive fifteen miles an hour over the speed limit at this time of night?"

"I apologize, sir. Didn't realize how fast I was going."

"And where *are* you going?"

He'd thought about this one. "Well sir, my daughter Myriam, she is at a sleepover but hasn't been able to get any sleep. Scary movies, you know how it goes. My wife made me come out at this hour, bring her home." It was close to the truth. *See, I'm a regular suburban dad, just like you.* That was the idea, at least.

"Mind if I take a look in your trunk?"

Haddad exhaled. Guess that strategy hadn't worked. "Sure, of course." He reached down and pulled the lever.

Thirty seconds turned into a minute. What was he doing back there? Haddad knew he had dropped off all the supplies in storage unit twenty-six, three days earlier. Even if there had been some little thing left behind, why should a county policeman get worried about eggs, alcohol wipes, or insulin syringes? Unless the whole operation was already compromised, and this guy was just playing with him before the arrest. But how? They had been too careful, for too long, for it all to come crashing down so quickly.

The little Chevy shuddered with the impact of the trunk slamming shut.

"You've got quite a collection back there, Mr. Haddad." The tone of his voice had completely reversed. "Always nice to find another man who can appreciate the quality sounds of old vinyl."

Haddad couldn't believe what he was hearing. The hobby was usually something he was more embarrassed about than anything, digging around the hidden corners of thrift shops and used bookstores for classic records from the sixties and seventies. But this time it just might save the day. He let himself laugh, a real laugh. "I know every album that was back there, so if I find one is missing…"

"Don't you worry, I've got too many of my own." The policeman handed the documents back through the window. "Why don't you get out of here and go find that daughter of yours."

"Thank you," Haddad said. "You are a good man."

"Just be careful out here." The officer turned and took a few steps back to the cruiser, then stopped. "You know, Mr. Haddad, I hope you don't mind me saying, but it's really nice to come across someone with your…" He paused, and Haddad knew what was coming. "With your background, someone who embraces American culture like that. Kinda refreshing."

If he only knew.

Haddad pulled away, driving under the speed limit in the right-hand lane. He hated himself, knowing he was really in the process of doing just the opposite. Affirming all the stereotypes. He wanted nothing to do with this project—this horror—growing only a couple of miles down the road.

But now it was personal. Smart guys, these visitors from home.

And that would make any chance of escape much more difficult.

C ole threw himself down onto the loamy soil and wriggled into a narrow cavity against the old tree trunk. Not ideal, but it would have to do. He looked out just in time to see Proper Kambale's dark green uniform disappearing into a patch of wild celery. Innocence and Bonny were gone too, but Cole knew the bloodhound would be their biggest liability. As good as her nose was, she simply wasn't trained to hide out quietly like the military dogs he was used to working with.

The voices grew louder, then stopped completely. The men couldn't be more than fifty feet away now, and it would be easy for them to see the fresh boot prints and trampled vegetation along the path. Cole and the Kambales had not made any effort to conceal their tracks—there shouldn't have been any need, not this far from the main trails. Now hushed voices started up again, accompanied by the sound of more deliberate footfall fanning out through the clearing. Bonny would sound the alarm before long. He silently adjusted the butt of the rifle into a better position against his shoulder. Maybe it wasn't such a smart idea to hide after all. It would only make these guys think there was a reason to be suspicious. But the look the brothers had exchanged when Innocence returned moments earlier said it all. The odds were not good, eight men against three. Especially if they were really LRA.

So now they were hiding, and they were about to get found. Cole held his breath. Someone was walking along the opposite side of the tree trunk.

With the element of surprise on their side, they might have been able to take out a few of these guys first. Pretty decent chance of coming out on top. But that wasn't how war worked anymore. Unless there was confirmed evidence that this was really the enemy, acquired ahead of time and approved up the chain of command, American soldiers were not allowed to shoot first. Rules of engagement. And as hard as it was to hold back and wait, Cole cared too much to try to pull a Rambo here. If only the bad guys held themselves to the same standard.

A shout, and a scramble of tearing leaves and breaking stems.

Then Bonny's lusty bray filled the forest.

Game on.

A HEAVY COMBAT boot landed in the dirt right in front of Cole's face, followed quickly by a second. A man had climbed over the fallen tree, and he was about to take off running towards Proper's hiding spot. Cole acted instinctively, grabbing out with his free hand for an ankle just as it lifted off the ground. There was a surprised shout, and the whole leg swung back at his face.

Too slow.

Cole pushed out of the cavity, caught the boot squarely in the chest, and kept driving forward until he felt his right shoulder connect with the back of the man's knees. The man buckled, body folding over Cole's back and head whipping through the air until it connected solidly with the tree trunk behind them. Cole let go of the legs and spun around. Not the prettiest tackle he'd ever made, but it did the job. The man was unconscious, a trickle of blood coming from one nostril.

One down.

The clearing was alive with the chaos of confusion. Shouting from every direction. Bonny's frenzied barking. Bird cries and monkey screams sounding the alert across the forest.

Cole raised the rifle and caught another man in his sights. This one was running toward him, pistol turned sideways in an outstretched arm, a wild look in his eyes. He wore the same dark green camo as the first one. The debate flashed through Cole's mind in the millisecond it took to make a decision. He had no doubt these guys were up to no good, and a burst of automatic fire behind him confirmed the assumption. Cole moved his finger to the trigger and began to squeeze, tracking the man's running legs. It would take him down, but not kill him.

"Stop!" The word broke through the chaos, but it was too late. The old rifle bucked against his shoulder as a single round tore through the air. Cole released the pressure on the trigger and watched the man's momentum carry him a few feet further until he collapsed in a screaming heap. Cole brought the weapon around ninety degrees to the direction of the voice and immediately dropped it down against his chest.

They had Innocence. Three men surrounded the park ranger. Two of them with the muzzles of their rifles trained against his head, while the third was aiming directly at Cole.

"Put your weapon down and raise your hands in the air." Most Congolese didn't speak any English, so this was surprising. One more vote for the LRA hypothesis. Cole followed his directions. No reason to die yet.

But where was Bonny? He hoped with everything in him that those shots had not been directed at her.

"How many are you?" The short dark man spoke again, now striding quickly over to where Cole stood. He wore the same forest camouflage as the others, quality stuff but with no names or insignias anywhere. Not the uniform of any legitimate fighting force, but still a lot more professional than the Salvation Army look sported by most of the rebels in the area.

"Two." Innocence called out to him. "Only the two of us."

The man stopped and turned back toward Innocence. "I was not asking you, dirty fool."

"Well my answer would have been the same," Cole said. He couldn't believe none of the rebels had seen Proper, still hiding in the tall wild celery on the other side of the clearing. "We are scientists, working in this park with valid government permits. Please free us now."

The short man snickered. "Scientists, carrying loaded weapons?" He looked over to the wounded younger man, moaning on the ground and gripping a blood-soaked lower leg. "And shooting at my men? No, *monsieur*, I cannot believe it is like this."

Cole clenched his teeth. He should have taken charge from the start—confronted this group out in the open. But it was too late for second-guessing. "I fired only in self-defense. This soldier of yours was going to kill me."

"Maybe you will wish he succeeded, before we finish with you." The leader smirked, a deranged smile that reminded Cole of a psychopath serial killer, then signaled to three other men. "Come, tie them. We can reach the camp tonight."

"Myriam, my daughter." She stood against the only bare wall left in the small storage space. Haddad closed the distance between them in three long steps, but she put an arm out, hand extended, and turned her face away. "Did they harm you?"

She held her silence. It had always been her most effective tool, but now it hurt worse than ever. He gently pushed her hand down and put both of his own on her shoulders. More slowly this time: "Did they harm you?"

Myriam shook her head from side to side and started sobbing. She wasn't completely gone, then. Haddad turned back into the room and took in the scene for the first time. The two visitors sat on folding chairs against an old wooden desk they had scavenged from the office, staring at him with calculated passivity. They couldn't have been older than thirty, not even born when he left Lebanon to start this long waiting game that was finally coming to fruition. The two men both wore close-cropped beards and looked like they were better suited to a seaside cafe in Beirut than the rocky hillsides of the Bekaa. But what did he know anymore?

His throat caught when he saw movement at the door. Was it a trap after all? No, almost worse. His cousin Adel strode in, gave a curt nod, and quickly averted his eyes from Haddad's gaze. It was obvious. He was complicit, but ashamed of his role. Haddad felt utterly alone.

"I couldn't say no, Fadi." Adel reached into a white box on the floor and pulled out a form-fitting face mask. "They could have done much worse."

He held it out for Haddad, who only then noticed the others were already wearing them.

"*Shukran.*" Thank you. Haddad reached for the mask and continued in Arabic. "What do they want with Myriam?"

"Ask them yourself." Adel had immigrated to the States with him in the early eighties, two undercover Hezbollah operatives striking out together, part of the organization's unprecedented surge of sleeper cell creation that was barely utilized but always ready and waiting. Theoretically ready and waiting, at least. Haddad suspected that more than a few of their counterparts, scattered around the U.S. and Europe, had gone completely native after being neglected for so long. But somehow he and Adel had stayed true, kept up communication with their faceless handlers as one decade spilled into another. As the comforts and security of a successful American life piled up around him, Haddad knew it would be hard to finally answer a call to action. Adel was different, though. He had never married, never really integrated himself quite so fully or shown much appreciation for their new life. Now Haddad wondered if he should have done the same.

One of the younger men stood up. He had introduced himself the day before only as Ahmad. "Your daughter is our insurance. We could not be confident in your cooperation without more leverage."

"Confident in my cooperation?" Haddad didn't want to believe they were so perceptive. "Haven't I provided everything you asked? Risked my own business and safety to support this Jihad?" He almost said *cowardly Jihad* but caught himself.

The other man, Faisal, spoke from his chair. "Risked your own business and safety. . ." He paused. "Yes, I can see that we were right. You have lost perspective, my brother. Do you want to know what we have not only risked, but lost?"

Haddad lowered his eyes. He realized that in all the fear and stress of preparation he had never stopped to wonder why this attack, why now.

"You are not unaware of recent events in our home, I don't think. First these foreign rebel Sunnis in Syria reaping destruction across our borders. And now the Zionists come from the south again, terrorizing our villages with their tanks and missiles."

"I know. And I cry with you over the innocents lost." This was true, and Haddad welcomed the rush of emotion caused by the man's words.

Ahmad spoke again: "They are not nameless innocents to us, brother, though they may be now for you, so long removed from our realities. Three weeks ago, a missile flew through the window of my own home while I was away, fighting outside Damascus. Killed my sleeping wife and two daughters, just like that." He spoke through clenched jaws, the muscles in his cheeks pulsing. "And do you know where this missile came from?"

Haddad only shook his head.

"Yes, maybe it was fired by a Zionist pilot, but the weapon itself, and even the jet it flew out of, they are all from America. Manufactured here, then given so generously to their friends in Israel."

Faisal stood now. "My brother was killed also, by a sniper on the border. And for what? He was only a boy, making foolish pranks with friends."

"Then why do you come here?" Haddad said. "Why not take the fight to Jerusalem, where it belongs?"

Faisal spit at his feet. "We have been taking it to Jerusalem for sixty years. You should know that."

"Now we must bring justice to the *kafirs* of America. Maybe they will learn to choose their friends more wisely."

"Or maybe they will come back to Lebanon for revenge," Haddad said. "That would not be a good solution for any of us." He had a hard time believing Hezbollah's leadership could really be behind such a foolhardy mission as this. But he had no way to know. Nothing but the anonymous words in his Gmail account.

"Let them try, after we are done with them." Ahmad gestured to the rows of shelving that took up a quarter of the room.

Haddad looked more carefully at the setup. He recognized his egg boxes lined up along the shelves. Forty-eight eggs to a tray, eight trays deep in each box. Almost eight-thousand eggs altogether. The sight of the space heater plugged into the wall made him realize he was sweating profusely. It must have been almost a hundred degrees in the small space.

What was growing in those eggs, injected so carefully into each one with a tiny needle that didn't even break the shell? And what would they do with it all, supposedly ready for use in just a few short days? He knew they had already gone to his cousin's workplace the night before to scout things out, but otherwise the ultimate plan was a mystery. They must have doubted his conviction from the start to keep him in the dark like this. Haddad didn't care, though. The less he knew, the better.

"I'm taking her with me." Haddad walked back to Myriam and put a hand on her arm.

Ahmad took a step toward them, then stopped. "No, brother, I'm afraid we cannot allow that. We are honorable men. She will not be harmed, unless you prove yourself a traitor."

Haddad looked to his cousin, who again avoided eye contact. "You can't just keep her here, a captive."

"We can," Ahmad said. "And we must."

"You will bring her food, and whatever else she needs from home to be comfortable." Faisal looked her up and down, spending too long on the tanned legs and shoulders left bare by a tank top and skirt even Haddad was ashamed of. "Make sure you bring her something appropriate to wear. This girl is our sister, even if she has abandoned the faith."

Myriam sobbed once beside him. Haddad looked at her, wanting to embrace this sweet daughter whose world was changing forever. But the hatred in her eyes kept him away. He had failed her.

She pulled her arm out of his grasp and backed away. "I never told you, Aba, how my friends used to tease me in school. *Is your dad a terrorist?* they would ask. I defended you with every ounce of strength I had." She shook her head slowly as a single tear rolled down her cheek. "But now I know they were right all along."

It was too much. Haddad brought his hands to his face and wept.

Tiny splinters of cheap nylon twine dug into Cole's wrists. They already felt raw, and he couldn't help but wonder just how much skin remained to protect the big veins from the steady sawing motion. His arms were stretched tightly around the bulky pack behind his back, and each step down the forested path was an agony of screaming muscles and burning skin.

He strained to look over the two young rebels directly in front of him. One of them limped painfully, his lower leg now bandaged and the bleeding stopped. The bullet had gone straight through the muscle of his calf and would heal with time. The other man had a large round knot on the back of the head, evidence of his unfortunate run-in with the tree trunk. He glanced back at Cole, hatred in his young eyes. But more than just hatred—they were bloodshot and unfocused, and his whole body shivered every couple of minutes. Aftereffects of the concussion? Cole remembered the same early signs when Marna first started getting sick. Had these guys been exposed to the virus too?

Ahead of them, Innocence's shiny bald head bobbed along steadily. Cole wished he could see his face—that would give at least some indication of just how much trouble they were really in. What had happened to Bonny?

And what was Proper plotting, hopefully tracking silently behind them even now?

"You doing okay, my friend?" Cole spoke in a soft and nonthreatening voice. Time to test their captors, see what kind of communication they would be able to get away with.

A sharp jab from the rifle muzzle behind him provided a quick answer. "No talking!"

Cole caught Innocence's quick look over the shoulder, and an almost imperceptible nod that accompanied it. He was a hard read, this man who had seen so much in life. But there seemed to be some confidence remaining in his dark eyes, and Cole took comfort in that.

A shout came from the front of the line. Something in Acholi again, but whatever it was caused the rest of the men to stop. *Men* was a generous term. Apart from the leader, none of these fighters could have been more than twenty years old. Two of them sat down right where they were, while another pushed into the thick foliage at the side of the path.

"Toilet?" The leader stood in front of Cole, sadistic smile still plastered across his face. Cole did need to go. More importantly, it would be a good opportunity to see what kind of vulnerabilities he and Innocence might be able to exploit.

"Yes." Cole nodded.

The man pulled a long *panga* from its sheath along his leg and stepped around Cole's back. He pulled roughly against Cole's hands. Was that the blade scraping against his skin? The smallest misstep could prove fatal. *Focus here. Quiet submission.* The time for fighting would come. In seconds, he was free, and his hands dropped limply against his sides. The burning tension was gone, replaced by an achy feeling in his shoulders as the blood rushed back into the dead weights of his arms. The short man stepped over to Innocence and did the same thing.

First mistake—never free multiple captives at the same time. The rule had been drilled into Cole during the detainee operations training before his first deployment. It seemed obvious, but for these rebels who were more accustomed to dealing with traumatized village children it was probably never an issue.

Not this time around.

MINUTES PASSED AS they waited for one last man to return from his sojourn in the woods. The leader called out.

No response.

Cole looked at Innocence, but his face was a mask of indifference. Another case of untreated water or undercooked jungle rat working its magic on this teenage rebel's intestines? Or was Proper out there, silently subduing one of the enemy?

Another man took off back down the trail, calling to his friend. Second mistake—never investigate a suspicious situation alone.

A surprised shout echoed through the forest, followed immediately by the pop of a single shot.

Proper.

Chaos broke out again for the second time in less than an hour. Cole pulled at his hands, tied again even more tightly behind his back. No way out that way. The leader was shouting over his men, motioning wildly with his hands. Three of them ran back in the direction of the gunshot, while the leader and two wounded stayed to guard Cole and Innocence.

Go now, Proper. Cole sent his words out into the trees. *Melt into the forest and wait for the next opportunity.* Proper had the upper hand, the elements of surprise and stealth securely on his side. But the bond between those brothers was strong, and it was clear they had some unique associations with the LRA. Maybe too strong to allow for rational decision-making in a situation like this. Yes, he had grown up in these mountains, and he was experienced in the guerrilla warfare the environment required. But so were these rebels. Six against one—the odds were not good.

Cole looked to Innocence and raised his eyebrows. *What should we do?* The park ranger shook his head side to side. Nothing yet. Wrong move now, and they might be shot on the spot and left for the hyenas. Maybe miss out on even better chances of escape later on. It would be easier for their captors that way—simply kill them and be done with it. And nobody back at the camp would be any wiser about the lost ransom opportunity, as long as this leader could convince the others to keep their mouths shut.

More shouts erupted in the distance, muffled by the dense vegetation that marked this lower elevation along the northern slopes of Mount Karisimbi. Did they discover bodies? Cole hated the feeling of being totally ignorant of what was going on.

"Get down!" Proper's voice, close by. Cole threw himself into the thick nettles lining the edge of the path. Now the rapid crack of the Kalashnikov.

Deliberate single shots.

A gasp, then choking, and the young fighter with the wounded leg fell beside him, blood spraying from a gaping wound in his neck.

They might just make it. Cole rolled over the dying man and kicked out at the leader, who was returning fire with his own automatic rifle. Cole connected solidly with the man's knee, then rolled again right into his legs. The man struggled to maintain balance as he jumped and swung the weapon's muzzle in Cole's direction, but it was too late. He tripped over another prostrate form and fell into the nettles.

Cole flipped over on top of the rebel leader, holding him to the ground with his own body weight. He looked up just in time to see Innocence charging through the brush in the direction that his brother's shots had come from. The park ranger was calling out in his native Lingala, but there was no response.

Thudding footsteps signaled the arrival of the other three men, and in seconds they had pulled Cole off their leader. He was pinned to the ground by two of them, the familiar cold steel of another AK-47 pressed roughly into his temple. A crashing of branches and more shouting, then Innocence was pulled back onto the trail. His whole body was bucking and spinning, his legs like writhing pythons in the hands of the two men who struggled to restrain them.

"They killed him!" Innocence choked out the words between hoarse yells, anger mixing with grief as he slowly stopped fighting. "My brother… they killed him."

G ive it to me straight, Chuck." The president sat motionless at his desk. That desk. Anna still couldn't believe she was really inside the Oval Office, watching the inner workings of the United States government in action. But the summer had already been full of surprises of both the personal and professional variety, and she wasn't complaining. She followed the president's eyes from the stack of papers he'd been paging through up to the intimidating face of the man seated across from him. "Does this outbreak honestly present any danger to our national security?"

"Not at this time, Mr. President."

Charles Howard was fairly new to the job as national security advisor. Retired as a four-star and chairman of the Joint Chiefs the year before, Howard was the president's closest—and some said only—confidant when it came to the nation's defense. He'd long been a persona non grata among those responsible for shaping the president's public image. *Too much confidence in his own moral paradigm*, was how Andrew Mills described it. Anna wasn't sure such confidence was a bad thing, but his apparently conscious effort to avoid interacting with anyone below his elevated status on the power spectrum made it hard to like the man.

"Other than a small number of troops with the Kony task force, we have very few citizens anywhere near Goma. Those soldiers all received the smallpox vaccination prior to their deployment and should be protected if the virus is indeed related."

Anna had to stifle the urge to jump right in and inform them about another very important American citizen who was also in the area. Wasn't Cole's presence reason enough to justify a full CDC mission, at the very minimum? *Wanted you all to know that Marna died yesterday.* The words from his e-mail the night before had been on repeat in her mind ever since, mixing themselves with those awful images on CNN from the dying patients in Goma.

"Then I really don't see why we should invest any more resources in the investigation." President Rogers set the papers down. "Let the French take care of it, if they're so concerned about that unlucky aid hospital. Isn't that one of their former colonies?"

"Belgian, sir."

"Okay, then the Belgians can send a team, save the world this time around. Or what about the WHO? Isn't this kind of thing exactly why we keep those millions of dollars flowing to Geneva year after year? We have too much going on to worry about one more headline-grabbing virus in Africa."

"I agree. Between the Lebanese conflict, this hurricane, and Sunday's big event, you have more than enough going on for one week."

Mills stepped forward from where he and Anna were standing along the wall. "Since I'm apparently the only one concerned about headlines in this office, can I propose a compromise?"

The national security advisor turned his chair just slightly in their direction, a scowl on his face. "Always with the compromises, Andrew."

The president looked more interested. "Let's hear him out at least."

"Don't worry, this is the best kind—one that doesn't require any funding or effort on either of your parts."

The scowl on Howard's face softened.

"We're going to get questions about the outbreak at the press briefing later today, whether we want them or not. Scary diseases are exciting. A hell of a lot more exciting than our ongoing support to this dubious Israeli involvement in Lebanon, and maybe tied with coverage of your plodding response to the waterlogged southeastern United States."

"And your point is?" The national security advisor looked at his watch.

"Let me focus on what we're already doing to respond. It may not be much, but it's better than ignoring the story completely."

The president looked surprised. "That implies that we're doing something? I was under the impression that no one could even get into Goma."

"That's true," Mills said. "But it was a USAID-funded scientist who made the initial identification of monkeypox in the dead gorillas. And we have an infectious disease doc with the CDC flying back to Atlanta right now with samples for further analysis. So it's not like we're just sitting on our hands doing nothing."

"This is why I keep you around, Andrew." The hint of a smile crept into the corners of President Rogers' mouth. "Go ahead and play up those stories this afternoon if you think it will help."

"Your administration has a wide reach, sir. You know as well as I do that we've got to take credit whenever credit is due."

Anna couldn't stand it any longer. She didn't realize her boss knew about Cole at all. Did he honestly not make the connection between their last names? She raised her hand just slightly, then changed her mind. No reason the bigwigs needed to be involved in this.

Too late.

"I think our lovely little intern from Wyoming has something to say?" The president's words startled Anna. Had he really been watching her that closely? Flattering, and a little creepy. The unwelcome image of another White House intern doing the unspeakable in this same room flashed in front of her eyes. She wanted to melt into the creamy paint on the wall behind her.

"Thank you, Mr. President, but it's something I can tell Mr. Mills offline." The words came out much more smoothly than she was expecting, but this didn't seem to have any effect on the look of disbelief that was still plastered across the national security advisor's face.

"No, I'm curious now," the president said. "It must have been important if you thought it worth sharing in this context. Please, go ahead."

Anna took a few steps forward. Deep breath. "Well, it's just that the USAID-funded scientist that Mr. Mills mentioned is my brother." She paused, trying to gauge the response of these men to her decidedly insignificant revelation. The president's cocked head and furrowed brow were enough encouragement to go on. "His name is Cole McBride, and he's a veterinarian studying emerging infectious diseases in central Africa. He's also in the military, so I just thought maybe we could do a little bit more to make sure he's safe and support the investigation?"

"What do you mean, in the military?" The president directed this question to her boss, standing beside her. She didn't dare to look at his face.

"Mr. President, this is news to me too. Sounds like we may need to track down a few more details on this thing."

"He's on active duty," Anna said. "But this is some sort of academic break for him to get a PhD."

"Do you know where he is now?" She could see the concern in the president's eyes. His kids were about the same ages as her own siblings. "Is he in any danger?"

"I don't think so, sir. He sent an e-mail last night from the defense attaché's house in Kigali, but I'm not sure what he was planning to do next. The South African woman who died was a close friend of his."

President Rogers looked back to the national security advisor. "Chuck, if this guy, this Cole—"

He paused.

"Cole McBride, sir," Anna said. "Captain Cole McBride."

"If Captain McBride is really military, this falls right in your lane."

"Roger, sir."

"I want you to track him down, make sure he's healthy and safe, and see if there's anything else we can do, within reason, to keep this virus from getting out of control."

Howard looked back at Anna and shook his head slowly. The look in his eyes made her feel like vomiting. After what seemed like minutes, he turned back to the president. "Yes, sir. I can tell you, though, this Captain McBride isn't going to be too happy to find out about his kid sister's meddling. It's never a good thing to have someone like me on your tail."

"Mr. President." Anna gripped the edges of her suit jacket. Why couldn't she have just minded her own business? "General Howard is right. Maybe it would be better—"

"I'm sorry, Ms. McBride, I've spoken my mind, and that's that. Thank you for letting me know about your brother." The president looked down at his desk and picked up another paper. "Now if you'll excuse us."

Anna stood frozen in place until she felt a tug on the sleeve of her jacket. She turned to see that Mills was already on his way out of the room.

So that was that.

It really wasn't very different from so many of the video games he'd grown up with. Thumb-operated controls, handheld touchscreen device, obstacles to avoid, and even bad guys to look out for. Except this was real life, and Captain Jake Russell was controlling a miniature drone currently circling a few hundred feet above a terrorist camp deep in the Congolese jungle.

"Now if only this thing was armed," he said. "I wouldn't mind taking out a few of these guys right now."

"I hear ya." Master Sergeant Mike Denison sat beside him, eyes on the ground control station's screen even as he steadily typed their observations into another laptop sitting on his own knees. Rico lay quietly on the other side, head resting across a front paw, eyes closed. "You're pretty convinced they're LRA, then? Too bad we can't just get a clear photo of Kony himself and be done with it. Bring in the big guns and call it a day, right?"

"Exactly." Jake turned the screen slightly. "You see that?"

He pointed to a spot on the bottom edge of the live video feed from the Puma UAV's camera.

"Yeah. See if you can zoom in a little."

Jake pushed a tiny joystick forward with his left thumb to make the adjustment. "Visitors, you think?"

"No, they're walking right up like they own the place," Mikey said. "Must have been a group that left before we got on target this afternoon."

They'd been watching the drone's footage for a couple hours already, and it was almost time to bring her back for another battery swap. Not much seemed to be happening in the camp itself, but they had done some exploring of the surrounding area and found what appeared to be an active pit mine just a few kilometers away.

This was interesting, though—a small group of men approaching the camp along a freshly bulldozed dirt road. "Looks like they got a couple wounded." Jake hit a button to bring up the menu again. "I'm going to lower her down to two hundred feet."

"Go for it."

The tiny moving shapes got blurry as the Puma lost elevation over a couple slow circles. Jake tapped a finger against one leg. *Come on already.* A video game wouldn't make you wait so long for something simple like that.

"Woah, woah, not too low or they'll be able to hear her." Mikey leaned in closer, and Rico opened one eye. How did the dog always seem to detect even the slightest tension in his partner's voice?

"There we go." The picture focused, and Jake strained his eyes to take in every detail. Something wasn't right. "What's up with the packs those two guys are wearing?"

"Nice gear," Mikey said. "But not just the packs. See this one's hair?" He pointed to the screen. "Hundred dollars says he's not black."

"Shit, you're totally right." The textured brown on top of the man's head stood out in stark contrast to the uniform black of all the others. "Those two are walking kind of funny too. No motion in the arms, almost like their hands are tied."

Jake brought a hand to his forehead and pushed it through his own hair.

"That would be bad." Mikey nodded as Rico stood up on all fours, tail raised. "Very bad."

"You have the sat phone?"

"Right here." The master sergeant set his laptop down and picked up the phone.

"Okay, see if you can get him."

Jake looked back to the screen. The group was only about a hundred feet outside of the barricaded entrance to the main camp.

A series of tones, then long beeps. Mikey had turned the speakerphone on.

Fifty feet from the camp's entrance, the group stopped. A chaos of movement, and then it was clear. The packs were off the two men's backs, their contents strewn across the ground.

A click from the phone, followed by a chorus of shouting voices. Rico turned to the phone and whined softly. He knew. Then it went silent.

"Oh man," Mikey said softly. "Things just got seriously complicated."

B ill, I could do this with my eyes closed." Travis Grinley stood up. Time to get the ball rolling.

"I'm sure you could. Promise me you won't try it tonight, though." Bill Shackleton sounded tired, and Travis knew he had probably woken his boss with the phone call.

"I'll be fine. But yes, I promise. No blinking for me tonight. You have my guarantee."

"Let me know as soon as you get anything." Bill paused. "And be careful."

It was a ten minute walk through a maze of aging corridors from Travis's office to the Special Pathogens Branch's Biosafety Level 4 laboratories. The styrofoam sample box in his hands was just like so many others he had processed over the last few years. One more treasure chest waiting to spill its secrets. Monkeypox? Probably. But there were sure to be some surprises hidden away in the virus's genetic code. There always were. It was amazing how even one little mutation, a random error in the transcription of a single base pair, could end up changing a sleepy virus in equilibrium with its environment into a bloodthirsty killer like this one. But that's all it took—natural selection at its finest. Travis shook the box gently. Only a few more hours, and this virus would be a mystery no more. His little piece of the disease detection puzzle would be complete, and he could pass the results over to the rest of the team. People like Leila, who didn't really give a damn about the DNA but might be able to use the information he delivered to stop this thing from spreading any further.

Leila. Their reunion at the airport had been a total flop. She barely looked at the roses and only managed a half-hearted side hug before pushing the box into his hands and turning away.

"Don't want to miss my flight." She pulled her hand out of his and walked off toward the line for security.

"Leila." He didn't quite shout, but it felt loud, his voice echoing across the vast space of the departure hall. No response, and a minute later she was gone.

Sure, he got it. She was tired and stressed out. Her mother was sick. But still. That wasn't the Leila he'd been dating for almost a month. Yes, it had taken a while to break through her outer shell, the general aura about her that most people incorrectly assumed was straight-up bitchiness. He'd gotten to know the real Leila, a surprisingly affectionate genius who had finally spent the night for the first time before leaving for Africa a week ago.

That's who he'd been expecting at the airport. And who did he get instead? Something in her expression—that final look at the airport—made him wonder if she would ever be back.

BSL-4: AUTHORIZED PERSONNEL ONLY! The large red words printed across the door were followed by an oversized universal biohazard symbol. Three interlocking circles with a fourth at the center—kind of like a leaky Venn diagram. Even after all this time, it was still hard to believe that he was actually one of those authorized personnel. Travis Grinley, a one-time high school dropout from the backwoods of eastern Tennessee. He swiped his ID card and waited for a click before pushing firmly on the heavy door.

Fluorescent lights flickered on as he stepped into another hallway. He was alone. It had taken some convincing, but Travis knew his boss didn't really want to spend all night twiddling his thumbs in BSL-4 just to meet the buddy system requirement. Emergency situations called for emergency measures, and that sometimes meant bending the rules. Not that he was worried—the tasks ahead only required the most basic laboratory skills—stuff molecular biology grad students across the country were doing every day. True, they rarely got their hands on pathogens like this one, but the techniques didn't change.

Travis stopped at the end of the corridor in front of a heavy-duty transparent airlock door set at waist height in the wall. He swiped his card again and entered a six digit PIN on the adjoining keypad. There was a hiss as the door to the fumigation chamber swung open. He set the sample box on a conveyor belt, pressed a button, and closed the door. The chamber's decontamination cycle of poisonous gas and ultraviolet radiation would kill everything except the samples themselves, bagged and sealed safely inside the box. When the cycle ended, the box would arrive at an identical door on the other side of the chamber, where Travis could retrieve it after he got inside the lab. This complex system sometimes seemed like overkill, but its design was necessary to ensure the biological purity of the working spaces inside. No living thing of any size could enter or exit the laboratory without Travis's full knowledge and cooperation.

A minute later, he was undressing inside a small locker room. Undressing all the way. The first time through, he'd glanced up in shock to see his older female mentor stripped down to her birthday suit right in front of him. But now it was simply another part of the daily routine, and he was usually quite content to keep his eyes to himself.

He put his street clothes into a locker and stepped into the next room. Shower in and shower out. The hot water pounded against his shoulders and back, clouds of steam filling the small room. He tried to clear his mind of everything but the tasks ahead.

It was going to be a long night.

The water turned off seven minutes later. All the showers were on automatic timers—a necessary control the scientists implemented to keep themselves from cheating by not staying in long enough. He stepped into another changing area. Disposable socks and underwear, then a fresh pair of scrubs from the shelves beside the door.

Ready for stage two.

Travis wrestled a biohazard suit off its resting place on the wall in the next room. The thick blue polyurethane provided necessary protection, yes. After seeing those videos of the dead and dying from the hospital in Goma, he was glad for that. But it was also incredibly heavy. Travis was a pretty average guy in the size and strength department, and getting into the suit by himself was always a hassle. How did Leila manage to do it so easily?

Leila.

She'd be in the air now, flying overnight all the way back to Amsterdam. Would she be able to sleep? Or could she ever sleep on planes? They hadn't been together long enough for him to know even this most basic fact.

Getting the hood on was easy compared to the rest of the suit, but it marked the real transition into the alternate reality of BSL-4. Once it was zipped and sealed into place, Travis popped the end of his air hose adaptor into the complementary piece on a coiled green hose snaking down from the ceiling. With a loud whoosh, the whole suit began to fill. It was fully inflated in seconds, and he took a deep breath of the cool dry air. The process was kind of like getting geared up for a dive—wetsuit, weights, and tank, all heavy and awkward—but then slipping into the water and feeling like a new man.

Travis started waddling across the room. "Shit!" He tripped over the long end of an overboot and grabbed for another hose hanging above him. Catastrophe averted. Wouldn't have been the first time to completely bite it, but at least no one was there to laugh at him this time. He smiled, remembering a less fortuitous experience involving an escaped rat that ended with him sprawled across the floor. He'd taken crap for months over that one. So maybe the diving analogy wasn't perfect—unfortunately, the addition of pressurized HEPA-filtered air into the biohazard suit did not provide nearly as complete a transformation. He passed through the chemical shower, its stainless steel walls covered in nozzles that would foam the contaminated suit with a deadly mix of sanitizing agents on the way out. The final door into the lab always seemed to take forever to open. Even without a shower, the settings in the room required a full circulation of air before letting anyone through.

BSL-4 was not a fun place for those in a hurry, but then, that had never really been a problem for him. *You can take the boy out of the South, but you can't take the South out of the boy.* His mom's favorite phrase, repeated ad nauseam every time she called him during those five years of grad school in New York. He'd shot her down each and every time. *No, Momma, sorry to say I've fully converted.* But when the job offers came through, and it came down to Boston versus Atlanta, the familiar call of home was just too strong to turn away.

The heavy door slid open, and Travis stepped through. He disconnected his air supply from the shower room's hose, now stretched taut behind him, and popped it into a new one inside the lab. The silence of his late-night sojourn was gone, replaced by the steady loud hiss of air that served to drown out any other sound. In the past, this constant white noise made it nearly impossible to communicate using anything but hand signals, but the recent addition of a pretty decent integrated headset developed by NASA made a big difference. Of course, that was assuming there was someone else in the room, or at least in the building, on the same channel.

Not tonight.

Travis retrieved the box of samples from the airlock chamber and brought it over to one of several cabinet hoods inside the laboratory. The hoods each had their own vacuum filtered air system, making it that much harder for any adventurous virus to even think about escaping. Layer upon layer of safety precautions, each one building on and adding to the one before it—that was BSL-4. They didn't make his job very easy, but he had seen what these pathogens could do. The oozing skin, bloody coughs, and dissolving internal organs. Not just in pictures, or videos, either. He welcomed the redundancy.

Travis set the box under the hood and began pulling away too many layers of packing tape with practiced double-gloved fingers.

Finally, the real work could begin.

THERE WERE EIGHT sets of sealed bags, each labeled with a fine-tipped black Sharpie in Leila's neat handwriting. Travis picked them up, one by one, and set them out across the counter. First in line: blood and viral culture tubes from Marna Van Wyk, the now deceased South African helicopter pilot. He wished he could have heard more from Leila about what happened that night on the drive to Kigali. How did a healthy young woman like her crash so quickly? But he knew Leila wouldn't want to talk about it, not yet at least. She was too quick to blame herself when something went wrong, even if there was nothing she or anyone else could have done to prevent this woman's death.

Next up were the blood, scab, and tissue samples from the infant mountain gorilla. This little orphan was still alive and on the road to recovery, according to the last e-mail from the Gorilla Doctors vet in Musanze. And finally the scabs, tissue biopsies, and viral culture tubes collected from the dead adult gorillas in Virunga National Park.

The viral culture tubes would go into an incubator. Pretty unlikely that anything would turn up there—viruses were tough to grow outside a real animal body. Still worth a shot, though, and they would need to get their hands on live virus eventually either way.

The rest of the samples would all be processed in basically the same way. Travis picked up a small biopsy cup holding a tiny piece of black tissue floating in a transport medium. This was supposed to be straight from an active lesion on the infant gorilla's skin. Of all the samples, this one had the best chance of revealing the mysterious culprit. He unscrewed the lid and used a sterilized set of stainless steel forceps to lift the tissue out of the biopsy cup. It could be anything, this little piece of unidentifiable gunk at the end of the forceps. He brought it up right in front of the hardened clear mask of his biohazard suit's hood. Crazy to think that this was really diseased skin from an endangered baby mountain gorilla, taken from the poor little patient himself less than twenty-four hours earlier on the other side of the world in Rwanda. And even crazier that the minuscule piece of tissue could hold the key to halting the continued spread of what was rapidly turning into an outbreak with genuine pandemic potential.

Travis carefully placed the skin biopsy into a new container, this one filled with a special solution of chemicals that would extract the DNA and break it up into standardized lengths in preparation for purification and genomic sequencing. The technology advanced every year, and he loved working in a place that stayed well-supplied with all the newest equipment. Whether or not the federal government could afford these fancy toys was a question way above his pay grade. Pretty sweet, though, to know he would have answers before the night was over, rather than the days or even weeks of waiting the sequencing process might take somewhere else.

The next hour passed by in a focused blur of meticulous activity. Pipetting minute amounts of liquid from vial to vial, concentrating the target DNA into ever more purified solutions. These repetitive manual steps of preparation could quickly get boring, but Travis had been doing it long enough to know how important it was not to let his mind wander. Even the smallest mistake would mess the whole process up and require starting over from the beginning. At least there were no live animals, needles or scalpels required this time—that's when things could really get dangerous when working alone.

He squeezed the automatic pipette's trigger one final time and watched as the last drops of liquid were deposited into an open well. The plate looked almost like a miniature muffin tin, each tiny depression in the plastic holding a library of purified DNA fragments just waiting to be read.

"And done," he said out loud, placing the plate into a sliding tray on the side of the HiSeq 2500 genome analyzer. He pushed a button and watched the samples disappear into the imposing million-dollar machine. Literally. The complete set-up had a sticker price of just over a million dollars, even if the CDC probably didn't pay full price.

A flat screen display lit up with a new message. TIME TO COMPLETION: 5 HOURS, 23 MINUTES.

Travis yawned and unsuccessfully tried to bring his hands above his head in a stretch.

Damn suit.

Time to get some sleep.

FRIDAY, JULY 2

Morgan Andrews brought both hands to her face, covering her eyes for a soothing five-second break from the glowing panel of screens in front of her. She moved her fingers over her temples and massaged in slow firm circles. The headache had been growing steadily more intense over the last few hours, and now it was almost unbearable.

A deep breath, and she opened her eyes. *This is what I signed up for.* No way a little sleep deficit was going to stand in the way now. Morgan had accepted this entry-level position at the National Security Agency's Central Africa desk straight out of Caltech three years earlier. And for the first time in those three years, she finally felt like she was really contributing to something important.

The fun started when she showed up for what was supposed to be just another day at the office, almost forty-eight hours earlier. The automatic alert was waiting on her main screen: a target level had been hit, and exceeded. This time it was outgoing calls from the DRC to Iran. Interesting, but not necessarily worth getting excited about yet. The week before it had been calls from Rwanda to Pakistan. That one turned out to be a brother's death and the ensuing coordination with extended family who owned a restaurant in Kigali. Did she ever imagine turning into such an expert on the cost of a fancy religious funeral in Islamabad? No, but that's what made the job fun. Something different every day—looking for needles in the haystack. Anytime the number of calls crossed a pre-set limit for each combination of countries, she would get one of these alerts.

This one stood out almost immediately. All the calls routed through a couple of towers in rebel-controlled North Kivu, and all of them going to a hot-listed number in the Iranian government. That wasn't normal. Now she had spoken with everyone from the CIA's chief of station in Kinshasa to a special ops colonel in Djibouti, and the NSA's global surveillance capabilities were sharpening their focus on her forgotten little region. She had gotten home to sleep for a few hours the night before, but no such luck this time around.

Morgan took another swig of her lukewarm coffee. *Beep beep.* Another message popped up, but this was a different type.

Target number detected. Connecting now.

She slammed the paper cup down on her desk, sending a geyser of coffee up across one screen. Whoops. Good thing no one was there to see it. She reached for a headset and pulled the earpieces over her dark hair. Not quite fast enough.

"—never mentioned that this plague would also spread outside of Virunga. Do you know we now have several cases even here in my own city? Am I to die also?" The words spilled quickly from a heavily accented male voice. Morgan had listened in on enough conversations to immediately place the accent as foreign-educated Congolese, and a large world map spread across a second tier of three screens confirmed this conclusion. Large red orbs pulsed silently over both Kinshasa and Tehran.

"My friend, calm down please. You should not have called me here." This voice was smoother, more polished.

"Simply suffer in silence, then, until you have wiped out my entire country? No, Dr. Torabi, that will not do."

Morgan looked from one screen to the next as new information appeared with every passing second. The number in Tehran was the same one that had been tried again unsuccessfully just twenty minutes earlier from their unknown location in Virunga National Park. Someone was screening calls. And now this new mobile phone in Kinshasa was publicly registered to Mr. Frederic Mulumba, Minister of Mines. Could someone in the government really be so completely off his rocker, clearly up to no good but not even following the most basic rules of international intrigue?

"Enough. I told you never to use my name." Apparently the Iranian agreed with her assessment. "We made an arrangement, and the operation is moving even more efficiently than we thought."

"Yes, but —"

"When the gorillas are gone, there will be no further objections to our project. You have my guarantee of that."

"It is not only the gorillas that are dying. You —"

"Will it really be such a tragedy if a few among your trouble-making population don't survive? And you will be a rich man, you must not forget this most important detail."

No response. Morgan checked the connection. Still active.

"We both have much to lose," the minister finally said. "You must not forget that, either."

A click, and the connection went dead. Morgan sucked in deeply, not realizing she'd been holding her breath.

This was big time.

Cole woke with a start. They were back. He heard the shuffling of footsteps on the tent's dirt floor and tried to open his eyes. No luck. His captors had tied on a snug blindfold almost immediately after the incident with the satellite phone, and his whole head throbbed with an aching pain from the constant pressure on his eyeballs. He shifted his body and felt the dead weight of both arms flop across his back. *Come on hands, stay with me now.*

How many times had the man come back during the night? The visits all blended together in a fuzzy blur. Why couldn't he just accept that Cole wasn't going to change his story? He was a scientist, investigating a disease outbreak among the mountain gorillas, escorted by two Virunga park rangers and their detection dog. It really was as simple as that. But this mysterious boss man was smart, that much was obvious. He was also scared, too desperate for someone who was supposed to have the upper hand. And that was the only weapon Cole had to work with. It wasn't much, but he would keep exploiting it with every bit of psychological strength he could muster.

"So you're an American?"

Cole lifted his head from the dirt. This was someone new.

"Don't worry, I'm on your side." The voice sounded European. Maybe German? "You're lucky to be alive, from what I hear."

A firm hand touched his burning shoulder, then moved up the back of his head to begin working at the knot in the blindfold.

"Is that right?" Cole said. The canvas fell away from his face, and he slowly opened one eye. It hurt, but not unbearably so. A patch of bright sunlight danced across the dirt floor, streaming in from the tent's half-open door flap. The man was still behind him. "Help me up?"

"Let me finish with your hands, first." Cole felt a slight tingling sensation at the tips of his fingers. "Must be careful not to free them too quickly. You know about reperfusion injury?"

"Yeah, pretty classic in horses that get stuck on the ground for any length of time."

"Huh?"

"A hoof gets caught in a halter, or the legs are jammed up against a stall wall—happens all the time. The weight of their own bodies cuts off circulation to the limbs, and then that rush of blood when they're finally helped up can totally destroy the muscles."

"Not a lot of horses out here in the jungle, you know."

"Same thing happens transporting big game, if you're not careful. Never let a rhino lie down in the back of a moving vehicle." The tingling spread up his fingers. No pain yet—that was good.

"And what do you know about that?"

"I'm a veterinarian, an animal doctor."

"You bloody kidding me?" The man stood and stepped around Cole, then crouched down right in front of him. He had a deeply tanned face with close-cropped blond hair and stubble. "Monkeypox outbreak in the gorillas. You know something about it?"

"I guess you could say that." Cole nodded. What was that doctor's name, from Doctors Without Borders in Goma? "Cole McBride, working out of Musanze with the Gorilla Doctors. I'd shake your hand if I could."

«And I'm Lars. Lars Olsson.»

"Wow." This was definitely him.

"My thought exactly," the doctor said. "We were supposed to be making each other's acquaintance under different circumstances three long days ago. As you can see, I ran into a slight problem along the way."

"We were worried, but there was nothing to do. No one can get into Goma right now."

"I figured as much."

"The journalist? Is she here too?"

Olsson shook his head. "Silly girl thought she could escape and got shot down by one of these boy soldiers."

"Here at the camp?"

"No, outside Goma. We were making a run for the border—trying to get those samples to you—when they found us. Guess that means her body hasn't turned up?"

"Not as of yesterday morning, at least. Only news out of Goma was the ongoing disaster at your hospital."

Olsson looked up. "Disaster?"

"According to a blurry mobile phone video being played on repeat by CNN, the disease is spreading like wildfire through patients and staff. I'm sorry."

Olsson closed his eyes and bowed his head. "I should be there." He pounded a fist into the dirt floor. "But instead? I am a prisoner, helpless doctor to a few dying rebels."

"You're helping me," Cole said. "And what about my friend, a tall black man named Innocence? Have you seen him?"

The anger left Olsson's face as quickly as it had arrived. "Yes, he is just across the camp, held like you overnight but unharmed. He told me about your capture and his brother's death."

Cole felt his heart rate speed up, a curtain of anger dropping over his burning eyes. What had Proper done to deserve such an end? Nothing. He was one of the best—kind, strong, thoughtful. And now he was gone too, one more body added to the ever-growing pile of corpses littering the graveyard of Cole's mind.

The doctor moved behind him again and loosened the rope a little more. An overwhelming sensation of pins and needles flooded both hands.

"Can you move your fingers?"

Cole tried to send the message down his arms. "Can't tell yet. Any motion back there?"

"Barely, but that's all we need. You should be fine."

"Thanks." Cole felt his hands drop to his side. Freedom.

"Assuming you don't get killed in the interim, that is."

The doctor rotated him onto his back and placed his arms along both sides. They were coming back to life more quickly now, and Cole could feel the blood pumping all the way down to his fingertips. *Thank God.* It would have been tough to be much of a vet without them.

"And you think that's a possibility?" Cole said.

"Oh definitely. Something's going on here that's making this Lukwiya character go crazy. And it's not just the disease that's killing off his army, either."

"Hang on," Cole said, sitting up. "They've got it here too?"

"Doctor!" The harsh shout was accompanied by a low moan.

Cole looked to the tent's opening, and Olsson jumped to his feet. They had been talking for close to an hour.

"This man is sick." Cole recognized the voice of his overnight tormentor and watched the tall man push into the tent. So this was the guy Olsson called Lukwiya, some kind of high-level officer sitting just below Kony himself. He was surprisingly well dressed in jeans and leather jacket—not exactly the faux-military getup Cole was expecting—and sported an expensive-looking watch. Yes, Olsson was right about new money. Lukwiya yanked on a rope, bringing a much shorter captive sprawling across the floor. The man sobbed for a moment and then lay silent.

"Sick, or wounded?" Olsson knelt down beside him.

"Just don't let him die," Lukwiya said, backing out of the tent. He stopped in the opening and looked up, dark eyes meeting Cole's own. "Take a good look at this man, Mr. Animal Doctor. There are ways to make you talk."

Cole held his gaze. *One one-thousand, two one-thousand, three one-thousand.* He watched as Lukwiya violently cleared his throat, positioned the resulting mucous, and sent it flying. Cole felt it land on his cheek, warm and wet. The resulting stench of rotten mouth and chewing tobacco was almost overpowering. But still, he didn't look away. Finally, the tall man shook his head, turned around, and was gone.

"Good to see you two hit it off well last night." Olsson handed him a dirty rag.

"Thanks." Cole wiped his face and threw the cloth into a corner. "Yeah, he seems to think there's more to my story than just the dying gorillas."

"And is there?" The doctor looked at him, eyebrows raised.

"Maybe," Cole said. "It's not that I don't think you should know. Just better, for your own sake, that you don't have any extra information to get beaten out of you." He crouched down beside their new companion. "That what happened to this guy?"

"Yes," Olsson replied. He had a hand on the man's forehead. "I saw it, yesterday morning. I'd be surprised if this fever is related to his wounds, though."

"Really?" Cole was staring at the side of the man's head. The ear was completely gone, its former position marked by a gaping mess of oozing flesh surrounded by blistering skin. "That thing looks ripe for a nasty localized infection."

"Of course, yes. And I have antibiotics for that." The doctor was pulling an odd assortment of medications out of a large box. "My pharmacy. Everything under the sun except those missing antivirals and the exhausted anti-inflammatory drugs."

"And the fever?"

"Seems too hot, too soon, to be the secondary bacterial infection that's brewing in that wound. I'm guessing he's coming down with your pox virus. Less than twenty-four hours since he would have been first exposed by the sick LRA here in camp."

"Which is exactly what happened with my colleague, Marna. Have you ever seen something with an incubation period this quick?"

"Not in thirty years of tropical medicine." Olsson shook his head. "That's the scariest part of this whole thing. Even if the smallpox vaccine really is protective, the virus is spreading too fast for any public health response."

"Any idea what kind of vaccine stocks they have here in central Africa?"

Olsson laughed. "If only there were such a thing. You might have enough for a few million Americans hidden away under some mountain in the U.S., but it will take months to ramp up supply for the rest of the world."

"We don't have months," Cole said. "For us or the gorillas."

A flash of white from the wounded man's newly open eyes caught Cole's attention.

"Gorillas?" The man's faint voice was slow but clear. "You know about sick gorillas?"

"You speak English?" Cole was surprised.

"A little."

"Well yes," Cole continued. "My teammates and I found the sick gorillas here in Virunga. Do you know something also?"

The man grimaced as Olsson smoothed some white cream over his wound. "Give me medicine for the pain, and I will tell you more."

A SOFTENING AROUND the man's eyes let Cole know the drugs were beginning to work. Maybe now he was ready to talk.

"So about the gorillas?" Cole didn't want to push too hard. He thought back to the basic instruction on interrogation techniques he'd received early on with 10th Group. Broad, leading questions. Active listening. It was simple stuff, but it worked.

"Yes, I like the mountain gorilla." The man looked almost comfortable, leaning against the side of the tent. "Never hurt one myself, no."

"That's good." *Don't push him too fast.*

"I take many tourists to see the gorillas. Cheaper for them to come with us, no need to pay for official permits. And still plenty of money for me."

"Where was that, only in Virunga?" This was interesting, but not a surprise. Cole knew that several of the rebel groups had been providing illegal gorilla tours to penny-pinching backpackers and the unscrupulous wealthy for years.

"Yes, only Virunga. Too many rangers on the other side."

"Okay, that makes sense." And it did. Economic development and relative stability in Rwanda and Uganda had enabled those countries to build up the security presence in their most valuable national parks to the point where this sort of illegitimate activity was almost impossible.

"Last week, my friends take some tourists into the park. They want to see big gorilla family, up close."

"You were not with them?" Olsson asked.

"No, I was in Goma. I set the tour up. But a good woman, she needed my attention." One corner of his mouth turned up in a slight smile. This was good—he was relaxing. "So I sent them with my friends this time."

"Tell me about the tourists," Cole said.

"There were two of them, young men like you."

"Like me? You mean in age, or race, or language?"

"Yes, they were young like you. And fair-skinned, but not white."

"Not white?"

"Darker, with short black beards." The man brought a hand to his own face, then pulled it away quickly when his fingers reached the heavy layer of cream now protecting the wound. "And they spoke French, like me, but also something else to each other. Maybe Arabic, I do not know."

Ding ding ding, we have a winner. The addition of young Arab men made any twenty-first century story that much more interesting. Cole caught Olsson's eye and saw he was thinking the exact same thing. *Don't press the point yet, though.*

"Okay," Olsson said. "But what do they have to do with the gorillas getting sick?"

Cole tried to get the doctor's attention again and gave a little shake of his head. *Not yet.*

"And why should I tell you this?" The man sat up straight, his face hardening. "You think we need more white people interfering here? This is our country, our business. You have no place here."

Shit. It was textbook. Push too hard, and you would lose any chance of obtaining actionable intelligence. Time for the salvage attempt.

"Sir," Cole started. Show respect, establish camaraderie. "We don't even know your name yet. I am Cole McBride, and this is Lars Olsson. We are both captives here, like you." He could see the suspicion in the man's eyes, but he tried to maintain a kind and interested expression in his own.

The seconds passed. Waiting. Until finally, the man spoke. "You do not need to know my name. But yes, we all hate the same man."

Cole tried to pick up where they had left off. "So you sent these tourists out of Goma with your friends?"

There was another pause as the man looked from Cole to Olsson and back to Cole again. "Yes, they went into the park with two other FDLR, men who also know the gorillas and make money in this way."

"And when did you see them next?"

The man raised a hand again, held it in the air beside his missing ear, and then let it drop to his side. "I did not. I did not see them again, except for one, three days later."

"Which one?" Cole was whispering now.

"My friend, one of the guides. I found him near Rumangabo, shot many times through his body and almost dead."

Cole saw Olsson's eyebrows go up. *Just give him time.*

"I'm sorry," Cole said. Was that neutral enough? It was hard not to look as desperate for the rest of the story as he actually felt.

"I put him in a truck, for the big white hospital in Goma." The man shook his head slowly. "I do not know if he made it there alive."

"Again, I am so sorry. I have also lost many friends this week." Cole put a hand on the man's leg. He wouldn't have done it to another American, but African men were different, more tactile in their expressions of brotherly concern and affection. "But he must have told you something about what happened, yes?" Another gamble.

"It is a strange story," the man said. He looked up at Cole again. "I do not know what to believe."

"And we won't either. But give us a chance. Maybe it can help us get out of here, together."

"My friend, he tell me the tourists try to spray the gorillas."

What in the world? "Spray them? What do you mean?"

"Yes, I asked him also. He said they use spray bottles, like for cleaning. They spray something at many gorilla faces until the animals run away."

Cole felt a sharp pain and saw that his fingers had turned up a tiny shard of broken glass in the dirt floor. Spraying the gorilla's faces. Arab men. Unusual pox virus outbreak. He wiped the hand against his beige hiking pants, leaving a streak of blood along with the dark African soil.

"Then they took guns and shot my friends. Left them for dead in the forest."

"But one of them didn't die." Cole's heart was racing. "The killers messed up."

The man leaned back against the side of the tent.

"Yes." He placed a rough hand on top of Cole's own. "And now you know the story."

The soothing tones of a solo cello broke into Travis Grinley's disjointed dreams.

Leila has the virus. She's sick.

He half-opened one eye as the slow melody continued.

She needs me.

Bach's Cello Suite No. 1, the Prelude. It was the best ring tone his old flip phone could manage, and as beautiful as those familiar notes were, Travis hated alarms. He reached blindly for the phone and started pressing buttons.

Silent relief, and the darkness enveloped him again.

Where is she? I left her for one minute, and now she's gone. Iran.

He was running through the Atlanta airport.

Leila!

The melody started again, louder now, and he reached for the phone again.

One more snooze?

No. He opened both eyes this time. The faint glow from a computer screen illuminated the room just enough for him to remember where he was. He sat up straight. Five and a half hours weren't enough for a good night's sleep, but that was all the HiSeq 2500 needed.

The sequencing results were ready.

TRAVIS ROLLED OVER and pulled himself up off the floor. It wasn't the first time he'd spent the night, and he knew it wouldn't be the last. He sat down at his desk and popped an ID card into the keyboard. The wonders of technology. No need to go through the hassle of getting back into BSL-4 anymore, only to stand there for hours reading results and running reports on the genome sequencer itself. He could do it all remotely, from the comfort of his own windowless basement office. He looked around at the bare walls as the desktop loaded up. At least it was better than the cubicle farm he'd toiled away in for the first couple of years.

It always took forever for his computer to establish a secure connection and then load the data from the sequencing machine. What was Leila up to? Probably landed in Amsterdam already, waiting for the next flight on to Tehran. Schiphol International. Flower shops. That's all he remembered—bulbs and kits and fresh tulips in every color under the sun. He'd been through a couple of times, traveling to and from Africa on quick missions like the one they missed out on earlier in the week. They would have been there now, braving the horrors of the hospital outbreak in Goma, maybe squeezing in a quick safari on the side. But no, stupid hurricane had to come along and screw him out of the adventure.

Initial Sequencing Successful.

The message never failed to give him the warm and fuzzies. Nerdy? Yes, but he didn't care. He was a well-paid nerd using his skills for a purpose, and that was more than most could say. The message confirmed that these skills were still intact—that all those hours in the biohazard suit were not suffered in vain.

He scrolled through the summary report. The good news was that all the samples contained identical viral DNA, which meant the dead pilot, the live baby gorilla, and the dead adult gorillas were all infected with the same thing. That was about as good as it got in terms of confirming zoonotic transmission between the gorillas and the woman.

Viral Identification.

Travis frowned. This was where the machine took a stab at figuring out what exactly it was dealing with. It compared its own sample results with an online database made up of thousands of already-mapped pathogen genomes. Normally there was an easy match, and he could call it a day. Maybe a few mutations here and there in some of the less important genes, but nothing to write home about.

But this was different.

Instead of showing the exact species and strain that the samples matched most closely, the report only listed the much larger genus name, *Orthopoxvirus.* This was like searching for the newest thriller by James Rollins on Amazon and getting a results page that showed every book ever written by an author with the first name James. Not so helpful.

Time to dig in a little further. A few more clicks brought him to the page he was looking for.

Travis brought both hands to his mouth, elbows leaning on the desk in front of him. *This is weird.* On one line, the report showed a 99.9 percent DNA match with an old monkeypox sample that had been isolated from a sick child during an outbreak in the Congo way back in the nineties. Right, that's what they expected.

But the next line told a different story.

VARV: 99.1%

Variola virus. The causative agent of smallpox.

Travis pushed away from his desk and exhaled slowly. He picked up the phone.

"Bill, you're gonna want to see this."

VIRUNGA NATIONAL PARK
2:01 P.M.

H ear that?" Jake Russell kept his voice to a barely audible whisper. "Voices—on the road."

"Yup," Mikey said. "Guys said they concealed our route, but of course that doesn't mean much when our friendlies here keep traipsing back and forth for no good reason." The Special Forces sergeant glared at the small group of Congolese soldiers sitting in plain view on a nearby log.

They weren't exactly the cream of the crop, that was true. But they would have to do. American troops were not allowed to engage the enemy by themselves here in the DRC, or anywhere in Africa for that matter. So instead they got to babysit these scared shitless city boys from Kinshasa who had never set foot in the jungle and wanted nothing to do with Joseph Kony or the LRA. These particular soldiers had volunteered, or rather been volun-told, for the mission by their commanding officer the night before. Unlucky for them. After a couple hours' frenzied planning and coordination, the whole group had started into the park. Virunga, oldest national park in Africa, and one of the biggest, too.

Unfortunately, there wasn't much chance to enjoy the scenery. They bumped along through the night packed like sardines in the back of two old logging trucks, barely able to breath under heavy tarps and accumulating more bruises than any of them had managed to collect in jump school. Fun times. When they finally reached the drop-off point, there was only an hour of darkness left. Not much time to cover almost five miles, especially since they were fully kitted up in combat gear, but they managed. When the first rays of sun began filtering through the trees, they were safely hunkered down just three hundred yards outside the camp.

Rico looked across his handler's body in the direction of the voices, ears up and an intense interest in his eyes. Poor dog, he'd been waiting a long time to see some action. But this was not the time, not yet at least. The operation would start at dusk with an admittedly risky infiltration attempt, but the actual assault, and Rico's chance at getting his teeth dirty, wouldn't come until the camp had settled down during the quiet hours after midnight.

"They're coming closer," Mikey whispered into his throat mic. "Stay quiet, stay covered. No confrontation here."

The rest of the team was already concealed in the underbrush, arranged in a staggered diamond formation over about fifty yards. Every angle of approach covered. Jake sat up on one knee and signaled to the Congolese soldiers. They were equipped with the same high-speed earbud radios as his own guys but apparently didn't see the need to keep them in their ears. Maybe because that made it too hard to shoot the shit with the guy sitting next to you? Jake tried not to be overly critical—"tried" being the key word. Finally, they saw him.

"Get down and stay quiet," he whispered. "Don't let these guys find us."

The one English speaker said something to the others in French, and they all dropped down into the vegetation. *Thank you.* They really weren't so bad to work with. Just untrained and undisciplined. Send those two motivated ones back to Bragg for the Q Course and they'd do just fine. No doubt about that. Unfortunately, they didn't have six months to spare, and tonight's rescue mission would require a flawless performance. Jake hoped they had it in them.

A MINUTE PASSED. The unseen animal life that had been providing a steady soundtrack through most of the day went silent. Then a high-pitched shriek tore through the heavy air from somewhere high in the canopy. A bird? Monkey? Either way, something didn't like what it saw down below. Military working monkeys. MWMs. That's what he needed in a place like this. Dogs had their place, sure, but they were totally out of their element here in the rainforest of central Africa. He'd have to ask Cole about it, if they got him out of there alive tonight.

Not if. When.

A cough—a loud one—sounded from where Jake knew the Congolese soldiers were hiding. Seriously, now? Then another, followed by a whole series of them. *Shit. Here goes nothing.* The voices started up again, men shouting, and then the sound of leaves and branches breaking.

"Sir," a voice came over the radio. "Request permission to apprehend target now."

"Roger, go for it." Jake brought one leg up, ready to move. "Remember, no weapons." Their compact MP5 submachine guns were equipped with silencers, but he wanted to avoid casualties at all cost. Even enemy wounded required medical care, and that would probably mean aborting the mission.

In an instant, the forest came alive. Jake jumped up, rifle at his eye. He and Mikey made up the center of the diamond, and they would cover the other ten men.

There. Fifty feet away.

Three of his guys were tearing through the underbrush, converging on what looked to be just two armed men in olive fatigues. A fourth appeared behind them, diving across the final distance to hit one of the combatants squarely across the back.

It was over in seconds.

No shots fired.

"Nice work," Jake said, arriving on the scene. This was what his team was trained to do. Elite warriors of the twenty-first century.

"They'd better hold still if they know what's best for them." Mikey gave Rico a generous lead, and the dog leapt between the two men, his vigorous sniffing only interrupted by an occasional low growl.

"I'm just glad it's not me," Jake said. "I'd be shitting myself right about now."

The captives didn't resist as the team finished securing zip-ties, gags, and hoods.

"Now what?" Mikey pulled Rico away.

"We're not going to let them go, that's all I know." Jake crouched down beside one of the men. "I have no desire to reenact *Lone Survivor* out here."

"I think we'd all agree on that, sir." Sergeant Eric Olmsted was one of his EOD techs—explosive ordnance disposal experts—a fresh-faced twenty-three-year-old out of Maine. Good guy to have around.

"You the one who made that flying tackle?"

"Might have been," Olmsted answered, a ridiculous grin plastered across his face. "They made it too easy."

"And we're sure there's just the two of them?" Jake looked around. This was not the time to get complacent.

"Rest of the team is out hunting," Mikey said. "They'll let us know."

BACK IN POSITION. The two prisoners were laid out on their backs, right between Jake and Mikey, with Rico keeping a close watch. The dog seemed to revel in his new assignment. He sat up straight, mouth closed, eyes flicking from one man to the next. Every time one of them dared to readjust or let a moan slip from his gagged mouth, Rico responded with a quick snarl. Maybe he was somewhat useful out here in the jungle after all.

"So what do you think?" Jake said. "Stick with the plan?"

"Hell yes." Mikey took a long suck from his CamelBak. "Bump in the road, that's all that was."

"Still, gotta hate it when things don't go just like they're supposed to."

"Sir, mind if I tell you something?"

"Preach on."

"That's just the nature of our game. We make a plan, sure. But we're prepared for every contingency. You'd do well to stop expecting things to go our way every time."

"I know, you're right." And he was. Mike Denison had deployed ten times in as many years. He was the kind of guy you knew you had to listen to. "Thanks man."

"Just doing my job. That's what I'm here for." The master sergeant reached up to press a button at his neck and lowered his head. "Radio check. All clear out there?"

One by one, the rest of the team called in. Nothing to report. Jake hoped no one would start missing these two rebel fighters. From what he knew about the LRA, they were used to traveling in independent groups of twos and threes, even blending into the local communities, until the time came for an actual raid. Best-case scenario was that these two had been return-ing to the camp unexpected after an absence. They'd been searched, more thoroughly than they probably would have liked, and didn't even have a mobile phone between them.

"Might as well get this thing called in while we can," Jake said. "Will you get the boss on the line?"

"Sure thing." Mikey pulled the satellite phone out of its case and dialed up a series of numbers. "All yours."

"Sir, Jake Russell here." He sat up a little straighter. It was ingrained, that reaction. He just couldn't report to a senior officer, full-bird colonel, no less, without feeling the nervous tension leftover from all those years of training.

"Jake." The colonel's rough voice came through his earbud clearly. "I was wondering when we'd hear from you."

"Sorry about that. I know I'm late on the call."

"What's happening over there? We're getting all kinds of images from the Global Hawk above you, but not a lot to report on this end. Still no sign of our guys in the camp."

"We've had some excitement, actually. Tied us up for a few minutes."

"Go on."

"Two armed combatants came off the forest track and discovered our position." Jake's hands were sweating. He knew he would take some crap for that.

"How in the hell?"

"My fault, sir. Didn't control our host nation soldiers as well as I should have." No reason to go into the details.

"I assume they've been neutralized?"

"Roger. Right beside me here, if you'd like to say hello?"

"I'll pass." Colonel Alsina's steady tone was tough to read. "Any wounded?"

"Negative. My guys are hot shit." He knew that would be good for a chuckle, at least, and he was right.

"You've got me to thank for that, Captain. I knew they'd have to make up for your deficiencies." Now Jake could hear the smile in his boss's voice.

"Ain't that the truth."

"So you're still on for tonight then? I assume you'll just lay low with those prisoners?"

"Roger, that's the plan. We'll send our two high speed Congolese into the camp just before sunset—see what they can do for us in terms of intel."

"And then the snatch and grab later on."

"Exactly. Quick and dirty. We'll be in and out of there before these sleeping terrorists know any better."

"That's the goal, at least." At the colonel's words, Jake saw Mikey look up and give him a nod. He was listening in to the conversation on his own headset. Expect success, but plan for failure. Of course he was right. "But Jake, you know this is a risky mission. Be smart and think on your feet. I had to pull some strings to keep JSOC from stealing this one."

"Thank you, sir. We won't let you down."

"The Ospreys are already on standby at Entebbe, ready to fly whenever you give the word."

"Roger." The CV-22 Ospreys had only recently joined the hunt. They were heavy-duty armed transport aircraft—futuristic hybrids between a helicopter and a regular plane—complete with their own Air Force special ops crews on loan from Uncle Sam. "Any more intel on our man Kony?"

"No, best we can tell he's not around. If you're lucky enough to find yourself in that position, though, you know the rules—grab if you can, shoot if you must."

"Will do." Jake looked over at Mikey, who was making little circles in the air with a gloved index finger. *Time to wrap things up.* "Okay sir, I'm out for now."

"Hang on, Jake, just opening up a high side message now, looks like it might be relevant." The high side was military-speak for a secure classified network. Usually meant something important. There was a pause. "Yeah."

And another one. "Shit."

"Sir?"

"Change of plans."

ATLANTA
7:55 A.M.

If Travis was right, all hell was about to break loose.

Bill Shackleton hit the elevator call button for the third time, watching as the numbers above the closed doors kept climbing in the wrong direction. *Crap.* He didn't have time for this. The tall director of Viral Special Pathogens turned quickly and half jogged to the stairwell entrance. Four floors down, deep into the soggy Georgian clay. He took the stairs two, sometimes three, at a time, wincing all the way. The bad knee was getting worse every year, but he was still a long way from being convinced that a joint replacement would do him any good.

Finally, basement level B4. He stopped for a second before opening the door. No need to sound any alarms yet. A few early risers were settling into their cubicles as he strode down the open hall. Pleasant nods and even a couple good mornings—just another day at the CDC. Shackleton knocked once on Travis's office, hand already turning the doorknob.

"That was fast." Travis looked up from his monitor and pushed away from the desk. "Grab that chair and have a look."

"I may have exceeded the speed limit once or twice," Bill said, sitting down beside his hotshot molecular virologist. "Just one of many sacrifices I make in the interest of national security."

"Right. Well there may be plenty more opportunities for that kind of thing over the next few days."

Shackleton pulled his reading glasses out of a front chest pocket. He wouldn't start wearing those all the time until he really needed to, either. "Show me what you've got."

"This is what first tipped me off," Travis said, pointing to a box on the screen. Shackleton hadn't done much work on the new sequencing machines himself, but he recognized the interface. "Those are the percentages of matching nucleotide sequences, comparing our samples with both the monkeypox and smallpox viruses."

Shackleton turned to look at Travis. "This would be a great time to come clean."

"Huh?"

"Come on, just tell me this is all some kind of drill. You know, test the system, keep the boss on his toes, that kind of thing?"

"I wish I could, sir." Travis held his gaze easily, and Shackleton instantly knew he was telling the truth. "I really do."

"Okay, so how does this happen?" Time to figure this thing out. "Some kind of contamination, maybe?"

"With variola virus?" Travis raised his eyebrows. "You of all people should know that's supposed to be impossible around here."

Shackleton was one of only three people in the world with access to the CDC's deep-frozen stock of old smallpox scabs. And he knew the vaults hadn't been touched in years.

"What about natural contamination?" the director asked. "Any chance there's been a little pocket of transmission going on there in the Congo, posing as monkeypox all these years?"

"Faking out the scientific community for forty years?" Travis clicked through a couple of pages on the screen. "Don't think so. And that's not what we're looking at, anyway."

"What's this?" Shackleton moved closer to the screen, trying to interpret a series of nucleotide sequences labeled with different percentages.

"The intact variola virus is not actually in our samples."

"Then how do you explain the fact that the machine found 99.1% of its DNA?"

"I know it looks like that initially, but the number is misleading. You remember that the central genome of every orthopox virus is highly conserved across species."

"Is that a question?" Shackleton didn't like being talked down to but appreciated the reminder. "Of course I remember."

"Which means the smallpox and monkeypox viruses already share a large percentage of their genes. The only real differences come at the more variable ends of the genome."

"The areas that determine host range, transmissibility, and pathogenicity." It was coming back to Shackleton now. Very small differences in some of these genes had big effects on which types of animals any given virus could infect, how easily it spread between them, and the severity of the disease it caused. The monkeypox virus had a wide host range and was capable of infecting all sorts of rodents and primates, including humans. But it wasn't as contagious and didn't kill very many of its victims. Smallpox, on the other hand, could only infect humans, and it was deadly. His role as a caretaker of this ancient scourge of humankind was not something Shackleton took lightly.

"Exactly," Travis said. "So even though our samples contain 99.1% of the variola genome, we really only have a few extra genes tagged onto a regular monkeypox virus."

"Tagged on. Meaning—"

"Spliced in. That's what these sequences are." Travis pointed at the screen. "Intact smallpox genes, very obviously transplanted right into a monkeypox virus."

Shackleton stared at the long string of letters running across the screen. *Obviously, of course.* But he trusted Travis—he had to. T, A, G, and C. The letters would be meaningless to the vast majority of the population, infinite combinations of gibberish that in reality represented the building blocks of life: thymine, adenine, guanine, cytosine. Or death, as the case might be.

"The entire genome of this hybrid, or chimera, is just a little longer than either of its sources. Somehow, its designer figured out how to add in these genes without messing up the basic structure and function of the virus."

"And would that be easy to do?" Shackleton wiped a drop of sweat from his forehead.

"No, but with enough time for plenty of trial and error, combined with the right equipment, it's well within the capabilities of any halfway decent molecular biology lab."

"Problem is, there are only supposed to be—"

"—two labs in the world with access to the smallpox virus." Travis shook his head. "Trust me, I know."

"Us here, and the Russians, at VECTOR."

"You really think they could be behind this?"

"No, I don't." There was no way. The Russians had been showing plenty of bravado recently, this was true, but the intentional release of a genetically engineered superpox virus? That was a stretch.

"Then who?"

Shackleton stood up. He needed to go—start making calls. His hand was on the doorknob when it hit him. A terrible thought, starting small but immediately bursting out with violent clarity, quickly obscuring every other possibility.

"Travis." This was going to be hard, but Shackleton knew it was his own fault. Why in the world had he authorized her, of all people, to fly across the world with this plague? "What do you know about Leila's family?"

"Sir?" The younger scientist looked up at him, confusion written across the lines of his forehead.

"Her family, what has she told you?"

"They're Persian, live in Tehran. She doesn't say much more than that."

"You know her dad is in government? Farrukh Torabi, head of their nuclear programs, of all things. And her brother, he's a molecular biologist, like you."

"No." Travis started shaking his head.

"The brother trained at Harvard years ago, but totally off the grid ever since. Did Leila ever tell you how hard it was to get her clearance approved?"

"No way." Travis moved his clenched hands under the desk. "Her mom is dying."

"Maybe. Odd timing, though, isn't it?"

"That wouldn't make any sense, even if—"

"Did she say anything to you at the airport last night? Any indication that something wasn't quite right?"

Travis's eyes dropped. He couldn't have been clearer.

A buzz in Shackleton's pocket broke the tension.

"Bill here," he said, phone to his ear.

"Bill, it's Jen." Jen Vincent, his boss and director of the Division of High-Consequence Pathogens and Pathology. "I just got a call from someone at the National Security Agency. How soon can you get in here?"

"I'm downstairs—give me three minutes," Shackleton said, opening the door. "You're not the only one with bad news this morning."

Any luck?" Morgan Andrews walked into a dimly lit room full of glowing monitors. Her big break on the overnight shift had kept her running all over the NSA's massive campus ever since.

"Yep, looks like her flight landed at Amsterdam Schiphol early this morning, right on time." Rajiv Kumar had gone through initial orientation with her and was a magician when it came to following suspicious people around the world.

"And on to Tehran from there, right?" Morgan had called him up on a whim after receiving the CDC's surprising message an hour earlier. *They really think this Epidemic Intelligence Service officer has gone rogue?* At this point, anything was possible. She'd been given free reign to start tracking down every possible lead that might help connect the dots and shed more light on the night's intercepted conversation between Kinshasa and Tehran.

Rajiv pushed away from the desk and looked up at her. "Well hang on, don't you want to see how she spent the layover in Amsterdam?"

"At the airport, you mean?"

"Yeah, I was just starting to track her from the arrival gate when you came in."

"Track her," Morgan said. "You're serious?"

"You doubt me?" An exaggerated wounded expression appeared briefly on Rajiv's face. "Let me show you."

A high-definition image of a crowded airport scene appeared on one of the screens in front of them. Rajiv drew a quick circle with a finger on the trackpad in his hands, and a white circle appeared on the screen.

"That's your girl, Leila Torabi, just getting off the flight from Atlanta."

The image quality was good enough for Morgan to see that he was right. She'd already gone through the background check and clearance documents required for Dr. Torabi's work at the CDC, and she recognized the woman's regal face and short dark hair.

"Now watch." Rajiv tapped the keyboard, and the image started moving. For some reason, Morgan hadn't realized it was a video, but of course it would be. Security cameras were everywhere in a big international airport like this, and the Netherlands was a close ally of the U.S. in the global war on terror. She leaned a hand against the desk, watching as the doctor's petite form moved across the screen, leaving the busy gate area and almost getting lost among the masses of fellow travelers heading down a wide hall.

"Pretty cool." Morgan stood back up. "But can you find her again?"

"Ha, you have no idea. After I confirmed her identity using that first shot, our facial recognition system kicks into high gear."

"Meaning..."

"We can follow her every step until she gets on that next plane." Rajiv smiled up at her. She knew he'd nurtured a hopeless crush on her all through their orientation, but that was three years ago now. *Please tell me he's not just doing this to impress me.* "It should be done patching all the clips together now, if you have a second."

Morgan wasn't sure that she did, and she also didn't want to provide any encouragement in the romance department. She was scheduled to brief her section head in just twenty minutes, and all she really wanted to know was if the doctor actually got on the flight to Tehran.

"Sounds amazing, but I've got to run. She did make it on the next flight, right?"

"Definitely." Rajiv sounded hurt again. "Already confirmed that from the airline's passenger manifest."

"Awesome," Morgan said over her shoulder. She felt bad, but now it was time to focus on the essentials. This was her moment to shine.

An elevator was waiting for her down the hall. She hit the top floor and held down the *Door Close* button.

"Morgan!" A hand shot between the closing panels. Rajiv stood there panting, like he'd just sprinted down to catch her. She hoped he wasn't really that desperate. "Was Leila Torabi supposed to meet anyone in Amsterdam?"

Phew. Work—not play—that was a good thing. "Not that I know of." She thought about it. "No, probably not."

"Because I just watched her have a long conversation over coffee with someone at the airport."

"Someone?"

"A man, looks to be of Middle Eastern descent."

Morgan took a deep breath. This was probably worth few minutes, after all. She stepped out of the elevator. "Okay, show me what you've got."

IT WAS STILL her, there was no doubt in Morgan's mind. The woman had been browsing the displays of a flower shop for several minutes when she suddenly picked up her bag and strode purposefully across the walkway. Outside a Starbucks, she greeted a man who indeed looked the part—dark face and beard, along with some sort of headdress that screamed *terrorist*. Morgan had finally come to accept the National Security Agency's undisputed title as global champion of racial and religious profiling. No reason to make their job more difficult than it already was.

"So what do you think?" Rajiv didn't seem to be holding it against her.

"You're totally right," she said softly. "More than a little concerning."

"Look, they're leaving Starbucks together."

They watched as the pair of travelers moved through the airport. It was clear that they were still talking to each other as they walked, but now every pause and gesture seemed to carry a greater weight.

"Why does she keep looking behind her?" Morgan said.

"I was just thinking the same thing. It's almost like she's afraid of being followed."

"And did you notice he doesn't have a carry-on? Strange for an international traveler."

Morgan looked at her watch. Five minutes until the meeting.

"Look at that," Rajiv said, pausing the video.

The image showed the pair standing against a strange-looking wall, with the man pulling something out of his pocket. *What in the world?* Then it hit her.

"Storage lockers," she said.

"Yep."

He started the video again. The man pulled a suitcase out of the locker and bent over it. The CDC physician was next to him, messing with something in her briefcase.

"You can stop it there." Morgan had seen enough. "We need to call this in right now."

"YES, SIR." MORGAN hoped she didn't sound as nervous as she felt. Her supervisor had passed her on to his own boss, who proceeded to put her through directly to General Charles Howard, national security advisor to the president. "This is Morgan Andrews, intelligence analyst with the NSA."

"Ms. Andrews, I've just seen the footage. Quite impressive."

"I can't take credit for—"

"Don't be modest. Are you one hundred percent sure that this woman is Dr. Leila Torabi from the CDC?"

"One hundred percent, sir."

"Then we're going to call the airport, hold her there in Amsterdam. Great catch on this."

"Sir, we're a few hours too late."

"Too late?"

"That video wasn't from a live feed." He didn't know? Morgan felt her heart race. "Our target landed in Tehran ten minutes ago."

The Azadi Tower. Leila Torabi peered through a grimy cab window at the giant white marble structure looming ominously over a wide expanse of manicured green lawn. It was the first real vegetation she'd seen since they left the airport. She reached up to adjust the *hijab*'s thin fabric pressing into her forehead. One duty free shop in Amsterdam had clearly embraced its role of supplying headscarves to all the imminently repressed women heading for the Muslim world, and Leila picked up a plain-looking three-pack in the *rusari* style.

"You know the Azadi Tower?" The driver spoke Farsi, but she could tell he was suspicious. Why was this woman in Western dress traveling alone in Tehran? The black sedan behind them probably had something to do with his wary looks, too. "Built in 1973 to celebrate the 2500th anniversary of the Persian Empire. Very nice museum inside."

Azadi was the Farsi word for freedom. Leila bit down hard on the inside of her cheek. *If only.* She hadn't been back to Iran in almost fifteen years, all in the pursuit of this shadowy ideal. Freedom. Was it really worth everything she'd given up?

The rest of the drive was a blur of drab buildings and crowded streets. There were pretty parts of Tehran, she knew that. But this was not one of them. The cab slowed, and Leila caught sight of a large white sign proudly identifying her destination. The sprawling brick campus of the Imam Khomeini Hospital Complex took up several city blocks.

"Which entrance do you need?" The cab crept along with a line of cars approaching the hospital.

"I didn't know there was more than one," Leila said. "My mother is at the Cancer Research Center." That would give him something to tell those guys in the sedan, at least.

"You should have said so—it's on the other side." He tapped twice on the horn and pulled back out into the road. Leila caught his glance in the rearview mirror. "She will be glad to see you."

"Sorry?"

"Your mother. She must be happy that you have come home."

Leila blinked back unwelcome tears. "Hope so."

THE WARMTH OF the summer evening surprised her. Tehran was a cold and barren place in her memories. She knew this was simply because most of her childhood trips home had been during the winter, but Leila still had a hard time reconciling this hardened vision with the reality now before her. She climbed a set of stairs and paused outside a more modern glassed foyer. *Here goes.*

"I'm here to see a patient, Yasmin Torabi."

The man at the reception desk looked past her to the two men in dark suits she knew were standing conspicuously just outside the entrance. The corners of his thin lips turned downward. "You are alone?"

"Yes."

His fingers moved quickly on an ancient keyboard across the desk. For all its external grandeur and proud proclamations of collaboration with a variety of European universities, the research center had clearly been short on funding for more than a few years. That would be hard for Maman, always the self-proclaimed sophisticate and proud global citizen. Paris, New York, Tokyo, and now this, her final vigil, in an outdated hospital of the world's pariah state.

"Fourth floor. Room 415." The man stared at her, his bushy graying eyebrows raised. "You are a friend? She also has other visitors."

"I'm her daughter." She stepped away and turned towards the single elevator just visible through a doorway. "Thank you."

THE STERILE SMELL of sanitizing chemicals hit her nose sharply as the elevator opened on the fourth floor. It was a familiar relief. Leila had spent time in hospitals all over the world during med school and residency—another benefit of the American passport—and this artificiality was much preferable to the more natural odors wafting through many of those overcrowded wards.

A young woman in pressed blue scrubs sat at a long desk just opposite the elevator. The charge nurse.

"Can I help you?" Again, the curious, prying eyes. How did they all know, so immediately, so instinctively, that there was something different about her? Was her fifteen-year absence really that transparent? Leila had made a concerted effort to stay away from nosy Persian-American communities over the years—to do away with anything that might identify her with the family and country she'd rejected so completely—and now she could see that her efforts had been successful.

"I'm here to see my mother, Yasmin Torabi."

The woman inhaled quickly, her wide eyes glancing down the hall.

No. Leila tasted vomit in the back of her throat. She followed the woman's look and saw a small group of people leaving one of the rooms. Maman.

"Excuse me," Leila managed to mutter, already walking in their direction.

"Wait!" The nurse's shrill voice rang out behind her. "You can't—"

Leila followed the numbers. 407. 409.

A female doctor reached for her arm, but she pulled away.

411.

And then she saw him. Baba. He was outside the room, talking quietly with a man she didn't know.

413.

He looked up and met her eyes. In that first instant, his face seemed more fragile than she'd ever seen it.

415.

She was there, standing next to him.

"Baba."

In the pause that followed, she saw a hundred internal debates playing on repeat over a thousand sleepless nights, all coming to a climax deep within his piercing eyes. This was their only chance.

His mouth tightened, followed by a quick, almost involuntary jerk of his head to the side.

"No," he said, straightening up and looking back into the room. "No."

The simplest of words, and yet it meant so many different things in that instant.

And he moved past her down the hall.

"Maman!" Leila choked on the word as she flew through the open doorway. "Where is she?"

There were others in the room, crowded around a simple hospital bed, and they stared at her silently. Even after fifteen years, she instantly knew their faces. Uncles, aunts, cousins, and there, at the head of the bed, was her brother, Sohrab. But none of them mattered now. The only one she cared about was stretched out on the sheets, unmoving, her beautiful wilted face already frozen in what every physician would immediately recognize as the deceptive peace of the newly dead.

"No, Maman." She sobbed, pushing in beside her brother and stroking a cool wrinkled cheek before finally lowering her face into the crook of her mother's frail arm. "I'm sorry."

B ill Shackleton dug through the dark leather briefcase at his feet for a pair of Ray-Bans. Relief. It was bright out there. Bright, hot, and humid, now that the last rains trailing behind the hurricane had made their exit. He stared out at the wall of lush green summer foliage pressing in along both sides of the highway. The park-like setting made it hard to believe they were just minutes outside the nation's capital.

"You know Ken Alibek?" Colonel Sam Simmons had been talking almost non-stop since picking him up at Baltimore-Washington International Airport half an hour earlier. "Russian guy, mostly does his own consulting these days."

"Not personally," Shackleton said. "But I know his story, yes."

"Then you probably see where I'm going with this."

Shackleton leaned back into his seat as the USAMRIID commander stepped on the gas and pulled the wheel left, easily passing an old minivan with Missouri plates. The new Audi R8 GT purred contentedly. A pre-retirement gift to himself, Simmons had said. After thirty years in the Army, he was finally scheduled to take off the uniform next month. And then this, the unlikely event his Research Institute for Infectious Diseases had been preparing for since it first came into being almost fifty years earlier.

"Yeah," Shackleton replied. "And now I'm afraid he was right."

Ken Alibek, formerly Colonel Kanat Alibekov, was a Kazak military scientist who defected from the USSR in the early nineties, bringing with him a treasure trove of information on the secret Soviet biological weapons program. There were doubters, though, and Shackleton himself had always wondered if some of the man's reports might have been exaggerated for the benefit of his overzealous debriefing interrogators. Alibek claimed that the Russians had been experimenting with weaponized smallpox all along, producing huge quantities of aerosolized virus capable of being loaded into a warhead and sent across the Pacific. Not just smallpox, but Ebola, Marburg, and anthrax too. It was every infectious disease scientist's worst nightmare, and even more so for Shackleton and Simmons, charged as they were with protecting their country from superbugs like these.

"Long as we're on the same page for this afternoon's briefing, then," Simmons said.

"Unfortunately, yes." Shackleton looked back out the window just in time to see a large blue sign towering over the narrowing highway. *Welcome to Washington, D.C.* It marked a change in scenery as well, the thick Maryland forest replaced by a grungy industrial area.

"Sorry," Simmons said. "Not the prettiest route into the city this way, but it'll get us to the White House in fifteen minutes flat."

Shackleton glanced at his watch. "Should be right on time."

"Why don't you start us off, Bill. How about a two minute summary of what you found in those samples this morning." The president looked at him intently. *Bill.* So now he and the POTUS were on a first-name basis? That relationship probably only went one way. He'd heard that President Rogers was unique in this regard—he liked to get his information directly from the source. But it was still surprising when he got the call that morning. *The President wants you up here ASAP.* Not his boss, or his boss's boss? Hell, it really should be the Secretary of Health and Human Services herself giving this briefing. But no, the president wanted to hear it straight from the horse's mouth, and that's how he found himself sitting at a long mahogany table in the White House Situation Room.

"Well sir, I really only need about thirty seconds." The president raised his eyebrows. "We analyzed a variety of gorilla and human tissue samples from this outbreak in the Congo, and they all revealed infection with the same chimera pox virus."

"Chimera?" The president leaned in, elbows on the table. "What exactly do you mean by that?"

"It's basically a monkeypox virus that has been artificially manipulated with the addition of a number of smallpox genes." There it was, the simple truth that would change everything. "A single organism created from two genetically distinct sources."

"I hope," a hard voice said from the other end of the table, "you've selected those words carefully."

It took Shackleton a second to identify its source. Retired General Charles Howard—the new national security advisor. He looked just as mean in person as he always did on TV. Shackleton tried to contain a nervous smile.

"What he means," the president said, "is that this allegation has serious implications for all of us."

"Trust me, Mr. President," Shackleton said. "Those implications have been clear to me from the very beginning. My team is running the virus through another sequencing machine now, just to confirm what we've already seen. And Colonel Simmons here has his folks at USAMRIID doing the same thing." He'd handed off the samples to the colonel's deputy at the airport in Baltimore.

"How can you be so sure that this is a manmade virus?" the president asked. "Don't these things happen in nature all the time? Seems like a day doesn't pass without your type sending up another briefing about some hybrid new bird flu."

Shackleton paused. How to explain these fairly high-level molecular biology and genetics concepts in this context?

Colonel Simmons jumped in just as he was about to start talking. "Sir, as you know, the smallpox virus is only supposed to exist in two places in the world: Bill's lab at the CDC, and Russia's VECTOR lab."

"That's what I've been told."

"The gene sequences that Bill's team identified this morning—they're smallpox genes. Previously mapped, recognized the world over as such. So in order for these genes to find themselves within a Congolese monkeypox virus, they first have to get to the Congo. That's a long way to go for a lonely little virus, all the way from either Atlanta or Siberia. Yes, there are a few small changes in the coding sequences, but we believe those are also artificial modifications, developed in a lab specifically to cause the extreme behavior we've already seen in the chimera virus."

"Like?" General Howard again.

Simmons continued, "Short incubation period for one. Natural monkeypox viruses need almost two weeks from the time of infection to the first signs of disease. And the increased mortality rate, of course. Based on the initial rough data coming out of the hospital in Goma, we're talking about over ninety percent of victims dead within three days."

"But how do we know," President Rogers said, "these changes are not just natural mutations of a free-living monkeypox virus?"

"I wish that were the case, sir. I really do." Shackleton was impressed—the president had all the right questions. "First, viruses with this combination of characteristics simply don't occur in nature. They would burn through their host populations too quickly. Once the last victims died, what's the virus going to do next? No, they have to leave enough survivors to allow continuous reproduction and transmission over time."

"Just because it's rare," General Howard said, "doesn't make it impossible."

"True." Shackleton turned to look him straight in the eye. Time to pull out the trump card. "But there's something else. People have been playing around with the DNA of viruses and bacteria for a few decades now, long enough that the scientific community has come up with a bunch of generally accepted rules governing how we do things. There's also a whole toolbox of commercially available products that make the work of splicing and dicing these genes a lot easier than you might expect."

"And that means what?"

Shackleton could see the impatience written across the national security advisor's face. "It means that when we see certain sequences of nucleotides—the building blocks of DNA—at the start and end of a given gene, we know that it was inserted into that genome artificially. Kind of like a signature for whichever method of molecular manipulation is being used." He paused. Had he lost them? "Now, if I were going to create my own biological weapon, I might choose to get rid of those signature sequences— make my genome look a little more natural. But that's not the case here."

The President spoke again. "The sequences are still there?"

"Exactly," Colonel Simmons answered. "This superpox virus was created by someone who knows enough to be dangerous, but isn't exactly on the cutting edge of the molecular biology community. The key piece of information for us is that they had access to some seriously nasty smallpox genes."

"And that brings us back to this morning's crazy phone call to Iran." Shackleton knew everyone in the room had already been briefed on the NSA intercept, probably before he was, but he wasn't sure if they had really put the pieces together yet. "If we accept the Congolese mining minister's allegation that this outbreak was somehow purposeful, started among the gorillas to clear the way for an Iranian mining project in Virunga National Park, that gives us a pretty clear culprit to point—"

"Dr. Shackleton," General Howard cut in. "While we appreciate your input as it relates to the virus itself, I think we're quite capable of addressing the higher-level national security implications on our own. Thank you both for coming this afternoon." He looked pointedly at Shackleton and Simmons, then to the door.

"Hang on, Chuck," the president said. "I'm not sure we're done with them yet. I still don't see how Iran could have gotten these smallpox genes, if that's what we're going to assume now. Does this mean Russia is tied up in the game as well?"

"Not necessarily." Shackleton tried not to glare at the national security advisor. Didn't he realize they were playing for the same team? "We do have a pretty good theory, a way to explain that piece without blaming the Russians, at least not directly."

"Go on."

"With the end of the Cold War and subsequent crash of the Russian economy, there were thousands of government scientists newly out of work—no way to support themselves or their families. Most of these scientists were former Biopreparat, employees of the USSR's massive biological weapons program." Shackleton paused. It was important that they understood this now, before any hawks like Howard started getting ideas about World War III. "So what do you think they did? A bunch immigrated to Europe and the U.S., that's true. But most of them have simply disappeared. It doesn't require much of a stretch to imagine that one hungry scientist may have made his way to Tehran, a tiny vial of weaponized smallpox hidden away in his briefcase."

"That's all it would take?" The president shook his head slowly.

"And now twenty years later, Iran decides it has a good reason to try out one of these bugs they've been playing around with. They're running out of yellowcake uranium and don't have any legal means of procuring more. *When the gorillas are gone, there will be no further objections to our project.* Isn't that what this government official said on the call we all heard?"

"Farrukh Torabi, Deputy Minister for Nuclear Energy." General Howard nodded. Maybe he'd finally stop being such a doubter. "It's a crazy story."

The president brought a hand to his forehead, pushing the fingers through thinning silver hair. "But it might be the best one we've got."

ANNA MCBRIDE HAD to force herself to keep from hovering outside the imposing double doors. The rest of the aides and interns lounged easily, taking advantage of the break to discuss Fourth of July plans or check their phones.

Not Anna. Her boss, Andrew Mills, was in there—so why wasn't she with him? Of course, he'd made some comment about the discussion being above her clearance level, but she thought it probably had more to do with her *personal interest* in the situation, as he'd put it so delicately. The news of Cole's capture had been hard to bear, sure, but the worst part was not being able to tell anyone else in the family—not even Chase. How keeping her in the dark was going to help anything, she didn't know. Right now, it was only making her even more stressed than she'd already been.

Cole, her invincible older brother, overpowered, probably wounded, and unable to escape from a remote jungle prison. She bit her lip. And here she was—just a few feet away from the people making decisions that could have life or death implications for him—yet totally powerless to have any impact on the outcome.

Anna wasn't used to feeling so helpless.

"You heard right," Shackleton said. "Her father, the very same Farrukh Torabi, was a grad student here at George Washington University when she was born. That was just before the hostage crisis and severing of diplomatic ties, so Leila has been an American citizen all along."

"Pretty nice cover, if she's really been playing for their side," General Howard said. "I just can't believe they really cleared her for this type of work, given that relationship."

"It seems obvious now—I realize that," Shackleton said. "But there was no reason for us to be suspicious, and I still have a hard time understanding how she could have been involved. Yes, it's odd that she's run off to Iran right at this moment, but—"

"And that she was observed collaborating with a known terrorist sympathizer," Howard said. "Yes, that's more than odd, I would argue."

"Who also happens to be a respected Syrian surgeon and former classmate of hers at Oxford," Shackleton said. That piece of intel had just come in as the meeting got underway.

"Which gives us all the more reason to question her motives from the start."

Shackleton knew Howard was right. Much as he hated to implicate one of his own, there was no way to get around the eyebrow-raising nature of Leila's recent activities. The buzz of a smartphone on the glass-topped table in front of the national security advisor interrupted the conversation. He glanced at it briefly, then turned to the president.

"Sir, your assault team is prepped and ready in Uganda, all set to move out on your command."

President Rogers didn't even bat an eye. "Let's do this."

L eila could use a drink. Not the hot milky tea in front of her, either. A real drink. She speared a dripping chunk of watermelon and brought it to her mouth. Refreshing, sure, but it would be so much better soaked in vodka. How in the world did Sohrab survive like this, year after year abstaining from the glorious ability to self-medicate through life's frustrations? They'd grown up side by side, enjoying the comfortable cosmopolitan existence of diplomats' children, but they might as well be living on different planets now.

Sohrab's tall form appeared through the back door again, and the only light in her parents' sprawling mansion went out. She'd been surprised to learn that he was living there too, but it made sense. They had moved in when Maman first got sick, his young wife insisting on taking care of her new mother-in-law by herself. The kids were already asleep when Leila arrived from the hospital that evening, and now she didn't know if she would even get to meet them.

"Still not home?" Leila asked as he walked up to the small patio table where she was sitting. The manicured gardens stretched out behind her, and the scent of jasmine hung heavy in the night air.

"No, he may not come at all. He's been spending a lot of nights away these last few months."

"And the other guys?"

"They're still here, out on the street." Sohrab sat in a chair across from her. "As long as you stay out of trouble, they won't give you any themselves."

"I thought you said Baba gave his blessing for my visit."

"He did." Sohrab lifted the delicate porcelain mug to his mouth and took a long sip. "But then he learned about your trip to Rwanda. Why did you bring those virus samples back to the States before beginning your journey here?"

"Excuse me?" Leila was confused. Why would Baba know or care about the outbreak? "I didn't know Maman was so close to the edge."

"I told you in my e-mail."

"And I thought there would be time. Of course I would have come straight here if I knew there was a chance I'd be too late."

"That's not it, Leila."

She felt his stare drilling straight through her eyes and into the back of her skull. Like she was supposed to know something else, as yet unspoken. The same look he used to give her years ago, unfairly accusing her of losing a favorite book, or later, at the Singapore International School, when he found out she was hooking up with that French boy.

"Yes, he was upset that you didn't arrive in time to say goodbye, fulfill her final wish. But that's not the real issue."

Leila shook her head. "You've lost me."

Sohrab leaned across the low table toward her. "I'm on your side. It will be better for both of us if we can speak freely."

"Speak freely? What do you think I'm doing?" She clenched her jaw. "I'm here because I wanted to say goodbye to my dying mother—maybe even start the healing process with the rest of our screwed up family. I have nothing to hide."

"And the virus?"

Even in the late-night silence of the shadowy garden, Sohrab's voice was barely audible.

"The virus is my job." She had to control the urge to shout. "That's it."

Her brother's questions were the last thing Leila had expected. She knew reconciliation wasn't going to be easy—maybe not even possible—but what did the week's nightmarish adventure in Rwanda have anything to do with it?

Sohrab's eyes had been locked on her own for what felt like an eternity, but now he dropped them and sat back into his chair. "You really don't know. I believe you."

"Thank you." Leila took a deep breath, willing her pounding heart to slow down. "Now what in the world are you talking about?"

He scooted his chair around the small table until he was right beside her, both of them facing the back of the darkened house. "You know I'm a microbiologist, yes?"

"I heard that much, at least," Leila said. "Can't believe Baba let you go off to Harvard, though, after putting up such a fight with me."

"He didn't have any reason to worry on my behalf. I was his faithful son." He took another slow sip of tea. "Still am, I think."

Leila looked at him questioningly. *You think?* She'd let it slide, for now. "So what do you work on?"

"I'm at a military lab outside the city. You wouldn't have heard of it. No one has."

"Following in Baba's footsteps, I guess?" She tried not to let the skepticism drip too heavily from her words, but she knew it was there.

"Something like that. The government is one of our only stable employers." Sohrab's face hardened. "It means I can provide for my family. But I know you don't understand that sentiment."

"I'm sorry." She really was. They were actually talking now—no reason to risk this baby step in the right direction. "Please, go on."

"We study biological weapons." He slowly stabbed a fork in and out of the last piece of watermelon on their little plate. "Defensive use only, just like at your own military labs." A pause. "That's what I thought, at least."

Leila followed his eyes back to the house and then out into the gardens around them. He was scared. Her big brother was scared of something, here at his own house.

"DO I REALLY want to hear this?" she said. "I mean, I appreciate your honesty, but I'm a doctor. Not a reporter. Or a spy."

"If you care about the oath you took to become a doctor, then yes, you want to hear this."

"Okay, but—"

"Just listen." She'd always hated when he said that. "The virus that killed those gorillas in the Congo—"

"Not just gorillas. A woman died in my arms, Sohrab, only two days ago."

"I created it." Her brother closed his eyes. One of his knees shook uncontrollably. "I've been working on it for years."

Leila stared at him, her mouth slightly open. She suddenly felt lightheaded, and grabbed for the edge of the table. "You created it."

"Crazy, I know." He looked up at her, then back over his shoulder again. "But I never thought it would see the light of day. It almost became a game, seeing how I could improve this composition with each new generation."

"Improve?" She could barely hear her own voice.

"Making it more contagious, giving it a shorter incubation period, generally increasing the efficiency with which it kills its victims. The virus is a lot hardier now, too. It can survive for hours in the environment after being dispersed in a simple aqueous base."

"Those don't sound like improvements to me."

"It hasn't all been successful, though. My current project is figuring out how to get around the pox vaccine's protective effects, but I'm not there yet."

"Thank God."

"Or Allah."

Leila snorted. "Right." Did he really still believe all that?

"But yes," Sohrab continued. "I agree with you on that, at least. Better that the vaccine is still effective, with an uncontrolled release like this."

"This vaccine is the only reason I'm not dying right now in front of you you," Leila said, rubbing the raised scar on her left shoulder. "I mean, we tried to be careful with the patient, but I'm sure I was exposed."

"And that was the idea. We wanted something that would spread fast through a population, impossible to stop without mass vaccination or the strictest of biosafety controls."

"But why monkeypox? If Iran wanted a biological weapon..."

She didn't realize how loud she was speaking until he put a finger to his lips and shook his head vigorously.

"I could be executed for telling you this," he said, even quieter than before. "And it's not only the monkeypox. The virus has changed over the years, picking up modified genes from a slightly more dangerous cousin. But your colleagues at the CDC have surely figured this out already?"

Leila lifted her phone off the table and shook it in front of him. "I wouldn't know." She hadn't been able to connect since turning it off on the plane in Amsterdam. "Are you telling me you've created some kind of hybrid, then? A viral chimera?"

He nodded. "I promise you, though, I thought it was for a doomsday scenario only. Your Americans put boots on the ground here in Tehran, something like that. We retaliate by releasing the virus in the States, or even just sending infected martyrs that direction."

"My Americans."

"Yes."

A light went on in the house, and Sohrab stood up. She'd never seen such terror in his flashing eyes.

"Wait," Leila said. "How did it get to the Congo? Why the gorillas?"

"You're better off asking Baba about that."

"Should I?"

"No."

"Then what?"

"Leila, what is Baba's position?"

"Okay..." Deputy Minister for Nuclear Energy. She still didn't see how it was related.

"And what is the biggest hurdle standing in the way of his success?"

Leila knew she should have stayed better informed about Iran's nuclear ambitions, but the topic usually fell into the conscious denial category with the rest of her family history. "Something about the centrifuges?"

He shook his head, clearly disappointed with her inability to make the connection. "Raw materials. We haven't had a legal source of uranium for decades."

And then Leila saw it, the whole messy story unfolding itself before her. The sour taste of vomit crept into the back of her mouth. Could her father really have been so shortsighted? To believe this was the best route to nuclear sovereignty?

"Sohrab, are you there?" Her sister-in-law's shrill voice cut through the night.

"We need to get you out of here," he whispered. "Before it's too late."

SATURDAY, JULY 3

Cole was still awake. Not because of the vicious mosquitos that wouldn't leave him alone, or the achy throbbing in his swollen hands. Annoying, sure, but nothing worse than he'd slept through before. No, he was awake because of the crazy story the FDLR captive had told them earlier in the day.

America.

This final piece of the puzzle only came out after even more persistent questioning, just minutes before Lukwiya returned to retrieve him. The captive's dying friend heard the two Arab tourists repeating the word to each other several times during their long trek up into the park to find the gorillas. When asked why they were so interested in America, all the men would say was that they were heading there next.

If true, and there was no good reason to doubt it, the story needed to be passed on to people who could act on it. Not buried here in the jungle.

He had to escape.

The camp had been quiet for at least an hour. Cole stood up and crept to the tent's opening a few feet away. A dark human form lay across the space. With most the camp sick now, this kid was all they could spare to guard him.

Bad decision. But then, they probably didn't think a white guy would be stupid enough to try anything alone out here in the jungle.

Cole watched him for several minutes. Definitely asleep. But how light a sleeper? He felt along the dirt floor at the inside edge of the tent. The afternoon's rain meant his fingers came up sticky with wet mud. *There we go.* A rock. He tossed it through the cool night air, right over the sleeping guard and against the side of an overturned plastic bucket about ten feet away.

The man stirred, his small black hand moving slightly against the stock of the old rifle held closely against his chest. But that was it. His eyes never opened. The breathing pattern didn't change.

Now or never.

Cole took one final look around the tent for anything that might come in handy. No such luck. They had taken his backpack, weapon, and even the KA-BAR Mark 2 holstered to his calf. Assholes. That seven-inch blade had been around the world and back with him. He scooped up a handful of the richly scented soil—so different from the hard-packed rangeland of the Wyoming prairies back home—and smoothed it over his face and arms. Within seconds, he was a different man, capable of melting into the night.

Cole lifted a leg high, extended it out well past the guard's free hand, and placed it toes first on the ground outside the tent. Not a sound. The other leg wasn't quite so easy, thanks to a cowardly kick to the knee from Lukwiya during his laughable attempt at interrogation the night before, but Cole still managed to lift it silently over his sleeping captor.

The moon was already low in the sky, but it still cast enough light to make things dangerous. Cole reached the shadow of another tent in three long strides. He inched around a corner, careful not to let his back brush against the canvas.

Now to get oriented.

He'd been blindfolded on his way through the camp the night before, so he had no frame of reference to work with. On one side, the tents opened up into what looked like a central gathering point. The other direction looked more promising—just a few rows of large tents, then a tall dark forest edge looming against the clear night sky. Easy enough to get that far, but what kind of perimeter fencing would be there? Not electrified, that much was obvious. Concertina wire? Tough to navigate, but nothing a few sutures couldn't mend.

But what about Innocence and the Danish doctor? Not an easy decision. Cole knew he'd have a better chance of successfully finding his way out of Virunga with the park ranger by his side. But the risks of going tent to tent looking for his fellow captives were too great. That would be a good way to get them all killed.

The tree line beckoned. Time to move.

Cole heard it before he took the first step. A dull thumping roar he'd recognize anywhere.

But he wasn't the only one.

A shout.

Change of plans.

And he hit the dirt.

"LET'S MOVE." CAPTAIN Jake Russell spoke softly into his throat mic. "Stay in the trees until I give the word."

It had been a long afternoon and evening, hiding out in the oppressive jungle while waiting for just this moment. Jake still couldn't believe that his little Kony-hunting expedition had blown up so quickly, first into a rescue mission and now a full-spectrum antiterrorism operation with global implications. Biological weapons from Iran, here in the Congo? There were some seriously messed up people out there. Not a surprise, that realization, but it did feel good to know that his team was about to play a key role in something way bigger than themselves.

He caught a glimpse of Mikey and Rico crawling through the understory about twenty yards ahead. His night vision goggles reflected their moving bodies in an eery yellow-green glow. Some of the guys were pissed that their role had shifted from primary assault force, but Jake was okay with letting the big guns go in first. At least for Rico, their new role monitoring the perimeter and preventing anyone from slipping away could end up being a lot more fun. Pity the fool who found himself on the wrong end of the dog's combat tracking experience and nasty bite. Maybe even Kony himself would do them the honor?

The Ospreys were close now, the sound increasing every second as their tilt-rotors shifted into an upright position to allow for stationary hovering. Shit was about to hit the fan.

COLE DID HIS best to burrow into the soft earth against the outside of the tent. The camp was quickly becoming a frenzied hive of activity. Much as he wanted to jump up and start shouting—*I'm here!*—his SERE school survival training was engrained too deeply to let him make that rookie mistake. Better to lay low, shelter in place, and wait for the rescuers to come to him.

A pair of skinny bare legs ran right by Cole's hiding spot, one foot landing just inches from his face. Would have been so easy to reach out and grab it, make quick work of the unsuspecting teenage rebel and come out with a weapon in his hands. But then what? It would only make him more likely to get shot in the coming chaos.

And chaos it was. Angry shouts of running men. A child's scream. More legs running past him in both directions. Crazed anticipation, but no real action yet.

A single shot rang out. Cole raised his head just slightly and saw the dark silhouette of a lone rebel, holding a rifle above his head with the muzzle pointed into the sky. *Good luck with that.* The shot was followed by a quick burst, faint pings of metal on metal just audible over the deafening roar of the Ospreys.

The response was instantaneous—a low growl emanating from the belly mounted mini-gun on the closest aircraft—and the foolish boy was cut down where he stood. It was like the earth rose up to swallow him, a cloud of soil and rock flying into the air with the impact of the 7.62-millimeter shells fired at over three-thousand rounds a minute.

And then the whole camp exploded around him. Blinding white light and deafening booms. Cole felt like someone hit the power button inside his head, and for a split second he worried that this was no rescue mission at all. They were blowing the whole place up, sanitizing the earth from the dual scourges of the virus and the Lord's Resistance Army. Even as the thought flew through his throbbing head, Cole knew he was wrong. *Flashbangs.* The

M84 stun grenades were the first and often only weapon used in this type of rapid nighttime assault, shocking surprised targets into submission with only the occasional burst eardrum to worry about afterward. They'd done wonders in the mud hovels of Afghanistan, often leaving a room full of militants wetting their pants and begging for mercy. Now on the receiving end of their simulated destruction for the first time, Cole could understand why the devices were so effective.

As his vision returned, he began to see the forms of his rescuers fast roping in from two hovering Ospreys. A true air assault. At the same time, an amplified male voice shouted from the heavens. "Lay down your weapons. You are outnumbered and outgunned. Get on the ground, face down, hands on your head." The voice spoke slowly and clearly, first in English, then French and something else. Maybe Acholi?

But it wasn't going to be that easy. Another set of legs ran by and then stopped. A man threw himself down against the same tent, just ten feet ahead of Cole's own position. The fighter set up his AK in front of him, aiming right into the main clearing where the Americans were still coming off the ropes. *Screw shelter in place.* Cole wasn't going to sit and watch his own guys get mowed down by this bastard. Not only that—any returning fire would have a good chance of taking Cole out too. He brought a leg up under himself and dove forward, one elbow coming down hard on the top of the fighter's head, while his other arm knocked the weapon from the man's unsuspecting hands.

The elbow wasn't enough. Cole's chest landed squarely on top of the fighter's back. He was shouting, trying to turn over, but Cole's combatives training—the Army's hybrid martial art loosely based on Brazilian Jiu-Jitzu—came back to him fast. Cole brought both hands up along the man's shirt, gripping the collar tightly and pulling it against the underside of his neck. Then a quick rotation of the wrists, and the pressure was on. The man kicked wildly for a couple seconds, then went limp. *To kill or not to kill?* Cole let go. This kid was not the real enemy.

The sound of the Ospreys faded a bit as they moved up to a higher altitude. Time to let the guys on the ground do their thing.

And then a voice—a good southern American voice—rang out behind him. "Think I found our guy!"

IT WAS REALLY happening. Much as he hated to admit it, Vincent Lukwiya knew that this was the end. Twenty years hiding out in these jungles, and now the game was up. At least the prophet wasn't around. The Americans wouldn't be that lucky.

Lukwiya looked out into the darkness. The shouting of his ragtag bunch of fighters was dying down, along with the scattered gunfire that represented their worthless efforts to fight back. They were foolish, but not stupid. Maybe some of them even realized that the assault could turn out to be more of a rescue in their case. Not for Lukwiya, though. He wouldn't get off that easily. Especially not after his recent business dealings. Was that how the Americans finally tracked him down? He knew he'd stayed in one spot for too long, but he couldn't just leave the mines. Not when the uranium was his only thread of hope left.

Time to move. Only thirty meters separated his accidental hiding spot in the pit latrine from the camp's front gate. The odds weren't good, but he had nothing to lose. Better dead than extraordinarily rendered to some lonely Egyptian prison for torture. Or worse.

It was impossible to see very far beyond his hiding place, but the straight line between him and the gate looked clear.

Go.

Lukwiya leapt out of the tiny aluminum outhouse, legs pumping faster than they had in years.

Twenty meters.

His left calf burned, the old knot of scar tissue from his one real battle wound stretching painfully.

Ten meters.

The forest rose up sharply on either side of the narrow dirt road just beyond the gate. If he could just make it into the trees, he would be safe.

Freedom.

He dove into the dense vegetation. There was no indication that the invaders had even seen him. No bullets flying at his feet or shouts in his direction. *Maybe there's still a chance.* After a minute to catch his breath and listen, he stood up into a crouch and started pushing through the darkness. His exposed skin stung from the ever-present nettles, but he didn't care. As long as he didn't run into a sleeping snake or prowling leopard, he would be just fine.

Lukwiya looked back. The lights from the camp were barely visible through the trees. He would only go a little ways further, then hole up for the night.

And then he heard it. There was something, or someone, moving through the brush behind him.

He froze.

The sounds continued. Leaves brushing against each other, unnatural on a windless night. Now a soft breathing. No, more like panting.

An animal.

Lukwiya started to walk faster. He couldn't risk firing his pistol for fear of raising the alarm back at camp. No way he'd hit something totally blind like this anyway. It was probably just a little forest rat, or a monkey. Did they roam around at night?

The ground cleared a little as he got deeper into the forest. He looked back over his shoulder. Nothing. The canopy above was too thick to allow even the faintest hint of moonlight through.

A deep growl sounded from the darkness behind him, and he took off running.

Not this. Anything but this.

Something firm and heavy hit Lukwiya in the center of the back, sending him flying through the air just as he felt a sharp pain in one arm. He landed hard on his chest, desperately trying to free the arm from a snarling iron grip that only seemed to get stronger.

Weren't leopards supposed to bite at the neck? Straight for the kill? But this didn't smell like a wild animal. No, it was more familiar.

A dog. It was a fucking dog.

The harder he fought, the more painful it became. There was no way out. He only screamed when he heard the horrific sound of his own bone crunching between the dog's teeth.

Finally, Lukwiya gave up and lay still. As if it had been waiting for just that response, the dog stopped fighting too. It didn't let go of his arm, but at least there was no more flinging him around like a piece of rope.

"Out." The dog released its bite. "Good boy, Rico." The American voice came from somewhere behind his head. "Don't try anything stupid. That dog would be happy to chew up your other arm, too."

Vincent Lukwiya obeyed. He didn't want to. But he was out of options.

COLE LEANED INTO the night, trying to find Innocence in the chaos of moving shapes on the ground fifty meters below the hovering aircraft.

"There he is," he shouted. "Tall bald guy in olive camos. He's coming with me!"

"Sir, we're under orders not to evacuate anyone else from this location." The young Air Force pararescue jumper was trying to pull him away from the Osprey's open hatch. "CBRNE teams are inbound now. They'll take care of him."

Chemical, Biological, Radiological, Nuclear, and Explosives. They were putting the whole camp under quarantine. He'd overheard something about taking precautions for nuclear radiation, and they knew about the virus, too.

"No way—he'll be guilty until proven innocent down there." Cole pulled against the harness holding him inside. "We've got to bring him up with us." He wasn't leaving Innocence behind, not after everything they'd been through together. Not while the man was still dealing with his own brother's death.

"Sorry, sir, we're already late."

The camp started getting smaller. They were leaving. Strong hands pulled him further into the Osprey's bay and forced him down onto a stretcher.

The last few minutes had been a total blur. First the initial verification of his identity, then this guy had strapped him into the harness and they'd both been pulled straight up into the Osprey.

"You guys are assholes," Cole said. "He was my friend."

„You're welcome—for the rescue, I mean." The airman shook his head. "Your guy's in good hands. I guarantee it."

Cole tried to control his anger. It was finished. He was safe. And Innocence would be, too. "Where we going, anyway?"

"Entebbe airport." The pararescue jumper started cutting off his filthy clothing. "C-17's already there, waiting just for you."

"Huh?"

"You're going home, sir. President's orders."

TEHRAN
6:29 A.M.

"KLM Royal Dutch Airlines is pleased to announce that Flight 3575 to Amsterdam is now ready for boarding." The woman's friendly voice came over the intercom first in English, then Farsi, her accent flawless in both languages. Leila slipped into the line already forming at the gate. She'd gotten in the habit of waiting until the final boarding call—no need to waste so much time standing around—but not today. Each little step felt significant in distancing herself from the palpable danger that seemed to be lurking around every corner.

She was surprised how smoothly the whole process had gone. Baba never came home—probably for the best—and Sohrab's own driver picked her up at an ungodly hour for an uneventful drive out to the airport. Maybe the Iranian government really didn't care about her after all, just another Persian-American back in Tehran for a family emergency.

But did every visitor get a tail like hers, the silent suited men who just happened to show up in all the right places? She'd last seen them at the security checkpoint and was even tempted to flash a little wave goodbye before thinking better of it. No reason to raise any final flags in their minds.

A tired group of men stood in line ahead of her, their business-class tickets trumping her elite SkyMiles status in boarding priority. Most were middle-aged and looked distinctly Persian, but there were a few exceptions. The branded carryon bags gave three of them away. European auto executives, returning home after making a big sale? The new trade embargoes were clearly not having their desired effect.

She followed the eyes of one Scandinavian-type to a large muted flatscreen hanging from a column in the waiting area. It was an early morning news program, state-run like them all, but at least this one featured an attractive female anchor. The woman looked especially excited to be talking about something, but wasn't that her job? Then the image changed. A large mansion in the Mahmoodieh neighborhood almost filled the screen, its gated drive blocked by the typical black SUVs of the Revolutionary Guard. *Uh oh, someone's in trouble.*

"Excuse me." The large man directly behind her nodded and pointed to the moving line. She turned away from the screen and took a few steps towards the gate.

That house looked way too familiar.

Leila stepped out of line and set her bag down. She hadn't seen it in the daylight the night before. Hell, she'd barely looked at it at all. But it was the right shape in the right neighborhood. Two strikes.

The driveway's gate started rolling open, and there he was. Sohrab. Held closely between two brutish uniformed men, arms behind his back. They tucked him into one of the waiting cars, and the image flashed back to fancy Ms. Iran at the studio.

Her brother's face appeared in the top left corner of the screen, along with his name and a single word written in Farsi: *Khaen.* Traitor.

SHIT. SHIT SHIT shit. What had she done? *Shit.* What could she do? Nothing. That was the point. She was powerless. The only thing that mattered now was getting back to the States in one piece. She felt for the scrap of paper deep in the pocket of her loose cotton pants. *Go to this address immediately on your arrival,* Sohrab had said. *Tell him about me, the virus—everything you know. He'll take care of you.* It was a simple street address in Cambridge, Massachusetts. Someone from his grad school days?

"Boarding pass and passport, ma'am?" The gate agent was looking at her with an impatient expression.

"Sorry." Leila handed her the documents.

"There's no visa in here," the woman said, holding up her American passport. "You must have entered Iran on a different document?"

Leila's heart skipped a beat. Of course she had. Iran didn't recognize dual citizens, so she'd come in on her old identification card.

"Whoops." Her attempted chuckle sounded more like the croak of a dying frog. "Here you go."

The woman took the old laminated card from her hand and looked at it closely. "They really let you through immigration on this?"

"Yes, no problems at all." That wasn't entirely true. She'd been informed that the obsolete identification cards were not supposed to be used for international travel anymore, but after a few calls it had worked in both directions. Risky—especially with all the reports of Iranian-Americans being detained on suspicion of espionage in the last few years—but it was her only option.

"Well." The agent took one more look at the card, then handed it back to Leila. "Enjoy your flight."

LEILA LOOKED OUT over the runway from her window seat at the back of the plane. She'd torn the *hijab* off the second she sat down, but the sweat still dripped from every pore. She reached up and twisted the tiny air vent all the way open. Just minutes to go until she was free. It didn't help that she and Travis had watched that horrible movie about the hostage crisis just a week earlier, the night before she left for Africa. The final scene replayed itself in her mind, Ben Affleck and the rest of them sitting on this very same runway, waiting to know their fate.

Then she saw it. A blue flash of light in the distance. *No way.* But that couldn't be for her. It was just a movie. No one cared that much. Did they? Still, she couldn't pull her eyes away from the window.

The engines kicked in, and the plane crawled forward. But there were more lights now, dark vehicles speeding across the tarmac. Did Iran's security forces make a habit of tearing around the international airport, just to scare people off from ever coming back? She sat back in the seat. Or maybe it was a hallucination. That watermelon was the only thing she'd eaten in twenty-four hours.

The plane was picking up speed.

She peeked out the window. Still there. The cars were coming in fast at a sharp angle. She gripped the seat cushion with all her might, willing the plane forward, hoping against hope that it was too late to stop.

And then they were airborne.

It was over.

She was free.

CAMBRIDGE, MASSACHUSETTS
7:10 A.M.

The sun's first rays hit the rain-soaked garden in an explosion of dancing brilliance. A beautiful summer morning. Arthur Attenborough stepped off the front porch and closed his eyes as the fragrant aroma of his prize-winning roses settled over him. He'd bought the rambling old Victorian forty years earlier, back when faculty could still afford to live on these sacred blocks tucked away between Harvard Square and the Charles River. He was a lucky man, and the home's welcoming location had served him well. Not only him, but his family, his university, and even his country.

Now where was that paper? Even after all these years, he couldn't do without it. *The New York Times*, print edition of course, delivered faithfully by hand in the wee hours of the morning, ready and waiting for his immediate consumption over strong black coffee. The long winter found him in a rocker by the wood stove for this daily ritual, but for six glorious months from May to October, he relished the spacious porch's more public setting.

No sign of the paper along the faded brick walkway, or nestled under the overgrown lilacs so delicately guarding the front gate. *Ah yes, the rain.* Attenborough opened the wood shingled mailbox and reached inside. Success. It was silly, this wave of endorphins that rushed through his aging body every time. But he was old enough to understand that the simple pleasures of a comfortable routine were among life's greatest gifts. And by all outward appearances, he had enjoyed many of them. Tenured for almost as long as he'd owned this house, Attenborough didn't concern himself with the petty competition and academic back-biting of university culture. He was employed to teach students and pursue his own scholarship exploring the impact of Shia-Sunni relations on Middle Eastern politics, and that was exactly what he did.

It was also why he always turned first to the *World* section, where he soon found himself staring at a brief story—hidden below the fold on the third page—reporting on an Iranian scientist's very recent arrest.

As a Berkeley undergrad during the counter-cultural height of the mid-60s, Attenborough had quickly fallen in with hippie protester crowd. It made sense at the time, an immature understanding of the nature of evil in the world informing his opinions about the role of the United States in foreign conflicts. Disillusionment with his decidedly less serious contemporaries soon followed—they were usually more interested in finding the next party than in bringing their rhetoric to a higher level. And then a younger brother was drafted and killed in the Tet Offensive, followed by a childhood best friend, shot down somewhere over Cambodia. What was the point of all this loss? Wasn't there a better way to deal with disagreements between nations? The weight of a confused moral responsibility crept uninvited into the back of his mind.

Years passed, the war finally ended, and Attenborough continued on the fast track to academic success at Harvard. Quickly reaching that triumphant goal of tenured full professor, he celebrated for exactly three days before realizing there must be something else for him in life. A chance meeting with a top Agency official at an alumni event led to conversations and then agreements he'd never even imagined. Finally returning to Cambridge after several months of training at Camp Peary, he knew he'd found that something.

So it was with great curiosity that he read and reread the half-column article in front of him. Sohrab Torabi. The name brought back a great wave of memories. Good ones, of long summer nights out on this same porch, debating Iranian politics over milky tea and cookies. And not such good ones, especially that final conversation in which Sohrab reaffirmed his decision to decline the recruitment, choosing instead to return to his country a faithful citizen.

They had met on a hot August morning when Attenborough welcomed another group of international graduate students to their new lives in the United States. His role as Dean Emeritus of International Student Affairs made natural interactions easy, and he took great care in handpicking potential candidates. The university was a magnet for the world's best and brightest youth, many of whom might not be completely content with the ways their own countries were being administered. And they all turned in the end. The offer was just too good—work for the genuine good of their own countries while being paid a healthy stipend and, best of all, carrying a get-out-of-jail-free card just in case the going ever got too rough.

All except Sohrab, that is. Three years into the microbiologist's doctoral work on some mundane technique of molecular virology, Attenborough had been convinced that Sohrab was ready to commit. He was upset with the results of recent national elections bringing a crazy religious extremist into power and—even more importantly—angry with his father over the de facto disowning of a younger sister.

A perfect combination.

And yet somehow he just wouldn't take that final step. The numbers being thrown around at the end were incredible, with a signing bonus that would have been more appropriate for a Red Sox rookie than an unproven research scientist. But it wasn't the science that Attenborough's handlers in Langley were interested in. It was the fact that a real live Iranian citizen with top-level connections and a guaranteed government job was even considering their offer. That kind of intelligence was priceless, at least as far as they were concerned.

At the end of the day, it wasn't about the money. Sohrab loved his father and his country, and the simple fact of it was that he couldn't bring himself to turn on them. Not yet, at least. He graduated with honors, promised to stay in touch, and hadn't been heard from since.

What happened? Attenborough read the article one more time. Just three short paragraphs, noting that the story had been extensively covered by the Iranian media, and that Sohrab was suspected of sharing classified information with enemies of the state. No mention of the nature of his work or his father's position in the government.

So who had finally gotten to him? And how? Attenborough couldn't help but feel somewhat vindicated, after all the criticism he'd taken for failing to close on the recruitment. He'd planted the seed, after all. But that feeling paled in comparison to the empathy he felt for Sohrab's current position. *Be strong, my friend.* He knew enough about the current regime not to wish that fate on anyone.

A persistent mockingbird sang from its perch at the top of the lilac bush. Each melodic phrase repeated several times, then on to something new. Attenborough checked his watch. His contact wouldn't be there yet, down at that monstrosity of a building hidden in the woods outside D.C., not for another hour. And much as he wanted to learn more, Attenborough knew they wouldn't tell him much anyway. That was not his role in the game.

At the end of the block, a small crowd was gathering outside the local bakery. He stood up and stretched his arms.

A blueberry muffin might be just the thing.

Fadi Haddad sat down on a tall stool behind the cash register and wiped his forehead. It was already busy at The Lonely Cedar, and he simply didn't feel like being his usual effusive self. But Ahmad made him promise to show up at the restaurant, just like always, and generally keep up appearances in every other way, or Myriam would suffer. Sweet, dear Myriam. It was a cruel way of guaranteeing his cooperation, but effective. They knew a Muslim father would give his own life before bringing harm to his only daughter.

At least she seemed to be doing okay so far. Ever the charmer, she'd convinced the guys to let him bring her laptop—no internet connection—along with a stack of DVDs, and set up her own little space in the unit across the hall from the makeshift lab. But would she ever forgive him? The cold hatred in her eyes didn't leave him with much optimism.

And Nour. She knew something was going on. How could he hide it from her, the woman who stood behind him so faithfully all these years? He made up some story about Myriam going to a friend's lake house for the week, her phone going overboard off a kayak, and that would have to do. So far she did not seem to be making a connection to his quick temper and long absences, and he knew she would never go to the police behind his back.

"Fadi, not even a greeting for your favorite press secretary today?" He looked up to see Andrew Mills standing in front him, along with the same young girl he'd brought before. "If you had any idea of the stress I've been dealing with this week, you'd already have a plate of hummus and some of that savory minced lamb ready and waiting."

Haddad jumped to his feet, beaming a wide smile he hoped looked genuine enough. "*Marhaba, marhaba*, Andrew. And you, young lady, welcome. Twice in one week?" He moved around the register and extended both hands. "To what do I owe this great pleasure?"

"Other than serving the best Lebanese food in town, you mean?" Mills said, laughing. "Anna here made me bring her back."

"It's true," she said. "Best hummus I've ever had!"

Now Haddad's smile was genuine—funny how a simple compliment could lighten the mood so quickly.

Andrew kept hold of both offered hands, longer than normal, and then pulled him in closer. "I also need to pick your brain on something." His voice was lower now, almost conspiratorial. "See if you might be any help in tracking down two unsavory visitors recently arrived from the land of the cedars."

Haddad tensed and froze for a split second. *What do they know?* Then all smiles again.

"Of course!" he said, guiding them to an empty table. "But first, you must eat something—these conversations are much better on a full stomach. What can I get you started with?"

ANNA SIPPED AT a tall glass of ice water. In spite of all that gushing, her stomach was in too many knots to make even the most appealing hummus plate look appetizing. Andrew had dragged her along for the excursion, apparently thinking his friend Fadi's connections in the immigrant community might produce some leads the federal intelligence agencies weren't already tracking down. Fat chance.

But Cole was safe, that was the important thing. And he was on his way there, to D.C., even now. Andrew wouldn't fill her in on all the details, but she had learned that her brother was rescued late the night before from the LRA camp and that he passed on some kind of vague intelligence about a possible bioterrorism threat. The very same threat they were now naively trying to investigate through an unsanctioned interview with this poor restaurant owner.

"So what do you think, Fadi?" Mills paused to shovel another scoop of the lamb into his mouth. His appetite had not been negatively impacted by the week's events. "Anyone else in the area you might be able to connect us to?"

Anna thought the owner looked nervous, but of course she'd only ever met him once before. The restaurant was packed, and they were keeping him from his other customers. Andrew's questions seemed a little presumptuous—as if every one of the thousands of Lebanese people in D.C. knew exactly what was going on with all the others. She didn't imagine that Haddad appreciated the assumption very much, either.

"You know, Andrew, it's been a long time since I came here from Lebanon. You have even visited my birthplace more recently than me, I think?"

"Guess that's right," Andrew said. "You've never been back since you first came over?"

"Not even when my father died, no."

"And you don't know anyone who has stayed more connected to events back home?"

"My home is here. But what I can do is this." Haddad placed both hands on the table. "I will talk to my imam this evening. See if he has heard anything worth passing on." He stepped back. "In all honesty, I don't like to be involved in this."

Andrew leaned across the table. "I can appreciate that, I really do." He pulled out his wallet and handed the man a business card. "That has my cell on it. Call anytime."

What do you mean, hanging out here for a few days?" Cole was leaning against the tall hospital bed in his negative pressure room at Walter Reed, but stood up straight now. "With all due respect, sir, I'll be damned if I'm going to sit in this shoebox watching Oprah while the powers that be decide if they're going to take this thing seriously. I've seen what the virus can do, way too close for comfort."

"And that's exactly why he doesn't want you out and about, potentially spreading it around yourself." Colonel Sam Simmons, USAMRIID commanding officer, stood next to Bill Shackleton from the CDC. Cole's welcoming party. "Just be thankful you're not in the Slammer up at Fort Detrick. At least here you'll have a bunch of pretty young Navy nurses taking care of you."

"But I don't need taking care of, that's the point."

Cole caught the glance exchanged between them.

"Cole, I'm going to be straight with you here," the colonel said. "Bill and I both agree there's not a good reason to keep you cooped up like this. You've been vaccinated, you've never had a fever, and the rapid test results don't show any signs of viral DNA in your blood or sputum."

"So what's the issue?"

"It wasn't our call," Shackleton said. "The national security advisor felt differently."

"General Howard?"

"Retired General Howard, yes." Emphasis on the *retired*. It was clear the colonel was not a fan.

"Even though you're the subject matter experts."

"Yep. Let's just say the medical concerns might not have been the only factor in his decision." Colonel Simmons looked at his watch. "I do feel bad, but the decision's final. And we should let you get some rest."

"Ha," Cole said, moving quickly in front of the door. "You really think you're going to get out of here that easily?"

"What do you think?" the colonel said, turning to Shackleton. "You need to be anywhere?"

"No, and it's only fair we bring him up to speed." The director of Viral Special Pathogens put a hand on his stomach. "But you haven't let me eat anything all day. I'm famished."

"Tell you what," Simmons said. "Let's grab something from the galley, just downstairs, then we'll come on back up to chat a little more. You want something, Captain?"

Cole didn't want to let them leave, but he trusted these guys. They'd be back. "Something really American, that's my only request."

THE LAST TWENTY-FOUR hours had been a total blur. The Air Force had wanted to transfer Cole straight onto a waiting C-17 Globemaster after the Osprey landed in Uganda, but he insisted on finding someone to tell his story to first. That someone turned out to be the Kampala deputy station chief, already at the airport with a team of Ugandan military intelligence waiting for the next hop back to Virunga. The Ugandans would be escorting Vincent Lukwiya to an undisclosed location to begin his interrogation, and the CIA wasn't about to let that happen without one of their own along for the ride. Cole hardly had time to blurt out the details before she was being called up into the same Osprey he'd just gotten out of.

"Promise me you'll pass this on?" he shouted.

"I'm on it—that's my job." He could barely hear her over the rotors, and then the ramp was raised and they were gone.

Cole still didn't know what had come of the information, other than Colonel Simmons' implicit reference to some kind of homeland threat when the two of them first walked into his room. They were the only non-medical people he'd seen since getting off the plane at Andrews. He'd been expecting a more immediate military or intelligence debriefing on his experience of the last few days, but there was no sign of any interest on that front. An ambulance was waiting for him on the runway, and they took him straight to Bethesda. It was almost as if Simmons and Shackleton had come more as a personal favor than because they thought he might have any actionable intelligence to share.

He sat down on the edge of the bed, then lay his head back on the pillow. A knock at the door startled him. That was fast.

"THIS AMERICAN ENOUGH for you?" Shackleton set a white styrofoam container down on the bed, opening the lid to reveal an overstuffed hamburger surrounded by a mountain of fries. "Burger night downstairs. They were out of beer."

Cole remembered Shackleton's dry sarcasm from the month he spent as an intern at the CDC, way back in vet school.

"Perfect, thanks doc." He tore into the burger, savoring the familiar taste of home. Not free range Wyoming-quality, but it would do for now. "So what else can you tell me?"

Ten minutes later, he'd heard the whole thing. A weaponized chimera pox virus—that explained a lot about what he'd seen in both the dead gorillas and Marna's rapid demise. He'd tried to keep any nagging thoughts of her as far away as possible over the last couple days. There would be plenty of time to mourn, but this wasn't it. Even still, the confirmation that her death was not a completely natural phenomenon only served to harden his resolve. This thing wasn't over yet.

And Leila? They hadn't exactly gotten on like best buds there in Rwanda, but he never would have pegged her as a spy. Not in a hundred years. She was book smart, no doubt about that, but not street smart like an Iranian agent in the States would have to be. The pieces didn't quite fit together either. If Iran were responsible for the virus—and there didn't seem to be much of a question about that now—why would she have high-tailed it back there so fast and blown her cover? No, he wasn't convinced yet.

This was all fine and good. But they still hadn't given any more indication of much concern about an imminent threat here at home. Time to get some answers.

"And what about the story I passed on from Uganda?" Cole asked. "I assume you heard something about it, based on what you said when you first came in."

The colonel raised his eyebrows, then walked over to shut the door. "That's being treated as very sensitive information."

"Makes sense. But not if you're trying to keep it from me. I'm the one who got the story in the first place."

"And you'll be recognized for that, trust me."

"Recognized for it?" Cole set his soda down on the bedside table, a little harder than he meant. Maybe before all this he would have cared, wanting to be sure he got everything he was due—military awards, some good press, maybe even a phone call from the president. But not now. Not after Marna, and Proper, and so much more than his own success on the line. "That's the last thing on my mind. I just want to make sure the right people are in the loop—that they're taking this seriously."

"Oh, everyone's in the loop," Shackleton said. "We spent a good hour down in the Situation Room earlier today. Lots of debate over just how serious the threat is."

"Debate?"

"Your story checked out, Cole," Simmons said. "A couple whiz kids over at NSA managed to make some educated guesses based on your information. French-speaking Arabs with a connection to Iran—apparently that was a pretty good indication these guys are Lebanese."

"That's what the Danish doctor thought too."

"Well, he was right. We have two adult males traveling on Lebanese passports from Beirut through Paris and into Kigali about a week and a half ago."

"So what connects them to the incident in Virunga?"

"Same guys left out of Kinshasa just four days later. No one travels across the Congo that quickly." Shackleton said. "Another layover in Paris before they caught a direct flight to Dulles earlier this week."

"Dulles, like Washington Dulles?" This was bad. "That's only half an hour from here."

Shackleton nodded. "Not exactly a very common travel itinerary."

"And did you find them? They have a good explanation for all those flights?"

"That's the tricky bit," the colonel said. "They've been pretty tough to track down."

"Tough meaning it took the FBI more than a couple of hours? Or tough meaning they're still missing?"

"The latter."

"Well shit." A pile of cold fries still covered the bottom of the carryout box, but Cole wasn't hungry anymore. "I hope they're pulling out all the stops now to find these guys?"

Colonel Simmons rubbed his chin. "A task force has been created, and they're starting to track down potential leads, yes."

"Starting—"

"Short answer is no," Shackleton interrupted. "The threat has not been given the priority any of us think it probably deserves."

"But it *is* being handled," the colonel said quickly. "Cole, I've already said more than I should have. You're supposed to be spending these next few days recovering from your ordeal, not worrying about something that doesn't really need to concern you anymore."

"Doesn't need to concern me?" Cole sensed the tension between the two older men. It was clear the career Army officer felt more of a duty to support his commander-in-chief's decision than his civilian counterpart did.

"I don't mind telling him like it is." Shackleton stepped away from where he'd been leaning against the wall. "Not everyone agrees that this situation should eclipse some of the president's other priorities right now, and they've come up with a whole list of reasons to play down the threat."

"Like what?" Cole couldn't believe what he was hearing.

"Questions about the credibility of this FDLR prisoner you spoke with, for one. Could he really distinguish Arabic from Farsi? Or was he just telling you what he thought you wanted to hear?"

"That's a possibility, of course," Cole said. "But it makes sense that the Iranians wouldn't want to send their own guys in for a dirty mission like this. Why not task their adoring little proxy Hezbollah with the job instead?"

"That's the assumption we're working under, yes," the colonel said. "But that doesn't explain why they would come straight over here to the U.S. No one thinks Iran is that stupid. Kill off a few gorillas in some forgotten corner of Africa, so they can stay in the nuclear game? Sure. But not attack us here at home."

"But what if Iran doesn't have anything to do with their trip here?" Cole was at the window, looking out over the wooded grounds surrounding the nation's premier military hospital complex. "Couldn't they be acting on their own now? Finally going to stick it to Uncle Sam now that they got their hands on a real weapon? I mean, I think it's pretty safe to assume they aren't very happy with the president's support of Israel's recent incursions into southern Lebanon."

"Yes, but—"

"Isn't that what we've always been most worried about? Some rogue non-state agent getting hold of a biological weapon like this? We can put the pressure of international law and sanctions on a sovereign nation, but that doesn't work for people who don't play by the rules."

"Cole, you don't have to convince me here," Colonel Simmons said. "I've spent my career trying to prepare for a situation exactly like this one. But not everyone's persuaded."

"What else are they saying?"

The colonel shook his head. "This is the worst one. The president's team apparently has a hard time understanding how our guys could even bring the virus into the States, passing through international airports with their post-9/11 security restrictions."

"Do they need a briefing on all the illegal drugs still getting smuggled into the country every day, in baggies or capsules inside people's bodies?"

Cole was pissed. "Hell, how about a mini-shampoo bottle or toothpaste container? When was the last time the TSA opened up one of those?"

"They don't want to hear it," Shackleton said. "They've got their task force, and they're going to do things their way."

"Still doesn't make any sense," Cole said.

Shackleton lowered his voice. "Do you know what we're celebrating tomorrow, Cole?"

"I haven't been gone that long, thanks."

"But do you know what makes it special? The president's been planning the biggest event in years—going to be quite a party down there around the Capitol."

"Nothing to do with this being an election year, I guess?"

"Let's just say the president doesn't want to let anything rain on his parade. This thing starts getting treated seriously, and he thinks he'll be forced to cancel the whole shebang."

"Good to know his priorities are lined up right."

"And if something happens anyway?" Shackleton said, lifting his shoulders. "We all know what a little terrorist attack can do for a president's ratings."

Colonel Simmons shook his head. "Watch yourself, doc."

"Is that why they're trying to keep me cooped up here like an invalid?"

The colonel placed a hand on his shoulder. "Your reputation precedes you. After that little foray into the Congo this week, they don't want you stirring up any more trouble."

A KNOCK AT the door, followed by a husky female voice. "Captain McBride?"

Cole opened it to a fierce-looking older woman in scrubs. A beefy military policeman stood against the wall outside the door. So much for the pretty and young Navy nurses. He forced a smile. "Could you give us a few more minutes?"

"Sorry, visiting hours are over." She pushed in and motioned to the doorway. "Gentlemen?"

Shackleton was hunched over the windowsill on the other side of the room, like he was writing on something. He turned around with a nod.

"We'll touch base in the morning," Colonel Simmons said. "Do yourself a favor and get some rest."

Shackleton reached out to shake his hand. "Don't do anything stupid."

Cole felt a folded piece of paper against the man's expansive palm and closed his fingers around it. "Wasn't planning on it."

The evening just got slightly more interesting.

CAMBRIDGE
7:51 P.M.

L eila caught the cab driver looking at her in his rearview mirror. Was she just being paranoid, or did it seem like everyone was out to get her all of a sudden? When it was finally her turn to step up to the immigration counter back at Logan, the officer had done a double take at his computer screen before regaining his composure and handing the passport back to her. He managed to mumble a "Welcome home, ma'am," but she caught him picking up the phone as soon as she started walking in the other direction. Then on her way through customs, another uniformed guy looked straight in her direction and nodded his head, radio to his mouth.

"You have a reason to think you're being followed, Miss?" She recognized the Haitian accent immediately.

"Huh?" Leila glanced over her shoulder, then looked back. "I mean, no, why?"

His dark eyes held her gaze for a second. "I been doing this job a long time. The black Suburban a few cars back don't blend in too well."

She turned again. There it was, just coming off the bridge and following them onto Memorial Drive. So now she was on the Americans' bad side too. Why even let her off the plane, then? Maybe they thought she was leading them right into some terrorist nest at home. As if the Revolutionary Guard chasing your plane down in Tehran weren't bad enough. Leila still hadn't decided if that had actually happened, but she knew she wasn't making up Sohrab's arrest. His face also appeared on the BBC at the KLM lounge in Amsterdam, right as she was trying to switch her onward flight from Atlanta to Boston. At least she didn't run into any old classmates this time around. That had been a little awkward, walking all the way across the airport to the temporary storage lockers just so Khaled could switch out his sample merchandise for the next convention. He seemed to be doing pretty well for himself, at least.

Focus.

She'd been doing this all day, her mind racing off in odd directions right when it most needed to concentrate on the present. Whoever was following her would find out the truth soon enough. She was an American. A faithful one, forsaking family and religion for the country she believed in. Even when it hurt.

"I don't know," she said. "Please, just take me to that address on the paper, and I guess we'll find out there."

"Almost there. 81 Bradbury Court, yes?"

They had turned off Memorial, crawled passed a few of the old brick university buildings leading up toward Harvard Square, and were now on a quiet residential street lined with a mix of quirky old Victorians. *Did Sohrab really know someone here?* He'd given her the impression that he trusted this person completely—and that's all she had to go on.

The taxi slowed and then stopped. "You sure you want to get out here?" The driver looked at her again, genuine concern written in the lines of his forehead. "I take you to a police station, maybe they help you out?"

"No, this is fine." She opened her door. "Thank you, I appreciate it."

The sweet scent of lilacs hit her immediately, bringing with it a flood of memories. Saturday afternoons studying for med school finals at the arboretum. The backyard full of them during those idyllic years as a child in Paris. *Focus.* Two large bushes grew up on either side of the trellised archway leading up to the house, their branches laden with heavy clusters of blossoms in every shade from white to deep purple.

"They stopped around the corner," the driver said, motioning down the street with his head as he lifted her luggage out of the trunk. "I stay until you get inside."

Up the short walk, past an equally impressive collection of roses, and onto the classic wraparound front porch. Leila raised a fist to the door. She'd never wanted to follow her father into the murky sea of politics and international intrigue. A big part of the decision to become a doctor was that it seemed like such a black and white way to make a positive contribution. Science and medicine to the rescue. And yet here she was, right in the middle of a world she'd done all she could to escape. But this was for Sohrab, for her adopted country, for that poor South African girl who died in her arms. Whatever bit part she'd been cast in the week's crazy drama, this was her moment to shine. Her chance to make things right.

ARTHUR ATTENBOROUGH HAD just poured himself a glass of Scotch when a light knock sounded at the front door. Strange, he wasn't expecting anyone. But given his position, he often had international students stopping by for the comforting combination of a listening ear and strong drink. And ever since Jane's death, he was even more happy for the company.

He rose slowly from the soft leather recliner—the old knees weren't quite what they used to be—and called out in a loud voice. "On my way." At the hall closet, he reached behind an assortment of hanging jackets to flip a small switch.

Just in case.

The Agency had set him up well, even if he didn't always appreciate the inherent invasion of his own privacy. Just part of the job. The switch started a sound recording on the house's integrated surveillance system and also sent an automated message to the Boston field office. They could theoretically listen in live to his conversations with potential recruits, but he doubted anyone was ever that interested. It was only when Attenborough reported to his handlers about an especially appealing candidate that he began getting the calls with advice and coaching on how to close the deal. After almost thirty years in the business, though, he'd realized he was a hell of a lot more experienced than most of the young intelligence analysts trying to tell him what to do. He knew who would make a good spy—who would be willing to turn on their own government—usually from the first meeting.

Except for Sohrab—his only mistake.

The morning's news was still replaying itself at the front of his mind, but he hadn't been able to find anything more than the most basic information about the arrest. Tomorrow he would make some calls, see what he could learn.

Attenborough looked through the peephole. A young woman, maybe thirty, looking quite overwhelmed. Maybe Pakistani? He didn't know her.

The solid wood door opened with a creak.

"Can I help you?"

THIS OLD MAN with a thick shock of silvery white hair was not who Leila expected. His long face had blue-blooded Ivy Leaguer written all over it. Only now, as he stood there towering over her like some kind of WASPy giant, did she realize she'd assumed it would be another Persian. Not that Sohrab couldn't have gotten friendly with a regular old American, but it was still a surprise.

He repeated the question. "Can I help you?"

"Um, yes, sorry." She looked over her shoulder. The taxi driver was still there, but no sign of the Suburban. "Do you mind if I come inside?"

He gave her a questioning look, then stepped to the side and gestured through the door. She pushed it shut behind her.

"Thank you." Leila stood there for a few seconds, choosing her words carefully. "I believe you might know my brother, Sohrab Torabi."

The man's bushy eyebrows shot up. "Please, come on in."

She followed him into a quaint farmhouse kitchen and nodded gratefully when he offered her a chair at a little breakfast table looking out into the backyard.

"Something to drink?"

"No, thanks," she said. "I don't think we have much time."

He pulled out a chair on the other side of the table and sat down.

"Forgive me, I didn't even introduce myself." He reached a hand across the space between them. "Arthur Attenborough. I teach here at the university."

"And I'm Leila, Leila Torabi. It's a pleasure."

She could feel his penetrating eyes moving over her face, as if he were trying to decide if she were really who she said she was.

"I knew Sohrab had a sister, that she had lost touch with the family after some youthful rebellion, but I didn't expect her to show up at my door, today of all days."

His words made her feel a little better. The fact that he already knew this much meant he was probably the right guy.

"Let me get straight to the point." Leila rested both hands palms down on the table. "I need your help. I don't know why Sohrab chose you, but he's in trouble. We're all in trouble. And you're the only person he trusts with the information I'm about to share."

Fadi Haddad sat in his old Chevy, staring out into the trees as he waited for the melancholy folk ballad to finish. *A Prairie Home Companion* was broadcasting a special late show live from Wolf Trap, courtesy of the local public radio station, and he hated to miss it. But the team was expecting him, and Myriam would be hungry. He reached into the passenger seat for the carryout bag. Sushi rolls, with a side of miso soup—her favorite. He was doing everything he could to make up to her.

His life's new mission.

The parking area was bright—too bright. He'd always hated those glaring flood lights, mostly because they burnt out far too quickly. Changing the bulbs required a precarious reach from the top of a rickety ladder, and that was a task better left to others. His shadow followed him up to the entrance, stretching and then shrinking again behind him.

Here goes.

He unlocked the door and felt a welcome rush of cool air as he stepped into the hall. *Climate-Controlled! 24-Hour Security!* The words on the billboard, towering above the forest from the building's roof, shouted to bored drivers sitting in traffic on the parkway below. A funny business, this, not one you would ever find in Lebanon. Did people really need to accumulate so many things, in such quantities that they could not even keep them in their own homes? But it had been lucrative over the years, supplementing the more temperamental income from the restaurant to provide a comfortable lifestyle for his family. And it was perfect now—finally serving the purpose for which it had been purchased so many years ago—providing a safe and secluded place for the hidden project currently underway in unit number twenty-six.

Adel sat outside the closed door, a pistol resting on one knee. They had each accumulated a small collection of weapons, legally purchased over the years at gun shows around the state, but Haddad always left his own in a locker in the backyard cellar at home. He wished he'd thought to get one that evening, though he knew the others wouldn't have let him keep it. They didn't trust him.

"Cousin, we were beginning to wonder," Adel said, eyeing the bag in Haddad's right hand.

"Sushi, for Myriam."

Adel stood, pulled a key from his pocket, and knocked hard on the opposite door.

"It's your father."

Her angry voice answered immediately. "I don't want to see him." It sounded weaker than usual.

Haddad stepped to the door. "I brought you some dinner."

He pushed it open and stepped inside. The dancing reflections from a movie playing on her laptop provided the only light in the room. His daughter lay on a single mattress in the far corner, the blankets pushed up in a pile at her feet. *If Nour could see us now.* He felt against the wall for the switch.

"Mind if I turn on the light?"

"Yes."

"Myriam, I just want to see you, talk for a few minutes."

"Go away."

"I brought you sushi."

No response. Fadi walked slowly toward the bed, the bag stretched in front of him.

"Aba, I don't feel good."

The words hit him like a train. It was a strange combination of terrifying fear for her health and joy that she was finally trusting him with something, anything. He knelt down and put a hand on her forehead. She pulled away at first, then rested back on the pillow. The skin felt warm, but he didn't even know what was normal. In their unspoken division of parenting duties, that initial determination on the presence of fever had always been one of Nour's tasks.

"When did it start?"

Silence. He could imagine the debate raging inside his daughter's head—hold on to the anger and continue punishing him, or give in to the temptation be a sick little princess again?

"Just this afternoon. Headache is killing me." She brought a hand up and massaged her temple. "And now my throat is hurting, too."

He closed his eyes, cursing silently.

"It's the virus, isn't it?" she whispered.

He was still clueless about what was growing in those eggs across the hall. Not because they wouldn't tell him. He just hadn't wanted to ask. Better not to know—but now he was curious.

"What have they told you?"

"Nothing." The bitterness in her voice was almost gone, replaced by the calm pragmatism of one resigned to her own fate. "But I listen to them talking, through the door. It's a virus, and they're going to kill us all with it."

She began to cry suddenly, a full-body weeping that caused the whole mattress to shake. Maybe she hadn't given up yet.

Haddad pushed his fingers through her smooth black hair, just like he'd always done while putting her to sleep as a little girl.

"I'm sorry, my daughter." He squeezed her hand and stood. "I am so, so sorry."

HADDAD CLOSED THE door gently, then leapt across the hall.

"What have you done?" He was on top of Adel, both hands around his neck, before the other man had a chance to react. "You promised me you would take care of her!"

He felt the steel muzzle of his cousin's weapon dig into his ribs.

"Stop—I don't want to hurt you."

Haddad released his grip and fell against the wall. "You promised."

"She's only tired," Adel said. "That's all."

He spat at his cousin's foot. "That's a lie, and you know it. She says it is a virus."

"I've spent much more time in this room than she has," he said, placing a hand on the opposite unit's door. "And I am doing just fine."

"She's only a girl," Haddad murmured. "My only child."

"This is the life you wanted, cousin. I chose to keep things more simple."

Haddad staggered to his feet and turned, beckoning for Adel to follow him toward the entrance. Adel stood and watched him silently for a few seconds, his face an impenetrable mask. He took one hesitant step, then came down the hall after him.

Outside, the tree frogs had taken up their nightly chorus.

"We don't have to do this, you know," Haddad said. This was his last chance. They'd been through a lot together, he and Adel, and though they always had their differences, he never imagined it would come to this. "I know someone in the White House, a powerful man. One call, and we could be protected witnesses. A plea bargain, maybe a year or two behind bars, and then freedom. True—"

"Stop, Fadi." Adel put a firm hand on his shoulder. "Stop. This is what we were called to do, and the opportunity has finally arrived. We will avenge the deaths of the innocent. This is our time."

"But it's been thirty—"

"Enough," Adel said. "Come, there is much to be done for tonight's mission."

HADDAD SHUDDERED AS he entered the room. The heat and humidity were overpowering, but it wasn't only that. There was something else in the air, an unidentifiable aroma somewhere between a rotten egg and a forgotten beer fermentation. He could almost see them—tiny sperm-like viruses floating invisibly around him, filling his lungs with certain death even in that very first breath. Where were those masks? He reached into the box on the floor beside the door. Empty.

"It's no use," Ahmad said. He was sitting at the desk, a stack of eggs crates in front of him and a five-gallon green plastic fertilizer bucket at his feet. "At this concentration you will be exposed whether you like it or not."

Haddad glanced at Adel, who gave a single nod, lips pressed tightly together.

"Then this has become a suicide mission?" He tried to keep his voice from sounding as strangled as it felt.

"For you and your cousin, perhaps, yes. We were more thoroughly prepared for the task." The other one, Faisal, sat in a second folding chair, stirring something rapidly in an identical bucket. "But maybe you are old enough to have received the vaccine?"

"Vaccine?" Fadi's mind raced through the possibilities. What virus could be vaccinated against? Would Myriam also be protected? For the second time in ten minutes, he hated himself for leaving all the medical aspects of family life to his wife.

"It's possible some small memory lives on in your blood, maybe enough to fight off the infection." Faisal stood. "Take my place here."

Haddad moved slowly across the room. Could he take them all? No, there was no way. These were young, strong men. They would kill him—or at least leave him locked up behind—and then any opportunity to redeem himself would be gone.

He sat down and looked into the bucket at his feet. It was filled about halfway with a thick yellowish liquid that looked nothing like normal eggs.

"Just keep stirring until it goes easily, like water," Faisal said, turning back to the shelves where he picked up another box. "We still have many hours ahead of us."

Haddad could see that he was right—over half of the egg boxes still sat on the shelves untouched.

"I'm allergic to eggs," he said.

It was true. He'd suffered through several surprise episodes of anaphylactic shock in the many years since that first incident as a child.

Ahmad laughed. "Well then, I would advise you not to eat any of it."

Haddad took the long whisk from where it leaned against the inside of the bucket and began to stir, grimacing at the slick wetness on his fingers. No precautions now.

Adel went back into the hall, leaving them to work in silence. Faisal sat beside a new bucket, the box of eggs beside him. He opened it, carefully lifted one tray out, and set it on the floor. Then he began to crack the eggs, one by one, against the side of the bucket. The inefficiency killed Haddad, competing even with his fear and worry for Myriam next door. It took everything in him to keep his mouth shut, not march over there and show them the simple one-handed crack that would double their speed. He'd been working at the restaurant too long. But there was no reason to promote efficiency in this operation. No, every minute lost was a minute he could think and plan for some way out of this hell. It was clear now that Adel was not going to change his mind, but there might be another way.

The contents of each egg poured out easily, already having lost most of its viscosity, and there was no remaining distinction between yolk and white. Something was at work within them, eating away and destroying them as it reproduced itself millions of times over since those initial tiny injections four days earlier. The thought had never crossed his mind that these simple eggs could be used to grow something other than a chicken, but it made sense. They were the perfect balanced diet, an ideal medium for life of any variety. Life, not death. And yet here he was, participating in the production and mass replication of some sort of biological monster.

The buzz against his leg startled him. *Nour.* Only two people in the world called him at this time of night, and one of them was stretched out sick and without her phone across the hall. He pressed an elbow against it, trying to hit the silence button without letting the others catch on. Finally, the buzzing stopped.

He knew she would call right back, and they'd be sure to hear it if they hadn't already. This was it.

"I need to use the bathroom." Haddad spoke softly, doing his best to project complete innocence in tone and expression. He stood, wiping a hand against his pants.

"But brother, you've only just arrived." Ahmad smiled at him. It was not a kind smile. "We are not slave drivers, though. Of course, you can go."

That was easy.

He was halfway to the door when the phone started buzzing again. Hanging freely in his pocket, the sound was unmistakable. *Just keep walking.* Hand on the knob.

"Leave the phone."

Fadi closed his eyes, resisting with all his might the urge to simply take off running. There would be other chances, but not if he had a bullet in his back. He turned around, reached into his pocket, and tossed the phone across the room into Ahmad's slimy hands.

The younger man flipped it around and pried open the back panel. "I don't think you'll be needing this anymore." He popped the battery out and threw it behind the shelving into a far corner of the room. "Now, please enjoy your break."

SUNDAY, JULY 4

The hall outside Cole's room was quiet. *At last.* Around midnight, the same bossy nurse had come in to take vitals and a couple more tubes of blood, promising it would be the last time she'd bother him until morning. Then a few soft footsteps right at one, some unlucky patient with hourly treatments, and now silence. It was only a lull, he knew that, but it was the best he was going to get. This was the trouble with hospitals—they never really went to sleep.

Wouldn't stop him tonight, though. It couldn't. Not with so many lives at risk while those in power twiddled their thumbs or maybe worse. He stuck a hand in his pocket, feeling for the folded paper Shackleton had given him earlier. Still there.

Cole felt bad for the Navy security guard standing watch outside his room. He was going to take a lot of crap when someone finally realized what happened. Of course, no one ever actually said Cole was supposed to stay under strict confinement—there was a whole other ward of the hospital for those patients—but it was pretty clear that this was Howard's intent.

Retired General Howard. *How'd I manage to get on his bad side?* Sure, the mission into Virunga didn't turn out quite as planned, but a lot of good had come of it, too. So why was he being punished for this?

Cole walked back to the door and popped his head outside.

"Hey man, mind if I close this? I'm having a tough time sleeping in here."

The poor kid looked momentarily startled, as if he'd been caught daydreaming. He must have been just about the twins' age. Chase and Anna were only a few miles away, but Cole hadn't been able to see—or warn—them yet. If everything went according to plan, that would soon change. The young sailor stood up straight. "No problem, sir. Make my job even easier."

Simple enough. Cole closed the door gently and waited a couple of agonizing minutes just in case the kid changed his mind.

Nothing.

He climbed into his high-tech hospital bed and pulled the hanging curtain all the way around it. They'd have to have a pretty good reason to disturb him before the morning vitals check.

And by that time, he'd be long gone.

COLE STOOD ON the bed and placed one foot onto the heavy-duty headboard covered with outlets and attachments of every kind. It held him easily. The styrofoam ceiling tile felt almost weightless in his hand as he lifted it up and over into the crawl space above. Was this really as easy as they always made it look in the movies?

No time like the present to find out.

He hoisted himself up onto the top of the wall separating his room from the next one over. The crawl space was about three feet tall—plenty of room to maneuver, if he could just find a way through the maze of oxygen tubing, electrical wiring, and central air ducts. And avoid putting a hand or knee down in the wrong spot, of course. That would make for an unpleasant surprise for some poor old lady sleeping in another room.

Cole pulled his legs up and leaned over the open hole looking down on his bed. Silence. He carefully lifted the tile from its temporary resting spot and replaced it back in its original position. Perfect.

Now to get his bearings. The outer wall of the building made for a hard stop about fifteen feet in front of him, but back over his shoulder and on either side the space seemed to go on almost indefinitely. He closed his eyes, trying to remember the trip into the hospital that afternoon. The entrance to this unit was a ways off to the left, he was sure about that, with an elevator lobby just beyond it. If he could just make it there, past the nurses' station to the lobby beyond, he'd be in the clear.

He slowly turned around until he was facing in the opposite direction, toward the hallway. At least he knew he'd have a solid wall beneath him to follow all the way out. One hand up and over a tight coil of wires, then the other one, and finally the legs, always careful to gently test the surface before letting his weight down on top of it.

It was slow going, but not difficult. The most important thing was to minimize any sounds that might be detected by his guard or a passing nurse in the hall. This wasn't like the old cabin on the ranch, where strange noises in the ceiling were expected and best ignored.

It opened up a little bit at the intersection where his room hit the hall. The careful turn was just about complete when his left knee came down too hard right on the edge of the framing. The adjacent tile shifted slightly, and with it a harsh crunching sound of styrofoam on metal. *Crap*. It sounded like a train whistle in Cole's ears and set his heart racing. He froze and started counting. Sixty. One-twenty. At three hundred seconds, and with no indication that anyone below was any wiser to his efforts, he started to move again. Even slower now, and more deliberate, if that were possible.

TWENTY MINUTES PASSED before he got to the massive bank of elevator shafts piercing through the crawl space. He found what looked to be a far corner above the lobby and gently lifted one tile up a few inches.

It was empty, and the door into his unit was closed. Sweet relief. More quickly now, he moved the tile all the way to the side, turned around, and lowered himself most of the way down through the hole. One more check over his shoulder, and he dropped to the floor. He punched the elevator call button and watched the numbers steadily rise. Almost there. What would he say if his favorite nurse happened to be coming off a snack break, riding that same elevator back to her floor? That wouldn't do—no reason to risk an awkward confrontation until it was absolutely necessary.

The door to the stairwell was just around the corner, and Cole was already at the next landing before it closed behind him. It felt good to be on the move, warming up muscles that had been confined too long. He flew down the stairs, taking them two and three at a time, watching the floor numbers decrease until finally he was at the lobby level. The original plan had been to walk right out the front entrance, but as he looked down at the blue scrubs and white disposable slippers they'd given him, he began to question that decision. Sometimes the best disguise was no disguise at all, and at some hospitals it might have worked. Not at Walter Reed, though. There would be more security guards at the entrance, and the slippers especially might raise some eyebrows. Much to his annoyance, there'd been no sign of his own clothes or gear anywhere in his room, but at least they'd returned a little Ziplock bag with his wallet in it.

No, there had to be another way.

He continued down two more levels until the stairs ended in the bowels of the building. The door opened onto a darker hallway, and the thick scent of industrial laundry detergent filled Cole's nose.

This might work.

The first door off the hallway opened into a large room filled with tall shelves stacked high with clean linens. A long row of super-sized washers and dryers stood silent against one wall. But what about the stuff that was just too far gone to wash? There had to be some way to get rid of it, along with all the other thousands of pounds of trash produced every day in a hospital of this size.

He backtracked to the hall and followed it to the end. A thin line of bright light was visible under wide double doors. *Integrated Waste Management Department*. This was more like it. Every warehouse needed a loading bay, and that meant a way out.

The door opened easily into a tall-ceilinged warehouse that smelled surprisingly clean given its function. It was quiet, but not silent. The soft thuds and rustling of garbage being sorted echoed in the empty space.

Cole slid inside and moved quickly into the shadow of an enormous trash compactor. The noises continued unchanged. So far so good. He crept to the edge and looked around. There it was, just fifty feet away—a tall overhead door and beat-up iron ramp leading out to where the trucks must come to pick up their loads.

"Excuse me, sir, can I help you?"

Cole did his best not to jump. He turned around to find an older Asian man staring up at him, a skeptical expression on his face.

"Oh, good," Cole started. Time to think fast. He extended a hand. "I'm Dr. Davis, one of the new residents up in surgery."

The man just stood there.

"Can you tell me where I could find the regular trash collected this evening?" Cole said, trying his best to project acute embarrassment. "Think I tossed my ID badge along with whatever I didn't finish for dinner."

The man visibly relaxed. "Which floor?"

"Third," Cole guessed.

"Over here."

Cole followed him past the loading dock to a series of dumpsters along the same outer wall.

"Probably this one," the man said, pointing, "but you sure this is worth it?"

"I'll give it a try anyway. Don't worry about helping me—I know you probably see enough of this stuff as it is."

The man didn't move as Cole lifted the top and started pulling bags out. Once he had a nice collection of them, he tore into the top of one and started sifting through the contents with both hands. It was mostly filled with plastic wrapping and a few empty water bottles—so much for the recycling program. Not too bad yet. The second one was a little worse, with sticky food containers and a few used tissues. Did people really get that sick in the heat of summer?

Finally, the man gave him a nod and walked away. Cole didn't wait long, only ripping through a couple more bags before deciding it was time to make his move. The regular door beside the loading dock was locked, just like he expected. Only the night manager would have a key, and Cole had no intention of seeing him again. But the overhead loading door itself hadn't made it all the way down to the ramp, and he could feel a draft coming through the remaining six inches or so as he lowered himself down.

It would be tight, but definitely worth a try.

His left arm and most of the leg went easily, but that was it. Was there any give at all? He drew his arms under him and started to press against the ramp, lifting his back up into the hard edge of the door.

There it was, a slight shift, and then the door began to move. Cole slid under it the rest of the way and dropped over onto the concrete.

Free at last.

THE LOADING AREA was lit, but there was no one around. Cole took off at a fast walk around the side of the building, sticking to the shadows, and within minutes he reached the complex's front security entrance. It was much easier to get off of a military installation than onto it, and he planned to take full advantage of that. Now the scrubs might be an asset—he was just another tired doctor who didn't feel like changing, heading out to catch the Metro home after a late shift at the hospital.

The gate guards didn't even glance at him. Or at least they didn't say anything. Cole didn't look back to find out, but continued down the sidewalk until he came to the intersection with Rockville Pike. The entrance to the Medical Center Metro station welcomed him from across the street, and he didn't wait for the crosswalk.

Cole almost flew down the two long escalators, only slowing when he came into view of the ticket area. It was Saturday night, so the trains were running late, but the deserted space proved this place wasn't much of a hot spot for the D.C. party scene.

Two old pay phones were tucked away against the wall beside the ticket machines. He'd waited a long time for this.

Cole pulled the folded paper out of his chest pocket and opened it up. A phone number, that was it. He just hoped whoever was on the other end wouldn't mind accepting the collect call.

"This is Morgan." A woman's voice. Didn't sound like she was sleeping.

"Hi." Cole paused. "I was given this number by Dr. Bill Shackleton from the CDC. He seemed to think you might be able to help me."

WASHINGTON, D.C.
2:26 A.M.

You sure we won't run into any cops over here?" Haddad whispered. He looked across the wooded glade separating their parking spot from the low red brick structure in the distance. Seemed like a long way to go, especially lugging the two heavy containers at his feet.

"I'm sure," Adel said. He closed the truck's door quietly and lifted his own fertilizer drums. "I've been out here every night this week—the foot patrols are every hour, on the hour, and that's it."

Ahmad smirked beside him. "Just watch out for those Capitol Police dogs—they can smell an Arab like you from miles away."

"Right." Haddad knew he was kidding, but the thought still sent a shiver up his spine. He'd never liked dogs, not since that fateful afternoon when a pack of them slaughtered his favorite ewe's newborn lambs while he napped in the hills above the village.

Even though the risk was minimal, they had decided it would be best to look as official as possible. The four men all wore extra pairs of Adel's green work coveralls, each one printed with the Architect of the Capitol's large stylized logo. He'd been working there almost twenty years, starting out as an assistant gardener in the Botanic Gardens and working his way up to general foreman of the grounds keepers. The job wasn't as lucrative as Haddad's entrepreneurial pursuits, but it fit Adel's personality better. They'd always known this position right at the center of the government's beating heart might one day come in handy, but Haddad never imagined there would be such a direct link between a future operation and his cousin's line of work.

They followed a paved footpath through the tall trees. Not a single tourist around now, but the next night it would be a totally different place.

Every break in the thick foliage gave him another glimpse of the gleaming white dome looming overhead, its perfect shape complemented by a fluttering halo of stars and stripes just below. And off to the other side, blocking his view to Reflecting Pool, he saw the massive stage set up and ready for the next night's performances.

A Capitol Fourth.

Haddad couldn't fend off the nostalgic feelings the sight evoked inside him. He'd brought Nour and Myriam to the annual celebration many times over the years, and it always left him feeling proud and glad to be an American. Even a messed up American sworn to betrayal. Those were the nights when he did his best to forget his true purpose there in the land of the free. Not to revel in being one of them, but to punish and avenge for the injustices this nation had inflicted on his own true people. If they were caught now, how would he explain himself? That he meant to tell someone...tried to stop them...was just waiting for the right moment? His opportunities to act were slipping away.

The thin wire handles of the heavy buckets dug into his hands, but he kept walking. There was nothing else to do.

Adel led the way through an ornately patterned arched entryway into the small courtyard of the short hexagonal brick pavilion. The Summerhouse, he'd called it, built in 1880 and designed by the same man who did New York City's Central Park. It was mostly ignored by tourists hurrying between bigger and better attractions, but much-appreciated by local joggers who often stopped for a cool drink at the water fountains.

There were no joggers now.

Haddad set his buckets down, stretching his fingers as he watched Adel dig into a pocket and pull out a large set of keys. He chose one and fit it into a small lock at the corner of the wrought iron grating blocking the entrance into the Summerhouse's most unique feature, the Grotto.

"WE'RE GOING IN there?" Haddad was skeptical. Behind the grating was a dimly lit scene that didn't belong there in the shadow of the Capitol dome. In fact, it would have fit better tucked away deep within a hidden *wadi* cutting through the hills above his family's village. Lush vegetation surrounded a small waterfall that trickled out from a rocky cave, first into a shallow pool and then a narrow stream. The water disappeared under the foundation beneath him before apparently feeding into the decorative fountain in the center of the Summerhouse.

"The Grotto, yes, as I told you," Adel said quietly. "Just watch your step if you plan to keep your feet dry."

Haddad followed him in, climbing up through the opening before picking his way down the rocks and into this unexpected oasis. The sweet scent of honeysuckle filled his nose as he felt the reaching vines brush against his face. The other two were right behind him, nearly filling the small space. Adel set his buckets down in the stream and crept back to the entrance, pulling the grating shut and sticking a hand back through to lock it.

No escape now.

"Faisal, you will stay here in the shadows and radio if there is any activity." Adel placed a hand on the younger man's arm. "No weapon unless we are already compromised."

Haddad caught his cousin's eye as he pushed past him. Did Adel really think he had already turned them in? He bit the inside of his cheek, wishing with all his might that he had.

Adel bent down under the overhanging rocks and disappeared momentarily into the darkness. A hand reached out. "Give me the buckets."

Haddad passed all eight of the heavy containers into his cousin's waiting hands, then ducked beneath it himself. The cold water was refreshing, soaking what was left of his hair and running down his sweaty face. Just past the cave's opening, a short flight of stairs went down into a larger space. Or at least it felt larger, but he couldn't even see the hands in front of his face. The air had a slightly stale, earthy smell that reminded him of the hidden cellar under the shed in his own yard. Now what? There was a creak of rusty hinges, and a faint crack of light appeared a few feet away, Adel's body silhouetted against the opening doorway.

"The back entrance," his cousin said. Haddad could hear the smile in his voice. "They'll wish they had sealed this up long ago."

HADDAD WAS BREATHING fast when he finally reached the bottom of the three-story spiral staircase for the second time. They'd realized it was impossible to carry two buckets at once due to the tight curve and steep angle of the descent, and he'd been terrified of tripping over his own feet the entire way down, back up, and down again.

A red emergency exit light over a door in the distance gave the entire grounds maintenance department an eerie glow, and the steady hum of large machinery added to the unwelcoming ambiance.

"So this is where you work." It was more a statement than a question. Now that he thought of it, he realized that though Adel had been to his restaurant and storage units countless times over the years, Haddad never once expressed an interest in visiting his cousin on the job.

"This is it, for one more day."

Was there a hint of regret in his tone? Maybe so, but Haddad knew it wasn't enough to change anything now.

"Where's the access point?" Ahmad was already on the other side of the room, both hands running along a large cylindrical tank towering above him.

"All in good time," Adel said, using another key to open up a wall-mounted control panel beside the tank. "We have to flush the system first—I don't think the genuine fertilizer in here will be good for your virus."

Haddad watched his cousin punch a series of numbers on the keypad. There was a short beep, and then a small screen lit up in front of him. A minute later, the mechanical whirring of a pump started up, followed by the sound of liquid draining out of the tank.

"That'll go straight into the Potomac," Adel said. "And people wonder how those mutant catfish get so huge."

When it was finished, another series of commands resulted in a tinkling spray of water filling the tank from above.

"What's that?" Ahmad asked.

"Just water—cleaning her out." Adel picked up the large black duffel bag he'd carried slung across his back and ducked underneath the tank. "This will take a few minutes."

Haddad heard the zip of the bag, then the knocking sound of metal on hard plastic.

Weapons.

"Are you staying here?" He hadn't even considered that possibility, but it made sense. But did this mean he'd have to leave alone with the other two? Somehow, his cousin's presence had given him a sense of security that was about to be pulled away completely.

There was a grunt from behind the tank, but that was it. So this was Adel's last stand. A suicide mission to conclude all these years of patient waiting and preparation. Or maybe not. Maybe no one would think anything of a sprinkler system malfunction in the middle of the next night's festivities, and they could all continue with their normal lives until sometime in the week ahead, when people all over the country started getting sick. Maybe there was still a chance of preventing this thing from happening at all. *Please, Allah, give me this chance.* Haddad brought a hand to his face and wiped the water that was still dripping into his eyes.

The rinse cycle finished, and the tank stood silent again.

"Now?" The edginess was obvious in Ahmad's voice. "Every minute we are here is one too many."

Adel came out from under the tank and pointed to a built-in ladder climbing up one end. "Fadi, you will do the honor."

Haddad tilted his head to the side, eyebrows raised.

"Climb up the ladder, and we will pass you the fertilizer drums."

Now he understood. Of course, they would give him this task. Then there would be no chance of defending himself against the charges. *Material support for acts that are dangerous to human life and intended to intimidate or coerce a civilian population within the territorial jurisdiction of the United States.* He had become very familiar with the PATRIOT Act's definitions.

Haddad hated ladders, but he climbed anyway.

The round access port opened easily, and he leaned down to lift the first bucket from Ahmad's raised arms. He balanced it on the top of the tank, unscrewed the cap, then tilted it precariously into the larger opening. The egg solution gurgled out of the bucket, filling his nose with that same evil scent from earlier in the evening. If he weren't already exposed to the virus, there was no escape now.

His arms began to shake with the fifth bucket. *Steady now.* It went in like the others, but he didn't know how he would manage the last three.

"That's long enough," Ahmad said.

Haddad had requested a short break before lifting the final bucket, and the muscles of his arms and back burned like they never had before. He reached for it, swinging it up and onto the tank just as he had done with all the others. This time, the cap popped off on its own, and a fountain of liquid death shot out of the opening and showered down over his head.

The smell and taste were overpowering, and Haddad had to swallow back the vomit that immediately filled his mouth. He teetered on the edge of the tank, desperately trying to keep his balance while holding the bucket in place with one hand.

"*Yekhreb betak!*" Ahmad swore loudly—may Allah destroy your house. He'd been hit by the geyser too.

Haddad willed his arms to lift the bucket one more time. *He already has.*

Finally, it was done. There was no turning back now.

He sat against the wall trying to clean the last of the slippery mess from his hair and face, only half-listening as the other two men finished their final preparations.

"—prime the system with a regular water-only cycle first," Adel was saying, "so the solution is already mixed and ready at the sprinkler heads tomorrow night."

"And what if you are discovered before the time has arrived?"

"I won't be. My men are not the types who come into work when they are not needed."

"But what if?"

Haddad rose to his feet and walked unsteadily over to where they were standing in front of the control panel.

"The cover will be locked and I've changed the startup PIN. It would have to be manually reset by a technician from the manufacturer, all the way down in Florida."

Adel pressed some numbers on the keypad, and a time appeared on the screen. 10:00 p.m.

"There," Adel said, hitting a green enter button and closing the panel's cover. "The system is programmed and locked for a new fertilizing cycle set to start tomorrow night."

Haddad closed his eyes. He might as well be dead already.

He followed Ahmad and Faisal back to the truck in a daze, only briefly noticing the heavy mist spreading through the air as it jetted out from evenly spaced sprinklers on either side of the path. *Priming the system.* Haddad imagined the organized network of pipes hidden in the earth beneath his feet, filling even now with a slowly diffusing solution of biological terror.

The same terror that was coursing through Myriam's veins back in Fairfax.

He had to get back there.

WASHINGTON, D.C.
3:03 A.M.

The distant beat of dance music carried through the cool night air as Cole stepped out of the Metro's 1st Street NE exit. It only took a few seconds to get his bearings. Union Station's grand white marble towered over him, and a few blocks south he had a clear view of the Capitol dome rising up above the trees. In spite of the nonstop trouble he'd faced since landing at Andrews just twelve hours earlier, it felt good to be back home. Broadly speaking, of course. He'd take the grand mountain vista from his parents' kitchen window over this one any day of the week.

A lonely cab idled around the corner in front of the main entrance, its driver leaning against the hood, hands in pockets, staring into space. When he saw Cole, he stood up and raised a hand.

"Looking for me?" he called.

Cole shook his head. "Sorry, just a quick walk from here." He felt bad leaving this guy without a fare, but it should be an easy ten minutes to the twins' apartment, and he didn't have any cash.

Not dollars, at least.

He was halfway across Massachusetts Avenue, deep in thought about the imminent reunion with his siblings, when the piercing squeal of tires broke the silence. An old Ford pickup tore around the corner right behind him—not even a hint of a stop at the deserted intersection. He leapt to the side just in time, missing the truck's front bumper by inches but catching the passenger side window with a somewhat purposeful open-handed smack. *Assholes.* Teach them to pay attention where they're going. A fleeting glimpse through the window as the truck raced past revealed three Arab-looking guys—two of them about his age in the front, eyes focused on the road ahead, while a third older man stared right back at him from the rear bench seat.

Cole tried to catch the license plate number before the truck disappeared around the circle, but all he could see was the distinctive Maryland blue crab.

Three guys, not two, like the ones they were looking for. Still, his heart was racing.

The conversation with this Morgan chick from NSA had convinced him even more than he'd already been that the threat was way more serious than anyone was taking it. Even though Cole didn't normally like to get too caught up in political dramas, he'd still let Morgan know what he thought of the administration's decision to stall the investigation. He hated to assume the worst of people, but it was hard to see this in any other light. And even though she didn't come out and say so, it was clear Morgan felt the same way. Still, unless she could track down some useful information about where these two Lebanese guys were hanging out, it wouldn't matter how many people agreed with their assessment.

Cole started to jog, passing a few surprised stragglers sitting on the curb outside a bar, and continuing through Stanton Park before turning down 10th Street. The only reason he even remembered their address was because it sounded so perfectly D.C.—1000 East Capitol.

He slowed to a walk as he reached the intersection. There it was, a stone-fronted Victorian with the classic corner turret he recognized from Anna's Facebook photos. At the door, he found the buzzer for unit three, pressed the button, and waited.

This would be fun.

S o where'd you find this gas guzzler?" Leila looked a little awkward, standing there on the curb watching Cole lift her small carryon bag into the bed of Chase's new Silverado V8. At least she let him help her this time around. He'd pulled up at Reagan National's arrivals area just minutes before she walked out. After the reunion with his siblings and a few hours' sleep on their couch, he'd been chasing dead-end leads from Morgan all morning.

"My brother's—he's here in the city for the summer."

"And drove this thing all the way from Wyoming?"

Cole hopped up into the cab and put the truck in gear.

"Great to see you too, Leila." He'd been hoping for a change in her attitude after their less-than-friendly collaboration in Rwanda—some implicit acknowledgement that they'd been through a lot but were definitely on the same team now. That was really the only reason he'd agreed with Morgan's recommendation for her to fly down to join him. *She's the only other person in the U.S. who has seen what this virus can do. The fact that she's also immune means you can both get right in the middle of things if that becomes necessary.* And so here Leila was, right off the plane from Boston after being released from what sounded like an epic all-night interrogation. "Just so you know, I never believed you were really working for the other side."

"Not sure I should take that as a compliment, but thanks." Leila looked like she hadn't slept in days, but she still managed a smile. "Good to know at least one person in the U.S. government wasn't quite so quick to label me a traitor."

"They were worried, and reasonably so." Cole followed signs for Interstate 395. "From what Morgan said, that exchange they got on video at the airport in Amsterdam was pretty damning."

"Bad timing for a chance meeting with an old friend, that's all."

"I'm just glad the story checked out, for your sake. No way the FBI would have let you out on your own this quickly if that friend of yours had any genuine terrorist connections." He paused. "Really sorry about your mom, by the way."

"Thanks." She leaned back into the seat. "I still feel so guilty for everything that's happening. Guilt by association, I guess, seeing as my own family is behind so much of it."

"We can't choose our families, Leila."

"I know you're right, but that doesn't help anything right now. Not Marna, not those gorillas, not my brother, locked away and suffering in some desert dungeon. He didn't mean for the virus to be used, you know. I hope you can believe that."

"I want to believe it. That's the best I can do."

They were silent for a minute. Cole tried to imagine what it must be like for her, torn between family and country, beaten back and forth by both sides.

"Heard you had quite an adventure yourself over the last few days," she said.

"You could say that." He wasn't sure how much Morgan had already told her but didn't feel like rehashing the whole story now. "How was Boston?"

"Good as six hours of nonstop interrogation can be expected to be. Just wish I knew something that might have been more useful."

"Me too." The flash of a smile crossed Cole's lips. Based on what Morgan had said, most of what Leila learned from her brother simply confirmed the predominant theory about the virus's Iranian origins, rather than adding much that might help with the day's more pressing threat. But she was here now, for better or worse, so he was going to make this work. "Still glad you were able to come—it'll be good to have you on board when I finally get to reconnect with Shackleton and the colonel. Sure, those video clips from Goma making the rounds on CNN are powerful, but that hardly makes the threat feel real for most people here in the States."

"Which is probably why—"

"—it's been hard for the right people to get excited about it and realize what we're actually facing."

"Exactly," Leila said. "Sounds like there may be other factors too, though. Morgan seems pretty convinced the investigation is being delayed by a self-interested election-year politician."

"Much as I hate to acknowledge it, I think she's right."

The burner phone from 7-Eleven started ringing. Same number Cole had been getting calls from all morning.

"It's Morgan." He pulled off into a little parking area looking out over the Potomac. The bright midday sun beat down on a wide expanse of steely blue water. In the distance the gleaming white dome of the Jefferson Memorial welcomed a steady stream of cars coming across the bridge into D.C. It was a beautiful summer day. "Let's hope she has something good for us this time."

"SORRY, MUST BE in a bad spot." Cole said. "Could you repeat that?"

Leila caught his eye and mouthed the word *speakerphone*. If she was going to be any help in stopping this thing, Cole needed to trust her. Wasn't that why he agreed to let her come down? Not that she would have taken no for an answer, after those two soul-searching flights on the way back from Tehran and then her conversation with Professor Attenborough the night before. Sure, it would be nice to be back in her own apartment overlooking downtown Atlanta, sleeping the whole thing off. But she couldn't go on living as if she were the only person in the world who mattered. Not anymore, not when she was implicated so deeply in the week's events.

Cole pressed a button, and the NSA analyst's voice filled the cab.

"—picked up a call from a woman name Nour Haddad. Parents immigrated here from Lebanon years ago, but she was born in the States."

"One more time, who got the call?"

"Fairfax County Police. Our system alerted when it discovered that this lady's husband has been on a terrorist watch list for years."

"What—for being Lebanese?"

"He'd been distantly connected to a few suspected Hezbollah operatives at one point, but no criminal record or recent flags on him. Looks like an otherwise respectable small business owner."

A quizzical expression grew on Cole's face.

"Okay," he said. "But what happened this morning? Why'd she call the police?"

A pause.

"Her husband never came home last night. First time since they were married, she swears. And her teenage daughter has been missing all week. Apparently—"

"Huh?"

"Apparently, Mr. Haddad told his wife their daughter was on vacation with a friend. After worrying herself half to death all night, she finally called the friend's parents this morning."

"And?"

"Daughter's not with them either. She—"

"Sounds weird, yes, but I'm still not seeing a huge connection to our two recent travelers."

Leila felt the same way. She wanted Morgan to be right—wanted this to be the big break they'd been looking for—but it wasn't adding up yet.

"You said he's a small business owner?" Cole continued. "What kind of stuff?"

"Stop interrupting me, and you'll see where I'm going with this," Morgan said. "He owns a restaurant in downtown D.C. and also a self storage facility out near their home in Fairfax. Cops have already checked out both spots. Didn't see anything suspicious, but they did run background on a rental vehicle at the storage place. It was picked up at Dulles on Tuesday morning."

"Where'd you say it was?" Cole handed the phone to Leila and pulled the truck out into traffic. "Tuesday morning—that's the same day our two guys arrived from Kinshasa. Can you send me a photo of the husband? Driver's license, passport, anything. Just message it to this same number."

"Hang on," Morgan said. "Okay, it's right on Fairfax County Parkway, near the intersection with Route 29."

Two tones chimed a few seconds later—photo message alert. Leila held the phone up so he could see the picture that had just come through. A broad dark face stared back at them.

"That's him—the older guy from the truck last night."

The pickup swerved into the left lane, its engine roaring.

"Cole, FBI's planning to send a team out there later this afternoon."

"Later this afternoon isn't good enough."

"Cole—"

"We're already on our way."

Fadi Haddad sat on the floor beside his daughter's mattress, one hand resting against her sweaty cheek while the other held a bottle of water to her lips.

"Drink, Myriam, you need to keep drinking."

She had dutifully sipped from the bottle ever since waking up a few hours earlier, but her movements were getting weaker even as her breathing sped up and the coughing fits got worse.

This time, she didn't respond at all.

"Myriam, you must keep fighting. We will be out of here soon—to a hospital. Back to real life."

Still nothing. Her eyes stared vacantly at the ceiling, no longer even trying to follow the silent movie playing on the laptop beside her.

Haddad wasn't sure if he believed his own words. After a silent drive back from D.C., Ahmad and Faisal had locked him in the storage unit with Myriam. That was the last he'd seen of them. They were still there, across the hall in unit twenty-six, but it didn't sound like they would be for much longer. Myriam was right—it was possible to pick out a few words from their hushed conversations through the door. There'd been a debate about if and when they should leave the area at all. One of them—he thought it was Ahmad—wanted to stay and appreciate the effects of their efforts, maybe even going back into the city itself that evening. The other argued that they should stick with the original plan of leaving immediately to begin the long drive to Mexico.

And now they were leaving.

He glanced down at Myriam's bare arm, then looked more closely. A faint spotty rash was appearing on her perfect olive skin, almost as he watched. It hadn't been there five minutes earlier, at least, he would swear to that. Was this one of the virus's normal symptoms? He hated himself for not knowing more about the monster eating away at his daughter right before his eyes. And she was only the first of so many.

Haddad struggled to his feet at the sound of a key in the door. The floor flew up to meet him, and he stumbled to a knee before regaining his balance. It was just the lack of sleep, and food, that was all. He felt fine.

"It is time to go." Ahmad stood in the doorway. "Say goodbye to your daughter."

Haddad just stood there, shaking his head slowly. No, they couldn't do this. Would they kill him now, or drag him all the way to Mexico, maybe back to Lebanon for some kind of ultimate punishment? He didn't know which would be worse.

"No, I won't leave her, not like this."

"Fadi, brother."

"Don't call me that. I want no part of this anymore. "

"This?"

"This game, in which innocent lives are traded back and forth and back and forth on and on into eternity. I've had enough of it. I want out."

"Brother, you are far, far too late to make that decision." Ahmad moved into the room and put a hand on his arm. "Come on your own, or we will have to use more forceful means."

A cloud of blackness momentarily danced before Haddad's eyes as he felt a long-forgotten surge of rage rush through his body. He brought a fist up hard into the younger man's jaw, sending him staggering back a few steps, and followed it with a quick jab right at the nose.

The open door was only a few feet away. He leapt through it and turned down the hall, only to be met head-on by Faisal's broad shoulder slamming squarely into his stomach. Haddad felt himself falling over the smaller man's back, his momentum carrying him forward even as he gasped for breath.

A wave of dizziness swelled up within him, and he was tempted to stop fighting right there—collapse on the floor and be done with it.

But it receded just as quickly, and he kicked hard as he scrambled over Faisal's shouting face. That would leave a mark. He was rising to his feet again when the full weight of Ahmad's body landed on his back, forcing him to the floor. Twisting and thrashing, he tried to free himself, pushing back desperately, trying to ignore the heavy fog that threatened to engulf his throbbing head. There was a sharp pain in one shoulder as his arms were pulled violently behind his back, then the ripping sound of packing tape flying off the roll as it went layer after layer around first his wrists and then his ankles.

He only realized he was shouting when they threw a final wrap of the tape over his mouth and around the back of his head. He could barely breathe through his nose. He had to stop fighting.

It was finished.

They stood panting in the bright hallway for what seemed like hours, until finally Ahmad broke the silence.

"Didn't he say he was allergic to eggs?"

HADDAD DIDN'T FEEL the first prick, only knowing it was over when Ahmad's hand pulled away from his neck, an empty syringe between his thumb and forefinger.

"If you weren't already infected, this should do the trick," the younger man said, his face just inches from Haddad's own. "Not that the virus will have much time to act, if this allergy is as bad as you claimed."

Haddad just stared up at him. Was this really how it would end? He knew eating an egg could push his excitable immune system over the edge, but getting injected with such minuscule amounts of the stuff? He'd never even imagined the possibility.

The next one stung a little on the way in.

He failed them. Not just Myriam and Nour, but every person in the country that had so carelessly adopted him as one of its own. He'd waited too long for the right moment, rather than simply making the call and accepting the consequences. A coward—that's all he was.

The two men continued to draw the vile liquid up, syringe after syringe injected into every bare piece of skin in his body. The last one was the worst, a forceful jab straight into his temple. At the same instant, the dull headache already there burst in an explosion of searing pain and overwhelming pressure.

He let his head fall back against the floor and closed his eyes. It wasn't worth pretending he could fight any longer.

They must have sensed the change. He heard them walk back to unit twenty-six, and then a minute later close the door and pass by him again. The main door opened and closed.

He was alone.

Haddad felt the steady drum in his throbbing head slowly increase as the minutes passed by. That wasn't good. His heart should be slowing down now that the excitement was over, not moving in the other direction.

The soft tissues of his nose and sinuses were starting to swell, making each breath a little more difficult than the one before it. Just like that first terrifying ride in the back of a taxi as a young boy, speeding from his village to the nearest hospital. He'd been through it enough times that the symptoms were unmistakable. Anaphylactic shock—his body's misguided reaction to the harmless proteins of a chicken egg.

His lungs screamed for oxygen, but he couldn't force enough air through the narrowing spaces inside his head.

Each breath was a battle, and he was losing the war.

A black curtain hung before his eyes. He couldn't resist it any longer.

THE SOUND OF shattering glass behind him broke through the silence. Footsteps running down the hall, then a woman's face bent over him while a hand ripped the tape from over his mouth.

Haddad tried to inhale, anticipating the sweet relief of precious air filling his lungs. Nothing. His throat was sealed shut with its own swollen flesh.

A man's face appeared, shouting something, but it was gibberish to his muddled brain.

The curtain stirred, then fell, enveloping him in a weightless darkness.

It was time to go.

COLE DUG HIS fingers deeper into the man's neck, searching for the pulse that would prove his oxygen-starved heart was still beating.

"Think we can bring him back?" he shouted.

"Not without an airway," Leila said, tearing through the first aid kit she'd found in the front office.

Cole emptied his pockets, searching for something, anything, that could be used to cut into the man's neck for an emergency tracheotomy. Keys? Maybe. But of course, it was pointless without a tube of some sort that could be inserted through the wound and into the trachea itself.

Leila leaned over the man's body, placed both hands on top of the sternum, and began to pump. Up and down, up and down. Cole heard a rib crack. She was giving it all she had—he had to respect that. Blood started to trickle from the man's nose.

"Think that might be it." Cole put a hand on her shoulder.

She did a few more compressions, slowed down, then stopped.

"There goes our best chance of figuring this thing out."

"I know," he said. "But that's not going to bring him back."

Cole jumped to his feet. Halfway down the hall, the door to one of the storage units stood open. It was dark inside, but a laptop screen flickered in the far corner. He flipped on the overhead light.

"Here's the girl!"

He knelt down and felt for a pulse. Still alive. But she was hot. Way too hot.

Leila crouched beside him just as he noticed the rash on the girl's bare arm.

"She's got it too," he said. "Here, in the U.S. of A."

Leila pulled out her phone. "I'm calling for an ambulance."

"Sure, but let them know they need BSL-4," Cole said. "If you stay with her I'll check out that light from the unit across the hall."

He dashed out into the hall and tried the handle.

Locked.

One step back, then he brought a heel up with all his strength, hitting the door just to the side of the handle. There was a crack, but no movement. Again he kicked out, and this time the door swung open.

A wall of hot, putrid air rushed out to hit him like a train. He threw an arm up over his mouth and nose and stepped inside. It was a small room, about the size of a two-car garage. A space heater glowed from its position on the ground just inside the door. Along the back wall, a shelving system was empty except for a few boxes. More boxes were piled everywhere, mixed in with the dimpled cardboard inserts that could only be used for one thing.

Eggs.

A large outdoor trash can stood in one corner. Cole almost didn't want to look inside, didn't want to believe it, didn't want to confirm what he already knew to be true.

It was filled to the brim with more broken eggshells than he'd ever seen in one place. He kicked the can over on its side, sending the shells flying across the floor. Not just shells. Hundreds of tiny insulin syringes spilled out too.

This was it. Bioterrorism 101.

Eggs had been used to efficiently reproduce viruses and bacteria since the earliest days of experimentation with biological weapons after World War II. They were cheap, available, and effective—almost every pathogen under the sun seemed to grow in them. Given enough eggs and a few days in a warm incubator, a single drop of infectious material could be transformed into an almost unlimited quantity of live viral culture. A deadly solution primed and ready for distribution using whatever discrete method its creators desired for achieving their devastating goals.

He dug into his pocket for the phone. If this didn't convince them, he didn't know what would.

A tired male voice answered. "Colonel Simmons here."

"Sir, this is Captain McBride."

"Cole, where the hell are you?"

"I apologize, sir, but I didn't see an alternative."

"Like hell you didn't. Always the maverick, isn't that it?"

Cole took a deep breath. *Here goes.*

"You think you've still got any influence over at the White House?"

"Excuse me?"

"Because we're going to need it. You won't believe what I'm looking at right now."

Anna McBride had to pinch herself to confirm that this wasn't just some strange nightmare. First Cole's late night surprise at the apartment, then the morning's realization that his escape had somehow made him public enemy number one around the White House, and now a half-hearted reversal of opinion with his preemptive find of the terrorist's lab.

She tried to melt back into the wall of the Situation Room. Her interim top secret clearance had finally come through that morning, and this was the first time her boss had let her stay for a high-level briefing. No reason to make herself too obvious, though.

"So it's really that easy for a couple lone rangers to brew up a biological weapon like this?"

Anna had never seen the president so angry. She really did feel bad for him, poor old man. He was only trying to throw a good party, after all. Yes, it was probably more for his own benefit than the American people's, but that didn't mean he deserved this.

"They think they can bring our great country to its knees," he continued. "Well, they're wrong."

Colonel Simmons motioned with his hand from near the other end of the long table. He was the one Cole had called first this afternoon, and it was his team from USAMRIID that was already there in Fairfax now. "They're wrong, Mr. President, because they won't have a chance to bring this country to its knees. Not if you do the right thing and cancel tonight's festivities."

"Colonel Simmons," General Howard said. "I think the president has already made it clear that this option is not on the table." He turned to President Rogers. "Am I right, sir?"

"You are. Canceling the event would mean the terrorists have won. Game over."

"With all due respect, sir," Simmons said. "The terrorists win if this hybrid pox virus is released into our population. We're talking thousands sick within days, hundreds of thousands in a couple of weeks. There goes the economy, and with it any chance of a second term."

The president pointed at her boss. "Andrew, tell us again how the media would handle this last-minute cancellation?"

"There's no way we could keep the threat under wraps, even if we tried. This event that was supposed to be a crowning triumph would be portrayed instead as yet another failure on the part of your administration." Anna could see that he was wrestling with the implications of his own words. "But even in light of this cold hard truth, I have to side with—"

"Thank you, Andrew," the president interrupted. "That will be enough."

The president had already shot down both his FBI Director and the Secretary of Homeland Security, so Anna knew her boss didn't stand much of a chance. But she was glad he made the effort, and she knew it probably had more than a little something to do with the news of his friend Fadi Haddad's death.

"If we cancel this event," the president continued, standing up, "the terrorists will have achieved their primary objective, which is sowing fear in the hearts of the American people. We will not let them change our way of life."

He looked down the table to his national security advisor.

"Chuck, I trust you'll work together with this group to neutralize whatever threat might face us tonight."

"Of course." Howard looked slowly around the table. "And I expect full cooperation."

C ole looked out over the sea of bodies spread across the West Lawn of the Capitol. The still air felt heavy with moisture, but there wasn't a cloud in the sky. It was deceptive—just another warm summer evening perfect for the rousing patriotic spectacle ahead. The calm before the storm.

"Really packing themselves in down there," Leila said.

"And this is just the tip of the iceberg." Cole pointed beyond the stage and Reflecting Pool to the long open park stretching all the way to the towering Washington Monument and beyond. "Capitol Police are estimating four hundred thousand people between us and the Potomac right now."

"You scared?"

He thought she might be playing with him at first, but the expression in her eyes said otherwise.

"Not so much scared as pissed," he said. "Everything we've been through this week, and all these lives still at risk just because a few guys in suits didn't have the balls to make the right decision."

The distant clatter of a helicopter reflected off the wall of windows behind them. They were positioned at the northwest corner of the Capitol's sprawling terrace, standing just a few feet from a couple of quiet Capitol Police officers. Cole glanced at their weapons again, trying not to be jealous.

One held an M4 carbine loosely in both hands, while the other was already set up with his bolt action Remington 700 sniper rifle. Bill Shackleton and the colonel were on the opposite corner of the wide terrace, and the rest of the grounds were swarming with undercover FBI and Secret Service.

"Hear that noise?" Cole said. "Those birds will be making low circles over the city all night, starting right here and continuing out about five miles."

Leila looked up higher into the sky, and Cole followed her eyes.

"You said there are jets up there too, right?"

"Yeah, the F-22s should do a fine job of keeping the airspace over the city clear."

"So no crop duster flyby or something ridiculous like that."

"No, no crop dusters."

"But that's still not enough."

"Nope. Even if we did have eyes on every rooftop in the city, what's to stop someone from using a high-powered pressure washer out the window one floor down? These guys have already proven themselves creative, so even if their original plan is unworkable now, they've got to have a backup."

Three radios crackled to life at once.

"This is an all hands alert. I repeat, all hands alert."

He didn't recognize the voice. Colonel Simmons had given Cole a handheld transmitter from his biological threat team, and all the federal services involved in the night's operation were tuned in to the same channel.

"Two suspects have been detained at the northeast entrance after resisting our request to turn over their water bottles. The bottles are filled with an unidentified white milky fluid."

Leila was shaking her head.

"Requesting urgent on-site evaluation to assess the threat."

Now Colonel Simmons' voice came through the speaker. "Deliver the bottles securely to the temporary lab behind the Library of Congress, and we'll have an answer within twenty minutes. Over."

"Roger—" The voice cut off, then continued. "No. No! Don't open that!"

"What's happening?" A third voice cut in. Deep and intense.

"Sir, everyone, it's a false alarm." There was some laughter in the background. "Vodka and cream—white Russians. Just a couple college kids trying to get drunk during the show tonight."

"Shit," Colonel Simmons said. "Still shouldn't have opened it there in an unprotected environment."

"Won't happen again, sir. Out."

Cole closed his eyes. That kind of slip-up was not okay. What if they were in fact the terrorists, and had simply popped the caps off and sprayed the liquid out over the crowds of people still waiting to get through security? The exposure would be limited, and probably containable, but even thirty people were too many.

"Could be a long couple of hours, right?" he said.

"As long as that was the last scare, I'll be fine." Leila answered. Her lips turned up in a half smile. "Couple of my favorite bands are playing tonight, so that's my real interest in hoping these Lebanese guys changed their minds."

If she could crack a joke, after everything she'd been through, maybe he should try to lighten up a little, too. The entire anti-terrorism apparatus of the United States government was focused right here. He'd done his part—now it was time to let the big boys run the show.

There was a flash of lights from the stage, and a male announcer's voice broke through the roar of thousands of excited voices squeezed onto the lawn below.

"Ladies and gentlemen, the moment you've all been waiting for. Please rise and join me in welcoming the president of the United States of America!"

9:36 P.M.

Ten incredible entertainers, each performing two American classics, and now it was coming to a close. The cheering died down as the presenter announced a short break for the set change. The orchestra was next, scheduled to accompany first a couple of famous classical singers and then what had been billed as the most elaborate fireworks display in U.S. history. Cole had to give it to him—the president did know how to put together a good show.

He blinked his eyes and continued to move his gaze purposefully across the scene below. It wasn't easy to keep scanning the audience, trees, and sky, now that the sun had set and the lights on stage pushed everything else into darkness, but he'd done his best.

They were almost in the clear.

Something wet and soft pressed itself into the back of Cole's knee, and he reflexively spun around, kicking out with one foot as he turned.

Bad decision.

A tall brindle Malinois caught his shoe in its mouth, throwing him off balance and sending him flying to the marble-tiled floor.

"Out! Tyson, out!" A young black guy in smart civilian clothes spoke firmly to the dog, who released Cole's shoe and sat down on his haunches, a toothy grin on his face.

"What the—" Cole said, jumping to his feet. A familiar laugh came from behind the pair, and his sister Anna jumped out and ran straight for him.

"I'm so so sorry!" she said, wrapping her arms around him, still laughing. "When did you start reacting to a dog's innocent sniff with that kung fu kick?"

"Innocent?" Cole said, trying to contain his irritation. He was too wired to play around. "Who are these guys, anyway?"

Anna stepped back and gestured to the man, who came forward with a hand extended. Cole noticed the pistol holstered to his belt.

"Special Agent Danny Walker, Secret Service." He reached down and scratched the dog between the ears. "And this is Tyson. Sorry about that—I think we're all lucky he didn't catch you just a little bit higher."

Apart from Bonny and the rest of the Virunga bloodhounds, Cole hadn't seen a real working dog team in over two years. It was a refreshing reminder of his last assignment with 10th Group, and this was a good-looking dog.

"But wait, how'd you know I was up here?" he said, putting an arm around Anna's shoulder. "And why are you even here? I thought I made it pretty clear that you and Chase needed to steer clear of D.C. tonight."

"You did. But we're not your kid siblings anymore, so we made up our own minds. Chase is up on the next level with the rest of his congressman's staff."

"And now with the president's team gone, I'm allowed to let her tag along with me," Agent Walker said.

The president was gone? Cole had assumed he'd stick around to see the show after those rousing introductory remarks.

Anna shrugged out from under his arm and stepped toward Leila. "I'm Anna, Cole's sister."

Leila looked a little nervous with the dog sitting right there, and Cole remembered her initial fear of the gorillas back in Rwanda.

"And I'm Leila. Leila Torabi, with the CDC."

Cole thought he saw Anna's eyebrows go up just slightly. They'd barely covered the basics during their early morning catch-up at the apartment, and he couldn't remember if Leila's complicated role in the week's events was completely worked out. Who knew what Anna had heard, working there in the White House. But ever the family politician, she broke into a wide smile.

"So nice to meet you!"

The low sound of a rolling tympani started up from the stage. It quickly grew in speed and volume, ending in a bursting climax of sound as the entire orchestra broke into a patriotic medley.

"So how do you two, or three, know each other anyway?" Cole asked, nodding at Tyson, who seemed to have forgiven him for the unexpected kick.

"It's all his fault," the special agent said, tugging playfully at his dog's ear. "Guess your sister here can't resist a handsome canine, especially after getting to know a certain three-legged hero she told me all about." He gave Cole a perceptive look. "Thanks for that."

"I just wish you could see his mad skills with the Frisbee," Anna said.

"Whose? Agent Walker here or the dog's?"

She punched him in the arm.

"Both, actually. They were showing off for me right out on that lawn earlier this week. You should have seen Tyson's hilarious reaction when the sprinklers came on!"

"Sprinklers?" It hit Cole before he even finished saying the word.

"Well, more like misters, in this case," Anna said, turning to Walker with a smile. "We were going to tell someone about that, right?"

Cole saw that Leila was on to it as well. She stepped closer, concern written all over her face.

"Hang on, Anna. Slow down and tell me exactly what you mean by these misting sprinklers."

An operatic rendition of God Bless America was at its peak volume on the final chorus, forcing them to shout. Cole didn't hear the cell phone ringing in his pocket, but he did feel it start to buzz. He pulled it out and saw the familiar Maryland number.

"Sorry, I've got to get this." He stepped away from the group. "That you, Morgan?"

"Yep, just got something, but you're going to have to move fast. You know they're interrogating the wife, Nour Haddad, right now?"

"Guess so, yeah."

"She just told them about a cousin of her husband, frequent visitor and close friend of the family."

"And?"

"He's been employed there at the Capitol for over twenty years. Currently works as some kind of supervisor in the grounds maintenance department."

"Shit."

"My thoughts exactly."

COLE GRABBED THE Capitol Police sniper's shoulder. "Hey man, you know anything about the sprinkler system out there?"

"What the hell?"

"We just got a lead on this terrorist threat. Do you?"

"Only that it stopped working right a few days ago. Maintenance guys were out to check it but water's still spraying out too fine. If it weren't for last week's storms that grass would be yellow already."

"Do you know where the system is controlled from?"

The policeman shook his head. "I'm guessing somewhere down off one of the basement levels, but no clue."

Cole looked over his shoulder. "Agent Walker, is there an alternate secure channel for radio transmissions tonight? Something an employee at the Capitol wouldn't have access to?"

"Yeah," he said. "Try eighteen."

Cole spun the dial until the number appeared on the small LCD screen. "This is Captain Cole McBride at the northwest terrace. Anyone on this channel right now?"

A woman's voice answered. "Go ahead Captain McBride. This is the operations center."

"We have a new lead that needs rapid action. One of the terrorists has a cousin, an Adel Massoud, who is employed in some type of groundskeeper position here at the Capitol."

"Go on."

"I just confirmed that the sprinkler system has been spraying a fine mist this week rather than the normal droplet shower. This is a viable route for aerosol dispersion of the viral agent that needs to be neutralized immediately."

"We have someone from that office here now. Please hold for a response."

A recent American Idol winner was starting the second verse of her overly dramatized version of the Star Spangled Banner.

Cole pointed to Leila and Anna. "You two get to the other side to let Colonel Simmons and Shackleton know what's going on. We need to keep this off the main radio channel for now."

Leila shook her head. "I'm going with you."

"No way." Cole appreciated the courage behind her offer, but without any tactical training she would only be in the way. "Those guys need this update, and I'm not going to leave Anna alone. Agent Walker, you and Tyson are coming with me. And Anna, if she tells you to put a mask on, you put the mask on."

Cole took a few steps, then shouted over his shoulder. "We'll meet you right back here if we can."

He started to weave his way through the oblivious crowd behind them. What was taking the operations center so long with an answer? As the crowd thinned, he took off at a jog, continuing around the north side of the terrace with Walker and Tyson right beside him.

They were halfway down the east stairs when the radio started talking.

"Two of our officers just tried to enter the grounds maintenance department but found the locking mechanism jammed and the door possibly barricaded. A more fully equipped team will be on their way back down there very shortly."

The pop diva's soaring melody carried clearly through the night air. She was starting the final verse.

"Very shortly might not cut it," Cole said. "Who's there from the grounds office?"

There was a pause, then a gravelly old man's voice came through. "That would be me, Architect of the Capitol. Adel Massoud is one of my employees."

"Sir, is there another access point into the sprinkler control area? We're at the east stairs right now."

The man coughed. "There is another way, through the Summerhouse Grotto. But it's been locked up for years."

"Summerhouse?"

Walker was already running. "This way!"

He was fast, and the dog had no trouble keeping up. Cole had to sprint to catch them. They turned left down a dirt path that curved back around the north side of the Capitol building. The downward slope made it easy to pick up even more speed.

"Right up here!"

Cole saw a low brick structure hiding in the darkness under some tall trees. In all his visits to D.C., he'd never noticed it before. They tore through an arched entryway and came to a hasty stop in front of a small fountain. Tyson threw both front feet up onto its edge and looked quickly from his handler to Cole and back again.

"Where to?"

Walker had both hands on a black iron grating that seemed to block access to some sort of natural display. The distant stage lights reflected off moving water behind it.

"This is the Grotto, but it's definitely locked."

"Do you mind?" Cole said, reaching for the other man's weapon. Before Walker could reply, he pulled it smoothly from the holster and fired once directly into the lock. The shot echoed wildly in his unprotected ears, accompanied by an impressive shower of blinding sparks. He handed the weapon to a shocked Walker, put a hand on the grating, and pushed. It swung inward, and he crawled through the opening and down the other side.

"Stop right where you are!"

A new male voice shouted loudly, but Cole couldn't see where it was coming from. He ducked into the shadows of the rocky wall behind him.

"Secret Service!" Walker yelled. "We're on the same team."

"Ops center just sent us over here. It's just you and the dog?"

"No, another guy's already in there—military type."

Tyson's tall silhouette appeared on the edge of the Grotto's window before he jumped down to join Cole. Walker followed, and finally two Capitol Police officers.

"It's got to be back there in the cave," one of them said, splashing past Cole before disappearing under an overhanging rock. The moving beam of a flashlight flickered inside a second later. Cole ran right through the trickling waterfall and jumped down a short set of stairs into a large earthy space below.

"Master key's not working," the officer said, fiddling with another door at the far end of the cave.

Walker jumped forward, the dog sticking right by his side. "I'll do the honors this time."

The shot felt even louder inside the closed space, and Cole opened his eyes to see Tyson shaking his head vigorously. The vet in him couldn't help but hope the dog's eardrums were still intact.

"It needs another one," the officer said, spinning the broken handle around the still jammed door.

"Get back to the entrance," the second officer yelled. He dropped to a knee in front of the door, shouldered his breacher shotgun, and placed the muzzle in contact with the locking mechanism.

Cole and the others dove for the stairs as a deafening boom rang out. He turned back just in time to see the door swing open. The officer took off down a spiral stairway with Walker and Tyson right behind him. Cole followed them, and the other Capitol policeman took up the rear. The stairs were steep and narrow, and Cole tripped and almost fell as he tried to keep up with Walker's nimble form just below him. Their boots clanged noisily against the cast iron stairs, and Cole realized that all the sounds of the concert had faded out as they got deeper underground.

Suddenly, just below them, a burst of automatic weapon fire tore through the air, and the first officer cried out.

Another burst, followed by a loud thud at the bottom of the stairs.

"Man down! Man down!" Walker shouted, ducking down.

Cole stopped right behind him and crouched on a stair, looking out through the railing into the darkness. A faint red emergency exit light glowed on the other side of the room.

"Cut your light," he whispered to the officer behind him. The bright flashlight beam disappeared.

"Now what?" Walker said quietly.

"Assuming this guy pre-programmed the sprinkler cycle, he's got all the time in the world. We don't have that luxury." Cole felt Tyson's muscular body quivering against his leg. "You thinking what I'm thinking?"

"Yep," Walker said.

Cole heard the click of the dog's lead being released, then a whispered command.

"Go get 'em, boy."

Tyson leapt down the remaining stairs and shot across the room, his speeding form barely visible in the darkness. He was heading for a tall white tank against the far wall.

More shots rang out, but they didn't faze the dog, who dove under the tank. There was a fierce snarl, and then a man's horrified screams.

"Let's go!" Walker said, taking off running. Cole was right behind him, jumping over the first officer's motionless body at the bottom of the stairs

A single shot echoed through the empty space just as they reached the tank. Tyson barked once, then came around the side of it covered in blood.

Cole was on his knees in an instant, running both hands along the dog's neck, chest, and abdomen, trying to find the wound.

Walker stepped back around the tank. "He's dead. Bastard blew his own head off back there."

Cole jumped to his feet. "He must have been pretty confident that this thing was a done deal then. Time check?"

The second Capitol policeman called out from the bottom of the stairs, "9:51. My guy's gone—"

At that moment, the double doors under the red emergency sign flew off their hinges in an explosion of light and sound that blew Cole right off his feet even from forty feet away. Another method to breach a door.

Two heavily armed and armored men swept inside and took up positions on either side of the entry, weapons scanning the room. They were followed rapidly by the rest of the SWAT team.

"You're too late!" Cole shouted, raising his hands slowly above his head. "Terrorist is already dead."

One of the SWAT officers raised his goggles. "What the hell?"

"We beat you down here," Cole said. "But this thing isn't over yet."

Cole saw the control box mounted on the wall beside the tank.

"There!" He was beside it in a second, trying to pry the cover off with both hands. It didn't budge. "You guys have a crow bar or something?"

"No," the SWAT officer said, "but this ought to do."

He brought the butt of his assault rifle down hard against the cover's exposed hinges, shattering the plastic around them. Cole tossed the cover to the side and stared at blank screen. The keypad below it looked just like an ATM's. He pressed a green button.

The screen lit up. His eyes flew to the only thing that was changing—a countdown.

6:21

6:20

6:19

The simple text to the left of the numbers said it all.

Next cycle begins in:

6:16

6:15

"How do we stop this thing?" Cole shouted. He tried to press another button, but a message box popped up: PIN required. "I'm going to take a guess and say the dead guy on the other side of this tank was the only one with that number."

The SWAT officer raised his weapon to the screen. "Can't we just blow it to pieces?"

"No!" Cole said. "That'll only lock the current program into place. The virus must be out there at the sprinkler heads, just waiting to be released."

He racked his brain for a solution. Even if the program couldn't be aborted, the sprinkler pumps themselves must run off some kind of electricity, right? And without the pumps to push the contaminated water through the system…

He lifted the radio to his mouth. "This is Captain McBride. We need to cut power to the entire Capitol complex immediately!"

"Say again."

"We have about five minutes before a few thousand Americans are hit with a guaranteed death sentence. Cut the power!"

The SWAT officer beside him got on his own radio. "This is Officer Jenkins down in grounds maintenance. I'm confirming this request."

5:04

5:03

The old man's voice from earlier came through now. "It's not easy. The Capitol's source of electricity is protected like none other in this country."

"You've got to make it happen, sir." Cole was rapidly entering one four-digit combination after another, but the screen wouldn't unlock.

"There's only one possible way." The voice got quieter, like he was speaking to someone else in the room. "Get me our Pepco contact on the phone. Now." Pepco, the Potomac Electric Power Company, sole supplier of electricity to the city of Washington since the 1920s.

4:37

4:36

4:35

"I'm going back up," Cole said. He wasn't going to hang around down in this dungeon, not with the twins still up there, unvaccinated and unprotected.

"We'll go too," Walker said, taking hold of Tyson's lead.

The connection went bad as they sprinted up the spiral stairwell, but he could still make out a few words of the Architect's conversation.

"—urgent national security implications. Only three minutes before—"

They were in the cave, now splashing back through the artificial creek and up through the open grating. Cole recognized the slow opening melody of Tchaikovsky's 1812 Overture. Leaving the Summerhouse, they retraced their earlier run up the hill, even faster this time. He had to get back to them before it was too late.

"How much time do we have on the countdown?" Someone shouting over the radio.

Cole recognized the SWAT leader's voice: "Just under a minute. Power's still on."

And they were back onto the terrace.

The two girls were right where they had left them.

"Leila!" he shouted. "Anna! Put your masks—"

The radio's connection was back loud and clear. "Thank you. Yes, now. Right now!"

The night went black in perfect time with the Overture's first cannon blast.

Completely black. The Capitol, the monuments, every building lining the National Mall. The whole city was dark.

But then, the second cannon blast. And with it, the sky exploded in a sea of color and light. So these were the fireworks everyone had made such a fuss about. Now he understood why.

Cole glanced to the side. Leila's wide eyes reflected the flashing brilliance of the blazing night sky, and a beautifully genuine smile stretched across her face.

"We did it," he murmured. "We really did it."

He felt for her hand and gave it a quick squeeze before returning his own gaze to the spectacular celestial display.

Epilogue

The citywide loss of power at 10:00 p.m. on July 4th was a complete non-event, a mysterious blip in an otherwise busy news week that did not merit more than a passing mention by any media outlet. Most of the public simply assumed it was part of the show, a special effect coordinated ahead of time to make the fireworks even more magnificent than they already were.

This is how it needs to stay.

Members of the Senate Select Committee on Intelligence, your complete discretion in protecting this story from widespread release is required. There are those among us who may argue that a nation's leaders should never hide the truth from its citizens, but this perspective only stems from a willful naivety about the way the world really works. The enemy achieves his goal when he succeeds in spreading fear and insecurity among our people.

We must not let that happen.

SOME OF YOU have requested an update on the virus's spread in central Africa. As you know, the United States released several hundred thousand doses of smallpox vaccine to be used in a ring vaccination campaign around the Virunga volcanoes and North Kivu province. This strategy has proved effective, slowing and finally stopping natural transmission within the human population only last month.

And the mountain gorillas? It turns out the Iranians should have done more research on the ecology and behavior of these majestic primates before deciding to hinge their nuclear hopes on such a foolhardy plan. Even the most cursory reading of Dian Fossey or George Schaller would have led them to understand that gorilla families do not regularly engage in close physical interactions with other groups. The chimera virus killed off its mountain gorilla hosts too quickly, dying with the Rugendo family on the forested slopes of Mount Mikeno.

Of course, this famous silverback did not leave the world completely deprived of his dominant lineage. Little Endo made a full recovery and recently moved back with the other orphans to the Senkwekwe Center, where he will stay under the attentive care of Innocence Kambale, Dr. Antoine Musamba, and all the other dedicated rangers of Virunga National Park. Bonny the bloodhound also returned home with them. She was found baying lustily early one morning outside the Gorilla Doctors compound in Musanze, a full week after her disappearance.

Vincent Lukwiya is awaiting trial with other senior Lord's Resistance Army commanders at the International Criminal Court in the Hague. He was allowed to keep his treasured watch, but it now sits on the artificial wrist of a prosthetic left arm.

His captors, Captain Jake Russell, Master Sergeant Mike Denison, and their canine partner, Rico, are back in the Central African Republic, still hunting Joseph Kony but preparing to rotate out when another team arrives from Fort Bragg.

Sohrab Torabi presumably remains in prison in Iran. Our sources have been unable to track down any information about his status since the arrest.

After five days in the BSL-4 intensive care unit at USAMRIID, Myriam Haddad and her mother entered the Federal Witness Protection Program.

And Dr. Lars Olsson continues his work with Doctors Without Borders, currently managing a relief hospital on the outskirts of Damascus, Syria.

WE WERE LUCKY this time.

Or fortunate, or even blessed, depending on your understanding of our place in the universe.

But this threat, this great tragedy narrowly averted, was only one of many. We must remain vigilant, never assuming we can be fully prepared for every possibility, expecting success but planning for failure. We stand ready to enable and empower those noble Americans willing to raise their hands and confront whatever future dangers this great nation may face.

Again, Madam Chairman and Mr. Vice Chairman, thank you for holding this hearing. I welcome your questions.

Acknowledgements

This book had its earliest origin in wildlife photographer Brent Stirton's iconic image of a dead silverback mountain gorilla on a makeshift litter carried by a sorrowful group of local Congolese men. If you haven't seen the photo, go online and find it now. In the year between the event itself and *National Geographic*'s follow-up feature story, "Who Murdered the Virunga Gorillas?" by Mark Jenkins, I spent a full year away from the standard veterinary curriculum to study some of these same conflicts at the human-animal-environment interface while living and working in India and Mozambique. My first thanks are to these storytellers who inspired my own feeble attempt to continue shedding light on a part of the world that is too often ignored.

If it weren't for my own parents' ongoing subscription to this magazine and sacrificial support of their animal-loving son over many years, I would not even have been aware of the story, or more importantly, pursuing my lifelong dream of becoming a veterinarian. They taught me to read, write, and imagine the possibility of sharing my own stories with the world. Thank you, Dad and Mom.

I'm fortunate to call a number of scientists and veterinarians my friends, all of whom are much smarter and more accomplished than I am in the real work of making our world a better place. They were all kind enough to take time from their own commitments and busy schedules to read my manuscript and provide insights and suggestions to ensure its accuracy. Many thanks to Mike Cranfield and Fred Nizeyimana, both real Gorilla Doctors with many years of experience working to protect these incredible animals in their mountain homes of central Africa. Thanks also to my colleague Marlene Zähner, a Swiss veterinarian and lead for Virunga's CongoHounds project. Aaron Harris is a physician and alumnus of the Epidemic Intelligence Service who continues his epidemiological investigations around the world with the CDC. Cyndie Courtney, Sarah Churgin, and Nick Marsh are all fellow writers and veterinarians. My friend and colleague Hayley is an active duty Veterinary Corps officer like me who is currently pursuing a PhD in epidemiology while studying monkeypox in the DRC. Sound familiar? And yet Cole's character came into being long before Hayley and I even met!

The rest of my initial readers came from all walks of life and brought their own diverse expertise and tastes to bear on the story. Many thanks to Colin Basler, John Montague, Sean Tennant, Rachel Braddock Bayles, Drew Gideon, all my siblings, and parents-in-law.

Three literary agents took a special interest in this work and provided incredibly helpful feedback on the manuscript itself and the current state of the publishing industry. Thank you, John Talbot, Russell Galen, and Paul Lucas.

I owe particular gratitude for the support of James Rollins and Marty Becker, two other veterinarians who are already successful authors in their own very different ways. Maria Goodavage, Bob Mayer, and Richard Phillips are also authors who have been generous enough to share their names, encouraging words, and audiences with me.

I've had the privilege of serving alongside courageous Soldiers, Sailors, Marines, Airmen, and other operators, many of whom are handlers working with very accomplished canine partners. Thanks for everything you do to protect my family and my country.

Lena and Gil, I don't think you'll remember the occasional Saturday morning or hour-before-dinner that I was writing behind a closed door rather than playing with you. But I know your momma will.

Becca, thank you. You've pushed and encouraged me at every step, making this book possible alongside everything else in our life together. Home is wherever I'm with you.

ABOUT THE AUTHOR

Elliott Garber is a veterinarian and military officer currently assigned on active duty with a special operations command. He has lived in India, Egypt, Mozambique, and Italy and traveled to over 50 other countries around the world, including a recent deployment to Iraq. You can often find him under the water, up in the air, or out in the woods. Elliott lives with his wife and two young children in Coronado, California. This is his first novel.